Someone to Kill

Someone
to
Kill

Kurt Corriher

A Tom Doherty Associates Book / New York

SOMEONE TO KILL

Copyright © 2002 by Kurt Corriher

This book is printed on acid-free paper.

A Forge Book
Published by Tom Doherty Associates, LLC
175 Fifth Avenue
New York, NY 10010

www.tor.com

Forge® is a registered trademark of Tom Doherty Associates, LLC.

ISBN 0-765-30187-3

First Edition: January 2002

Printed in the United States of America

0 9 8 7 6 5 4 3 2 1

For Alicia

Acknowledgments

More people contributed to the making of this book than I could possibly list in a single page, but I would like to express special thanks to my agent, Mildred Marmur, for her energy and tenacity; to Daniel Rabuzzi for his extensive knowledge of international banking; to Sebastian Kropop for a wealth of information on the former East Germany and for tours of Berlin and his beloved Dresden; to Ted Blanton for guidance through the labyrinth of our legal system; to Hal Brodsky for medical expertise; to Frederic Young, Rosemary Waldorf, Deborah Mills, Marty Stevens, and Steve Bouser for critiquing the manuscript; to David Hartwell and Moshe Feder at Forge books for shepherding the book through the publication process; to Vladimir Volkoff for wise and patient encouragement; and especially to my best critic and best friend, Alicia Corriher, for believing in her husband.

KC

Someone to Kill

1

He called himself Mr. Greene. And just after 3 P.M. on a blustery day in March, he carried a black attaché case into the parking garage built onto the side of the Courier building. His stride was purposeful and deliberate—a man at home there, a man who knew where he was going, a man like a hundred others who would walk in and out of the parking deck that day. He was middle-aged, blue-eyed, and once blond, though strands of gray had robbed his hair of its earlier golden luster. All his life people had remarked on his eyes—striking, penetrating blue eyes that now were invisible behind green-tinted sunglasses.

He walked to the stairwell and climbed briskly to the third level, his footsteps echoing in the concrete silo. A sign with red letters a foot high read RESERVED—NEWSROOM. He strode past it, turned, and started down the line of cars. He saw the Honda almost immediately. It was a late-model Accord, gray, with black interior, license number CNA-431. Hitching up his sleeve as if to check the time, Mr. Greene stepped up to the passenger door. But the eyes behind the sunglasses never fell to the watch on his wrist. Instead they swept the garage from corner to corner. It was empty. And he knew already that there were no security cameras mounted in the rafters. His dry run the day before had confirmed that. With one last look around, he pulled a thin strip of metal from inside his suit coat. The metal slid down the glass with a quiet hiss and hooked onto the locking mechanism. A flick of his wrist disengaged the lock. So far so good. The locksmith's tool disappeared into the coat, and he drew a pair of latex gloves from his trouser pocket. A few seconds later Mr. Greene pulled the door latch with a gloved hand, climbed into the car, and lay across the front bucket seats, drawing his knees toward his chest to make room for the closing door. The attaché case just barely fit on the floorboard on the driver's side, tucked beneath the brake pedal.

The hand brake dug into his ribs, but he ignored the discomfort, clicked open the attaché case, and withdrew a lump of gray material, like modeling clay. His fingers slid it smoothly beneath the dash and over the top of the steering column, shoving the ends higher into the dash and molding them into the back of the instrument panel. No problems. No surprises. And why should there be? He had practiced this half a dozen times—in a different Honda, of course.

When the lump was secure beneath the dash, he pulled the tail of his coat from behind him, muttering at himself for forgetting to button his jacket. Not even practice made perfect. Something could always go wrong. But Mr. Greene anticipated glitches. In fact, he often told his associates that expecting the unexpected was precisely what separated professionals from amateurs. And Mr. Greene was not an amateur.

From his lower right coat pocket he drew a black plastic case about the size of a pack of cigarettes. Two thin wires trailed from the bottom, then met and vanished into a small brass tube, similar in size to a .22-caliber long rifle cartridge.

With his thumb, he shoved the tube deep into the plastic mass that now lay like a python, coiled above the steering column. A magnetic strip on the back of the black box clicked onto the steel brace that secured the steering column to the wall of the engine well. Once the magnet was attached, he slid the box gently forward, moving it along the brace until the wires were taut and invisible from the driver's seat. Finally, with the fingernail of his index finger, he tugged a tiny plastic switch aside and exposed the red warning tab beneath it.

Mr. Greene took a deep breath and held it. Hearing no footsteps, he sat up, climbed out of the car, slid the lock closed, and shut the door behind him with a satisfying *chunk*.

He had almost reached the Second Street exit when two men entered from a door at the far end and walked in his direction, lost in conversation. They were still a hundred feet away—too far for a good look at his face. He broke left and walked toward a farther exit onto Tryon Street, keeping his face in profile. He reached that exit without encountering anyone else, descended to street level, and breathed a sigh of relief as the welcome sunlight broke over him. He fell into the pace of the crowd on the downtown sidewalk, most walking north toward the soaring Nationsbank tower that dominated downtown Charlotte. A left on Second Street carried him around the corner of the garage.

His rental car was a Honda Accord identical to the one in the parking deck, except that it was white instead of gray. It stood in an open parking lot a block north of the Courier building, where he could watch both exits of the garage, the one to Second street, and the other to Church. Mr. Greene climbed into the driver's seat and started reading a day-old newspaper. The standoff at some cult in Waco, Texas, was still on, and there had been another arrest in the World

Trade Center bombing. He flipped to the local section and started reading a piece about how supermarket scanners in Charlotte were overcharging grocery customers. The byline read "Judith Lyles." The research in the piece, he noted, was painstaking, the style hard and aggressive. No doubt about it. The lady was good.

He pulled a pack of French cigarettes from his pocket and tipped one into his mouth. For the second time that day, he considered a cup of coffee at the cafe opposite the parking deck. After all, she wasn't scheduled to leave work for over an hour. But people didn't always behave according to schedules. Besides, it would mean more contact with people, more chances to be noticed and remembered. And anyway, he reminded himself, that dirty water Americans called coffee was hardly worth it.

He took a long pull at the cigarette and settled down to wait. At least the car was better than the motel room. Earlier that day he had watched a television talk show about a woman who had awakened from a three-year coma to find herself divorced and her husband married to her twin sister. American television. No, it was better to sit in a chilly car and pretend to read a newspaper.

At precisely 4:30, a woman in her late thirties stepped through the door of the *Courier* newsroom and turned left toward the escalator to the lobby. She was tall, with long straight hair, pinned back at the temples for a more professional look. A gray suit hugged shapely hips and accented a still youthful figure. Even the sleeping child on her shoulder did not disguise the suppleness of her body. Stepping off the escalator in the lobby, she walked left again and approached the glass door that led directly into the parking garage.

Fred Baines stood guard at the door, his uniform, as always, crisp and clean and buttoned down. He cast a not so furtive glance at her long legs, then shifted his gaze to the face. It was a stunningly handsome face, but the expression stopped him cold. The lips were tight and drawn, the eyes hard. He knew her, of course. Judith Lyles had made quite a name for herself with her fearless exposés. Fearless. And yet . . . He studied the face as she drew closer. She had never been the friendly type. The most he ever got from her was a cool nod. But today she brushed past him without even a look, her expression rigid and pale. And her eyes. Something was different. What was it? She looked . . . harried. No, *hunted*. Maybe it had something to do with the little girl. Funny. He had never thought of her as a mother.

Judith Lyles entered the parking garage and shifted the child, a little too roughly, from her left shoulder onto her right. The sleeping girl whimpered softly. Her mother's spike heels echoed loudly as she hurried down the long concrete corridor, casting nervous glances right and left. Her shoulders relaxed a little when she reached the car and ducked into the narrow space between it and the neighboring vehicle. She shifted the child higher, fished the keys from her purse, and unlocked the rear door. As gently as she could, she laid the little girl onto the back seat and covered her carefully with an overcoat.

A few minutes later she pulled into the rush hour traffic on Church Street and headed north. Four blocks later she took a left onto Sixth Street, then nudged the accelerator as she passed under the green light at Graham and headed for the curve. Traffic rolled as a unit, rounding the curve and merging into Fifth Street, each driver jockeying for a place as the two lanes fed into one.

Today there was no battle. A white Honda had been hovering beside and a little behind her for three blocks. She thought the driver, a blond man in sunglasses, might contest the merge onto Fifth Street, but he let her slide in ahead of him. A few minutes later she turned onto the northbound ramp of I-77 and pressed the accelerator to the floor.

Traffic was, as always, bumper to bumper on the expressway. She hit sixty miles per hour at the end of the acceleration ramp, dropped her little finger onto the signal lever, and began drifting toward a pickup truck on her left. The driver hit his brakes and she slipped in front of him. In her rearview mirror she saw his mouth working angrily, and for the first time all day, she smiled. Driving in heavy traffic was a challenge she enjoyed.

And it also meant that, for the next thirty minutes at least, she was safe.

Mr. Greene was not happy. He was four cars behind her and traffic was heavy. If he could have used the ignition . . . But no, his instructions were clear and emphatic. Under no circumstances were there to be incidental casualties. That meant that he had to control the timing of the detonation. It also meant that the danger of being seen and remembered climbed exponentially. With an ignition detonator he could have been out of the area—even out of the country—when the blast occurred. Now he had to be there, had to *see* it happen before he could make his escape. Oh well, risk was part of this business. He smiled. Risk also carried a very high price tag.

He had made visual confirmation on Sixth Street. It was

the target, and she was alone in the car. Now he just had to be sure she was isolated from traffic when he hit the button. Even so, there was some risk of incidentals. The car might cross the median—slam into oncoming traffic. He was good, but he wasn't God. With explosives you could never be sure. And he had made that clear. But he had promised to do all he reasonably could, and he had done so. Maybe a little more than was reasonable.

At the I-85 interchange, two-thirds of the traffic peeled off onto the exit ramps, but half a mile later the road narrowed from three lanes to two. Still, there was a net improvement. Mr. Greene breathed easier. He had almost twenty miles in which to make the hit—but very few exits to work with along the way. Of course, if he had to he could follow her off the interstate and into Avery. The problem was that college towns were always crowded with pedestrians, and pedestrians noticed a lot more than people whizzing along at seventy miles per hour in little tin boxes. No, he had to do it on the highway. And he had to do it today. The timing was another condition of this job. Today. Not yesterday. Not tomorrow. *Today*. And on her way home from work. Mr. Greene shook his head. People wanted the world for their money. If only they knew what they were asking.

After the Sunset Drive exit, traffic thinned even more, and he accelerated until only a black Toyota was between them. She was driving seventy-five miles an hour, sticking mainly to the left lane. That was good. The worst thing she could do would be settle into a pack of traffic and hang with it the entire distance. With her driving faster than the traffic flow, there were sure to be chances. Coordinating those chances with one of the few exits was the hard part. He could help his own cause by temporarily slowing traffic in one lane, but not in both—not without attracting attention.

He would have to have a little luck on his side if this was going to work the way he had planned it. He resolved to stay with her until the intersection with Highway 73, the last exit before Avery. If he couldn't make that exit, he would pass her and set off the blast behind him. He didn't like that. He needed a broad view of the area, not a keyhole sight in a rearview mirror. But it was still better than following her up the exit ramp and sending the bomb up in a small town.

Reames Road approached. He eased ahead of the Toyota. The target was now two hundred yards away and gaining on a tractor-trailer. Would she get past it in time? Far enough past? Big trucks could not stop very quickly. If the Honda was too close, the truck might jackknife when the driver hit the air brakes, slam into the bridge abutment, kill the driver. "Absolutely no incidental casualties." Easy to say. There was also the chance that the truck would block the transmission. Once he committed to the exit, he had to be sure the signal would reach the detonator. A car was no concern, but a big semi . . .

The sign said REAMES ROAD, ½ MILE. She was already past the truck but not signaling for the right lane. Not yet. Maybe she wouldn't. There was no one pushing her from behind. He was now the closest car. It looked good, except for the truck. The truck was doing at least seventy, and she was not pulling away from him fast enough. Still, half a mile was about twenty-five seconds. It might work. He nudged the accelerator closer to the floorboard. The road ahead of the target was empty for five hundred yards. No problem there. And yes, it looked like the truck would be far enough behind her. If he could just get ahead of it himself, then cut into the right lane in time to make the exit . . . It would be close, but it was going to work. Mr. Greene pushed the accelerator deeper and closed on the truck.

He could scarcely believe his eyes when the amber light began blinking on the left rear of the trailer. Almost immediately the big truck swayed toward him, and his foot leapt instinctively to the brake. Then he saw what looked like a bundle of roofing shingles flash past in the middle of the right lane. The driver had swung out just enough to avoid it, then eased back into the right lane. But it was too late now. Hitting his brakes had blown this chance. Mr. Greene cursed his luck and eased past the tractor-trailer as they crossed beneath the bridge that carried Reames Road over the interstate. One chance down. Three to go.

At the next exit she was tailgating a yellow Lincoln. The Lincoln was traveling seventy miles per hour and passing a string of traffic in the right lane. Lyles was ten feet off his bumper. Mr. Greene hung back six car lengths.

Two exits to go.

As Huntersville approached, she had just passed a Dodge minivan, and the van was still too close behind her at the ramp. Mr. Greene fingered the black transmitter in his right hand. Its leather case was damp from perspiration. As the Huntersville exit passed, he flipped the safety cover back over the red button for the third time. One exit to go. Highway 73 to Cornelius. If it didn't work there, he would pass her and hit the button as he took the Avery exit himself. There was only one mile between Highway 73 and the Avery exit, so he would have to accelerate to eighty-five miles per hour to get around her. That could attract attention, but there was nothing else he could do. For a second he considered letting her take the Avery exit in front of him, then hitting the detonator as he drove past. He could stay on the interstate until Mooresville, then double back. It would work, but it would mean cars following behind for miles until the Mooresville exit—all kinds of chances to take down his tag number, get a description of the car and driver. . . . No, better to blow the Honda on the road behind him where it would at least block pursuing traffic.

Up ahead the gray Honda passed a big green sign that said EXIT 28, HIGHWAY 73—1 MILE. Three cars were lined up in the right lane ahead of her. He checked the rearview mirror. The nearest car was in a pack of traffic at least two hundred yards back and fading. It was possible. If only she didn't overtake the three cars too soon. He glanced at the speedometer and muttered a curse. She was driving eighty now. At this rate she would be in the lane beside them at the exit.

Another big green splotch said EXIT 28, HIGHWAY 73—CORNELIUS—½ MILE. It wasn't going to work here. And at the speed she was driving he would have to put the accelerator to the floor to get around her before the Avery exit. That would be sure to attract attention. Mr. Greene pressed his lips together hard, as if someone were trying to pull a thousand-dollar bill from between them. Oh well, if it had to be, it had to be. Sometimes you took chances.

The exit ramp had just come into sight when she pulled even with the trailing car. Then it happened. The lead car in the right lane switched on its blinker. Almost immediately, the two trailing cars followed suit. They were all taking the exit! Was there still time for him to follow them? How would they react when the blast happened? Would they slam on their brakes, jam the exit, block his escape? In a few seconds he mentally reviewed the escape route. He would drive into Cornelius on Highway 73, turn south at the stoplight onto Highway 115 to Huntersville, then back onto I-77 toward

Charlotte and the airport. Yes, it should work. This was it.

With his right hand, Mr. Greene laid the transmitter on the dash, flipped the plastic cover from the red button and laid his index finger on top of it. With his left hand he steered the Honda into the lane behind the three exiting cars. The trailing car was now heading up the ramp, and the target was passing underneath the bridge. He had to be sure the concrete support pillar didn't block the transmission. He aimed the short black antenna, eyes flicking back and forth from the transmitter, to the target, to the ramp in front of him. His left hand nudged the wheel to the right and he started up the ramp. The concrete abutment was moving between him and the target. Now!

His finger plunged into the red plastic.

He saw shattered glass fly from every window in the Honda an instant before it vanished behind the concrete column. The crack of the explosion followed instantly. He slid the transmitter quickly off the dash and onto the seat beside him. The driver in front of him, a woman, was looking around in confusion but did not stop. All three cars continued to the stop sign at the top of the ramp, then turned left toward Lake Norman and the shopping centers on the west side of the highway.

Mr. Greene turned right, toward Cornelius. In his rearview mirror he saw brake lights gleaming. On the bridge, people were climbing out of their cars and running toward the railing. A plume of black smoke was rising over the interstate, about a hundred yards north.

He turned his attention back to the road in front of him. Downtown Cornelius and Highway 115 lay less than a mile away. A sign said WELCOME TO CORNELIUS, SPEED LIMIT 35 MPH. He eased off the accelerator. No speeding tickets now. Just another commuter ambling home from work.

2

Pavlak bolted upright when the phone erupted beside his
ear. A flame of pain shot through his neck and down his
right shoulder. He rubbed his neck with his left hand and
reached for the phone with his right, then hesitated as he
tried to remember where he was and what he had been
doing. By the fourth ring he had it all clear. He was in his
apartment, the one that had been his home for the last
three months. And he was sitting at a desk because he had
been reading through applications to replace Happy Harrington as track and field coach. The clock beside the window told him it was 7:15 P.M.

He snatched up the receiver. "Yes?"

"John?"

"Yes."

"This is Meg Alwyn. John?"

"Yes, I'm still here."

"Judith was supposed to be here for dinner an hour ago,
but she didn't show up. We're getting a little worried. Do
you know where she is?"

Pavlak rubbed his neck and cautiously tried twisting it.
The pain shot down his arm again and he resolved to look

straight ahead for the rest of his life. "I, uh . . . what? Judith's late?"

"Yes. Hollis and I invited her to dinner this evening, but she hasn't shown up. I spoke to her on the phone this morning, and she was definitely planning to come. We thought maybe she was out on an investigation somewhere, but I called the *Courier*, and they said she left work about four-thirty. Do you have any idea where she might be?"

He tried to shake the sleep from his brain and concentrate. "Meg, I have no idea where Judith is. I haven't even spoken to her in almost a week. You know how things have been lately."

There was a pause. "I know, John. But I don't know what else to do. I've called everywhere. There's no answer at her house. I called the day care center, and they told me Tasha was running a fever and Judith picked her up around ten this morning."

His mind scavenged for possibilities. "Did you call Diane Sweeney? She probably left Tasha with her."

"No, she didn't. I called Diane already. She hasn't seen Judith today."

"How about the *Courier*'s South Carolina newsroom? She's probably . . ."

"No, I called York already. I've called everywhere and everybody I can think of, John. I'm really beginning to get worried." The tone of her voice confirmed it. "Do you think . . . I mean, it has crossed my mind that maybe Judith just . . . you know . . . decided to disappear with Tasha or something. I mean that's not like Judith either . . . ," she added quickly. "But in her present state of mind . . ."

"No, Judith would never do that. She's smart enough to know that something like that could keep her from getting legal custody. Look, she's just out trying to nail some embezzler or something. You know Judith. She'll turn up."

"Well . . ." Meg answered doubtfully. "I hope you're right."
She hung up.

Pavlak walked to the kitchen sink and splashed some water on his face, then forced himself back to the office and
stared at the desk with its stack of résumés beneath a glaring
fluorescent light. He still had a couple hours of work ahead.
His skull pounded, and the pain in his neck lay in ambush,
just waiting for him to turn his head.

Then he caught sight of the portrait on the back corner
of the desk, and suddenly a beam of light washed across the
gloom on his spirits. The photograph was only a few months
old—taken on Tasha's fourth birthday. She beamed out at
him in a white dress, with dark hair cascading in generous
curls over her shoulders, and a pink rabbit squeezed against
her cheek. She was looking left of the camera, laughing—a
child's laugh, full of innocent delight. He remembered that
in less than forty-eight hours he would see her again—have
her to himself for an entire day. Those sparkling black eyes
would light up when he opened the door. The skinny little
arms would wrap themselves around his neck and squeeze,
and for a few precious hours he would be the most important, most needed, most adored man in the universe.

Then, as quickly as it had come, the light vanished, and
darkness thudded into its place. Judith was going to take her
away, and there was absolutely nothing he could do about
it. If he sued for custody, the court would award it to Judith.
She was the mother, she was an award-winning journalist,
and she earned twice his salary.

He walked to the mirror in the bathroom and ran his
fingers through his tangled hair. "You're a hell of a sight,
Pavlak," he muttered. "Pull yourself together, for God's
sake." He stepped into a pair of sweats and laced up his

running shoes. A couple of miles would wake him up—maybe even loosen the crick in his neck.

He hit the concrete sidewalk at an easy jog. The brisk spring air cleared his head. He decided to run to his office and back, taking a long, scenic route through the botanical garden. He couldn't find his new calculator anywhere. Maybe it was in a drawer in the office.

By the time he reached the Guthrie Athletic Center it was dark, but the pain in his neck, at least, was gone. He jogged up the stairs to his office, savoring the spring in his legs. As he approached his office door he heard the phone ringing and fumbled frantically for the key, found it, then snatched up the receiver as the door burst open.

"Mr. Lyles?" It was a man's voice.

"Uh, no. This is John Pavlak. I'm Judith Lyles' husband, though, if that's who you're looking for."

"Ah, I see. Yes. This is Detective Crane with the Mecklenburg County Sheriff's Department. Your landlady said I might find you at this number. Mr. Lyles . . . Sorry . . . Mr. Pavlak . . . I'm afraid I have some bad news for you."

Pavlak's heart slammed. "Oh God," he breathed and put out a hand to steady himself on the back of the desk chair. "What is it?"

"It appears that your wife has been killed."

He turned down Davis Drive as if in a dream and slowed at the house. Since the phone call, nothing was real, not even his house. It was a solid but unremarkable redbrick structure with a wooden porch in the front and a detached white frame garage at the back. It was fifty years old and had the tall, shady oaks leaning over the roof to prove it. Everything unmistakably middle class. Pavlak had loved the house from the start, but Judith was disappointed, hoping for something grander. It was ironic that when the separation came, she had insisted that he leave, and she stay. But Pavlak understood that it was for Tasha's sake, and he had agreed.

Now, as the old house drew nearer, he thought back to that last night. It was only three months ago, but it seemed longer. The arrangements had all been completed, the decisions made. For the moment the bickering and bitterness were put aside, and he and Judith had sat on the living room couch and held each other and cried. There were only two questions left. Would the separation be permanent? And who would keep Tasha? And both of them knew the answers. After thirteen years, something had gone wrong—slowly, but irremediably. It was over. And Tasha would go with her mother. That was the part that broke Pavlak's heart. He and Judith had been drifting apart for years, and the separation was like pruning a dead branch. But losing his little girl would tear at something living and vital. He would agree, he knew, because he couldn't bear to see Tasha caught in a battle between them, certainly not a battle that he was doomed to lose. Then they had heard the creak on the stairs and looked up to find Tasha's dark round eyes peering at them through the slats in the railing.

"What is it, honey?" Judith had asked, hastily wiping the tears from her cheeks. "Did you have a bad dream?"

For a moment there was no response. Then a small voice, so fragile and slight it was almost inaudible, had asked. "Are you fighting?"

They had simply stared. Then Pavlak had taken his arm from Judith's shoulder. "No, sweetheart. We aren't going to fight anymore." And Tasha had rushed down the stairs and flung her small arms around his neck. Pavlak had hugged her tightly and turned to Judith with a sad smile, only to be stunned by the cold resentment in her eyes. That was when he realized how hurt Judith was by Tasha's preference for her father.

After the detective's phone call, he had run back to Mrs. Ekelwood's house in record time and jumped straight into his car. Now he spun the wheel toward the driveway, and immediately glimpsed the highway patrol car parked behind the house. The sight of it, as cold and gray as a revolver, fired a shot of reality into his numbed brain. Tears came, but he fought them back. There would be time to cry later.

The patrolman was standing at the back door, apparently waiting for a response to his knock. When Pavlak stopped his car, the patrolman walked toward him in the purple glow from the street lamp.

"Are you Mr. Lyles?"

"My name is Pavlak. John Pavlak. I'm Judith Lyles' husband."

"Oh yes—right. Mr. Pavlak."

The patrolman said nothing for at least five seconds. He was tall, almost as tall as Pavlak, and swarthy. His uniform was crisp and clean, and his hair—as much as was visible beneath the broad-brimmed hat—looked as if he had just stepped from the barber shop. The only blemish on his military appearance was a heavy shadow of beard, noticeable even in the dim light.

"I'm very sorry Mr. Lyles—I mean, Mr. . . . ."

"Pavlak."

"Right, Pavlak."

A mockingbird sang in one of the oak branches above them. A mockingbird singing in the dark. The patrolman, the house, the mockingbird, his own voice—it was all part of a movie he was watching.

"The man who called me . . ." Pavlak began.

"Sergeant Crane?"

"Yes . . . Crane. He didn't tell me much. He said he would meet me here."

"He's been delayed, but he'll be here soon. Did you bring your house key?"

Pavlak ignored the question. "Listen . . . are you sure about this accident? Are you sure it was my wife?"

"Well—we're sure it was her car."

"When? Where?"

"About two hours ago. On the interstate. Just north of the Cornelius exit."

"What . . . I mean . . . what happened?"

"We're not positive. There was no other vehicle involved. Something seems to have happened to the car. There was an explosion."

"An explosion?" Pavlak said dumbly, staring.

"Apparently, yes." The patrolman picked his words. "There may have been a bomb."

"A bomb?"

"Maybe. We're not sure. I'm very sorry, Mr. Lyles . . . Mr. Pavlak. Very sorry."

"Thank you." Pavlak pawed absently at the door handle on his aging Toyota. The patrolman was behind him somewhere, fading out of the dream. "Thank you very much." Why was he thanking him? Oh yes, the man said he was sorry. It was proper to thank someone for being sorry. Strange.

Pavlak turned back toward him. "Uh, listen . . . Officer . . ."

"Yes?"

"Do you know where my daughter is? I mean, has anybody said anything about her? It's almost eight o'clock, and I don't know where my wife left her. . . ." The patrolman's expression stopped him.

"Mr . . . Pavlak. Didn't Sergeant Crane say anything about the child?"

Something invisible swooped at Pavlak out of the darkness. He fought it off. "No. What are you . . . ?"

"There appears to have been a child in the car as well. The bodies are badly burned. . . ."

Pavlak felt his knees strike the sharp gravel of the driveway, and an instant later the patrolman gripped his arm. He rested his forehead against the side of the car and stared at the ground, not seeing it. "It's not my little girl," he said firmly. A hand tugged at his arm, and Pavlak, feeling suddenly embarrassed, struggled to his feet.

"Is there someone you could call?" the patrolman asked. "Maybe we should go into the house and call someone to help you." The patrolman held his arm in a powerful grip.

A sudden rage seized Pavlak, and he wrenched his arm free. "I'm fine," he shouted. "I have to go. I . . ." He tried to open the car door, but the patrolman was leaning against it.

"Mr. Pavlak . . . ," he was urging gently, pulling on Pavlak's arm again. "Step away from the car."

Pavlak tried to pull free again, but this time the patrolman held on. He heard the crunch of gravel behind him and twisted his head to see another police vehicle—this one a county sheriff's car, pulling in beside his. Two car doors slammed in rapid succession. Pavlak planted his forearm in the patrolman's chest and shoved. The tall law officer stumbled backward and for an instant Pavlak was free, then suddenly there were more hands on his arms, pulling him away from his car. A flight would be nice, he thought. For a little while he could drown all this in passion and violence and the sweet distraction of physical pain. He was gathering himself to throw a punch when a calm voice stopped him.

"Mr. Pavlak? I'm Detective Sergeant Crane."

Pavlak let his shoulder drop and turned toward the voice. The hands on his arms fell away. Crane was dressed in street clothes—khaki trousers and a brown leather jacket. He wore a white shirt but no tie. Only the close haircut hinted at his profession—the haircut and the expression on his face. It was that empty, emotionless look of men for whom human tragedies are part of every day's routine.

"Thank you for coming, Mr. Pavlak," Crane went on. "I know this is very difficult for you, but the sooner we start our investigation, the sooner we can get to the bottom of this. You are the legal owner of this house, is that correct?"

"Well, we own it jointly, so I guess . . . yes, I'm the legal owner."

"And you have no objection to our searching the premises?"

Pavlak shook his head. "But why . . . ?"

"Unlock the door for us please, Mr. Pavlak."

They walked in a huddle toward the back door. The movement of a curtain in a lighted window in Diane Sweeney's house caught Pavlak's eye, but when he looked up the curtain was closed. His fingers shook, but he finally managed to fit his key into the lock and turn it. At least Judith had not changed the locks. He pushed the door open, flipped on the light, and froze.

The shelves to his right were empty, and books lay scattered on the floor at his feet. At first he thought someone had dumped bags of cotton on the couch, but then he realized it was the stuffing from the cushions.

"My God," Pavlak murmured and started forward, but Crane grabbed his sleeve.

"Don't touch anything," he ordered curtly. "Frank, get the van. You stay outside, Mr. Pavlak. Have a seat in my car. I'll drive you home in a few minutes."

"But . . . my car. I'm all right. I . . ."

"We'll get your car back to your apartment. You shouldn't drive now. Take a seat in my car. I'll be with you in a moment."

It was an order, not a request. Crane raised an eyebrow toward a deputy in uniform who nodded and turned. "Come with me, Mr. Pavlak," the deputy said firmly.

Pavlak's keys were still in his hand. As he followed the deputy toward Crane's car, he turned them quietly until the ignition key for the Toyota was pressed firmly between his thumb and forefinger. The deputy opened the rear door of the county vehicle and waited. Pavlak started forward then hesitated. The squad car was on his right, the Toyota two steps away on his left.

"Hang on a second," Pavlak said casually, turning left. "I have to get something from my car first." He pulled on the door handle, dropped in and slammed the lock shut behind him. By the time the deputy reached the car, he had the engine roaring and was shoving the gear stick into reverse. The deputy landed a useless slap on the windshield as he released the clutch, then he heard shouts and saw scurrying figures in the corner of his eye as the Toyota bounced over the gutter and into the street.

It was all a dream. Still a dream. He was conscious of going through familiar motions: shifting gears, turning the wheel. He had felt something like this during that first fire fight in Vietnam. Crawling forward, firing, fitting a fresh clip into his weapon and shoving it home—all as if the air around him had not been filled with death. Then he was spinning right onto Main Street. But something was wrong.

There were people in cars, driving slowly, stopping at red lights. And other people walking and talking on the sidewalk as if the world had not turned upside down. What was wrong with them?

Horns blared angrily and brakes screeched. Behind him in the distance he could hear a siren, and blue lights flashed frantically in his rearview mirror. "Just north of the Cornelius exchange," the patrolman had said. Ahead of him, the last traffic light before the I-77 intersection changed to yellow. He planted his palm on the horn and glanced at the speedometer. He was doing seventy. A car started to pull out from his right then lurched to a halt as he flew beneath the blazing red light. Only a few hundred yards now.

A highway patrol car with blue lights flashing sat defiantly astride the entrance ramp. The northbound lanes were closed. Pavlak ignored the frantic signals of the patrolman and ducked around the rear end of the patrol car, with the Toyota fishtailing in the wet grass before the tires caught on the concrete again. He accelerated to the bottom of the ramp, then almost immediately slammed the brake pedal. Yellow tape and a phalanx of flashing lights, police cars, and unmarked vans blocked his path. Beyond them, a section of the highway glowed brighter than daylight. Three banks of floodlights, mounted on half-ton highway trucks, provided the illumination. He saw a line of men on their hands and knees, dressed in white smocks, crawling across the lighted area in formation. Pavlak threw the door shut behind him and sprinted toward them. He hurdled the yellow tape and heard shouts, then shadows came at him from both sides. Someone grabbed his arm, and he flung the man aside. Someone else tackled his knees, and he felt himself plunging to the pavement. Bodies landed on top of him, and hands clutched at his wrists, his arms, wrenching them behind him. In the babble of voices he heard someone shout, "Cuffs!" and a few seconds later, hard steel closed around one wrist, then the other.

"Who the hell is he?" an angry voice demanded. "Anybody know this man?"

Exhausted, Pavlak stopped struggling and lay still, gasping for oxygen, his right cheek raw from grinding against the concrete.

"John?" a familiar voice asked anxiously, somewhere above him. "John—what the hell are you doing?" It was Paul Tower, one of Avery's three full-time cops. "John, for Christ's sake . . . What do you think you're doing?"

"Paul!" he cried. "Is my baby here?"

There was a silence.

"She's gone, John. The ambulance left half an hour ago. They're taking them to Chapel Hill for autopsies."

Suddenly it was there again, some beast, dark and huge and terrible, looming and leaping at his heart, and this time he couldn't dodge. "Taking who?" he pleaded. "It's not her, is it? It's not my baby?"

He felt Paul Tower's hand come to rest gently on the back of his neck.

"Judith and Tasha, John. They were both killed. I'm sorry—I'm really sorry. But you've got to get hold of yourself. There's nothing you can do now."

Pavlak was fighting again, fighting the Beast now. He banged his forehead sharply against the concrete. That helped. He did it again. Then again.

"John, stop it! Pull yourself together, for God's sake!" A forearm circled his neck and locked his head back. "Get him up." The weights rose off his back, and hands lifted him to a sitting position. Tower squatted in front of him, blocking his view of the technicians who were combing the lighted area. He gestured over Pavlak's head. "Get him a cup of coffee."

Pavlak let his head drop and closed his eyes.

"John . . ." It was Tower again. "Didn't Sergeant Crane talk to you?"

"Yes, he told me, but . . ." Pavlak tried to reach for Tower's shirt, but the handcuffs held his wrists behind his back. "Listen," Pavlak pleaded. "Are you sure? You can't be sure. Maybe . . ."

"It's Judith's car, John. The license plate is charred, but it's readable. And the patrol even radioed in the engine number, just to be sure."

"But . . . How do you know it was them in the car? It could have been anybody." His voice sounded strange, as if someone else were speaking through his throat. It was pitched far too high.

Tower was shaking his head from side to side. "They'll make a positive ID in Chapel Hill, John, but you've got to face it. They're dead."

"They can't be!"

"They *are*. They died instantly. From the concussion, if nothing else. It was a big bomb."

Pavlak looked up. "Bomb? Are you sure it was a bomb? Maybe the gas tank exploded or something."

"No, ATF is here. It was a bomb. Under the dash on the driver's side. That was the first thing their man said when he looked at the car."

"But who—I mean . . . ?"

Someone handed Tower a steaming Styrofoam cup, and he accepted it with a curt nod. "We don't know, John. Listen, you gonna behave yourself now? Can we take the cuffs off?"

Pavlak nodded silently. Whatever was coming, he was too tired to resist anymore. The handcuffs fell off his wrists, and

Tower gently fitted the Styrofoam cup into his fingers. "Drink this, and I'll take you home. There's nothing you can do here. These guys'll find out who did this. Just stay out of their way. Okay?"

Pavlak nodded again. He was staring at the burned-out hulk of an automobile that sat on the median of the highway, illuminated by the powerful floods. The drone of diesel generators shut out the usual stillness of night, just as the floods held back the darkness. A man in white coveralls was on his knees beside the car, his upper torso inside it. Another man knelt beside him, holding a long flashlight beside his ear and aiming its beam into the floorboard. It was like a night scene from an old war movie. Pavlak stood carefully, then absently brought the Styrofoam cup to his lips. The coffee scalded his tongue.

"Come on, John," Tower repeated, turning him gently away from the blazing lights.

Pavlak walked numbly toward a big black police car with the town seal of Avery painted on the door. Beside it sat a county sheriff's car, the blue light still whirling on the roof. The deputy who had chased him there leaned against the fender with his arms folded and gave Pavlak an angry stare. As Pavlak dropped the coffee cup on the ground, and climbed into Tower's car, he saw the deputy reach through his open window and pull a microphone to his mouth. Thoughts scrambled through his mind uncontrollably, irrelevantly, as the car began to move. He stared through the steel mesh that separated him from the front seat. The day care. He would have to call them. He should get Tasha's things. She had some papers or something there, didn't she? Some drawings or something. Maybe the day care center had the child seat. No, it would be in Judith's car if Tasha was with Judith. It would be blown up or burned up or something, wouldn't it? Or maybe it was still useable.

The absurdity of such thoughts penetrated to something still sane in his mind. Useable for what? He had no little girl, no wife, no family whatsoever—nothing to care for. Nothing to love. No beautiful child to watch grow and change. Nothing but himself again.

Tower turned into the street where his apartment lay. Suddenly Pavlak desperately wanted to avoid the place that his landlady, Mrs. Ekelwood, called a "penthouse" and that was lonely and empty enough, even when he had not just been told that his wife and child were dead. Dead. Murdered. The Beast leapt at him, and he flinched.

Mrs. Ekelwood's house was a two-story frame Victorian, the kind of beautiful, high-ceilinged dollop of history that dominates older residential streets in small towns throughout the South. The porch was twelve feet wide and circled the entire house. "Nice place to ride a bicycle in the rain," Pavlak quipped when Mrs. Ekelwood first showed it to him. She had stared at him coldly and was not entirely mollified when he explained that he was joking.

A late-model Chevrolet stood in his usual parking spot in the driveway. Tower eased the police car against the curb. Mrs. Ekelwood stood on the porch talking to a man whom he recognized by the brown leather jacket. Pavlak breathed a sigh of relief. Thank God Crane was here. He couldn't bear to face the apartment alone.

"You going to be all right now, John?" he heard Tower ask as the policeman held the car door for him.

"Yeah, I'm okay."

"I'll get your car back to you later tonight. That be all right?"

"Sure. Thanks."

"Dr. Pavlak, this gentleman would like to speak with you," Mrs. Ekelwood announced coolly as Pavlak climbed the wooden steps to the porch. "He's from the sheriff's department." Her eyes launched daggers of disapproval into Pavlak's face.

Pavlak nodded at Crane. "I suppose you have some questions."

"Just a few." He gave Pavlak a long, accusing look then glanced around. "Can we talk in private?"

"This way."

Pavlak brushed past the detective and led him up the creaking stairs to his apartment. With a visitor at his side, the first since he moved in, the apartment seemed suddenly shabby. He showed Crane into the kitchen and gestured politely toward a chair at the table, then offered the detective a cup of coffee. Crane declined with a curt shake of his head and seated himself at the wooden table. He flipped open a clipboard with an aluminum cover. Pavlak took the opposite chair and waited.

"That was a damned fool thing you did, driving off like that."

Pavlak said nothing.

"I could arrest you, you know that?"

Pavlak met his gaze. "Go ahead. You think I care?"

Crane looked away, and when he spoke again, his voice had lost some of its hardness. "You're upset. That's understandable. But you get control of yourself, all right? Pull something like that again, and I won't be able to let it pass."

Pavlak started to respond but found he didn't have the energy. And anyway, it didn't matter: Nothing mattered. He wondered vaguely if anything ever would again.

"Now, Mr. Pavlak," the detective began, then stopped and

pulled a small notepad from the pocket of his leather jacket. "I believe the patrolman gave you a brief description of the . . . of the incident."

"I saw the car. ATF says it was a bomb."

Crane gave him a long look. "Yes, well, it appears that your wife and child were murdered." He waited for a response, watching Pavlak silently.

Murder. That word again. Something in his brain kept toying with it, then spitting it out again. Murder. Intentionally, purposely killed by someone. Pavlak looked into Crane's waiting eyes and suddenly realized that he was a suspect— the estranged husband in a bitter separation. Oh God, he thought. Not that too.

Mercifully, Crane dropped his eyes to the clipboard and continued. "I'm sorry to have to bother you, but you understand that in a case like this, we have to start an investigation as quickly as possible."

"Yes . . . sure."

"I guess the first question is the obvious one. Do you know anyone who may have wanted to kill your wife?"

Maybe it was nervousness, but Pavlak laughed. "My wife was an investigative reporter, Officer. And she was very good. There are probably hundreds of people who would love to kill her."

"Anyone in particular?" Crane asked patiently.

Pavlak took a quick mental survey back through the years. "No," he said, shaking his head slowly. "Not really. She exposed a charity fraud a few years ago—people collecting money for starving children in Ethiopia, supposedly. Nasty bunch. One of them broke her nose—but I think that guy's still in prison. She's had lots of death threats, anonymous phone calls, that sort of thing. She never took them seriously."

"Did you?"

"I did at first, then it sort of got to be routine. You know . . . Hey, honey, Sears called and said the microwave was fixed, and some lady said she was going to blow your head off with a shotgun."

"Anybody lately?"

"I wouldn't know. We separated just before Christmas, and we've hardly spoken since then. I do know that she was working on an exposé of some evangelist who was bilking old women out of their money. And she was looking into that motorcycle gang . . . the Devil's Dogs or Satan's Sons or whatever cute name they have for themselves. Drugs and prostitution, I think it was."

Crane nodded. "The Devil's Dragons. I know about that investigation, Mr. Pavlak. In fact I knew your wife. She worked with the police quite a bit. She helped us . . . we helped her."

"Then you probably know more about what she was doing than I do."

"What about her private life? Did she have a boyfriend? I'm sorry. I have to ask."

Pavlak gazed to his right out the kitchen's only window. It was huge, with nine panes of old, distorted glass and genuine wooden mullions. The wood was painted, like the rest of the room, in a sort of army-surplus green that Pavlak suddenly realized he hated.

"I understand," Pavlak replied. "No. At least not that I know of. She had a girlfriend, though."

"A girlfriend?"

"Soon after we separated, she asked Diane Sweeney to move in with her. At least that's what I heard. Diane refused. She teaches here at the college. English."

"You mean she's a lesbian?"

"Who?"

"Sweeney."

Pavlak shrugged. "Not that I know of. She's about thirty-five—as far as I know never married. But then, she's a card-carrying man-hater, so I can't imagine what man could tolerate her—or vice-versa."

"A feminist?"

"I suppose you could call her that. I'm sure she considers herself one."

"What's her name again?" He was scribbling on the clipboard.

"Sweeney. Diane Sweeney. She lives next door to Judith . . . to where Judith used to live . . . the house." He made a vague gesture toward the window.

"I gather you don't like her very much," Crane ventured.

"You gather correctly. We clash over everything. Always have."

"Judith was something of a feminist herself, wasn't she?"

Judith. So Crane knew her on a first-name basis. "Yes. But she only got strident about it lately—since she started hanging around with Diane."

"I notice she didn't use your last name. But you were legally married, weren't you?"

"Oh yes. Legally. She made it clear fifteen years ago, from our first conversation about marriage, that she wasn't going to use my name. I didn't object at the time. Thought it a rather sexist custom myself."

"You were married fifteen years ago?" Crane was writing again.

"It would have been fourteen in May."

"Judith was a few years younger than you, wasn't she?" Crane asked casually.

"Eight, to be exact. She was a young reporter, fresh out

of journalism school. She came out to interview me when I was made athletic director at Avery. I was only thirty-one, and the paper thought that made me worth a feature article. We got married a year later."

"Why did you wait until you were, what—thirty-two—to get married?"

"It just worked out that way. College, the army, Vietnam, graduate school. . . . I had a girlfriend most of the time, but I guess I just wasn't ready to marry. Then Judith came along. . . ."

"I understand. Let's see . . . ," Crane frowned, "that means you were married . . . ten years before your daughter was born?"

Pavlak studied the grain on the wooden tabletop and wondered why the question made him uncomfortable. "I would have liked kids earlier," he conceded, "but Judith was very wrapped up in her career. Then after she turned thirty, she began to change a little. I guess she heard her biological clock ticking. Unfortunately, we had a hard time getting pregnant. It took a few years, even after she was finally ready."

"What about your daughter?"

The Beast swooped at him. He dodged and swallowed. "What about her?"

"Whose name does she . . . did she use?"

"Tasha is a Pavlak. Judith said she didn't care . . . and I believe she really didn't." He started to tell Crane how their marriage, stable if not passionate for nearly a decade, had hit the skids almost immediately after Tasha was born. He had since realized that it had never really been a marriage, just a loose companionship in which they were tied to each other by a very long rope while both pursued their own interests. He glanced at Crane, who was waiting for him to say more. Pavlak shrugged silently instead. It was all too complicated to explain—and irrelevant to the detective's investigation.

Crane adjusted his weight in the chair and pretended to study the notes he had made. "Tell me about the separation. What are the terms?"

"Terms?"

"You know . . . who got what? What about your daughter? She stayed with your wife, I take it. Was it hard to work that out?"

The direction of the question was obvious. Pavlak decided to lay it on the line. "Detective," he began, "the separation was reasonably amicable at first, but it got increasingly bitter—on Judith's side, not mine. Up until now I just let Judith have her way—tried to placate her, hoped that some kind of friendship between us, at least, could be salvaged."

"And?"

Pavlak shook his head. "Things only got worse since Diane Sweeney started spending more time at the house. And finally, about two weeks ago, Judith took a job in San Diego. She was working out a thirty-day notice at the *Courier*, and she was planning to move—with Tasha of course—late in the spring. I'm not exactly sure when. In fact, I only heard about the move from other sources. For the last month, Judith rarely spoke to me."

"Would you have let her take your daughter to California?"

Pavlak studied his fingernails and shrugged. "I couldn't have stopped her."

"Would you have tried?"

A small hangnail protruded from the ring finger on his left hand. He caught it between the thumbnail and index finger of his right and pulled. The flesh tore, and a thin line of blood formed in the furrow between the nail and the finger. He looked up. "Maybe. I don't know."

Crane probed aimlessly, or so it seemed to Pavlak, for more than an hour. They talked about Judith's job and her investigations, but Crane always drifted back to their marriage and Judith's personal life. He had scribbled eight legal pages full of notes when he clapped the aluminum cover over the clipboard and stood. "I guess that's it for now. There'll be more questions later." He held out his hand. "I'm very sorry we have to do this, but you understand how it is."

"Of course," Pavlak took the proffered hand.

"You . . . don't have any plans to travel soon, do you?" Crane asked.

"I'm not going anywhere." Pavlak waited, then plunged. "I suppose I'm a suspect, right?"

"Not really. We don't have any suspects yet."

"But you haven't ruled me out."

Crane looked straight at him. "I haven't ruled out my mother yet. If you mean it that way, everybody's a suspect. By the way, there's a possibility the FBI will take over the investigation. If so, they'll want to talk to you soon."

"The FBI?"

"Many of Judith's current investigations involve people across the border in South Carolina. In fact, she was in York County early this morning. It's possible that the bomb was planted there. Cross-state crime is a federal matter, and bombings are more their line. They'll call on ATF for expertise, technical resources, and so on. You understand."

Pavlak nodded absently as he escorted the county detective to the door and wished him a good evening. Then he turned to face the apartment. Emptiness and silence. And suddenly the Beast was there, behind him, beside him . . .

everywhere. His knees went rubbery, but he willed his legs to carry him to the refrigerator. He took out a can of beer and pulled the tab with trembling fingers.

The phone on his desk rang. Pavlak walked into the study and stared at it as if it were a creature from outer space. It rang six times, then stopped. He stooped to unplug the line from the phone jack in the baseboard, then tossed the useless wire onto the desktop. As he did so, Tasha's portrait caught his eye, and he heard a cry, a sort of hoarse gasp, escape his throat.

He set the untouched beer on the desk and reached for the photograph. That smile—he would never see it again. All he had hoped for her, dreamed for her, she would never become. All he had promised her, he could never deliver.

A pain too sharp to endure knifed into him, and Pavlak dropped the photograph face-down on the desk. This was it. The Beast. Another guttural cry erupted in his throat. He shut his eyes, stumbled toward the light switch and swatted at it blindly until darkness engulfed him. It didn't help. The Beast was still there.

He rushed to the bedroom and dropped onto the mattress on his back. Everything was gone. His life, his hope—everything. Taken away by someone invisible, someone living, breathing.

The pain swelled and grew until his heart burst, only to swell and grow and burst again. And each time Pavlak was sure he would die. He cried out in hoarse, throaty yelps. He pounded his head against the frame of the bed. Nothing helped. His little girl was dead. Beyond reach. Beyond hope. Taken by a hand that was *not* dead, a hand that might, for all he knew, be holding a glass of champagne at that moment, celebrating.

For an hour he twisted and wailed on the bed, while the

ache in him swelled and burst, again and again, until finally, like lava, his pain began to cool and harden into a grim resolve. The Beast curled up and settled inside him. Tasha was dead. But he was alive. And there was one reason left for living. One reason only. But it was enough.

3

Exhausted, Pavlak switched on the light and washed his face. He had just finished drying when a soft knock sounded at the door. It was Kenneth and Audrey Rankin. Audrey, at five foot one, looked smaller than ever. Her eyes were red and swollen, but when she walked through the door to Pavlak's apartment, they widened. "Are you *alone*?" she asked.

Pavlak lifted his palms then dropped them to confirm the obvious.

"Where have you been? We've been calling ever since we heard. Where's your family? Your brother . . . ?"

"At home, I suppose. I haven't called him yet."

Audrey gave him a motherly but reproachful stare. "Have you told your father, at least?"

"No. He's on a trip out West."

There was an awkward silence.

Pavlak motioned toward the sagging couch. "Have a seat."

"What can we do, John? How can we help?" It was Kenneth Rankin who spoke. Kenneth was tall and slender, with gray eyes and hands that seemed to rest perpetually in the pockets of his trousers. If he took them out, it was only to light his ever-present pipe. "Have you called Judith's family?"

"No. There really hasn't been time. The police just left a little while ago." Pavlak sighed and walked toward the study. When he returned, the telephone was in his right hand. He plugged the phone line into a jack beside the couch, then rummaged in a drawer until he found his address book. He took a deep breath and made the call to Chicago. Judith's mother answered. He broke the news as gently as he knew how. There was a thin wail, then the crash of the phone hitting the floor. After a few moments of confusion Judith's stepfather picked up the receiver, and Pavlak repeated all he knew. It was very little. Judith's mother was still moaning in the background when he hung up. Pavlak stared wearily at the carpet.

"Who else should you call?" Audrey asked quietly. There were fresh tears on her cheeks.

"My father, I suppose. I have his itinerary around here somewhere." He rummaged among the papers on the side table until he uncovered a blank deposit slip with dates and phone numbers on the back. He had written it down as Roser dictated it over the phone.

Pavlak dialed a number beside the word "Flagstaff."

"Gustaf Pavlak, please," he said to the hotel clerk who answered. The extension rang once and then his father's voice came on the line.

"Hello?"

"It's John. I have bad news, Dad."

There was a short silence. "What's happened?"

"Judith and Tasha are dead. Somebody blew up Judith's car. It was a bomb." He waited, but there was no response. "Dad?"

"Are you sure?"

Pavlak could not believe his ears. His father's voice was choked. Was he actually crying? In his entire life, Pavlak had never seen his father cry, not even when Pavlak's mother died.

"Both of them?" his father asked again. "Are you sure?"

"Yes, Dad, both of them. Tasha was sick and Judith picked her up early from day care. The bomb went off on the interstate just outside Avery."

Pavlak waited again in silence.

"My God . . . I . . . My God . . ."

"Yeah, I know."

There was another long silence, then the old man began to recover. "Listen, we'll fly back tomorrow. I'll hire someone to drive the car back. I don't know when we'll get there. I'll make reservations right now and call you back."

"Don't bother. You'll get here when you get here. They're doing an autopsy in Chapel Hill, so the funeral won't be for a few days anyway."

"You've called Tom?"

"No."

"Are you going to?"

"You call him. I've got to go, Dad."

Pavlak hung up.

Kenneth and Audrey studied the floor. "John . . ." It was Kenneth who spoke at last. "I know your father did some terrible things when you were growing up, but you could be civil to him at a moment like this, at least." Kenneth taught philosophy at Avery College. Pavlak supposed that Kenneth qualified as his best friend, at least as far as he could be said to have one.

"That *was* civil," Pavlak replied, standing. "Can I get you some coffee?"

"I'm serious."

Pavlak rounded on him. "Look, Kenneth," he said sharply.

"I've never gotten along with my father. Never. It's not possible. You think this will change anything?"

Kenneth took a deep breath, then let his shoulders fall in surrender.

Pavlak made coffee in silence. He had just handed Audrey a cup when the phone rang.

"It's Roser, John," a quiet, female voice announced. Pavlak liked Roser, his beautiful, black-eyed stepmother, who was a year younger than he was. In fact, she was probably the only reason he and his father talked at all anymore. Pavlak often wondered why she had married the man. Maybe it was for his money, though she didn't seem the type.

"I'm so sorry, John," Roser continued in her soft, Catalonian accent. To Pavlak it was indistinguishable from a Spanish accent, but when he once made the mistake of referring to it as such, she had scolded him for half an hour. Catalonians, she insisted, were not, never had been, and never would be, Spanish. That they lived within the political confines of Spain was merely her people's cross to bear.

"We're in shock," Roser was saying. "We just called Tom. He's stunned too, of course. He asked if he should drive to Avery . . ."

"Thanks, Roser, but . . . you know how things are."

"Yes. All right, John. We'll see you tomorrow. We've booked a flight out of Phoenix. We'll get to Charlotte early tomorrow afternoon and come straight to your apartment."

"Please don't, Roser. I don't . . ." He started to say he didn't want to see his father, but thought better of it. "I need some time to get this under control a little better."

"All right, John, I understand. Take care. We love you."

He hung up the phone and plopped heavily on the couch.

Kenneth cleared his throat. "Who else should you call? There must be other people who should know. Judith's friends? More family?"

"Her stepfather will take care of the rest of her family," Pavlak answered. "The police will notify the paper. And Diane Sweeney will tell everybody else. I don't think there's anyone . . . Wait—I suppose I should call Brigitte."

"Brigitte? Oh, her German friend."

"Yes. She and Judith were close. Maybe Diane called her already, but I doubt it." He looked at his watch. It was almost eleven. "Anyway, it's the middle of the night in Berlin. I'll wait till morning."

"Well," said Audrey, standing, "I hope you don't mind if I clean up a little." She didn't wait for an answer but disappeared into the kitchen.

They stayed with Pavlak until after one o'clock, answering the phone and fielding the shocked condolences of acquaintances as the news spread through the intimate world of a small college town. On Pavlak's instructions, Kenneth told everyone who inquired that John was not up to company yet.

When they finally left, Pavlak couldn't sleep. He went to the refrigerator for a beer three times and each time talked himself out of it. He wanted a clear head. He lay in the dark and waited for sleep, but sleep would not come. The silence weighed on him. At 1:30 he decided to call Berlin. It would be 7:30 there. Maybe he could catch Brigitte before she went to work.

They had met Brigitte in Marburg ten years before. The acquaintance resulted from one of those things that can happen when you work for a small college. As athletic director, Pavlak enjoyed faculty status and even taught a German class from time to time when one of the faculty was on sabbatical. Then a last-minute resignation had left the school's junior year abroad program in Marburg without a resident director for the coming year. Pavlak learned of the resignation from a casual remark the dean made in a private meeting. "I'll do it," Pavlak had laughed. It was a joke, really, but then he had ended up with a year's leave from his post as A.D. and two tickets for Frankfurt. Judith had taken leave from the newspaper with feigned reluctance, but Pavlak knew she was secretly delighted at the opportunity to spend a year abroad.

Brigitte lived across the hall in their apartment building in Marburg. She was a sociology student, and she and Judith became fast friends. They shared a passion for their definition of social justice, and the two young leftists—Brigitte four years younger than Judith—spent endless hours discussing politics, railing against the hidden economic motives of American and West German foreign policy, and generally reassuring each other of their moral superiority over a greedy and uncaring world. After Pavlak and Judith returned to the United States, Judith's friendship with Brigitte survived.

In 1990, Brigitte had visited them and announced that she was about to marry a man named Turgat Onat, a German-born Turk whose name and dark features brought both him and, subsequently, Brigitte into daily confrontation with Germany's still virulent xenophobia. After they married, her husband, an architect, found a job in Berlin, and he and Brigitte moved to Germany's once and future capital. The last time Pavlak had spoken to her, she had taken a job with the *Gauck-Behörde*, named for the man Germany's chancellor had appointed to sift through the tons of files collected by East Germany's former secret police, the "Stasi." Brigitte was now happily immersed in unraveling the evil of a state she had, in her radical student days, energetically defended.

Pavlak lifted the receiver and dialed a long string of numbers—international access code, country code, city code, number—then waited through the clicks and buzzes as AT&T danced its mating ritual with German Telekom. At last he heard the familiar elongated beep that signaled a ringing telephone in Germany. It rang five times, and he was about to hang up when someone lifted the receiver.

"Hier bei Onat," answered a sleepy female voice.

"Brigitte. Habe ich dich geweckt?" He quickly checked his watch again and recalculated. Did he have Central European time wrong? Maybe they were already on daylight saving time or something.

There was a long pause. Too long. Brigitte usually recognized his voice and the transatlantic hollowness of the connection immediately. It occurred to him that he might have dialed a wrong number.

"Who's speaking, please?" the voice asked in German.

"Excuse me, I was trying to reach Brigitte Onat."

"Yes, you have the right number. May I ask who is calling?"

"My name is Pavlak—John Pavlak. I'm a friend of Brigitte's. I'm calling from the United States."

"Ach ja," the voice said. "Yes, I remember. You are Judith's husband. I am Karin, Brigitte's sister. Brigitte often spoke of you and Judith."

Something cold clutched at Pavlak's heart. Why had she used the past tense? "Karin, yes. Is . . . is anything wrong?"

There was another silence. "I'm afraid so. Brigitte died two days ago. She was killed by a hit-and-run driver."

4

Pavlak awoke shortly after eight o'clock to a polite but persistent tapping at his door. He was still in his clothes and had slept no more than an hour. Stiffness gripped his neck again, and a fresh headache pounded inside his skull.

"Coming!" he croaked at the door. The knocking stopped. Pavlak lurched to the sink and swallowed three extra-strength Tylenol, splashed some water on his face, then jerked the door open.

A man in an impeccably tailored suit nodded and raised his right hand. Nestled in the palm was a leather folder, opened to reveal an identity card. The initials "FBI" in big blue letters leapt out at Pavlak, along with the seal of the United States Justice Department. To the left of the letters was a laminated, color photograph that matched the face of the man holding the picture. His hair was completely gray, but the skin of his face was only beginning to show wrinkles beneath the eyes, calm blue eyes that regarded Pavlak patiently.

"I'm sorry to disturb you, Dr. Pavlak," the visitor said quietly. "My name is Streat. Special Agent Streat. I'm with the Federal Bureau of Investigation, and I'm the case agent investigating yesterday's bombing. May I come in?"

Pavlak gestured wordlessly toward the couch.

Streat held his gaze on Pavlak's face a second longer, then walked through the door. He looked around, then decided on an armchair. Pavlak slumped onto the couch and waited. The FBI agent observed him silently, the cool eyes betraying nothing.

"I know this is a tough time for you, Dr. Pavlak," Streat began quietly, "but you understand that there is no time to lose if we're going to catch the people who killed your wife."

His headache and exhaustion were not this man's fault, Pavlak reminded himself, but he still could not keep the irritation from showing in his tone. "Look, I already told that detective everything I know. And as long as you guys think I killed my wife, you're just wasting my time, your time, and the taxpayers' dollars. You . . ."

"We're not investigating you."

Pavlak pulled up short. "Well, maybe *you're* not, but Crane thinks . . ."

"He's not investigating you either. We're investigating the bombing, that's all. Oh, and the break-in at your wife's house."

"So . . . what do you want from me now? I told Crane everything I know."

"Yes, but I need to hear it myself. Besides, I might catch some detail he missed, or say something that jogs your memory. You never know. You *do* want us to catch the people who did this, don't you, Dr. Pavlak?"

It was the third time the man had used his title, and Pavlak felt an internal alarm go off. "Of course I do. In fact, I'd like to be the one who catches him, and I'd like to catch him before you get there," Pavlak declared between clenched teeth, then checked himself and drew a slow breath. "As for the burglary . . ."

"It wasn't a burglary. At least, not an ordinary burglary."

Pavlak stopped, his mouth open. "What . . . I mean, how do you know? What was it?"

Streat shrugged again, a condescending shrug that said the reasons were obvious to any idiot, but since you asked . . . "A lot of reasons. Mainly the way the house was searched. Somebody knew what he was doing. My guess is he was looking for something specific."

Pavlak's headache relented a little as the Tylenol took hold, and his attention, which had been wandering, latched onto Streat's voice.

"Looking for what?"

"I was hoping you might be able to tell me."

It was Pavlak's turn to shrug. "No idea. I've been pretty much out of touch with my wife since the separation. I'd ask her colleagues at the newspaper, if I were you."

"I will. But in the meantime, I have a few questions—if you don't mind."

"Certainly."

Streat thumbed quickly through a pocket notebook. "We've been looking at her telephone records at the *Courier*—don't have them from the home phone yet, but we're working on it—and there seems to have been an extraordinary amount of activity lately. Lots of calls to various numbers in Washington, D.C., for example. We're tracking them down right now. . . ."

"That can't be all that unusual," Pavlak responded. "Judith was a reporter. She was probably hunting facts, laws, regulations—that sort of thing. She did that all the time."

"Yes, well . . ." Streat flipped through his notes some

more, then started again. "There was something else pretty odd. In the last two weeks, she made seven calls to Germany. All seven of them to the same number." Streat looked up questioningly.

Pavlak made a conscious effort to keep his hands resting calmly at his sides. "Do you have the number?" he asked as casually as he could. Streat dutifully read it from his notes, and Pavlak's heart, already pounding, took another leap. "That's Brigitte's number—Brigitte Onat. She . . . is a friend of Judith's. They've known each other for years." Something inside Pavlak wanted to scream that Brigitte, too, was dead, but something else cautioned him to stay silent. He waited.

"So," Streat began slowly, "you're saying there's nothing unusual about these calls?"

"Well . . . Judith and Brigitte were very close. They talked on the phone a lot. With the separation and everything, Judith probably just needed a close friend to talk to."

"I see." Streat held Pavlak's eyes a split second longer than necessary. "Well, we'll move on then. Tell me everything you remember about your wife's investigations."

Pavlak groaned. "All of them?"

"I'm afraid so."

For the next two hours, Pavlak repeated everything he had told Crane the evening before. A few fresh items waded up from the swamps of his memory, but none seemed significant to him. Streat dutifully wrote it all down. The main difference between this interrogation and Crane's was that Streat wrote in a leather-bound notebook instead of the aluminum clipboard Crane used.

"Okay, Dr. Pavlak, that's it for now," Streat said when Pavlak protested for the third time that he really could not remember anything else. "The next step is to inventory the house—see what's missing, if anything. Can you go with me now?"

Pavlak threw up his hands. "I haven't even had any breakfast yet. Let me get a cup of coffee and wash my face. How about if I meet you there in an hour?"

"Fine."

"So tell me," Pavlak asked as Streat rose to his feet. "What are you thinking about this case? Who kills with a car bomb? And what about the burglary, or whatever it was? Was that just a coincidence?"

Streat gave no sign of having heard the question, and for a moment Pavlak thought he was going to ignore it. The agent gathered his things, walked thoughtfully to the door, then turned. "I believe, Dr. Pavlak, that someone very professional came to your house, searched it for something, then either he or an accomplice set off the bomb that killed your wife and daughter. What he was looking for—I don't know. Why they killed her—I don't know. That's what we have to find out."

"Why are you so sure the burglary was related to the bombing? Did you get any fingerprints?"

"Oh, he wanted it to look like a routine burglary, all right. And you'll probably find some things missing when we inventory the house. No, there aren't any prints. That's not surprising—there almost never are anymore. You can buy latex gloves in any grocery store now. But professional burglars show up with a truck or van. They grab the TV, the stereo, the microwave, and the jewelry, and they're out of there in five minutes or less. An amateur—say a local drug addict—might break in and look for something valuable to stick in his pocket, but he would break a window or smash the door. He wouldn't be able to pick two locks—the dead bolt and the knob. There are marks on the tumblers that weren't made by a key."

Streat leaned against the door frame and scratched absently at his cheek with a thumbnail.

"And an addict wouldn't remove the light fixtures on the ceilings. He wouldn't take the grates off the heating vents or look behind the filter in the air conditioner. He wouldn't lift the ceiling panels in the basement. He wouldn't dig through the soil in the potted plants. Most important, he wouldn't try to hide that he had done those things. But this guy did, you see. He wanted to make it look like an amateur burglary, but even a pro can't make that kind of search without leaving signs. You leave scratches—microscopic in some cases, but scratches all the same. And you can't put all the dust back where it was. That's what made it easy." Streat straightened to leave. "Your wife wasn't the best housekeeper, was she?"

"She wasn't a housekeeper at all. I did most of the cleaning. Since I've been gone, I guess nobody did it."

Streat stared at the floor, lost in thought. "You know," he mused, more to himself than to Pavlak, "this guy had to know we would catch on. The burglary ruse was just a little cheap insurance. It might delay us a day or two. And who knows—he might have gotten lucky—an incompetent local investigator—that kind of thing. But he probably knew the odds were we would discover that he was looking for something, and that we would assume the bombing was connected. That gives us a fair amount of material to work with. Still, he was willing to take the chance. Somebody wanted your wife dead real bad."

"And my baby?"

Streat averted his eyes. "That was probably an awful coincidence. Ordinarily she would have been alone in the car, wouldn't she?"

Pavlak said nothing, and Streat turned to leave.

"Hey, Streat."

"Yes?"

"You're pretty good, aren't you?"

For the first time, the agent smiled. "I'm the best. See you in an hour."

When he was gone, Pavlak put on a pot of water to boil then washed his face and shaved. He fried some eggs, gulped down a cup of instant coffee, then drove to the house before the hour was up. Streat was there along with two other men wearing white coveralls. They carried odd little metal tools and spent the whole time collecting bits and pieces of this and that, putting it into plastic bags, and labeling them with arcane symbols.

Pavlak searched through every closet, cabinet, and drawer in the house. Most of Judith's jewelry was missing. He was familiar with it because he hated gift shopping and almost always gave her jewelry for occasions that required a gift. He remembered that Judith usually kept emergency cash in the pocket of an overcoat, and he checked there. The pocket was empty, but he told Streat he could not be sure there had been anything in it.

At noon he drove back to Mrs. Ekelwood's house alone. Exhaustion was setting in, and the headache was back with a vengeance. As he mounted the stairs, Pavlak decided to have a sandwich for lunch, then try to get some sleep. He unlocked the door, started pushing it open, then froze. Through the crack he could see the armchair where Streat had sat. Someone had turned it upside down. With his heart slamming against his ribs, Pavlak pushed the door the rest of the way open.

Every inch of the floor was littered with items from shelves and drawers. His books lay in heaps, some closed, some carelessly open. A closet door stood open and his clothes lay scattered on the floor.

Pavlak picked his way through the debris until he reached the phone and, with a shaking finger, pressed 911.

5

"Your landlady says there were two of them."

Streat handed Pavlak a cup of coffee he had made himself after crawling around on his hands and knees in search of the jar. It had rolled beneath a cabinet.

"They wore suits and ties and dark glasses. Both had beards—neatly trimmed—and hats. Only one guy spoke. He flashed a badge of some kind and ordered her to let them into your apartment. They said they were investigating your wife's murder."

They were sitting in the kitchen. Pavlak tried to raise the full cup to his lips, but his hand was too unsteady. He set it carefully onto the table. "And she eagerly obliged."

"Don't be too hard on her. She didn't know any better— and she was intimidated. Besides, they would have gotten in anyway, one way or another."

Pavlak lowered his face to the coffee cup and took two long slurps to lower the level enough for him to pick it up without spilling it.

"Mr. Streat," Pavlak began, straightening himself, "what the hell's going on here?"

The FBI agent frowned and stared out the window at the

oak tree. "I wish I knew. Well, at least we do know one thing now. Whatever they were looking for at your wife's house, they didn't find it. We also know they're desperate. And determined to get it. And that there are at least two men involved. We have descriptions. Poor descriptions, I'm afraid. She isn't even sure of their hair color. My guess is that the beards are gone by now. Might have been fake anyway. And of course the glasses kept her from seeing their eyes. Only one of them spoke. She said he had a strange accent. She thinks he wasn't from around here."

Pavlak spilled coffee on his thigh and leapt to his feet, swearing. Streat watched silently as Pavlak swiped at his trousers with a tissue.

"You were about to say something . . . ?" Streat asked when Pavlak took his seat again.

"No, nothing at all. Strange accent. Uh . . . what did she mean by 'strange'? Did she say it was a *foreign* accent, or what?"

Streat studied him silently for a moment. "She's not sure. Just said it was an accent. About all we know is that they were white, middle-aged, one maybe six feet tall and very slender, the other an inch or two shorter and stocky."

"Which narrows it down to a few million people." Pavlak jerked his head toward the door where a man was dusting the inside knob for fingerprints. A radio hanging on his belt crackled intermittently. Behind him, two other investigators, wearing surgical gloves, were sifting through the wreckage of Pavlak's belongings. "What's all this going to tell you?"

Streat shrugged. "Probably nothing. There won't be any prints. About the only other hope is that they dropped something—a matchbook maybe, something like that. Slim chance, of course. We've got men canvassing the neighborhood now. Maybe we'll get a description of a car, but even that's a long shot." He shook his head. "These boys know what they're doing."

"You'll pardon me if I find your admiration a little hard to appreciate."

"Sorry," Streat smiled. "But you don't often see cases like this. It's a real challenge. And don't worry—we'll get them."

Pavlak drew a deep breath. "All right, now what? What should I do?"

"Is there somewhere you can go? Not here in town, but somewhere far away—preferably not obvious. Not a close relative, for example."

"I was about to say that my father and brother live in Lake Elm. I could stay with one of them, but that's only thirty miles away—and pretty obvious, I suppose."

Streat nodded. "Too close and too obvious. Anywhere else?"

"I'll have to think about it. Look, I can't leave immediately. I've got to bury my wife and daughter." Pavlak swallowed once, hard, then went on. "And besides, what about my job?"

"That's the least of your problems just now. We want to make sure you're alive to keep your job, although, frankly, I don't think you're in much danger. They were after your wife. They started there and didn't find what they wanted, so they thought she might have given it to you—whatever *it* is. If they were going to kill you, they would have done it already."

Pavlak grimaced. "That's comforting."

Streat ignored him. "Still, I think it would be a good idea for you to get out of here for a while until we make some progress with this thing."

"And when will that be?"

Streat held out his hands, palms up, and lifted his shoulders.

"Terrific," Pavlak sulked. "I'm supposed to just beam myself away to some unknown location, far away and unobvious, and wait indefinitely until you catch some mysterious crooks who you admit are smarter than you are."

"I didn't say they were smarter than I am—just that they're smart. I'm smart too. Smarter. I'll get them."

Pavlak's eyes flashed. "But will I still be alive when you do? Hell, they walked into my apartment in broad daylight, an hour after you left it. They were watching me and they were watching you. It's a cat-and-mouse game, and it looks to me like the FBI is just another mouse."

Streat gazed calmly out the window. "Well . . ." he began after what seemed an eternity, "I won't deny that the score's two-zip right now. And I won't deny that this is a tough case. But that's because we haven't found the motive yet. We're just getting started, remember. And we *will* discover the motive. Somebody knows who would want to kill your wife, and that somebody knows why."

"Right. And the two goons who searched my apartment think *I'm* that somebody."

"Don't worry. I'll put a twenty-four-hour guard on you for the next few days, at least until after the funeral. But if you really want to be safe, take my advice and find a place to hide for a few weeks—maybe a few months—until we find out what's going on here."

Instead of replying, Pavlak stood up.

"Where are you going?"

"To Lake Elm. I have to talk to some people. I'm sick of all this. I'm sick of Avery. I'm sick of burglaries and bombs. I'm sick of . . . everything."

Pavlak kicked the chair away from the table, and it crashed to the floor as he strode through the open door. The man dusting the doorknob raised an eyebrow in Streat's direction.

"He's cracking," Streat said simply. "Give me the radio."

6

The drive to Lake Elm normally took forty-five minutes. Pavlak made it in thirty-five, and that included stopping for gas at a convenience store on the outskirts of Avery. While he was filling his tank, a gray Chevrolet sedan pulled past him into the parking lot and the driver, a sandy-haired man in a cardigan sweater, entered the store. He was searching through the beer cooler when Pavlak came in to pay for his gas.

Back on the open road, he pressed the accelerator to the floor. With all that had happened to him in the past twenty-four hours, he couldn't bring himself to be concerned about anything as trivial as a speed limit.

Lake Elm, the county seat of Rowan County, was a historic old town once visited by George Washington. The town had several streets lined with glorious antebellum mansions, not to mention a tiny wooden hut reputed to have been the law office, for a couple of months, of Andrew Jackson. The most curious thing about Lake Elm was its name. Visitors were often disappointed to find no lake in sight, other than an artificial pond built in a park in 1939 to attract ducks.

In 1945, Gustaf Pavlak, John Pavlak's father, had found

himself a prisoner of war at Fort Leonard Wood, Missouri, along with several thousand other Germans. He arrived a week before his eighteenth birthday. Upon his release he traveled directly to Lake Elm to visit a great aunt who had immigrated half a century earlier. Unfortunately, the old lady died a few days before he arrived and left her estate to her three grandchildren in Alabama. Gustaf nonetheless decided to stay in Lake Elm. He was determined to make his fortune in America rather than return to the heap of rubble that was post-war Germany.

Within a week he landed a job in a local tractor repair shop and quickly became shop foreman. His boss, Harmon Withers, took a fancy to the clever, ambitious young German, helped him apply for permanent residency, and soon included him in all decisions concerning the business. A year later, when Gustaf married Margaret Withers, Harmon's only child, the relationship was sealed. John Pavlak was born nine months to the day after the marriage. His brother Tom followed two years later, but the pregnancy was difficult and Margaret underwent a hysterectomy after delivery. A few years after Tom Pavlak's birth, his grandfather, Harmon Withers, died of colon cancer, and at the age of twenty-five, Gustaf inherited ownership of the tractor shop.

Up until his death, Withers and his German son-in-law supplemented the income from the repair shop with part-time farming, and although Gustaf's sons were destined to feed the hogs in his backyard pen for a few more years, the young German was determined to rise above what he saw as the ignominy of farming.

He quickly phased out the tractor repair business and began assembling small harrows instead. Within a few years he grew frustrated with the vagaries of a business tied to agriculture and abandoned farm equipment in favor of warehousing machinery, particularly forklifts. At the same time, he incorporated the company and changed its name from Lake Elm Farm Repair to Pavlak Equipment, Inc.

The timing was fortuitous. The economic expansion of the fifties and sixties made Gustaf Pavlak a rich man, along with several dozen Lake Elm families who bought into the initial stock issue for Pavlak Equipment. By the time Gustaf's older son John graduated from high school, the company employed six hundred people and earned annual revenues of over four hundred million dollars. Gustaf Pavlak built an eight-thousand-square-foot house on a hilltop near the Lake Elm country club. It was made of white brick, custom manufactured using a rare clay found only in the Appalachian mountains.

With his head still pounding, John Pavlak turned through the gate and aimed the Toyota's hood ornament up the steep hill toward his father's gleaming mansion. He had not seen the house in nearly a year. The Toyota knocked like a diesel and threatened to choke, so Pavlak shifted down a gear, then another until he was whining up the steep slope in low. The engine sounded as if it were straining to come apart, and Pavlak wondered if this time it would succeed. He finally reached the top and had just jerked up the parking brake when the massive front door swung open, and his father stepped out.

At sixty-six Gustaf Pavlak was still tall and straight. The once brown hair was now mostly gray, but the step and bearing were that of a man twenty years younger. Nordic blue eyes were Gustaf's most striking feature, and when he was angry, they could penetrate like ice picks. Those eyes had caused more than one calloused hand to tremble inside its rough glove. As a child, John Pavlak had often felt the fury of his father's glare, but Gustaf could not fire his sons, and so his anger toward his children had taken other, more violent forms.

"Why don't you get rid of that wreck and buy a real car?" Gustaf demanded as soon as Pavlak slammed the Toyota's door. His hard German accent had not softened, even after almost half a century in America.

"For the same reason I gave you the last fifty times you asked that. I can't afford it."

"Can't afford it," his father snorted in disgust. "You can afford anything you want."

"Wrong, Pop. *You* can afford anything I want."

"Fine, so let me buy you a car. In fact, I'll give you my five hundred SEL. I'm going to buy a new one this week anyway. You can . . ."

"Pop," Pavlak cut him off. "Don't start, okay? I don't want a Mercedes. I like my car. As for the money . . . that's part of the reason I'm here. Do you still keep that trust account for me?"

"I don't keep it. The bank keeps it. It's an irrevocable trust. You said I use money to control you, so I set up the trust so I couldn't touch it even if I wanted to. Half of it was distributable to you when you turned twenty-five. You said you didn't want it, remember? The other half was distributable ten years later. You haven't claimed that either, so the bank is simply holding it until you do. They can't do anything with it, and neither can I." Gustaf eyed his son carefully. "Are you telling me you're finally ready for it?"

Pavlak hesitated. Eating crow, especially in front of his father, was not an easy thing to do. "Not all of it. I just want access to whatever money I may need. How much is in the account?"

Gustaf shrugged. "The last time I talked to Hoke Morgan it was about ten million, most of it stock in the company, but Hoke put a third in other investments, and he keeps a million or so in cash deposits."

"Jesus Christ," Pavlak breathed, shaking his head.

"All you have to do is go down to the bank and sign a signature card. They've been holding the papers for—what—twenty years now? Everything is still the same as it was back when you . . ."

"Yes, Pop, I know," Pavlak cut in, his blood rising. "Back when I said I didn't want your money, then or ever. Well, I still don't. I haven't changed. But right now I need a loan. I intend to pay back every cent of it."

His father's blue eyes darkened and his jaw clenched. Pavlak waited for the inevitable explosion, but this time it didn't come. Instead, Gustaf drew a deep breath and looked off into the distance where the tree-lined streets of Lake Elm lay spread out before them. The trees were still stiff and bare from the long winter. The first sign of foliage was a week away.

"You're right," Gustaf announced grimly. "You'll never change." Then, as if waking from a dream, "Come in. Roser is in the den." He turned his back and disappeared into the darkness of the house. Pavlak wiped his feet on the mat and followed, but by the time his eyes adjusted to the light, his father was nowhere to be seen. He followed the long hallway to the den in the back of the house. It was about twice the size of Pavlak's entire apartment and featured two facing fireplaces made of polished marble. Despite the mild weather, a fire danced in each of them.

Roser rose to meet him. Her flawless Mediterranean skin betrayed barely a wrinkle. She was, Pavlak thought, as beautiful today as the first time he had laid eyes on his father's new wife. Why Gustaf Pavlak had been so taken with the charming young Catalonian widow was easy to see.

"John, I'm so sorry," Roser whispered into his shoulder as she hugged him.

"Thanks for your concern, Roser. Your husband hasn't even mentioned my dead family. We talked about cars and trust accounts."

"He's just as upset as the rest of us, John. But he hides it from you. I've never seen him as shaken as he was after you called. He's hardly slept since then."

"Considering how much he despised Judith, he was probably too happy to sleep." Pavlak held up his hand to block Roser's rebuke. "Sorry. Okay, that was unnecessary. Well, if it's any consolation to him, neither have I—slept, that is— at least not to speak of. Roser . . ." Pavlak took her hand and squeezed it. "Something very strange is going on. Two men ransacked my apartment this morning while I was over at the house with an FBI agent . . ."

A voice boomed from the doorway behind them. "What!"

They both started and turned. Gustaf Pavlak's face was drawn and pale. He seemed to have forgotten the paper he held in his hand.

"That's right, Pop," Pavlak confirmed. "Now I'm in this too. Most likely Judith stirred up a hornet's nest with one of her investigations. We know there's more than one person involved, and the FBI thinks they're looking for something— some papers, I suppose. Apparently they think I might have them. The FBI wants me to hide out somewhere for a while. That's why I need the money."

"Oh dear God." His father's voice trembled, and for a moment Pavlak felt his guard drop. Despite the bitterness, there had always been something between John Pavlak and his father, something Pavlak himself could not quite grasp, that kept him from casting entirely free of his family. It was like an invisible cord whose presence was felt only when Pavlak tugged against it.

"That's . . . unbelievable," Gustaf mumbled. "That's . . ." He stopped. Then the old aggressiveness came back into his tone. "All right, listen. You'll stay here. I have a twenty-four-hour guard on this place anyway, and I'll double it. We'll close all the gates . . ."

"No, Pop!" Roser gave him a stern look, and Pavlak lowered his voice. "I'm *not* staying here," he continued with forced calm. "I run my own life, remember?"

"John, listen to me." Gustaf took a step closer. His fist was clenched, and his face began to darken. "Listen to me," he repeated. "I'll leave you alone. I won't even talk to you, if that's what you want. I have the resources here. I can protect you here."

"Protect me, Pop? You? Since the day I was born, you were the greatest danger in my life."

"Stop being melodramatic. I was a little hard on you and Tom sometimes, but I wanted you to be strong. I wanted you to be survivors . . ."

"Please!" Now it was Roser's turn to plead. "Don't start all that again. Can't both of you just forget the past and start over? John . . ."

"I'm not staying here, Roser, and that's the end of the discussion. I have some business to take care of." Pavlak walked around his father toward the door, the two of them brushing shoulders without looking at each other. Gustaf turned.

"Where are you going?"

"I'm—not sure," Pavlak lied. "Something weird is going on. I have a suspicion, that's all. I'm going to check it out."

"You're getting yourself involved in this thing?" Gustaf demanded, his lower jaw dropping. "Are you crazy?"

"Some sonofabitch killed my wife and my little girl, Pop. I'm 'involved' whether I like it or not."

"But for God's sake, John," Gustaf snapped, "let the police handle it. What good would it do to get yourself killed too?"

There was a long silence as the two men looked at each other.

"What *harm* would it do?" Pavlak asked quietly. "Now can I get the money?"

Gustaf started to say more, then apparently thought better of it. He raised the hand with the sheet of paper in it. Pavlak noticed the company letterhead for Pavlak Equipment, Inc.

"Here's a note to Hoke Morgan," Gustaf said. "You don't really need it. It's your money anyway. But Hoke's a timid type. He'd call me if I didn't give you this."

"I'll pay you back when I can," Pavlak said, turning away. "Roser, watch yourself." He pointed at his father. "He attacks when you least expect it."

"John, for God's sake . . ." Roser whispered wearily. "Your father has never laid a hand on me in anger."

"You're lucky."

"I have never hit a woman, and I never will." Gustaf's voice rose. He folded his arms and glared at his son. "Women are different. Women don't have to be strong. They're meant to be weak. But boys have to be men or they wind up . . . ," he waved his hand in disgust, ". . . like you."

"Thanks, Pop," Pavlak replied. "Glad to see there's a little of the real you left."

It was starting. Despite everything, this visit was going to end like all the others.

Gustaf pointed a finger at Pavlak's face. "Get one thing straight. Despite all your whining accusations, I don't regret the way I raised you. Not for one minute. I tried to make a man of you, that's all. But in Germany we had a saying. You can't make a horse out of an ass."

Pavlak walked out.

Well, he thought as he stepped back into the late afternoon sun, at least there was a certain symmetry to his visits here. They always began with his father criticizing something, then ended with insults and bitterness and Pavlak promising himself that this was absolutely the last time he would ever set foot in the old man's house. Nothing had changed. Despite the bomb that had shattered his life, this corner of the universe was still on track.

After two unsuccessful attempts, Pavlak finally persuaded the Toyota to start. The engine was roaring when his father rushed out of the house and up to his door.

"All right, forget it," Gustaf snapped. "This quarreling is crazy. We're a family. We should stick together, especially in a time like this. Don't be a damned fool. Stay out of this thing until . . ."

"Good-bye, Pop."

He jerked the clutch and the Toyota roared away down the hill. In the rearview mirror he saw his father watching the car gain distance. For a moment Pavlak felt a twinge of regret. Maybe the old man really was reaching out this time. To a casual observer, Pavlak's abrupt departure would seem, he knew, rude and disrespectful—which it certainly was. But a casual observer would not know his father, would not know the egotism, the manipulations, the cold brutality of the man. If Pavlak were to stay in that house, even for a few days, his father would take complete control of his life. Not intentionally, perhaps, but it was the only way Gustav Pavlak knew. He had to control everything in his reach. And he did.

Once back on the street, Pavlak headed for Pavlak Equipment's main plant, threading his way down familiar avenues, echoes of a past that he had tried to forget. It had been over twenty-five years since he had left Lake Elm, never to return—or so he had thought at the time. Avery had been Pavlak's initial destination. He turned down a football scholarship to Penn State in order to attend the exclusive private college just down the road. During his three years there, he set every conference football record a linebacker can set, and capped it off by graduating a year early, third in his class. Graduate school was the logical next step, but by then he was determined to put more distance between himself and his father. Germany was the natural choice. He had loved Germany since childhood. Both he and Tom had spent every summer in Herringstadt, their father's home town in Franconia, not far from the East German border. Gustaf's sister, Renate, a plump, kindly, but childless lady, lavished on her two American nephews all the love, attention, and *Butterbrot* that they could endure. That annual respite from Gustaf's beatings and abuse was, Pavlak decided later, the only reason he and Tom had managed to turn out reasonably sane.

To Pavlak, then, Germany was an idyll, a fairy-tale land of green hills and gingerbread and plump, laughing Tante Renate who smelled of ginger and ripe plums. So it was off to Germany when the time came to start working toward his doctorate. He flew to Frankfurt, took a train to Tübingen, and matriculated in the university.

That was when the idyll began to crumble. He spent a semester in Tübingen, then another in Göttingen. During that year, Pavlak got to know Germany's less romantic side. He quickly wearied of the puerile anti-Americanism of his fellow students, whose arrogance was matched only by their colossal ignorance of American realities. Then in a park in

Frankfurt, three men walked up to him in broad daylight, pressed the point of a stiletto against his belly, and relieved him of his wallet. Not two months later, he visited a Pakistani friend in a hospital in Hamburg, where he was taken after thugs in the harbor district had beaten the man into an unrecognizable lump.

Then came the order to report for an induction physical, followed by his snap decision to take a serious sample of military life. He enlisted for a four-year hitch and volunteered for OCS and Special Forces training. Later he wondered what macho madness had come over him at that phase of his life. And yet, despite the hardships, he had enjoyed his military training. And he was good. His two tours in Vietnam earned him a chest full of medals. Those years were sojourns in another world, a raw and deadly world. He was a man who led men into the jungle to find and kill other men who were trying to find and kill them. Nothing in his previous life had prepared him for it, and nothing in his subsequent life could quite comprehend it.

After he was discharged, Pavlak returned to his studies, this time in the United States, and finished a PhD in German literature at the University of North Carolina. It was then that fortune cast him a curious blow. The job market for foreign-language professors had shrunk almost to nonexistence. Of his graduate-school class only one student, the top student in the class, actually found a job. That student was John Pavlak. And the job was not teaching German. It was a dual post as Assistant Athletic Director and Assistant Football Coach at his old *alma mater*, Avery College.

John's father was furious. Gustaf was willing to accept a professorship for his son. Professors, at least in the Germany he remembered, enjoyed great social status and even relative affluence. But a football coach? And John, perversely, had felt good about the job from the moment he saw his father's face darken in disapproval. Then two years later, Badin Powell, Avery's athletic director, retired, and the president quickly appointed John Pavlak to take his place. Pavlak wasn't exactly anxious for the job—even coaching had been more challenging—but once again his father's disgust gave him enough satisfaction to seal the deal.

At the gate to Pavlak Equipment's main plant, the usually cheerful guard waved him through with a solemn nod. Of course, Pavlak realized suddenly. The man knew. The murder of Gustaf Pavlak's daughter-in-law and granddaughter would be the only topic of conversation there for days. He sighed. Why had he not thought of that? The last thing he wanted to encounter now were the pitying stares of old friends. And yet it was one old friend he had come to see.

The secretary in the business office gave Pavlak precisely the sorrowful look and comforting words that he had feared. Worse yet, she told him that Arthur Trask was in Tom's office. Pavlak didn't hate his brother. He merely despised and disliked him. Tom had stuck by the old man, not, as Pavlak well knew, out of affection, but because Tom had heeded the siren call to wealth and power. "The reason I don't like you," Pavlak had told Tom after one argument, "is that you're a greedy sonofabitch." Tom had responded by aiming a fist at Pavlak's nose, but Pavlak, always the quicker and stronger of the two, dodged the blow and planted one of his own in Tom's belly, doubling him over. After that they didn't speak for nearly a year. Now Tom's attempts to play his father's role constantly got him into trouble. He had the old man's toughness, but lacked his cunning and instinct.

Pavlak opened the door to his brother's office without knocking. Tom was the first to see him, and Pavlak braced for the usual sarcastic greeting, but this time Tom's mouth fell open, then closed again without a word. Another man was leaning over a blueprint on the desk, his back to the door.

Arthur Trask had started as a welder at Pavlak Equipment and quickly worked his way up. His solid reliability had gained first the confidence, and then the friendship of Gustaf Pavlak. Eventually the two men became inseparable partners, although Gustaf was always careful to maintain the upper hand. For the past thirty years Arthur had served the company as plant supervisor, the man who saw to it that the real work got done. He was almost worshipfully loyal to Gustaf Pavlak, his friend and benefactor, but he also kept close ties to Gustaf's older son John.

Pavlak liked Arthur Trask. Huge and barrel-chested, Trask faced life with such unfailing optimism that no mishap could spoil his mood. He was a popular man on the factory floor, and largely because of him, the employees of Pavlak Equipment silently endured policies that would have brought militant unionism to other shops—especially since Pavlak's brother Tom had taken over the job of Chief Operating Officer of the company. Arthur's skill at management made him, in Pavlak's estimate, the most valuable man in the company. He was one of those rare creatures everyone wanted to have around—a happy man.

Trask twisted his head around, and Pavlak saw his face transform when their eyes met. Trask started up.

"Oh John, I'm so sorry." He took Pavlak's hand. "I'm so sorry. I—I couldn't believe it. I just couldn't believe it." Suddenly, to Pavlak's dismay, tears began to flow down Arthur's cheeks. "My God, John, we had that dinner with you two—when?—just before Christmas. I just can't believe it. Christ almighty. If I'd had any idea that would be the last time I would ever see Judith and Tasha . . ."

Pavlak was embarrassed by the tears, but appreciated them all the same. With Arthur Trask, what you saw was what you got. No wonder he was so popular with the employees. Pavlak wondered for the thousandth time how the man could endure working with his brother.

"Hello, Tom," Pavlak said, turning. Tom was watching Arthur uncomfortably.

"I was sorry to hear it, John. Really sorry," Tom said tersely. For a moment he seemed to want to say something else, but nothing came. He stared at the desk and shifted from one foot to the other. Social grace was not one of Tom's strengths. At that moment Pavlak truly wished things could be different between him and his brother. Other brothers were close. Why couldn't they be? And even as the thought played through his mind, he knew it would never be. His was a broken family, never to be mended.

"How's Edith?" he asked, turning back to Arthur.

Arthur had pulled a huge red bandanna from his hip pocket and was drying his face. He was a giant of a man, tall and thick and powerful, even now, when the shock of hair atop the massive head had grown completely white. "She's fine. In shock, of course, as we all are. Jesus." Arthur shook his head again. "I just can't believe it. Yeah, Edith wanted to call you, but I told her not to. I figured you had enough to deal with just now. I'm surprised to see you here."

"I had to get out."

"You okay, John? I mean—is there anything . . ."

"No, nothing. It's—just the way it is. Life goes on."

"God, it's tough for you, John. First the separation, then this. You're a better man than I am, John. I don't think I could survive it. If anything happened to Edith . . . And I loved Tasha, John. You know I did. I loved that little girl like my own daughter."

The tears started again. Arthur was taking it harder than he had expected. Pavlak began to have second thoughts about his plans, but he plowed ahead. "I was just wondering, Arthur, if you might have a little time for a drink somewhere? I just wanted to talk a little."

"Of course, John. Anything you want. Right now, if you want. . . ."

For a moment Pavlak wanted to hug the great bear in front of him, and would have if his brother had not been standing there, shifting his weight from left to right and scowling miserably at nothing in particular. Here they were, the stranger acting the brother, and the brother behaving as a stranger. Nothing could have pointed up the perversity of the Pavlak family more clearly.

"Yeah. If you can get away, that is. Let's go."

Pavlak turned to his brother and their eyes met. "See you next time around," Pavlak muttered. "Take care of yourself."

"Yeah. You too."

And that, Pavlak thought, as Trask pulled the door closed behind them, is as close to fraternal affection as we will ever get.

7

Gustaf Pavlak's son, the one whose family had just been blown to pieces in a car bomb, would be the object of unwanted attention anywhere in Lake Elm, so Pavlak and Arthur drove the sixteen miles to Varryville, a textile mill town where Pavlak's face would not be instantly known. He rejected Arthur's offer of his own home because, although he didn't say it, Pavlak didn't want to face Edith's tears and sympathy.

On the way out of town he stopped at Lake Elm National Bank. To his dismay, the door was already locked, but the manager, Hoke Morgan, suddenly appeared behind the glass with a key. Instantly Pavlak knew that his father had phoned and warned Morgan that his son was coming. Morgan, as Pavlak also knew very well, would have slept all night on the floor beside the door rather than risk angering Gustaf Pavlak.

The banker's obsequiousness was cloying, and Pavlak rushed him through the business at hand, using the excuse that Arthur was waiting in the car. When he left the bank thirty minutes later, Pavlak carried fifty thousand dollars in large bills stuffed in his pockets. Morgan had also drawn up a letter of instruction authorizing the bank to transfer five hundred thousand dollars to a bank in Basel, Switzerland, with which Lake Elm National Bank had a "direct correspondent relationship," whatever that meant.

And just like that, the financial worries that had dogged Pavlak's adult life vanished. The relief he felt was as seductive as a drug, and as he left the bank, he made a mental note to remind himself daily that he would pay this money back. He did not, of course, have the slightest idea how, since he was carrying more than his gross annual salary in his pockets. The alternative, though, would be to owe his father dependence and gratitude, and he dared not risk that. Gustaf Pavlak was a master at turning any obligation on someone else's part into an advantage on his own.

On the way to Varryville, Pavlak opened his mind to Arthur and released all the confused and rambling thoughts that had harassed him for the past few hours. Arthur listened in silence, but Pavlak's words laid a visible weight on the big man's usually carefree features.

"Good God, John," Arthur breathed, when Pavlak finished. "These guys are dangerous as hell, whoever they are. I'm glad you're getting out of here, and I don't even want to know where you're going to hide. Just make sure it's somewhere safe. If I were you I wouldn't tell anybody. Maybe call the FBI every few weeks—hell, maybe not even that. If this is about drugs or something, even the FBI might not be safe. Those drug guys have so much money they can buy anybody."

"I want somebody to know where I am, Arthur. That's one reason I wanted to talk to you."

"Oh, Christ." Arthur squirmed in the tiny bucket seat. "I'll do whatever you ask, John, you know that. But I don't mind telling you, this scares me."

"Don't worry, I'm not dragging you into it—but some-body ought to know in case I don't ever show up again. And you're right about the FBI. I already thought of that. Judith was investigating a motorcycle gang—the Devil's Dragons they call themselves. They're suspected of drug dealing. But . . ." Pavlak hesitated and focussed hard on the car in front of him, "there's something else that bothers me."

"Wait—are you sure you want to tell me this? Shouldn't you take all this to somebody else?"

"Who? My family? You know how things are. I'm sorry, Arthur, but you're it." Pavlak smiled. "Hang in there, old man. Remember, *I'm* the one they're chasing."

"And don't take me wrong, but I hope it stays that way. I mean I hope the FBI or somebody catches them, that's what I hope. Jesus, I was afraid something like this would happen one day. I told Judith a hundred times to be careful. I told her it was a dangerous business she was getting into, but she wouldn't listen. You know Judith."

"Yeah, I know Judith," Pavlak responded drily. They were silent for a full five minutes while Pavlak made the turns that took them into the parking lot of a trendy restaurant known for its New York strip steaks. It was still early, so the restaurant was mercifully deserted. It was a large shell of a building with an interior of unfinished wood, wagon-wheel chandeliers, and a wooden balcony surrounding the main floor. He and Arthur found a table in a dark corner of the balcony and ordered grilled chicken. Pavlak picked up the conversation again when the waitress was out of earshot.

"Anyway, Arthur, there's something else that's bothering me. I tried to call a friend of ours in Germany, a young woman named Brigitte who was very close to Judith. I'm sure Judith mentioned her."

Trask nodded, never taking his eyes off Pavlak's.

"Only I found out that she was killed by a hit-and-run driver in Berlin a couple of days ago. And then the FBI agent told me Judith recently made a flurry of phone calls to Brigitte. Normally Judith called her maybe once every two or three months. And there's another thing. My landlady said one of the guys who searched my apartment had an accent. It could have been German. Now maybe these are all just grotesque coincidences, but I don't think so. I think Judith's death and Brigitte's are connected somehow."

"How could they be?"

"I have no idea—but I plan to find out. That's where I'm going. Germany."

Arthur stared. "Wait a minute. What do you mean 'plan to find out'?"

"Just what I said. I'm going to find out what happened to Brigitte and whether or not there's any link to this bombing."

Arthur sank back in his chair and fixed Pavlak with an accusing eye. "That's not hiding out, John. That's walking in deeper. I mean, Germany may be a good idea, but just go find yourself a little Bavarian village somewhere and enjoy some spring skiing or something. For God's sake, don't go meddling around."

Pavlak examined the table. It was natural wood, very blond, coated with polyurethane a quarter-inch thick. "I can't do that, Arthur. I can't just sit down and vegetate. Tasha was my life, my world. And even Judith—in some way I loved her once. Now, in one fell swoop, I've got nothing. I'm going to find out who took everything away from me." He looked up and forced a smile. "Don't worry. I won't be in Germany long. Just long enough to check out Brigitte's death, then I'm coming back to the U.S. I'm not sure where to. Not back to Avery, that's for sure, but I'll be around."

Arthur said nothing for a long moment, then a slow smile spread across his broad face. "You shit, you," he chuckled. "You don't want to believe it, but you're your old man made over. You're more a Pavlak than your brother will ever be," he added, the smile fading. "All right, John. I know you well enough to know there's no point in arguing. I hope you know what you're doing. Just be careful, okay?"

Dinner arrived, and the conversation stalled while they dug into grilled chicken that was dry and baked potatoes that were soggy. Pavlak paid with a hundred-dollar bill and drove Arthur back to Lake Elm. The night guard at the gate was a stranger to Pavlak, but he nodded them through the gate when his flashlight beam crossed Arthur's broad face. In the parking lot, Pavlak switched off the engine and the two men climbed out.

"Listen, Arthur," he began, as Arthur crushed his hand, "I lied. I don't *want* to involve you in this, but the truth is—I may need your help. I'm not sure what for. Maybe nothing. But I need to know if I can call on you if I need something."

"Stupid question. How could I say no? I think you're making a mistake—my advice is to hide out and let the cops take care of this—but if you insist on doing something foolish, you know you can count on Uncle Arthur to bail you out if I can." He snatched Pavlak up in a bear hug, and Pavlak winced as his ribs bent under the strain. "Watch your ass, young Pavlak. Watch your ass." Arthur dropped him back onto the pavement and disappeared through the front door of the office annex.

Pavlak climbed back into the Toyota and made his way out the gate. As he passed Myrtle Street, a gray Chevrolet parked in the shadows began to roll and drifted lazily into the street behind him.

8

Kenneth and Audrey Rankin arranged the funeral. It was a small, simple ceremony at the gravesite where Judith and Tasha were placed side by side. For Pavlak, it came and went in a daze. As the crowd was drifting away he exchanged a few words with Judith's mother and stepfather, both of whom were too distraught for a coherent conversation. He spoke a few obligatory formulas to his father and brother. Then Edith Trask, a still youthful-looking woman, despite her white hair, gave him a tearful hug, while Arthur waited his turn to do the same.

"I'm sorry, John," Arthur choked. "I loved Judith, you know I did."

"She loved you too, Arthur—and trusted you. She named you executor of her will, did you know that?"

Arthur nodded. "She asked me about it before she changed the will. It was only a few months ago, after you guys . . ." He shuffled his feet and twitched his shoulders nervously. "You know."

"Yeah, Arthur. It's okay. I'm glad it's you. I know you'll take good care of her things."

Finally, it was over, and Kenneth Rankin drove him home.

Special Agent Darryl Streat was waiting on the porch of Mrs. Ekelwood's house when they arrived. Pavlak thanked his friend, then insisted that Kenneth leave.

"I'll be fine, Kenneth, really. I'll come by later for dinner if that's all right."

"Of course, John. Come whenever you're ready. We'll be expecting you."

As Kenneth drove away, Pavlak mounted the wooden steps.

"Just checking in with you, Dr. Pavlak," Streat intoned, extending his hand. His voice was full of somber respect. "How are you doing?"

Pavlak accepted the outstretched hand. "I'll survive. What do you want from me?"

"Just to know whether or not you've thought of anything you haven't already told me."

Pavlak shook his head. "Nothing."

"Okay, then tell me your plans. Have you decided whether or not to disappear for a while, as I suggested? You may not know it, incidentally, but we've posted a guard on you."

"Of course I know. By the way, which one drives the gray Chevrolet? That *is* one of your guys, I hope?"

A slow smile played across Streat's lips. "Yes, he's one of our guys. But how did you know? They're trained not to be detected."

"I may not be an FBI agent, but I'm not an idiot either. I'm not the typical chump you people deal with day in and day out."

"I wasn't aware we were treating you that way."

"Then tell me . . . If he's just there to guard me, why am I not supposed to know he's following me?"

"Two reasons. First of all, the surveillance needs to be clandestine so that the bad guys don't know we're there either. That way, if they're tailing you too, we may be able to spot them before they spot us."

"And the second reason?"

Streat grinned. "We need the practice. My men always try to be discreet when we're guarding somebody."

"Uh-huh," Pavlak grunted, unconvinced. "By the way, what has ATF learned from all the garbage they collected? Anything?"

"Not much yet. It'll take time to piece together details about the bomb. As for the two who searched your apartment, about all we know is that they both wore new shoes."

"New?"

Streat nodded. "New, and probably buried in a garbage dump somewhere by now."

"I get it. New shoes so you can't match the sole prints even if you catch the guys. And that's the sum total of your knowledge up to this point?

Streat's expression did not change. "Look, Dr. Pavlak, I'm as disappointed as you—but I said from the start that we weren't likely to get at them through physical evidence. They're too professional for that. We're looking for motives. I've got three agents interviewing everybody Judith talked to in the last six months. It'll take time, but sooner or later we'll get the lead that takes us somewhere."

"Any hints so far?"

"We're taking a close look at the motorcycle gang. She was making them very nervous—and there had been threats. We know that much. We also know they're heavily into cocaine trafficking, and that they have connections with Latin American dealers. Your wife knew that too, incidentally. We don't think the gang did it themselves, but they might have called on connections—might even have tapped into the Mafia for some talent, for all we know."

Pavlak picked at the peeling paint on the back of a rocking chair. "Anything that points anywhere else?"

Streat watched him for a long second. "Just the phone calls to her friend in Germany. Why didn't you tell me she was dead?"

Pavlak peeled off a flake of paint the size of his thumbnail. "What makes you think I knew?"

"Call it a hunch."

"Pretty good hunch," Pavlak conceded. "I tried to call her to tell her about Judith. Her sister answered the phone. I don't know why I didn't tell you. Maybe because I knew you'd find out anyway."

Streat grunted, but Pavlak couldn't tell if he was angry or suspicious or both or neither. Pavlak looked up. "You know, Mr. Streat, I'd love to help you out on this—I mean other than just answering questions. But I suppose you wouldn't let me, would you?"

Streat eyed him closely. "I'm not proud, if that's what you're asking. I'll take any help I can get. But . . . you're marked on this one. I mean, you're a related victim, remember? That's why we took over your case too. We thought from the start that the house search here ties in to your wife's murder. For all we know, you're still a potential target. There's nothing you could do without putting yourself into danger, and I can't allow that. I know you're a decorated veteran," he added, "but this isn't Vietnam." He looked off the porch into nothing, while Pavlak wondered how and why Streat knew about his military record. "I'm sorry, but there's nothing you can do."

Pavlak nodded slowly. "Right—of course. I know you're right. Still . . ."

"What?"

"Nothing. It's just that I'm . . ." Pavlak let the sentence

die with a vague gesture, but his jaw clenched involuntarily as a surge of rage swept over him.

Streat nodded. "I understand what you're feeling. That's a natural reaction. But leave it to us. We'll see that somebody pays, I promise." Streat's gaze was steady. "Now back to my original question. What are your plans?"

"I'm going away."

"When? Where?"

"Soon. And I'm not going to tell you."

There was a tense silence.

"Why not, may I ask?"

"Simple. I don't trust you. Oh, not you personally. But as you said yourself, there may be drug money involved. And you and I both know that Latin American drug dealers have people on payroll everywhere—including the FBI."

"This isn't a narcotics unit. My team is clean."

Pavlak shook his head. "Sorry."

"You're making a mistake. We may need you. You could be a material witness, you know. I have to know how to contact you."

"You'll hear from me."

"Listen, Dr. Pavlak . . ."

"Forget it," Pavlak interrupted. "I'm not telling you, and that's final."

Streat's voice lost its placid tone. "I could take you into protective custody."

"Maybe. But then again, maybe not. I would fight it."

"But I'd have you locked up for at least a few days, and that may be all we need to crack this."

Pavlak sighed. "Do you seriously think you'll nab these guys if I sit around another week? Besides, what good am I to you?"

"I don't know. Maybe none. But you knew Judith better

than anybody else—and it's you these guys went after next, wasn't it?"

"Exactly. That's why I'm getting out of here. Just like you suggested," he added, raising an eyebrow at Streat.

The agent drew a long breath. "Well, at least tell me when you're leaving so I'll know when to cancel the guard."

"That's easy. When your guards discover that they're not guarding anybody, they can go home."

A flash of anger broke through Streat's crisp facade, then quickly vanished. "When will I hear from you?" he asked flatly.

"Once a week or so."

"That may not be good enough."

"It'll have to be."

Streat whirled angrily and started for the steps, then stopped. "Don't do anything stupid, Dr. Pavlak. I say again: You'd be well advised to cooperate with us."

"I am cooperating," Pavlak responded with a conciliatory show of his palms. "I'm just not taking orders."

The FBI agent looked into Pavlak's eyes for a long moment, then wordlessly turned his back.

In his apartment Pavlak showered and changed into synthetic slacks and a sport shirt. The evening was mild, but he pulled on a wool sports jacket and stuffed the pockets with bundles of hundred-dollar bills.

Next he sat at the desk and wrote a note on a piece of lined paper. "Dear Kenneth and Audrey," it said. "Thanks for your help. I couldn't have made it without you. Sorry to leave this way, but some nosy people are interested in where I go, and this is the only way I can keep it from them. I may be back in a few days—maybe not for several months. Please pass that information to the president's office along with my apologies. Tell him I said Jerry is a great assistant athletic director and can handle the office until I get back. Take care of yourselves. Love, John." He folded the note and slid it into his shirt pocket.

When he walked to his car, the gray Chevrolet was nowhere in sight. He drove to the Rankins' house and parked on the street, then started up the redbrick walkway. Halfway to the front door he stepped off the walk and behind the thick trunk of a willow oak. A moment later, the gray Chevrolet rolled into view on a side street, engine dead and headlights shut off. Pavlak waited until it glided to a halt, then continued up the walk.

Audrey greeted him with a kiss on the cheek.

"Hi, Kenneth," Pavlak said as he stepped into the living room. "Excuse me a second. First thing I have to do is hit the bathroom." He smiled. "This may take a while."

The bathroom was at the back of the house. He closed and locked the door but did not turn on the light. Instead, he pulled the note from his pocket with two fingers, opened it, and laid it beside the sink. He set a ceramic soap dish on one corner of the paper to hold it in place, then slid the double sash window open and quietly removed the screen, pulling it inside. He climbed out on top of the heat pump that squatted beneath the window. Six long strides carried him through the shadows of the Rankins' back yard and to a low, chain-link fence that protected Audrey's flowers from stray dogs. The fence was an easy vault. Pavlak scrambled through a hedge, tiptoed through a neighbor's backyard, then emerged onto the sidewalk in the block behind the Rankins' house.

At a service station on Forsyth Street he called a taxi. The driver hesitated when Pavlak said "Lake Elm," but dropped the car into gear as soon as Pavlak waved a hundred-dollar bill in his face. For thirty miles, Pavlak watched the road behind them. If he was being tailed, the G-men were doing a hell of a lot better job than they had before.

He got out of the taxi at the Lake Elm bus station and asked the ticket agent for the next long-distance bus. One was leaving for Philadelphia in twenty minutes.

"Perfect," he told the man.

In the next ten minutes, he went back to the window twice more, once to ask if there was a bathroom on the bus, and then again to ask if the driver sold soft drinks. The agent answered yes to the first question and, annoyed, no to the second.

At the departure gate, Pavlak chatted inanely with a bored driver who took his ticket, tore out the carbon copy and added it to the stack in his hand. Pavlak told the driver a dirty joke, guffawed at his own humor, then finally boarded the bus and watched until a lady with a heavy, fabric suitcase approached the bus. The driver turned his back to take the case, and Pavlak stepped quietly back onto the pavement and slipped around the front of the bus.

Two bays down, he climbed aboard the shuttle bus for Charlotte just as the doors were closing. With his head down, he paid the driver the correct change and took a seat in the shadows at the rear.

The ride to Charlotte lasted an hour. From the Trade Street bus station, another cab carried him to Charlotte-Douglas International Airport where he purchased a ticket to Atlanta in the name of Roger Waldau from Gastonia. He had to sprint down the concourse, but just managed to make the flight.

It was nearly eight in the evening when the plane touched down in Atlanta. Pavlak made straight for the Lufthansa counter and inquired about the late flight to Frankfurt. Tourist class was sold out, but there were plenty of first-class

seats available. Pavlak glanced at the clock on the wall behind the ticket agent's shoulder. He had over two hours. He
thanked the agent, then took a taxi to the closest mall and
bought a suitcase that he filled with new clothes, carelessly
chosen. He had never liked shopping.

When he was finished, a taxi deposited him back at the
airport just in time to produce his passport and buy a first-
class ticket to Frankfurt. The flight was scheduled to arrive
in Germany at 1:06 P.M., Central European Time.

Pavlak knew he couldn't take an international flight under a false name without a false passport, so he was vulnerable when Streat—or someone else—traced him to Atlanta.
But that would take time. And at Frankfurt, the trail would
come to an abrupt end. Once he became just another face
in the teeming millions on Europe's mass transit, he would
be impossible to follow.

The plane rolled to the runway right on schedule. Pavlak
breathed a sigh of relief when the thrust of the engines
pressed him deeper into his seat. A few minutes later the
lights of the city were spread beneath him like a toy village
on a table.

"Good-bye to all that," Pavlak whispered, and instantly
wondered why that title sprang to mind. It had been twenty-
five years since he had read Robert Graves' book.

The seat reclined like a lounger, and Pavlak settled back
to sleep. But then an image of Tasha's dark round eyes appeared before him, and he turned his face to the window
to hide the tears that rolled on his cheeks. Since the funeral
he had stayed too busy to dwell on the pain. Now, with nothing to distract him for the next nine hours, the flight was
going to be agony. Then something almost miraculous happened. For the first time in forty years, he cried himself to
sleep.

When the plane touched down in Frankfurt, Pavlak's limbs felt heavy and his mind sluggish. Jet lag always did that to him. He struggled to focus his vision, dragged himself through customs, exchanged five thousand dollars for German marks at the currency exchange counter, then descended into the bowels of the terminal to the train tracks that run beneath the Frankfurt airport. Twenty minutes later, he climbed two steel steps onto a train destined for Berlin. He had decided to buy his ticket from the conductor on the train. An investigator might question the agent at the ticket window, but it would take weeks to interrogate every conductor on every train that passed through the busy station.

Pavlak found an empty compartment in a first-class car and stretched out on the plush cushions. The short nap on the plane was wearing off, and he was already drifting toward sleep again when the train burst from the airport tunnel and into the harsh light of day. He opened his eyes just long enough to take in the familiar red-tiled roofs passing by his window. Well, he thought, it's started. Whatever "it" is.

9

In Langley, Virginia, the director of the Central Intelligence Agency strolled into a spacious conference room and took his seat at the head of a long, polished table. Foster Denham was a small, fastidious man whose delicate appearance had fooled many into assuming him weak. His friends knew better.

Five other men were already seated at the table, three of them dressed in blue suits and two in gray. The first man on the director's right was Patrick VanderPohl, the deputy director for Operations. Opposite him, scowling furiously at his fingernails, sat Sean O'Grady, director of the agency's Office of Security. Beside O'Grady was Edmund Olafson, chief of Eastern Europe Division, then Harris "Parky" Parker, his counterpart for Western Europe. The fifth man, sitting opposite Olafson, was younger than the rest. His name was Christopher Hopkins, and he was assistant deputy division chief for Eastern Europe.

"All right," Denham announced crisply, taking his seat. "I've read the brief. How many times did she call?"

"Her phone records indicate six calls," O'Grady replied. "At least that's what the FBI says. We haven't had time to finish checking our own log. So far I've located two of the girls who talked to her. She was pushy and insistent—as reporters usually are—and she bullied her way through screening to Patrick's office. When Patrick realized she knew something about Fool's Gold, he came to me with it. He . . ."

"What did you tell her?" the director interrupted, turning to VanderPohl.

VanderPohl shrugged. "I didn't speak to her personally. A secretary fielded the call. She repeated standard policy regarding comment on Agency operations, and so on. The woman—what's her name?" He consulted the sheaf of typed pages that lay on the table in front of him, stapled in the upper left corner. "Oh, right—Lyles. Lyles gave her a hard time."

"Did she—Lyles, I mean—did she use the operational name?"

"No, but she knew about the transfers. She said she just wanted to know if *we* knew about it—said she wasn't asking for classified information, and so on, just a confirmation or denial. We didn't bite."

O'Grady interrupted. "That was four days ago. At that point, uh . . ." He hesitated. "At that point we decided to lay low and wait it out. I ordered daily monitoring of her paper, the *Charlotte Courier,* just in case. We expected that it would die there. She didn't seem to have any details, just—you know—a little garbage she picked up somewhere. I figured, uh—the odds were it would die right there." The room was cool, but tiny beads of sweat had risen on O'Grady's forehead.

The director drew a long breath and shook his head. His face wore an expression that asked, why me. "All right—and now she's dead. So the question is, who else did she tell—and who told her?" Denham picked up a yellow wooden pencil and bounced the sharpened lead rhythmically on the table. It was an unconscious habit—something he did when a particularly prickly problem occupied his thoughts.

"As far as the FBI is concerned," O'Grady responded, a little too quickly, "the answer to the first question is nobody. They can't find anyone who knows anything about those calls to us, not her co-workers at the paper, relatives—nobody. They called us only because of the phone company record."

"Not even her husband?"

O'Grady glanced nervously away to his notes, then back into the director's questioning eyes. "John Pavlak is the reason I—we—brought this to your attention, sir. The case agent—Streat . . ." He riffled through the papers in front of him. "Darryl Streat . . . suspects Pavlak may know something he hasn't told them. And last night he disappeared."

Denham's eyes widened. "Disappeared? What the hell do you mean, disappeared?" He glared at O'Grady who swiped quickly at his forehead with a handkerchief.

"Just that, I'm afraid, sir. They don't know where he is."

Denham picked up the brief and waved it in O'Grady's face. "I thought the FBI had him under surveillance."

"They did—but they lost him. He slipped away from them sometime last evening."

"When did you talk to the Bureau?" Denham asked.

"About an hour ago."

"And they still haven't found him?"

O'Grady shook his head. "They know he boarded a bus for Philadelphia—the ticket agent and the bus driver both identified a photo—but at that point he vanished. Nobody saw him get off. The bus made stops all along the line— Greensboro, Durham, Richmond, Washington, Baltimore . . .

They're looking, of course, but they have no idea where he is."

"Do they think it was Pavlak who killed his wife?"

O'Grady frowned. "I'm not sure. Pavlak and his wife were separated and apparently there was a child custody battle in the making, so he had a motive. But they believe the bomb was triggered by remote, and they don't think Pavlak detonated it. Still, he could be behind it." O'Grady shifted in his seat. The leather upholstery was beginning to irritate the backs of his thighs. He had never understood why anyone would put leather on a chair. "You see," he continued, "the trouble is, the killing was very professional—and there was the search of the house. Also a similar search at Pavlak's apartment. Somebody is looking for something. The case agent thinks it's possible Pavlak concocted the searches as an elaborate ruse to disguise his involvement in the murder. But he obviously doesn't have anything solid on him, and I gather he's not a prime suspect—yet."

"Then why did the man run?"

"Well, that's what worries me as far as our operation is concerned. Apparently he hinted that he might investigate his wife's murder on his own. Streat—the Bureau's man— says Pavlak is very intelligent, and we know he was an outstanding military officer. That's all in our file on his father. But Streat says Pavlak is angry. He thinks he's looking for someone to kill."

Denham glanced up from the paper in his hands. "Someone to kill?"

"That's what Streat told liaison."

The director frowned. "So we've got an angry academic type on the loose, possibly with information about Fool's Gold, who could conceivably blow that operation all to hell."

O'Grady squirmed, and the leather squeaked. "Academic type, yes, but . . . uh . . . not typical. Pavlak was a Special Forces officer. He's highly trained in a variety of weapons and in anti-insurgency combat. He won a Distinguished Service Cross in Vietnam. His superiors describe him as 'extraordinarily resourceful.' And Streat says he's kept up his military skills. Works out regularly, practices at a local firing range—that kind of thing."

"A Distinguished Service Cross? Isn't that just one step below a Medal of Honor?"

O'Grady hiked one eyebrow and nodded.

For the first time, Edmund Olafson spoke up. "Well, our operation itself is dead, of course. He can't . . ."

"But he can *expose* it," Denham interrupted irritably, "and if the press got hold of Fool's Gold—Jesus H. Christ—they'd have a field day."

Foster Denham knew the modern American press only too well. He had joined the Agency soon after its creation from the remnants of the OSS in 1947. As a junior officer in what was then called the Office of Special Operations, Denham had cut his teeth in Italy, funneling funds to the Christian Democrats in response to Soviet backing for the powerful Italian Communist Party. He firmly believed that CIA intervention abroad was necessary to counter the activities of the KGB. Thus Denham had never forgotten September 8, 1974. He remembered exactly where he was that morning, the way most people remember their whereabouts on November 22, 1963, when John Kennedy was shot. Denham was sitting in his office in Langley, eating an egg sandwich for breakfast when his secretary walked in and, without a word, laid a copy of the *Washington Post* on his desk. His eyes had gone straight to a column marked in red ink. The story contained a copy of a letter from Congressman Michael Harrington of Massachusetts to Congressman Thomas Morgan of Pennsylvania. In it, Harrington revealed secret testimony from then CIA Director William Colby about the CIA's role in Allende's Chile. That letter was the beginning of a long nightmare of persecution for the Agency. When it was over, Denham, who was by then a GS16—the equivalent of a general in the military—on the DDO's staff, had developed a deep and abiding distrust of the news media.

"Fool's Gold was one of our more successful operations," Denham continued patiently. "It was legal—in my view at least—and it brought in some valuable intelligence. But the press would ignore that and focus on the transfers. Can you imagine the headlines in the *New York Times*, for God's sake? 'CIA Supplied Weapons Technology to Soviet Bloc.' They'd go into a goddamned feeding frenzy."

O'Grady cleared his throat. "That's why we thought we should run all this by you before I take any action."

"All right. What exactly does that FBI agent want from us?"

"Anything he can get. He's just fishing for information. He got the telephone records, saw the calls to us, and decided to contact us. I got the impression he's not getting anywhere on the murder."

The director snorted, a short, derisive laugh. "I'm not surprised. What do you expect from a guy who can't even keep track of one . . . what is Pavlak now . . . football coach or something? Even if he was a hotshot soldier twenty-five years ago." Denham shifted in his chair. "All right, look. Our operation couldn't possibly have anything to do with Pavlak's wife's murder. Fool's Gold has been closed for four years. The Cold War's over. Who would care if she did expose it—except for the potential public relations problem to us, of course. And nobody would kill a reporter to prevent bad publicity—tempting as the idea might be."

A collective chuckle relieved some of the tension in the room. Denham turned to Olafson, chief of Eastern Europe Division.

"Ed, I think your office should handle this from here."

"But sir," O'Grady protested, "this is clearly a security . . ."

"Yes and no," Denham snapped without looking at O'Grady. "Fool's Gold was Eastern Europe's operation, and they know it best. Ed, you will of course stay in close touch with the Office of Security."

Olafson nodded an assent.

"Keep Sean well-informed," Denham added with a placating gesture toward O'Grady. "And keep *me* informed at every step. We've got to keep an eye on Pavlak and make sure he doesn't get out of hand." Denham leaned back in his seat. "Since Fool's Gold was a cooperative operation involving the West Germans, you'll need input from Parky's staff too." Denham looked straight at Edmund Olafson. "Is Hopkins here the man you've decided on?" He gestured toward the young man on his right.

O'Grady's eyebrows shot up and his mouth opened. This had all been arranged with Olafson behind his back. He started to protest, but thought better of it and pressed his lips together again.

"Right," Olafson confirmed.

There was a short silence. "Fine," Denham agreed, twisting to his right. "Chris, it's your baby. On this, you'll report directly to me. I'll expect daily briefings—more often if necessary. Got it?"

"Yes, sir."

"The first thing to do is get all the information we have from this FBI Agent—Streat. Talk to Sean about it, then get in touch with the man."

Christopher Hopkins' eyebrows ticked upward. "Directly? Bypass the Bureau's liaison office?"

Denham shook his head. "Ask their permission first. Tell them I requested direct contact. If they balk, let me know, and I'll handle it at a higher level."

"Yes sir."

"Tell the Fibbies that their dead reporter seems to have had some minor information related to a defunct intelligence operation, but that there's no conceivable motive for a murder there. You can't give him any details because it's classified. Tell him he's barking up the wrong tree. But let him know that we're concerned about Pavlak and the danger of his exposing some of our former agents. That's true enough. Ask him to keep us informed at every step of this case. And again, if you run into resistance, let me know. Be tactful, of course. Chris, I don't have to tell you—we can't let Fool's Gold get into the press under any circumstances. I'm counting on you to handle this with extreme care."

The director dropped the pencil onto the desk and laced his fingers together behind his head. Hopkins was scribbling furiously into a small notebook.

"Gentlemen, I can't overemphasize the danger here," Denham continued. "Public exposure of this operation could have devastating consequences for the Central Intelligence Agency. We can't let that happen. Got everything, Chris?"

"Yes, sir."

"And you better brief Frank Borning on this just in case Pavlak turns up in Germany. Bonn Station should know what's going on."

Hopkins nodded.

Parky Parker, head of Western Europe Division spoke up.

"What about Krueger at the BND? Fool's Gold was his baby, after all."

The director pursed his lips while his fingers searched absently for the pencil. "No, not yet. Leave the Germans out of it for now. No reason to panic. Pavlak's an ex-military man, not an intelligence agent. Even if he is looking into his wife's murder, the chances of his actually exposing Fool's Gold are slim. And anyway, the Fibbies will probably find him in a day or two. Let's hope so anyway."

Hopkins cleared his throat. "You know—the question is, who *did* kill that reporter? And what were they looking for?"

Denham shrugged. "That's the FBI's problem, not ours." He laid both palms on the table and stood. The others started gathering their papers. "Ed . . ."

The sound of Denham's voice brought all motion to a halt.

"Yes?"

"Is there any chance—any chance at all—that Fool's Gold wasn't clean? That there was something going on we don't know about?"

"I ordered the file before I came," Olafson replied. "It should be on my desk now."

"Good. Let Hopkins give it a thorough look. Priority one. Use Analysis if they can help you. I want a report tomorrow morning. But let me know immediately—and I mean *immediately*—if you find anything that even smells funny."

"Right."

The director strode out of the room. One by one, the other men followed. Sean O'Grady's face was grim and florid as he slid through the door. Public snubs left a bad taste.

Christopher Hopkins was the last man out the door. He

closed it behind him and headed down a long hall in the direction of his office.

At thirty-six, Hopkins was a rising star in the Agency, bright, capable, and absolutely dedicated to his career. Sixty—even eighty-hour work weeks were his norm. Now he could barely contain his excitement. This special assignment, reporting directly to the DCI, was almost too good to be true. It was a showcase for him, a chance to prove his stuff at the highest level. His mind raced ahead. Olafson was nearing retirement. If he played his cards right, he could be a division chief before he was forty, then maybe—who knew—DDO by the time he was fifty, let's say, and then . . .

A sudden thought burst into his reverie. He was supposed to leave on a Caribbean Cruise in a little over a week. It would be the first vacation he had taken in two years. Martha had practically threatened divorce to get it out of him. The plans were made, the tickets bought. Martha was already packing. Now something told him that the big white ship would shove away from that Miami dock without them.

10

By the time Pavlak's train arrived in Berlin, his legs felt like wood, and his head seemed to be stuffed with cotton. He climbed into a taxi, and with the driver's help, found an inexpensive hotel on Kreiderstrasse, a side street, ten minutes' walk from the *Kurfürstendamm*. Registering at a German hotel meant surrendering his passport and having his name entered into a computer, but he was gambling that the computer would not get the information for at least a day or two. The Germans were efficient, but not that efficient, and even if Streat really did pursue him all the way across the ocean, Pavlak should have twenty-four hours or more before having to make another move.

Berlin had dozens of hotels like the Eger where Pavlak took a room. The wallpaper was peeling, and the mattress sagged, but it was scrupulously clean. And he was lucky enough to get a room that looked out onto a filthy concrete courtyard in the back, away from traffic noise. He double-locked the door, fell onto the bed in his clothes, and slept.

Ten hours later, he opened his eyes and stared at the unfamiliar wallpaper. It took a full five seconds for his groggy brain to reconstruct the past few days, and when it did, he wished that he had not awakened. He wished he could hold his daughter in his arms again. He wished his life were not his life. He wished he had no life.

Pavlak grunted aloud and shook such thoughts from his head. With the knuckle of his index finger, he wiped a tear from his eye, then forced himself onto his belly on the cold floor and started doing push-ups. He flung himself up and down until the tears were driven from his eyes. With jet lag still fogging his senses and cramping his limbs, the workout required more self-discipline than usual, but it was worth it. When he stepped into the shower thirty minutes later, sweating and panting, visions of self-destruction had vanished from his brain, and he was ready, if not entirely willing, to pick up the burden of life again.

In the hotel dining room he downed three hard rolls with butter and jam, scooped the bright yolk out of a soft-boiled egg, and felt his spirits rise a little more. He had always loved the fat and calorie-laden German breakfast, and tearing at one of the chewy rolls was like a homecoming.

This trip should be bearable, he thought. He had money. He had time. No one on earth knew where he was—at least for the time being. He would take a hard look at Brigitte's hit-and-run accident, and if he could find no connection to the bombing, he would board another plane and move his hideaway to eastern Oregon. He loved the high desert, and he should be hard enough to find there.

When he remembered the need for secrecy, Pavlak frowned. He could not risk staying in the hotel more than one more night. Streat was probably looking for him, and for all he knew at this point, even the two men who searched his apartment might somehow have access to the German computer—especially if the accent Mrs. Ekelwood had detected was German.

If all went as planned, he would talk to Turgat in a few hours, and perhaps, though he had never met Brigitte's husband, he could wangle an invitation to stay there for a while. That would make it easier to gather information, and of course he would conveniently forget to register his whereabouts with the police as German law demanded. To his American sensibility, that particular law had always sparked a sense of outrage and resentment that his European friends found puzzling.

After breakfast Pavlak tucked a newspaper under his arm and walked out onto the street. The hum of traffic and the scent of exhaust fumes struck him immediately. Despite political turmoil, despite the trauma of destruction and reconstruction, despite division and isolation, Berlin never completely lost the desperate decadence for which the city is famous. It remains the one place in the world where, if one has the means, one can get literally anything the heart desires—whether of the spirit or the flesh, legal or illegal. Every quality of man the species has yet produced still swarms the streets and basement clubs and back-alley apartments of Berlin.

For an hour, Pavlak strolled through the streets the Hohenzollerns had built. It was his first visit to Germany since that dramatic night three years before when he had watched on television as jubilant Berliners swarmed over the city's infamous Wall. He headed straight for the *Reichstag,* rounded the northern corner of the grand old building, and froze in his tracks. The sidewalk in front of him simply continued on into an uglier, shabbier, Berlin. No trace remained of the ugly concrete that had always bisected that sidewalk and announced the end of the free world. Beneath him, where the Spree had once flowed through no-man's land, a sight-seeing boat loaded with tourists glided past. Toward the east, scaffolding climbed the walls of every third building, and construction cranes thrust into the sky as far as he could see. After five minutes he turned his back. This new world would take time to digest, and right now he had other business.

It was Sunday morning, the one brief period in the week when the city wears an illusory and seductive calm, so seductive that Pavlak almost abandoned his cautious plan in favor of simply walking up to Turgat's apartment and knocking on the door. But as he approached Kreuzberg, the district where Brigitte had lived, reality snatched his attention back to the dangers at hand. He rounded a corner a bit too briskly and almost stumbled over a shabbily dressed corpse in the middle of a sidewalk. At least, he thought it was a corpse. When he bent for a closer look, he noticed an empty bottle clutched in one hand, and the slow, steady rise and fall of breath within the rags. Life still struggled there, addicted and wretched, but life nonetheless.

The sight gave him pause. In the past week, reality had adopted new and unknown dangers. If Brigitte's death was in fact a murder and connected to the bombing outside Avery, then there could be no such thing as excessive caution. He reversed his steps, found a phone booth, and dialed Turgat's number.

He recognized the voice of Brigitte's sister immediately. No, she told him, Turgat was not at home. He had left Berlin the previous day to visit his parents in Turkey. He was devastated by Brigitte's death and might not return for some time. In fact, he might not return to Germany at all. Karin hesitated, then continued. Turgat was angry and disillusioned with Germany, the country of his birth. Pavlak said nothing, and Karin changed the subject. She was leaving for home in a few hours herself, taking the night train. She had stayed in Berlin a week to help Turgat manage things. After all, he had no close family of his own in Germany. She had almost finished going through Brigitte's possessions. Karin's voice faltered when she mentioned her mission there, but she quickly recovered and remembered to ask Pavlak how he was coping with his own loss.

"One manages," Pavlak replied curtly. He was disappointed that Turgat was not available. It threw a monkey wrench into his plans. But perhaps Karin would know something helpful. Better Karin than nothing. "Karin—I'm in Berlin. In fact, I'm calling from a phone booth not far away. I'm sure you're very busy, but . . . I would very much like to speak with you, if you could spare me a few minutes of your time. Could you possibly meet me on Schornstrasse—the Cafe Schuller—in, say, half an hour?"

There was only the slightest hesitation. "Of course, Dr. Pavlak. I would be happy to. Brigitte told me much about you and your wife. But—why are you here in Germany? Is there . . . is there something specific you wish to talk about?"

"No, not really. I'm just—well—I'm struggling too, like Turgat. I believe it would make me feel better just to talk for a while. Do you mind?"

"Of course not. In half an hour then."

Pavlak hung up the phone. The Cafe Schuller was directly behind him—which was how he had chosen it as a meeting place—but he stepped out in the opposite direction, toward Brigitte's apartment. Perhaps it was silly and paranoid, but he had come this far by being cautious, and he would take no chances now. Not yet anyway.

As he neared Turgat's address, Pavlak slowed his pace and began examining shop windows as if he were a casual, Sunday morning stroller. From time to time he sneaked a glance at the building that bore the blue tag with white letters that read "1105 Argenenstrasse." It was a faceless, gray apartment building, stuccoed and characterless. He saw nothing suspicious. A middle-aged woman in a fur coat was walking a Dachshund on a leash. When the dog squatted to defecate, she dragged it unceremoniously into the gutter, and Pavlak looked away. Two children played in a tiny park diagonally across the street from the apartment building. Their mother sat on a bench and watched them with an expression of vague disapproval. The father sat at the other end of the bench reading a newspaper. Perhaps thirty yards further down the street, a young couple sat in a cheap French-made automobile, a tin box with wheels and a twenty horsepower engine, still popular among European students. They appeared deeply engaged in a lovers' quarrel, and in any event, their backs were turned to Turgat's building.

Satisfied, Pavlak casually sauntered into a side street, then ducked into a doorway and waited. Karin would pass within view on her way to the Cafe Schuller. If she were going to be on time, as Germans usually are—something Pavlak truly admired about the race—she would have to appear within the next five minutes. Pavlak pulled out his wallet and began slowly searching through its contents, as if he had lost something. There was not much to search, so he hoped Karin would hurry.

She did not hurry. The minutes dragged on. Several people passed by on Argenenstrasse—an elderly man, a middle-aged woman, two insolent youths smoking cigarettes—but no young woman who might have been Brigitte's younger sister. Ten minutes passed. Twelve. Had she gone a different way? For the first time the thought occurred to him that she might have driven there in a car, even though it was only a ten minute walk—something unlikely for a German.

And then she appeared, a slender young woman with

short black hair, walking quickly. She flashed into view, crossed the narrow street where he stood, and hurriedly disappeared behind the corner of the building. Pavlak waited another two minutes. Nothing happened.

He was about to step into the street again when a man appeared, walking briskly in the same direction. Pavlak's heart pounded into his throat. It was the man on the park bench, the one reading a newspaper whom he had presumed to be the father of the playing children. There was no mistaking the dark, suede leather jacket, or the smooth, powerful jaw.

Pavlak leaned back against the wall to steady himself. He could feel the blood pounding through veins in his temples. Think.

Maybe it was just a coincidence. Maybe the man was not following Karin at all. But if he *was* tailing her . . . Pavlak's brain raced to sort out the implications and quickly gave up. There would be time for that later.

He shoved the wallet into his pocket and stepped into the street. When he turned the corner onto Argenenstrasse, Karin was nowhere in sight. The man in the suede jacket was a block ahead of him, walking very fast. If he were following Karin, he would take a left turn at the approaching corner. Pavlak kept pace with him and watched as the man reached the corner, stopped, looked right and left, then walked straight ahead across the street. Pavlak stopped in his tracks and looked in a shop window at a display of electric trains. From the corner of his eye he saw the man stop again on the opposite corner, then turn abruptly to his left and strike out again.

It was not a coincidence.

When the man disappeared behind the corner building, Pavlak darted out in a dead run down a parallel street. Cafe

Schuller was not far. He had very little time. After a block and a half, his lungs felt as if he were inhaling molten steel. He ignored the pain and raced on. At the next intersection he rounded a corner to the right, dodged an elderly lady who shouted angrily at his back, and sprinted toward Schornstrasse. The man in the suede jacket should be at least a block behind him now. The question was, where was Karin? Had she already passed by this street?

As he approached the corner, she appeared suddenly, walking across his path from the right, not thirty feet away. She gave a small cry when she glimpsed him running toward her, but Pavlak pulled to a halt and did his best to smile. She quickly looked away and kept walking. He rounded the corner behind her and, as he did so, caught sight of the suede jacket about fifty yards away. Pavlak was four steps behind Karin and matching her pace. The cafe was coming up. He had to act quickly.

Still panting for oxygen, Pavlak spoke as clearly and quickly as he could. "Don't turn around. Just keep walking."

Her steps faltered at his command, then she resumed walking, with only a new rigidity in the stride betraying that she had heard him.

"I'm John Pavlak. A man is following you. We can't meet here. Walk past the cafe and turn left at the next corner."

She did not turn her head, but murmured several words straight ahead. Pavlak could not make them out.

"Just listen to me. Walk left at the next corner. Whatever you do, don't look behind you."

It occurred to him that he was asking an awful lot. This woman had never seen him before. And she had not seen the man in the suede jacket behind them. Why should she believe him?

"Please trust me," Pavlak pleaded, as the corner drew

near. "I *am* John Pavlak," he repeated. His mind was racing. "Brigitte told me once she used to call you *'Eselchen.'* "

Little donkey. It was the only thing he could think of on the spur of the moment that might convince her. She had reached the corner. To his horror, she stopped dead in her tracks, and for a moment he was sure she would turn around—maybe even scream for help. Then she glanced both ways, like a woman unsure of her directions, and turned to her left. As she did so, Pavlak glimpsed the side of her face. It was pale as death.

He followed her, waited three steps until the corner of the building hid him from the man in the suede jacket, then sprinted ahead and caught her hand. "Run!" he cried, dragging her with him.

By European standards, Berlin is a city of greenery. There are parks at every turn, some large, some small. A small one lay just ahead of them. Pavlak pulled her into it and searched desperately for something to hide behind. A line of low, dense shrubbery offered the only hope. He darted through a gap in the bushes and dove onto the ground, pulling Karin down with him. She lay with her back rounded against his chest, trembling and still. "Don't move and don't make a sound," he whispered into her ear. "Can you see the street?"

She shook her head wordlessly. Pavlak eased himself up on an elbow until he could peer through a gap in the foliage. "Look through here," he whispered hoarsely. She followed his instructions just as the man in the suede jacket appeared, jogging uncertainly. He stopped in full view and cast about him. Pavlak could see him well now. He was not tall, but he was powerfully built, blue-eyed with light brown hair.

The man's gaze quickly scoured the park, and for a second, Pavlak thought he had discovered them. Then the searching eyes moved on, and the anxious frown deepened. Finally the man rushed on, paused at the next corner, then sprinted down a side street.

The instant he was out of sight, Pavlak pulled Karin to her feet and half dragged her through an alley behind the park and out onto the opposite street. From there they doubled back toward the cafe, passed it at a brisk walk, and kept on in the opposite direction.

"Is there a taxi stand near here?"

Again Karin shook her head. She was a small woman with dark, almost black eyes, now round and wide with terror. Her face was still unnaturally pale.

Pavlak pulled her relentlessly through the streets of Kreuzberg, weaving back toward the *Kurfürstendamm*. He remembered a taxi stand on Bergsonstrasse, and it was there he was headed. They reached it at last and climbed into the first car in the line. Pavlak barked instructions and the taxi sped away in the direction of Schöneberg.

He glanced at Karin, and for the first time, her eyes met his. Pavlak smiled. She tried to smile back, but the smile died on her face. Pavlak realized then that he was still crushing her hand in his. She had made no effort to dislodge it, but he placed it gently on her lap and turned his full attention to the driver.

For twenty minutes, Pavlak led him down one street and up another, occasionally around in a circle, until the driver's annoyance grew obvious. When Pavlak was satisfied that no one was following, he ordered the driver to a cafe in Grunewald on the outskirts of the city. The drive took forty-five minutes, and the time passed in rigid silence. When the taxi at last drew up to the curb, Pavlak threw the fare and a generous tip into the front seat and pulled Karin onto the sidewalk after him.

"Well," he began as lightly as he could. "A bit of excitement to start off this Sunday morning."

"My God," she breathed, putting a hand across her eyes. It was the first time Pavlak had heard her voice except over the telephone. Something made him take her hand again and lead her into the Cafe Klatz. It was a grand old affair in the Viennese style, with elaborate wallpaper, upholstered booths, and crystal chandeliers. Pavlak had been there before with Judith. It was, he remembered now with a twist of irony, a Sunday morning. Karin ordered an espresso from a waitress in a black dress with a white lace collar, and Pavlak doubled the order.

While she searched in her purse for a mirror, Pavlak studied Karin's face. She was definitely Brigitte's sister. Her features were smaller and more delicate, but she had the same intelligent eyes and the same brief indentation in her chin. And somewhere in that face—he could not say exactly where—there lay the same potential for passion that had smoldered in Brigitte. But this face, despite its delicacy, was somehow stronger, quieter, less volatile. This, he guessed, was no radical utopianist, clinging to a romantic illusion of The Revolution. She was not beautiful, but she was attractive in a Mediterranean way. There was a careless grace in her movements as she brushed a bit of leaf from her hair. If he had seen her on a street in New York, he would have guessed her ancestry as Italian, or perhaps Greek—certainly not German. The color of her skin was too rich, her nose and jaw too sculptured to fit the stereotype of the German *fräulein*. Pavlak guessed her to be perhaps a year or two over thirty.

"So, Dr. Pavlak," Karin began when she was satisfied that her appearance was presentable, "I trust you are going to explain what just happened to me."

Pavlak immediately liked the understatement—something that is second nature to Anglo-Saxons with their inbred love of irony, but rare among Germans. And he was instantly captivated by the hint of a smile that accompanied it.

He drew a deep breath and started at the beginning. He talked for ten minutes, pausing only when the waitress delivered their coffee. Pavlak let his grow cold as he spoke. Karin sipped once, then ignored hers as well. She was watching him intently, and the intensity deepened as his story progressed. He sketched out the details of Judith's murder, the search of her house, and the apparent professionalism of the bombing. He told her about the two men who had ransacked his apartment, about Streat, about Judith's investigation of the motorcycle gang and the narcotics money that might be part of it. He had slipped away from the FBI, he explained, because he did not trust even them.

"And I came to Germany," he added, "because I want to find out if there could be a connection to Brigitte's death, and because . . ." Pavlak glanced away, then back again. "Because I want to find the man who murdered my little girl."

Karin watched his face, but said nothing. After a time, her gaze turned to a stare, and Pavlak realized that she was no longer seeing him but looking instead at something in her memory.

"Ich habe es geahnt," she whispered at last, barely loud enough to hear. "I suspected it."

"Suspected what?"

Her eyes flicked back into focus. "That they killed her."

"Who killed her?"

"I don't know. But Brigitte's apartment was searched too—much the way you describe. The police thought it was a burglary—there is much crime in Kreuzberg now. More all the time. I begged her many times not to move there, but . . ." Karin gazed out the window at the trees surrounding the cafe. In Berlin's latitude it would be May before they reached full foliage. "Some things were stolen," she continued. "A watch, some money, her jewelry."

"When was the burglary?"

"An hour after she was killed. While Turgat was at the hospital."

Pavlak's pulse was marching double-time. He took her hand. "Karin—what do you know? Tell me."

She shook her head slowly. "Nothing. And now your Judith . . ." She pronounced Judith's name as if it were German, turning the "J" into a "Y" and hardening the final consonant to a "t."

"Who is the man who followed me?" she asked suddenly.

Pavlak sighed. "I was hoping you could tell me. Have you ever seen him before?"

"Never."

"Are you sure? Someone has probably been watching you all week."

"Perhaps," she frowned. "I haven't seen anyone. Not until today. Maybe . . ." She looked at him. "Maybe he was waiting for you. Maybe he knew you would come—or guessed it."

Pavlak digested the idea. "I don't think so," he answered slowly. "No one knew I was coming."

"Yes, but maybe they were taking no chances. Why would they watch me, after all? I'm just a sister who lives hundreds of kilometers away and rarely saw Brigitte. But you are Judith's husband. You . . ."

She broke off with a gasp and her hand darted to her

mouth. For a second Pavlak thought the man in the suede jacket had appeared at the door, but she was looking straight into his eyes.

"What is it?"

"Turgat! Oh my God, Turgat!"

"What, Karin? What is it?"

"His father called last night. Turgat wasn't on the plane in Istanbul. I assumed he had missed his connecting flight in Munich and would catch a later flight. But he didn't call me or them. That's not like Turgat. We've got to call the police!"

She stood. Pavlak caught her wrist and held it firmly. "And tell them what, Karin? That Turgat missed his plane? They're not going to do anything about that."

"I've got to call his father."

She struggled, but Pavlak held tight. "Wait, Karin. If something has happened to Turgat, it's too late to do anything about it. And if he's okay, there's no need. We'll call later. Right now we have to think. *Think.* Did Brigitte say anything to you recently? Did you find anything unusual among her things?"

Karin hesitated, then reluctantly sank back into her seat. As she did, one hand rose tentatively toward her mouth and paused in mid-air. Pavlak noticed that it was trembling. He tried to appear calm and took a sip of the cold espresso. As he did, he noticed that his own hands were unsteady as well—whether from jet lag or anxiety, he wasn't sure. He decided to abandon the coffee and signaled the waitress.

"I can't think of anything unusual," Karin mumbled. "Nothing."

"I'm going to order a beer. Would you like one?"

"No, thank you. A cognac perhaps."

Pavlak barked the order in the cool, offhand manner that

worked best in Germany. Southern American courtesy, he had found, tended to trigger contempt in Europe.

"Did Brigitte say anything about Judith recently? Anything about America?"

A light went on in Karin's eyes. "The receipt . . ."

"What receipt?"

"A receipt for registered mail. She sent a registered letter or package or something. To Judith. I was curious about it."

"Do you still have the receipt?"

"I'm not sure. I think I threw it away."

"Was it recent?"

"Yes. A few weeks ago."

"Anything else?"

"I haven't gone through all her papers yet. Brigitte was a collector. She hated to throw things away. The papers are a mess because of the burglary. They were scattered all over the apartment."

The waitress arrived and conversation ceased. Pavlak took a long, thirsty pull from his glass, savoring the rich flavor. Why, he wondered for the thousandth time, could not, or would not American breweries produce a decent beer.

The noon hour was nearing, and the cafe was beginning to fill with customers. Pavlak was getting nervous. "We have to examine Brigitte's things, Karin. And you have to call Turgat's parents. Don't worry," he smiled. "He's probably sitting in Istanbul, drinking a cup of coffee that makes your espresso look like scared water."

She frowned. "The first thing we should do is call the police."

"We can't do that. Think about it. Two murders . . . three," he corrected himself, and fought down the lump that surged into his throat. "Five thousand miles apart. The two men who searched my apartment. The man following you.

I don't know who these people are, but they've got power and money. Lots of money. And money means influence. I came here because I didn't trust the FBI, and I don't trust the German police any more."

"We don't have any choice. We're helpless alone."

"But at least we're alive. Maybe Judith or Brigitte went to the police with something, and you see what happened to them. Somebody—we don't know who—knows where you are. And like you said, they may be looking for me. If they *are*, then I can't take a chance on being found. The man who followed you hasn't seen anything but my back. He still doesn't know I'm here—unless your phone is tapped. Anyway, we can't trust anybody at this point."

"Dr. Pavlak . . ."

Her hand came to rest gently on his arm. Pavlak looked into her somber eyes and found, to his surprise, a profound serenity there. Something untouchable that lay beneath the anxiety.

"You must tell me something. When you said you wanted to find the man who killed your little girl . . ." She stopped. "Your eyes frightened me when you said that."

"I'm glad to hear it," Pavlak responded instantly. "I hope they frighten him too, when I catch up with him."

Her gaze fell to the table. "Then I can't help you," she said firmly. "I'm sorry. I won't tell the police you're here, but I must go to them."

Pavlak was dumbfounded. "Why can't you help me?"

She shook her head and paused as her forefinger stroked a spot on the tablecloth. "Because I don't want to be part of a vendetta. I can understand how you feel . . ."

"Can you?"

She looked up sharply. "Why shouldn't I? Have you forgotten my sister?"

"Of course not. That's why I don't understand you. Don't you want to find the people who killed her? Don't you want them to suffer for taking her away from you?"

Karin's gaze returned to the stain on the tablecloth. "Yes," she announced at last. "I do. But I refuse to give in to that emotion."

"Why not? What's wrong with the desire for justice?"

"Nothing. But you're not talking about justice. You're talking about vengeance."

She was indeed Brigitte's sister, Pavlak thought. She had her opinions, and she was not going to back away from them without a fight. "I see," he answered. "And you view justice and vengeance as two entirely separate things?"

"They *are* separate."

Pavlak considered. "All right. Yes. They're not exactly the same thing. There can certainly be vengeance without justice, for example." He leaned in. "But there is no justice without vengeance, Karin. By definition."

"Agreed," she said simply, surprising him. "But vengeance can take many forms—and it's not necessarily your responsibility—or even your right—to impose it."

"Who then?" Pavlak demanded. "The legal system? That's a joke in the United States, and not much better here."

"There are other sources," she said calmly.

"Really? Who?"

She sat silently, never taking her eyes from his face.

"Oh Christ," Pavlak breathed. "Not . . . 'Vengeance is mine . . . ' ?"

"Why not?"

Pavlak set his beer glass onto the table. "You're a Christian."

"That bothers you?"

He shrugged. "It disappoints me a little."

"Why?"

"I thought you were smarter than that."

"I see," she said calmly. "You believe Christians are fools."

"Oh, don't feel singled-out," Pavlak responded with an edge in his voice. "I think you're *all* fools—Christians, Muslims, Jews, Buddhists—whatever. All of you with your childish faith in something that, if it does exist, couldn't possibly be benevolent." Pavlak picked up a light metal ashtray and tossed it aside.

Karin was still looking into his face. "Losing your family has made you bitter."

"No, I'm just a realist. I never fed on illusions. Never. Not even when I was a child. I always knew that God, if He does exist, certainly is not love." It occurred to Pavlak that his reaction was excessively emotional. He took a deep breath and forced himself to lower his voice. "You see, Karin," he went on, "I've had a long bath in reality—since the first thing I can remember, in fact."

"And what was that—the first thing you remember?"

Pavlak tossed the ashtray again and avoided her eyes. They were wasting time.

"The first thing I remember," he found himself saying, "is sitting in a high chair drinking a glass of milk. I think I was maybe three years old, something like that. I was playing with the milk, filling my cheeks and puffing them out—you know—just being a kid, lost in my own little fantasy world. I didn't know I was doing anything wrong. I didn't even see it coming. The old man hit me so hard he knocked me out of the chair. Milk flew all over everything." Pavlak waited, but Karin did not react. "I decided right then that nobody was ever going to catch me in Fantasyland again. Maybe I couldn't keep from getting hit, but the next time, at least I would see it coming."

"Who was 'the old man?' "

"My father."

"I'm sorry," Karin whispered.

"For what?"

"For you."

Pavlak laughed. "I should be sorry for you. At least I expect the blows to come. You tell yourself life is a rose garden, then you get caught off guard, again and again."

"No," Karin countered. "I know the blows will come. I just react to them differently. Maybe that's why I believe we should trust the police now."

Her mention of the police snapped Pavlak's attention back to his present predicament. "Karin, I need you," he pleaded. "I need to get into Brigitte's apartment and look through her things for a clue to all this. At least give me a day before you go to the police."

She shook her head. "I'm sorry."

He felt his blood rising. "You Germans and your authority worship," he snapped. "You still love men in uniforms, don't you?"

"The police are our only hope," she insisted, folding her arms firmly.

Pavlak's head began to feel like a bowling ball on his shoulders, whether because of Karin's intransigence, jet lag, or German beer he was not sure.

"All right," he sighed. "We'll go to the police together and tell them about the man who followed you. But I ask one thing. Help me search Brigitte's papers first. We can do it in an hour. One hour, that's all I ask."

"But . . . they'll be watching the apartment," she objected. "How can we get back there?"

"You can just walk in the front door. They don't know

we're onto them yet. Their man lost you, but he doesn't know it's because I spotted him."

"You mean . . . act like nothing's happened?"

"Why not? That gives us—and later the police—an advantage. Assuming this guy isn't a policeman himself," Pavlak added with an accusing glance. "If we panic now, they'll know they've been discovered and they'll lie low."

She had not touched her cognac. Now she swirled it in the balloon glass and stared silently into the golden liquid. "But I'm afraid to go back there now," she whispered.

"Shall I stay there with you? We can swing by the hotel and pick up my bag."

Karin considered only a second. "Yes. I would feel better that way. But we should hurry. I've got to call Turgat's parents—and I must call my husband."

Pavlak was startled. So she was married. Of course. She would be. He was not sure why the news surprised him.

He gave the waitress a ten-mark tip and asked her to call a taxi. While they waited on the sidewalk he tried once again to talk Karin out of going to the police, but it was no use. She saw no reason to suspect police complicity, she said. Begrudgingly, Pavlak admitted that he had no very good reason either. And perhaps she was right. Perhaps the events of the past week had made him paranoid.

The taxi arrived, and they climbed into the rear seat. Pavlak gave the driver the address of the Hotel Eger.

"Is there a way for me to get into your apartment unseen?" he whispered, with a warning glance toward the driver. "We have to assume they're still watching it. And if they *are* looking for me . . ."

"There's a back door from a courtyard where the garbage cans are kept. It leads down some stairs into a laundry room in the basement. But the courtyard is fenced in and the fence is topped with barbed wire. Kreuzberg is not a safe neighborhood. There's a gate in the fence, but it's always padlocked. I don't know how you could get into the court-yard, but that's the only possibility I know of."

They fell silent and watched the city slide past. The cab driver weaved through back streets for half an hour, then suddenly made a right turn, and Pavlak recognized the Ho-tel Eger, half a block away.

Karin didn't see his arm coming, and she gasped as he pulled her violently toward him and down. Her nose banged sharply against his knee, then Pavlak's chest crushed her into the seat.

"Don't stop!" Pavlak hissed frantically at the driver. "Drive on!"

At that moment the taxi was drawing even with a black Volvo parked across the street from the hotel. In it sat the man in the suede jacket. He was facing the hotel entrance, still pretending to read his newspaper.

11

"Still want to go to the police?"

They stood beside a sausage stand on Albertstrasse, each chewing on *Currywurst* and a slice of black bread. Pavlak was washing his down with a beer. Karin sipped a cola. She was pale again and—Pavlak thought at first—sullen. But he soon realized that her reticence sprang from fear rather than resentment, and he softened his tone.

"They found me through the hotel's *Anmeldung*, Karin. It's the only possible way. Whoever they are, they have access to police computers. Maybe they *are* the police."

"What do they want from us?" Karin pleaded suddenly, slapping her palm on the wooden board that served as a counter. "From *you?*"

"Me? He followed you first, remember?"

"Yes—as I was going to meet you. Maybe they were watching me because they didn't know where you were yet. Your *Anmeldung* wouldn't have been in the computer until this morning. And when he found you, he stopped following me."

"He stopped following you because he lost you. He had no choice. Look, they're probably watching both of us because they think either one of us might have what they're looking for."

"And what is that?"

"That's what we have to find out. We have to get back into Brigitte's apartment."

She shook her head firmly. "I'm not going back there."

"You have to."

"I can't."

"Why not?"

"Because I'm afraid!" Her vehemence startled him. "I just want to go home and get out of this. I'm exhausted and scared. I've half a mind to catch a train right now."

"Listen to me, Karin." He touched her shoulder. "You have no choice now. If they know my hotel, they certainly know your permanent address. They'll follow you home too. We need help, and we'll get help. But we have to find out who the bad guys are before we know where to turn. It has to be something Brigitte and Judith were doing. Think about it. Maybe these guys are looking for whatever Brigitte sent Judith by registered mail. If we dig a little, we can find it." Pavlak wished he really felt the confidence he was trying to convey. He took her shoulders and turned her gently toward him. "Don't abandon me now, Karin, please. You're all I've got. I need you—and you need me. Whatever the way out of this is, it's the same for both of us."

Afternoon traffic was picking up. It droned past them in an almost unbroken stream. A woman with three children in tow stopped and bought chocolate bars at the window. One of the children was a girl about three years old. Her hair was golden, and her eyes as blue as sapphire. When she saw Pavlak staring at her, she smiled. He turned quickly away.

"What is it?" Karin asked. "What's wrong?"

"Nothing. Listen, call your husband and tell him you've

been delayed. You need a couple more days to finish up here."

This time a full minute passed before Karin replied. "How will we get into the apartment?"

Pavlak breathed a silent sigh of relief. "The courtyard at the back—is it bounded entirely by fence, or is there another building that looks into it?"

"The fence is only on two sides. Another apartment building forms the side opposite ours. It's actually the side of the building around the corner on Röntgenstrasse."

"Any windows in it that look onto the courtyard?"

"Of course, but how would you get to one of them? They're probably all inside somebody's apartment."

"I don't know, but it's an idea. I'll figure something out when we get there. We have to wait until dark no matter what. If worse comes to worse, I'll pull a hat over my eyes and walk in the front door too."

"And me?"

"For you it's no problem. They already know you're there, so there's no point in trying to hide. Just act as if nothing happened."

"Suppose—suppose they grab me?"

Pavlak shook his head. "If they wanted to kidnap you, they would've done that already. They're hoping you'll lead them to something."

She nodded uncertainly.

Pavlak drained the last swallow of beer and looked at his watch. It said seven o'clock—he had not yet set it to Central European time. Seven plus six meant that it was now one o'clock in Berlin. "The question is," he mused, "what do we do for the next six hours until it gets dark? Care to join me in my hotel?"

She grimaced. "Sorry, but I'm in no mood for jokes just now."

"Who's joking? I have to go back there—they have my passport at the desk, remember? Their little guarantee that I'll pay my bill. Come on."

Pavlak pulled her toward a phone booth to call a taxi, but Karin insisted on calling Istanbul first to see if Turgat had arrived. For a moment he considered letting her use his long distance credit card but thought better of it. It would create another computer record of his whereabouts, and one of those was already more than enough. They pooled their loose change and ended up with enough for one minute of conversation in broken German with Turgat's parents. Turgat still had not arrived, his father told Karin, and they were frantic with worry. They had notified the Turkish police who had contacted their German counterparts.

After she hung up, Karin relaxed a little. Someone, at least, had pulled the police into the affair, if only indirectly.

"Aren't you going to call your husband?" Pavlak asked.

She shook her head. "Not yet. I've changed my mind."

"But he'll be worried if you don't show up on time."

"He doesn't know when I'm coming." She looked away, toward the *Fernsehturm*, the tower that grew out of the eastern horizon like an onion sprout. Once the pride of a brutal regime, it was still the highest structure in Berlin, a monument to socialist technology that had once towered over the Berlin Wall. "He's not really my husband," she confessed suddenly. "We've been divorced for almost three years. I wanted to call him because he's with the police."

"He's a policeman?" If there was one thing they desperately needed, it was a friend in the police whom they could trust.

"Yes—unfortunately."

"Why 'unfortunately'?"

"It's difficult to be a policeman's wife in Germany, especially in these days of skinheads and *Autonomen* and people whose primary goal in life is to hurt policemen."

Pavlak said nothing. He knew Germany's skinheads well. They were like American street gangs except that American gangs did not bother to romanticize their brutality with pseudo-political ravings. The same was true of the *Autonomen*, close cousins of the skinheads, except that they justified their hooliganism with left-wing, rather than right-wing political cant.

"Would he help us?" Pavlak asked carefully. "I mean, would he help us—without telling anyone?"

She nodded. "We're friends. He would help me if I asked."

"Good. Maybe we can call on him when we know something. Right now we have to get my passport. Come on."

The black Volvo was still sitting in the same spot, though its driver had abandoned the newspaper and sat motionless and bored in the driver's seat. Pavlak ordered their taxi driver to turn down a side street and circle the hotel. When they reached the far side, out of sight of the black Volvo, Pavlak and Karin climbed out. There was only one door on this side of the building. Pavlak tried it and found it locked. He knocked, lightly at first, then harder. Finally he pounded with his fist until an angry hotel clerk pushed the door open and demanded to know the meaning of the disturbance. Pavlak played the dumb tourist just trying to get to his room. The clerk jerked his head toward the corner. "Front entrance only," he barked.

"But this door's open now," Pavlak interjected with a smile, showing his key. "We'll just go in here."

"I said around the corner," the clerk ordered again, and

tried to slam the door. Pavlak was quicker and tore it from the smaller man's hand, shouldered him out of the way, and pulled Karin inside with him. The clerk started to protest but fell silent when Pavlak, who stood at least six inches taller, fixed him with an icy glare.

They took a hall elevator to the third floor. Karin waited while Pavlak arranged his things in the new suitcase he had bought in Atlanta. He had never really unpacked, so it only took a few minutes.

"That's it."

"Good. Let's go. We can leave by the same door. It's not locked from the inside. Fire regulations."

"I know," Pavlak replied, "but I still have to get my passport, and I can't go down to the main desk. They might have someone stationed in the lobby."

He picked up the phone and called the desk. "I'm in room three-twelve, and I'm running late. Send someone up with my passport and bill . . . Yes, I know, but I don't have time . . . Yes, but . . . Listen, I'm telling you I don't have time—and I've got a fifty-mark tip if my passport and bill are here in under five minutes . . . Yes. Thank you."

He hung up the phone and smiled. "Money works wonders. Come on."

He led Karin out of the room and around a corner into a wing that ran perpendicular to theirs. They waited no more than two minutes until the soft *ding* of the elevator sounded, followed by the rattle of the opening door. There were light steps on the carpet, then two raps on a door. Pavlak peeked around the corner. It was a desk clerk in uniform—the same one who had opened the side door.

"Here," Pavlak called to the startled clerk who jerked his head around and stared in frightened recognition. Pavlak took the passport from his trembling hand, replaced it with two hundred-mark notes, then smiled warmly at the clerk. They took the elevator back to the first floor and a few moments later hurried out the side door again, leaving the hotel and the black Volvo behind.

12

It was pitch dark when they finally left the Italian restaurant where they had dined on linguini and oyster sauce, and shared a bottle of chianti. Pavlak had the cab driver cruise past the apartment twice. As they were approaching it for the first time, he reached an arm around Karin and pulled her toward him. She stiffened.

"Pretend we're lovers," Pavlak explained in a whisper. "Look over my shoulder and search the left side of the street for anybody watching. I'll search the right. Keep your face out of the light."

At that she relaxed and brought her right hand up to hold the back of his neck, then melted into him with surprising ease. The cool, moralistic distance she had kept all day seemed to vanish in an instant, and the scent of her hair stirred something inside him. He squelched an impulse to kiss the warm cheek that lay against his, and focussed instead on the shadows on the sidewalk. If anyone was watching the apartment, he was well hidden. After the second pass, Pavlak ordered the taxi to halt six blocks away, and they climbed out. Karin set off nervously to walk in the front door, while

Pavlak circled around and approached the building from behind.

He was in luck. The apartment house behind Brigitte's had a window in the lobby that looked out into the courtyard between the two buildings. Pavlak waited while an elderly lady with an armload of packages struggled into the elevator, then he quickly pulled the latch, climbed out the window, and dropped twelve feet to the concrete floor of the courtyard. The landing jarred every fiber in his body.

"Any problems?" Karin whispered, as she pushed the basement door open from the inside.

"None that being twenty years younger wouldn't cure," Pavlak whispered, limping toward her. "Did you see anyone?"

"Not a soul."

"That worries me. I'd rather know where they are."

"Maybe they've gone—at least for the night."

"Maybe."

Brigitte's apartment consisted of one tiny bedroom in the back and a combination kitchen/living room in the front. It was cramped and dingy with age, but spotlessly clean. Cardboard boxes full of clothing were stacked neatly beside a chest of drawers in the bedroom, destined, Karin told him, for the *Heilsarmee*. She and Brigitte wore the same size, but she could not bear to put on one of her dead sister's dresses. And anyway, Brigitte would have wanted her things to go to poor people.

Another stack of boxes stood beside a desk in the living room. Those, Karin told him, were Brigitte's papers. She had gone through most of them, but only cursorily. Brigitte was an inveterate pack rat. The boxes contained all her notes from university, every financial record and every receipt from the past five years, all the personnel materials from her job, insurance policies—you name it.

Pavlak picked up a box and shoved it into Karin's arms. "One for you." Then he dumped the contents of a second box on the floor, and sat down cross-legged beside the heap. "And one for me."

"What are we looking for?"

"I have no idea, but be thorough. Study every sheet of paper, top to bottom."

"That could take all night," Karin protested.

"Got anything better to do?"

"Yes. Sleep. I'm exhausted."

"Me too. Maybe we'll get lucky and find something right away."

They were not lucky. Sometime between 3 and 4 A.M., Karin fell asleep on the floor. Pavlak pulled a blanket off the only bed and covered her with it, then opened the next box.

The soft, gray light of dawn was seeping through the curtains when he found it. It was a slip of paper torn from a scratch pad. Scribbled on the note in Brigitte's handwriting was the name "Schliemann, Siegfried Mathus." Below that stood a number, "2384708" followed by the notation "KD-2348" on a third line, and finally, at the bottom of the paper, *"Pavlak!"* The name was underlined twice and followed by an exclamation point. He laid the slip aside and spent the next hour finishing the boxes. There was nothing else of any interest. The registered mail receipt was nowhere to be found. Apparently Karin had, as she thought, thrown it away.

Pavlak rose stiffly from the floor and searched the cabinets for coffee. He found only a bag of loose tea, but no tea egg for brewing it, so he dumped half the bag into a teapot and poured boiling water over it After a few minutes he poured it all through a strainer into a second tea pot. It was much too strong, but he filled two cups and carried them to where Karin still slept on the floor.

"Wake up, Sleeping Beauty," he said in a soft voice and nudged her shoulder with his toe. She stretched and looked up at him through eyes still blurred with sleep. A strand of hair lay across her face, and she brushed it away with a feminine gesture that made his breath catch. Not a bad-looking woman, he thought. Too bad she and her sister were such idealists. In very different ways, to be sure, but idealists nonetheless.

Karin sat up, took a sip of tea, and grimaced. "God, that's awful."

"You're welcome. Here."

He handed her the note. She studied it for several moments with a frown on her face.

"Does it mean anything to you?" he asked.

She shook her head. "I never heard of Siegfried Schliemann."

"How about the numbers? What could they be? Driver's license? Personal identity card? Passport? Anything like that?"

"The first one could be from a *Personalausweis* maybe. I don't know." She handed the note back to him. "But why would Brigitte write down the number of a personal identity card if she already had the name?

Pavlak stroked the stubble on his chin. He had not shaved in three days now.

"What about her work? Could it have anything to do with the Stasi files?"

"We never talked about that. Remember, I hadn't seen Brigitte for nearly a year before she died. We spoke on the phone fairly often, but I never heard very much about her work. She was fascinated and horrified by the files, I know that. She told me I wouldn't believe all that had gone on in East Germany. I answered that I would indeed believe it—had believed it all along—and that she was the one who loved the communists. She got angry at that, and I dropped it. Politics was always a bad topic for us. I loved my sister, but . . ." Her voice trailed off, and she looked away. "She got into a left-wing crowd at Marburg. They were always defending the East German regime, saying that everything we heard about the secret police was just western propaganda. I was happy when she got this job, because I knew it would make her face reality. It did."

Tears welled in her eyes. Embarrassed, Pavlak walked to the window to give her a chance to compose herself. He peeked through a slit in the drawn curtain. The street was deserted except for a drunk sleeping in a doorway about a hundred meters away. In the distance he could hear the low rumble of Monday morning traffic coming to life on the major thoroughfares. He turned back to Karin.

"Do you know if she had any close friends at work? Anyone we might show this to?"

Karin blew her nose into a tissue. "There was a woman at the funeral. Ursula somebody or the other—Lund I believe it was. Yes, Ursula Lund. Brigitte had told me about her on the phone. They worked together. Brigitte liked her."

"Good. Let's find her. Get your coat."

"Now?"

"Why not? You cut me to the bone with that unkind comment about my tea. Come on. I'll buy you a cup of coffee, then after breakfast we'll give Ms. Lund a call."

"How do we get out without being seen?"

Pavlak walked to the window again. The drunk had changed positions but was still facing their building.

"We can't. But we can lose the tail if they follow you."

"Follow *me*?"

"Of course you. They don't know I'm here, remember? You leave first. I'll watch for a tail, then meet you some-where."

"And how will I know if they follow me?"

"You won't. Just assume that you're being followed. Walk to the Möckernbrücke station and get on the first train that comes through. Stand at the exit and wait until the doors start to close, then jump out at the last second. If anyone else jumps out too, take a walk to the KDW. It's a long walk from Möckernbrücke, so do some window-shopping. Duck into a shop now and then. You should be able to spot anyone tailing you, but don't let him know you've seen him. And don't worry. I'll be backing you up. Hunting the hunter, so to speak. When you get to the KDW, take the first glass el-evator on the right to the top floor, but don't get off. Just ride it back down again, then leave quickly by a different exit. That should shake him. When you're sure nobody's following you, take a taxi and meet me at the Cafe Klatz in Grunewald, where we went yesterday morning. I might be late. If I don't show up in an hour, you're on your own. You need any money?"

"What do you mean 'on my own'?"

"Just what I said. But don't worry—I'll be there. If there's anything here you might want for the next few days, take it with you. We're not coming back."

She drew a long breath and stared at the floor. "Okay," she said simply, and climbed to her feet. She spent ten minutes washing up and sorting through the suitcase that lay on the bed, occasionally sticking a small item in her purse.

She was ready to walk out the door when a loud beep

startled them both. It was the telephone on Brigitte's desk. Karin looked questioningly at Pavlak. He nodded.

It was Turgat's father calling from Istanbul. The police in Munich had found his son, floating in the Isar, face down, with his throat cut.

13

In Charlotte, Darryl Streat slumped disconsolately at his desk. His eyes were bloodshot, and his pulse pounded painfully in his right temple. Six hours staring into the eyes of a man who radiated hostility was not fun. Especially when the man weighed three hundred pounds and smelled like a goat.

For five hours, he had given his name as "Tiny." Just Tiny. When he finally broke, they learned his real name was Leroy Percy Adams. The computer showed him wanted for assault and battery in New Orleans, grand theft in Memphis, and three more counts of assault in Nashville. Adams was the leader of the Charlotte chapter of a motorcycle gang called the Devil's Dragons, a position he had won from his predecessor with the generous application of his two hammy fists. Adams finally admitted selling a kilogram of cocaine to an undercover agent of the Charlotte police, but if Adams knew anything at all about the murder of Judith Lyles and her daughter, he was a master at manipulating interrogators—something Streat doubted. The man was strong and stubborn and mean, but he was no Einstein.

And now no one was happy. The Charlotte narcotics unit

was not happy because Streat had pressured them into springing their operation early. "Just three more months," they had pleaded, "and we'll get the Colombian connection." Now they were barely speaking to him. Streat was not happy because his gamble had cost him a friendly relationship with local law enforcement and gained him nothing. And Adams was not happy because he was wearing handcuffs and leg irons and would have to take a bath.

"That bastard, Pavlak," Streat growled, slapping his palm hard on the desktop. The two agents sitting across from him were too tired to jump. "He knows something he wouldn't tell me. Now we're at a goddamned dead end again. We've got to find Pavlak, you hear me?" Streat glared at the man on his left who studied the floor intently. "What's the latest on Pavlak, anyway?"

Special Agent Lawrence Fortson squirmed and cleared his throat. "We know he flew Charlotte to Atlanta. We know he flew Atlanta to Germany and went through customs in Frankfurt. We know he registered in a hotel in Berlin. He checked out before the German police showed up to question him."

"Question him? What do you mean 'question'? I wanted the bastard arrested."

"I *told* you," Fortson shot back. "You'll have to charge him formally before the Germans will hold him."

"Tell them we want him on suspicion."

Fortson shook his head in an exaggerated motion from side to side. "They won't do that. It has to be a formal charge. And you can count on at least three weeks of red tape before we could get him back here, maybe more. If he fights it, it could take months."

"Are they still looking for him at least?"

A shrug. "They say they are. I expect they're just waiting

for him to register in a hotel again so they can pick his name out of a computer."

"Dammit, he won't do that! He just did it this time because he knew he had some lead time before we found out he was in Germany. Did you tell them that?"

"Of course I told them. But face it, Darryl, he's our problem, not theirs. They've got better things to do than look for some American nobody, who hasn't even been charged with a crime."

"You want him charged?" Streat glared. "Come up with some evidence. The magistrate would laugh in our faces if we asked for an indictment now."

"So what do you want me to do?" Fortson retorted, his voice rising. "Conjure him up? We're helpless. If the Germans don't get him for us, we don't get him. It's as simple as that."

"Not quite." Streat said, more quietly. "*We* can't look for him in Germany. But I know someone who can."

In Langley, Virginia, Chris Hopkins stepped into the office of the director of Central Intelligence and closed the door behind him. He had seen more of this office in the past thirty-six hours than in the ten years preceding the Pavlak affair.

"So what do the Fibbies want now?" Denham demanded. He was not a man to waste time on small talk, especially when he was in a bad mood. An open document lay on the desk in front of him, and Hopkins threw it a hasty glance before answering.

"Agent Streat has requested that we locate Pavlak."

The director's eyes fell shut. His right hand rose slowly from the desk to his face, reached his nose, and grasped the bridge between thumb and forefinger. "He wants *what?*" Denham asked quietly.

"He wants us to find Pavlak for them. He's sent a formal request through liaison."

One of the many amenities in the office of the director of Central Intelligence was a working fireplace. Surrounding that fireplace was a mantelpiece of pure white marble, quarried in the Shenandoah Valley. Sitting on the mantelpiece was an antique clock with a heart-shaped pendulum. Hopkins counted sixteen ticks before the director opened his eyes again.

"Did anyone inform Mr. Streat that we have certain rules about how we operate in friendly countries?"

"He knows that. But he says the Germans can't or won't locate him without a formal indictment, and he doesn't have the evidence for an indictment. The motorcycle gang has been scratched from the picture, and he says his investigation is at a dead end until he gets Pavlak. He thinks. . . ." Hopkins hesitated. "He thinks Pavlak knows something he isn't telling. And he thinks it has to do with us."

Denham stood stiffly and walked around the desk. He shoved his hands into his pockets, paced to the fireplace, spun on his heel, and paced back to the lavatory door. His black wingtips, shiny as polished glass, made no sound on the plush carpet. Hopkins started counting ticks again.

"I've just read your summary of Fool's Gold," Denham said suddenly, breaking the silence.

"Yes sir."

"You say it was a clean operation, but I couldn't help noticing a little—shall we say—'caution' in your language. You said . . ." Denham snatched up the document and flipped to the last page. " 'Thus Fool's Gold appears to have been an operation of substantial success. Over twelve years, the operation resulted in the interdiction of twenty-three illegal shipments, and indictments of seven Americans, three West Germans, and two Dutchmen on charges of illegal export of military technology to the Soviet Bloc via the German Democratic Republic, in violation of regulations formulated by the Coordinating Committee for International Export Control. It is also a textbook example of smooth cooperation with a friendly service. At this time there is no obvious reason to suspect additional, perhaps compromising revelations concerning the operation, other than those already known and approved in advance at the highest levels as a necessary cost of maintaining the operation.' "

He threw the report onto the desk like an empty banana peel.

"What is this shit, Chris? '*Substantial* success?' 'No *obvious* reason?' What's on your mind?"

Hopkins drew a long breath. "The report states the facts, and the conclusion is . . . pretty much the way I feel about it."

"But?"

"But I'm not real comfortable with it. Fool's Gold ran a long time and brought us some successes, but it was a frustrating operation. We never got the big score. American companies smuggling machine tools, the Dutch peddling radar components, Germans dealing in pesticide chemicals that *could* have been used for chemical weapons. But none of the really big stuff. Schliemann had plenty of excuses. He had no access to the bigger game, he always told us. And he always paired that with a plea for a bigger sugar sack from our side. If we would up the ante, he could get a higher clearance, and so on. We wound up giving him some pretty hot stuff to keep him going."

"Nothing they weren't going to get anyway—or build

themselves in time, right?" Denham was fumbling on the desk for a pencil but couldn't find one.

"Right. But still . . ."

"Wait a minute. Hold it right there." The director yanked open the middle drawer of his desk, dug out a yellow pencil, and, with a small grunt of satisfaction, took his seat and began bouncing the lead end on the desktop. "Are you trying to tell me we might have given them more than we got?"

Hopkins shook his head adamantly. "No. No way. We gave him small stuff, and we got—well, some good interdictions and indictments in return. Good. Not great. And it always seemed that the great one was just around the corner. But it never came."

Denham allowed himself a sigh of relief. "You scared the hell out of me there for a minute. Okay, so it boils down to something like a gut feeling that Schliemann could have been jerking us around, right?"

"Yes, I suppose that's it."

"But even if it's true, wouldn't he be doing it just to keep his payoffs coming? Fatten his Swiss accounts? And let's say he pulled it off. All well and good for him. Nobody got hurt too much in the deal. He was worth what we paid him. And there's still nothing there to kill a reporter over."

"Yes," Hopkins answered slowly. "If he was just pumping us for personal gain. But suppose he had another motive."

"What, for example?"

"Maybe he was a triple. Krueger and the BND thought they were running a double agent in place, but maybe Schliemann was playing with us. Maybe he hadn't really turned."

"Okay," the director dipped his chin. "Let's say Schliemann was an East German plant. What did he get out of us?"

"Our shipments."

"But you already said the shipments were penny ante."

"Right," Hopkins frowned.

"So what's bothering you?"

Hopkins threw up his hands. "I don't know. It just has an uncomfortable feel, that's all. It's probably okay—a pretty good operation with a mediocre double who gave us all he could. Just what it looks like."

"Hmm."

Hopkins could feel Denham's gaze burning into his forehead. It came at him through narrowed lids while the pencil drummed out something for a band to march to in quick time. After a moment Denham dropped the pencil. The great leather chair squeaked, and the director laced his hands behind his head. By now Hopkins knew the gesture well. Decision time.

"All right, Chris. You've succeeded in making me nervous." Denham smiled. "Let's get back to Pavlak. What does Streat want us to do with him?"

"Nothing. Just find him. He'll take it from there. He'll even fly to Germany to talk to him there—if we can find him."

"Does he know what he's asking? This breaks all the rules between friendlies. Technically we should ask the BND to find him for us. It's their country."

"The BND would just take it to the German police—and Streat has already done that. Of course, a request from their own intelligence service might get them moving a little faster."

A smile nibbled at the corners of the director's lips. "Neat little slip Pavlak pulled on the Fibbies. And the Germans don't seem to be doing much better." The smile faded. "But we can't let him expose Fool's Gold, no matter what. Even if Fool's Gold was clean, it's not the kind of operation you can explain to the public. And if it was dirty . . ."

He said no more, but Hopkins knew what he was thinking. Such a revelation would be devastating. Morale at the Agency had only recently climbed back to measurable levels after the controversies of the seventies, followed by Iran-Contra. Congressional liberals were already questioning the Agency's purpose, now that the Cold War was over. Another major scandal now could literally spell the end of the Central Intelligence Agency as he knew it.

"All right, find Pavlak," the director snapped. "Find out what he's up to."

"You mean—through the BND?"

The director shook his head. "No, leave the Germans out of it. And, for God's sake, don't let them find out we're tracking a man in their country. I'm looking down the road here. Who knows? In the long run, we might have to deal with Pavlak ourselves. In that case, the less the Germans know, the better."

"I see," Hopkins answered slowly. The phrase *deal with Pavlak ourselves* hung in the air. "So, tell the FBI we'll do it?"

Denham shook his head. "No. Give them our regrets. Nothing we can do, international agreements, and so on. If we don't want the Germans to know what we're up to, we damn sure don't want the Fibbies in on it either. Tell Streat he'll just have to work with the German police. That's policy. And after all, the dead reporter is not our problem." He looked up and fastened Hopkins' eye. "John Pavlak is."

Hopkins nodded and gathered his notes.

"Chris . . ."

"Yes?"

"Sorry about the vacation."

Hopkins shrugged. "No problem."

At least not anymore, he thought as he closed the door behind him. Martha had packed up the children and moved out the day before.

14

Pavlak watched from behind the curtains as Karin walked past the derelict who still lay in a crumpled heap on the opposite side of the street. The man stayed motionless until she was a hundred meters away, then stretched, rose casually to his feet, and moved off in the same direction. He was not the one with the suede jacket. This man was slender, with aquiline features and long, delicate limbs. From somewhere he produced an umbrella and now swung it casually at his side in a smooth gait, not the jerky wobble of a hungover alcoholic.

Pavlak examined the street again from doorway to doorway, then once more from window to window. If any others were watching the building, they were either hidden on his side of the street, or they were watching from behind a blind, as he was. He gave Karin a three-minute head start, then slipped out the front door and hurried in the same direction.

Pavlak stopped three times to examine display windows. After the third stop, he was satisfied that he was not being followed and strode out quickly toward the Möckernbrücke station. He dropped quickly down the concrete steps to the first level, brushed past the red ticket canceler that stood in the middle of the landing like a misplaced parking meter, then slowed his steps and slipped silently onto the platform.

Karin stood at the center, engulfed in the rush hour crowd. Her expression was calm, but her fingers nervously kneaded the pink subway ticket in her right hand. The thin man stood less than twenty feet to her right. From this distance Pavlak got a better look at him. He had thin, bluish lips and close-set, dark eyes. The fingers curled around the umbrella might have belonged to a concert pianist. He never seemed to look in Karin's direction, but Pavlak was sure he was watching her. A man trained in surveillance.

It was an old station. Pavlak stepped behind one of the massive square pillars that stood at intervals in the center of the platform. When the first train arrived, Karin hung back as the crowd surged forward. The thin man drifted toward the next car on her right and fiddled with his umbrella before entering the train a second after Karin stepped on. A loud electronic warning sounded, then the automatic doors began sliding shut. For an instant Pavlak was sure she had waited too long. Then in a surprisingly agile motion, she slipped sideways through the vanishing slit. Almost at the same instant, the doors in the next car caught on an umbrella. A beep sounded, and every door on the train slid open again. The thin man stepped casually onto the platform and, paying no attention to Karin, walked toward the opposite exit. Karin glanced once over her shoulder, and Pavlak knew by the look in her eyes that she had seen the man.

Pavlak leaned his back against the pillar, letting the smooth white tiles cool his skin. He forced himself to count slowly to thirty, then peered cautiously around the corner of the pillar. Neither Karin nor the thin man was in sight.

Plan B was now in effect. Pavlak rushed out of the station, taking the stairs two at a time. He turned left at the exit, onto the *Tempelhofer Ufer*, and set out briskly, searching every back on the sidewalk for some sign of the thin man. He was nowhere to be seen. Across the canal on Pavlak's right, a train from the U-1 line rumbled past on elevated tracks perched atop a network of ugly gray steel. Perhaps he had come up too soon. Maybe the man was behind him. He stepped into a *Konditorei* and examined the pastries from the back side of the window display. Still no sign of the thin man. He rushed out and doubled his pace, now afraid that he might have waited too long instead. Karin had been walking quickly. Perhaps they were too far ahead to be seen. Or maybe, he thought in a panic, someone had shoved her into a waiting car.

He brushed the thought aside and broke into a trot, ignoring the stares of other pedestrians. He bumped shoulders with a thick-necked man dressed in the ubiquitous dark blue of a German laborer and was just waving off a flood of curses when he caught sight of Karin's hair, bobbing among the crowd some fifty meters in front of him on Potsdamerstrasse. Thank God, he breathed silently. But where was the tail?

An uneasy feeling came over him. Was the thin man behind him after all? Was he, the watcher, now being watched?

Karin slowed her pace and finally stopped to gaze in a display window. Pavlak did the same, and as she glanced back, their eyes met for about as long as it took to bat an eyelash. At least she knew she wasn't alone. But where was the thin man?

Karin followed his instructions and adopted an erratic pace. When she walked into a *Schnellimbiss* and ordered something from the counter clerk, Pavlak crossed the street and bought a copy of *Der Spiegel* at a newsstand. He was getting more and more nervous. Surely the thin man hadn't just given up after the subway station. Why else would he have bothered to jam the doors with the umbrella? He had to be out here somewhere. But where?

Pavlak had one advantage. He knew exactly where Karin was going, and the thin man did not. He decided to let Karin move out of sight, then double back onto Kurfürstenstrasse and take a longer route to the KDW. At the pace Karin was moving, he should have no trouble getting there in time.

When she emerged from the *Schnellimbiss*, Pavlak let her drift away until he could no longer see her black hair bobbing in the crowd, then he dropped the magazine in a trash can and turned back in the direction he had come. A left at the next corner headed him back toward the KDW. He gave up looking for a tail and moved on at a brisk pace. If he timed it right, he should reach the giant department store just after Karin did—or maybe even a little before.

Pavlak took another left onto Urania, then a right into Kleiststrasse, and suddenly the big white *KaDeWe* on the side of the building loomed ahead. Patience, he told himself. Don't panic.

The *Kaufhaus des Westens*, familiarly known as the KDW, is the largest department store in Germany and one of the largest in the world. A major tourist attraction, it features six packed floors of goods in profuse, overwhelming display—everything from original art work to live lobsters. As Pavlak approached, Karin appeared, walking from his left, and turned into the main door on Tauentzienstrasse. She immediately melted into the crush of shoppers and tourists. If Pavlak had not known exactly where she was going, he would have lost her in the mass of humanity. As it was, he found her waiting in front of the elevator door with a dozen other people. He wandered to the left and pretended to examine a sable hat, imported from Russia and priced at a mere 3,200 marks. The thin man was still nowhere in sight. Pavlak picked nervously at the soft fur in his hands. Something was wrong.

The elevator arrived, and Karin was the first to step inside. Now, Pavlak thought, he has to show himself. Either he gets on the elevator, or he has to race up the stairs floor by floor. Pavlak had a good view of both the elevator and the nearest stairs. The thin man was not in the crowd at the elevator. He was sure of that, so Pavlak concentrated his attention on the stairs. The man would probably wait until the doors closed, to make sure she did not jump out again, as she had in the subway station, then he would have to hit the stairs in a hurry.

Loading the elevator took an eternity. There were too many customers to fit in the car, so some at the back of the crowd gave up and began to drift toward the stairs and escalators. One stocky man was the last to make it into the elevator, squeezing himself aggressively into the pack as the doors were closing. He twisted around to face front just before the doors hid his face, and Pavlak's heart slammed. It was the man with the suede jacket, now dressed in a businessman's blue suit. Of course! They had switched off. But where had this one been all along?

Pavlak carefully replaced the sable hat and picked up another made of rabbit fur. His main concern was Karin. Did she recognize the man? Had she even seen him? After the subway incident, her pursuers had to suspect, at least, that Karin knew she was being followed. No doubt that was why they switched tails. At least the man in the elevator did not know that Karin had seen his face from behind the bushes in the park.

But even so, they might decide to kidnap her now, as they had Turgat. And Turgat had not died quickly. He had been brutally beaten, Turgat's father told them in a tearful rage. Both thumbs were pulled out of joint, and each of the remaining fingers was broken. Someone had wanted information from him badly. Turgat could not give it to them, Pavlak knew, or he would have done so before they hurt him that badly. The Turks were a courageous lot, but nobody was that courageous.

If her pursuers intended to kidnap Karin, Pavlak reasoned, they wouldn't do it here, in front of hundreds of witnesses. Karin would scream and struggle—unless he shoved a gun in her ribs and ordered her to walk out quietly. Would she? Pavlak reconsidered. No, if they were going to snatch her, they would have done so on the street, not here. Or maybe they were following her until the time was right. Maybe they would attempt it after she left the store.

He picked up another hat, this one apparently made of some kind of synthetic fur, and the first one he'd seen that was even remotely affordable.

Would the man come back down the same elevator with her, or would he take another one, or walk down the stairs, or ride one of the escalators, or . . . Pavlak gave up trying to figure out all the possibilities.

He replaced the hat and wandered closer to the center of the first floor where he could keep an eye on several exits, as well as watch the elevator from a distance. If Karin followed his instructions, she would leave by a side exit, but he didn't know which one.

"Please, God," he muttered beneath his breath, "let her be on that elevator."

It took an eternity for the lift to return. When the doors finally slid open, the car was packed, and people began spilling out like grains of corn, shelled from a cob. At first Pavlak saw no sign of Karin, but she finally emerged. And three steps behind her was the stocky man in the blue suit. Pavlak saw Karin's eyes searching desperately for him, and he knew by the terror on her face that she had recognized her pursuer. He watched furtively as she walked to the exit on Passauerstrasse, pushed open a glass door, and turned to her left down the sidewalk. The stocky man drifted past the door and pretended to examine an alligator belt for perhaps fifteen seconds before ambling out the same door.

Good, Pavlak thought. He doesn't know she recognized him. It was a small advantage, but at this point he would take anything he could get. He still had seen no sign of the thin man and could only hope that he was drinking a cup of espresso in a cafe somewhere, his day's work done.

Pavlak hurriedly pushed his way to the opposite side of the store, stumbled through the exit and, with a groan, sprinted off down Ansbacherstrasse. He was in good jogging shape, but his legs and hips ached from yesterday's sprint, and his body took this opportunity to remind him that he had not slept at all the previous night. This time, at least, he would not have to run as far. He was hiding around a corner, still gasping for breath, when Karin appeared.

"Turn this way," he said as calmly as he could. His voice startled her nonetheless, and she jerked her head toward him with a small cry, hesitated only an instant, then turned toward him. Pavlak stepped backwards, out of sight, into the recessed doorway of a small Italian restaurant that was locked and deserted.

As she walked past, he whispered furiously. "Keep walking.

Don't look back. Take a taxi to Cafe Klatz. I'll meet you there."

Then she was gone.

Pavlak waited, his seared lungs still screaming for oxygen. He tried to breathe quietly and evenly. His only chance now was to surprise the tail and at least give Karin time to escape.

The first set of steps that approached belonged to a laborer in heavy boots. He glanced at Pavlak in surprise as he passed the doorway, then continued his way. The next set of steps was a long time coming. They had to belong to the stocky man, Pavlak reasoned. "Please, God," he whispered, as he squeezed his right hand into a fist and raised it beside his ear. "Let him be walking close to the wall."

The steps came nearer. Pavlak was tired. He had not slept for thirty-six hours. If he missed the first blow, it would be a tough fight. He was taller and probably a little heavier than his adversary, but the man looked thick and powerful.

Suddenly a face appeared in front of him in profile. It was his man. Pavlak fired his fist into the side of the head, and the man's knees buckled. Pavlak was on top of him instantly, pounding away with both fists. He landed half a dozen more blows before he realized that there was no resistance. The first punch had knocked the man unconscious. Ten yards away at the corner, a pedestrian stopped to stare, then another, and another. A small crowd gathered quickly. Berliners, like city dwellers everywhere, were not likely to risk their anonymity to help a stranger. But there was always the risk that someone might decide to play the hero.

Pavlak raised his fist as if to strike the man again, then pretended to lose his balance and flopped across the body. As he floundered, he slipped his hand into the prostrate man's inside jacket pocket. His fingers closed on leather, extracted the wallet, and slipped it into his own pocket. He was about to rise when his forearm struck against something hard. A few seconds later he pulled a pistol from a shoulder holster and shoved it, as surreptitiously as he could, into his belt, then covered it with the tail of his jacket.

Pavlak stood. "Now maybe you'll leave my wife alone, you Bavarian pig," he shouted. He spat at the unconscious man on the sidewalk, turned, and walked away. Not until he rounded the next corner did he risk a glance back. The man was moving one arm feebly. The crowd had stepped a few yards closer, but no one had yet come to his aid. As soon as Pavlak was out of sight, he clenched his teeth and broke into a run.

15

When Pavlak entered the Cafe Klatz, Karin was waiting at the door. She clutched his arm in both hands and leaned her forehead on his shoulder. "Thank God," she whispered.

"You'd make a great spy," Pavlak assured her, wrapping his arms around her slender shoulders. They were shaking.

"What did you do to him? I saw you kneeling over him."

"I told you not to look back."

"I couldn't help it. I heard you hit him. It sounded awful." She shuddered. "What did you hit him with?"

Pavlak held up his swollen right hand. "The one weapon I never leave home without."

"Did he see you?"

"I doubt it. Even if he did, he probably won't remember. Come on . . ."

He led her out of the cafe and into the surrounding park. A light drizzle had begun to fall from the low clouds that hung over the city. It was Monday morning, and the park was deserted. Pavlak put his arm around Karin's shoulders and turned her toward a gazebo that was hidden from the street by a phalanx of shrubs. She leaned into him, and Pavlak wondered if it was only her fear that made her acquiesce so readily to his touch, or if perhaps she was one of those rare women who could accept the comfort of a man— even one she does not know well—with graceful ease. The gazebo drew nearer. At least there they would be dry. He could feel her shivering beneath his arm.

"Cold?"

She shook her head. "No. Terrified. God, I was scared when I saw that man in the elevator. Then when we came down, and you weren't there . . . I almost didn't leave the store. I thought about screaming for help."

Pavlak guided her up the single wooden step and beneath the waiting roof.

"I'm glad you didn't. We wouldn't have this."

She looked at the wallet in his hand. "Is that *his?*"

"Not anymore. Let's see what goodies we have here."

They lowered themselves onto the curved, stone bench that hugged the wall of the gazebo. Karin leaned over his arm for a better view. The wallet contained 216 marks and some change. Pavlak hesitated before thrusting the bills in his pocket. He didn't need the money, and keeping it made him feel like a thief. But throwing it away would be an absurd gesture. He turned the wallet over and flicked a metal snap. A flap fell open, exposing a plastic window.

At the same instant, they both recognized the stylized eagle, emblem of the Federal Republic of Germany. The word *Bundesnachrichtendienst* stood out in bold print beneath it, then the name Klaus Joachim Lederer and the title *Sonderbeauftragter.*

Pavlak let the hand with the wallet fall onto his knee and leaned his back heavily against the gazebo wall. His head swirled. "What the hell . . . ?"

"Oh God," Karin whispered. "What have we done?"

"Well," Pavlak answered after a long silence, "you haven't done anything. I, on the other hand, just cold-cocked an agent of German Intelligence and stole his wallet." He shoved the wallet into Karin's hands and ran his fingers through his damp hair. "This has the makings of a bad day."

"But . . . why are they following me?" Karin protested. "I'm not . . ."

"Wait a minute," Pavlak interrupted, raising his hand.

"What?"

"Isn't the BND like the American CIA?"

"More or less, I think. Why?"

"Because the CIA is not allowed to conduct domestic intelligence against Americans. They can't spy on their own citizens—and counter-espionage is the FBI's responsibility, like it's the responsibility of the *Bundesverfassungsschutz* here, isn't that right?"

"I think so," she replied "but then . . . but then why is a BND agent following *me?*"

"Good question. And . . ."

"Oh no!" Karin brought the back of her hand to her mouth.

"What is it?"

"Turgat! Are they the ones who killed Turgat? Did the BND do it?"

Pavlak was silent for a moment. "I don't know. But if it was—and right now it looks that way—then we're in even bigger trouble than I thought."

"They would have access to the police computer, wouldn't they? That's how they found you at your hotel."

Pavlak nodded. "Maybe not official access, but I'm sure they would have ways. You know, Karin—I have no idea what this is all about, but I'm beginning to feel like we're a couple of rabbits being chased by a pack of wolves. Whatever we're going to do, we have to do it fast before they catch up to us."

"What *are* we going to do?"

"Well, first we find out about this." He reached in his shirt pocket and unfolded Brigitte's note. "We find out who Siegfried Schliemann is and what these numbers mean. . . . Karin?" She was staring blankly into the park. "Karin, are you with me?"

Her eyes found his again. "You won't kill him, will you?"

Pavlak said nothing.

"It's not them I'm worried about, Dr. Pavlak," she explained. "It's *you*. And it's me." She looked out into the park again. The drizzle had turned to light rain. "It's both of us."

"Why you?" Pavlak asked. "For that matter, why me? I'll be very careful."

A drop of water trickled from her hair, down her forehead, and onto her nose. She brushed it away without taking her eyes off Pavlak. "It's not the physical danger I'm worried about. Hatred is an obsession. It consumes." She raised both hands, then let them fall in frustration. "I loved my sister," she added, her voice breaking. "When I think of what they did to her . . . and Turgat. They *tortured* him!" Her eyes suddenly blazed with fury, and Pavlak stared at her, speechless. She spun away and crossed to the other side of the gazebo. When she turned, her eyes sparkled through tears, and Pavlak's heart caught in his throat.

"I want to let myself hate like you do. But Dr. Pavlak . . ." She shook her head and looked away into the treetops and the heavy sky beyond. "This hatred only prolongs the pain."

It was Pavlak's turn to examine the leaden, Berlin sky. "I've killed men before, Karin," he said slowly. "You should know that. I was a soldier. And now I'm a soldier again. Only this time, the war is private."

For a long moment there was silence, then she touched his arm, and he looked at her. To his surprise, she smiled.

"We must get to know each other better," she said softly.

For a second Pavlak was speechless. He put the tip of his forefinger beneath her chin and tilted her face toward his. She answered his gaze with open, honest eyes, and Pavlak found himself wishing he had met her under different circumstances. Finally he shook the thought from his head and took her arm. "Come on," he said, pulling her back into the rain.

From a phone booth Karin called Brigitte's work number at the *Gauk-Behörde* and asked for Ursula Lund. Pavlak leaned his head close to hers, and she tilted the phone away from her ear so he could hear the conversation. Karin identified herself, and, after a few seconds of confusion, Ursula remembered her from Brigitte's funeral.

"I need a little assistance clearing up some of Brigitte's things," Karin said casually. "Would you help me?"

"Of course. I'll do anything I can."

"Brigitte left a note to herself. It was dated the day she died. She wrote 'Take care of this immediately' at the top, but I can't make any sense of the note. Maybe you can help." Karin read the name and numbers from the scrap of paper Pavlak had found among Brigitte's things.

"Hmm," Ursula mused. "The name Siegfried Schliemann doesn't mean anything to me, but it probably refers to a file here. The first number sounds like a Stasi index number. You see, that's part of our nightmare. The files are not organized by name, but by numbers. And most of the keys to the numbers were destroyed in the transition days. The Stasi couldn't destroy all the files—there are millions—so they made it nearly impossible to find anything instead. Even the names in the files are often code names, not real ones. We have years of work ahead of us, just getting them sorted and organized."

"What about the last number, KD—two-three-four-eight? Does that mean anything to you?"

"Yes, that's lucky. That's a location code. The KD's would be in Brigitte's section. Tell you what—read it all off to me again, and I'll check into it. It was probably something she was in the middle of here at work. I'll take care of it, or at least see that her replacement knows where things stand."

"I'm awfully concerned about this," Karin protested quickly. "Maybe I'm just being silly, but . . . you know how it is. I feel very responsible. I want to make sure everything is done the way Brigitte would have wanted. I hate to ask this, but could you check on it while I hold the phone?"

"That's impossible, I'm afraid. It might take thirty minutes just to find it." She hesitated, then went on. "I tell you what. If you'll call back in an hour I'll let you know what I find out."

Karin looked at Pavlak, who nodded.

"Thanks so much. You're very kind." She snagged the receiver back on its hook. "Now what?"

"Now we get a late breakfast. I don't know about you, but I'm starved. Also tired. Let's find somewhere new."

Taxis were getting to be a way of life, as were cafes. Pavlak didn't mind. Cafes were one of the things he loved most about Europe, and missed most in the U.S. The driver recommended a small, quiet one in Schäferstrasse.

It turned out to be a hole in the wall that would feel crowded if more than a dozen customers showed up at one time. Fortunately, Pavlak and Karin were the only two there. It was dark, and the furnishings were disappointingly modern, but it was clean and smelled of cappucino and fresh pastry. As they waited for their coffee to arrive, an awkwardness settled over them. It was as if the tensions of the morning had granted them some sort of license for familiarity that was now suspended again.

"What do you do in real life?" Pavlak asked when he could stand the silence no longer. Before Karin could answer, the waitress arrived with their coffee.

"I'm a teacher. I teach the little ones—six to eight years old," Karin answered when they were alone again.

"Public school?"

"No. A church school."

Pavlak smiled. "Of course. What about the men in your life—other than your ex-husband, who doesn't count."

She looked up. "Why do you ask?"

"Just curious. Looks like we're going to be spending a day or two together. And you yourself said we should get to know each other better."

Karin stirred her coffee for a long moment. "I think you should know," she said carefully, measuring each word, "that I'm about to join a Franciscan order."

Pavlak's cup stopped halfway to his lips. He stared, then lowered it to the table untouched. "Are you trying to tell me," he asked slowly, "that you're a *nun?*"

"Only a postulant," she corrected. "The postulancy is the first step. Sort of a trial run, where you live with the community for a few months and decide if you want to go on. I'll move to the next step—the novitiate—in a few weeks. Assuming," she continued with a sardonic smile, "that I live that long."

"Why aren't you wearing a habit?" Pavlak asked, more sharply than he intended. He was trying to sort out his reaction. He felt betrayed somehow.

"As I said, I'm only a postulant. Even when I become a novice, though, I won't take my vows. I'll just be studying. The first vows are at least two years away. And even then I probably won't wear a habit. Hardly anyone does anymore, except for cloistered nuns—nuns who live in a convent."

"And why aren't you in a convent? If you're going to withdraw from life, why not do it right?"

"I'm not withdrawing from life," she answered smoothly. "On the contrary. I'm trying to embrace it more fully. *Real* life, that is. The soul and spirit of life, as opposed to the petty concerns that consume most people. But what about you?" she asked abruptly, wrenching the conversation onto a new course. "What do you do besides teach *Germanistik*?"

"I don't teach *Germanistik*," Pavlak replied. "My degree is in German literature, but I'm an athletic director."

"A what?"

Pavlak smiled. "It's hard to explain. You see, American universities have highly organized sports programs for their students. And the teams compete against teams from other universities. It's very popular in the U.S. Maybe too popular. It's big business. Anyway, I run the sports program at a small college."

"But . . ." Karin's brow knitted. "I don't understand. What do sports have to do with a university education?"

"That's a good question," Pavlak sighed. "Wish I had a good answer."

There was a pause. "Do you enjoy what you're doing?"

"It's a living."

"Aren't there other ways to make a living in America?" Breakfast had arrived, and Karin severed the top of a soft-boiled egg with an expert stroke of her knife. "Money doesn't seem to be any problem for you," she added with a sideways glance.

"This money's not mine. It belongs to my Dad. Karin . . ."

"Yes?"

"I don't understand why you object to my plans for the man who killed my baby, but I do hope you're not trying to convert me."

"I'm not trying to convert you," she answered immediately. "It just so happens that I rather like you. So why should I not object to your walking into disaster?"

"Rather more disastrous for him, I'd say."

"Possibly. Possibly not. There are worse things than death."

"And you think I'll be bringing one of those worse things upon myself if I kill the man who murdered my child?"

She cocked her head and gazed at him earnestly. "Let's look at it from a purely practical standpoint. Assume you find this man, and that you're sure beyond any doubt that he's the murderer—and that's assuming a lot. And then suppose you do succeed in killing him before he kills you. What happens then? Then you are a murderer, and you will have the police and probably prison to deal with."

"First of all," Pavlak responded, "you're assuming that I'll get caught by the police. I don't assume that. And if I am caught . . ." he shrugged, "then that's the price of justice."

"And is there no room for forgiveness in this justice of yours?"

"Why should there be?"

Karin gazed into her cup. "That's the question, isn't it? Why should there be forgiveness?" She straightened. "At this moment, I'm not sure. Part of me wants to join you. But there's another part that says don't abandon everything you've learned from the church." She stirred her coffee absently. "That's what's so hard for me now. I just can't fit what happened to Brigitte—and Judith and Turgat and your daughter—I can't fit it into what I felt a few weeks ago. But I know it must. It *has* to."

"For your sake, Karin, I hope it does someday. But you and I are very different." Pavlak jerked his hand aloft. *"Fräulein!"* he called toward the waitress, then turned back to Karin. "Let's go find out about Mr. Schliemann, shall we?"

Ursula sounded tense on the phone. She had found the file, a Stasi file on one Siegfried Mathus Schliemann, a resident of Dresden. Brigitte had examined, catalogued, and initialed the file over a month ago. Everything looked okay. Nothing to worry about.

Karin pressed her for details, and reluctantly, Ursula began to reveal them. Schliemann was manager of a state bakery until convicted of anti-socialist activities in 1982 because of his association with a church youth organization. Upon conviction, he received a two-year suspended sentence and was transferred to a road-paving crew.

"There are a million other details in the file," Ursula whispered into the phone, "information about his family, meetings with suspected enemies of the state, quoted comments about the socialist leadership, and so on—most of it provided by an informant with the code name *Adler*. It's a perfectly typical file. I've already told you more than I'm allowed—the privacy of the files is a very sensitive issue these days. Please understand."

"Oh, I do, of course," Karin assured her. "But there must be some problem with the file, or why would Brigitte leave herself this note? Is there nothing at all odd about it?"

"Well—nothing to worry about, really. Just . . ."

"Yes?"

"Well, we attach a form to each file listing its contents. That's so we can keep track of things when people ask to examine their files. Also to make it more difficult for old informants, or anyone else who feels threatened, to make things disappear if they get their hands on a file. There are two copies of that inventory. The original is attached to the file itself, and a photocopy is locked in a filing cabinet. A third inventory is entered electronically into a computer."

"And Brigitte had completed the inventory of this file?"

"Yes . . ." Ursula hesitated. "But . . . there's an odd error. One of the entries on the form is the total number of items in the file. That's very important, obviously, to keep things from being lost. Two people always count the physical items—sheets of paper usually—even though only one person—in this case Brigitte—actually skims through the materials in order to break the contents into general categories. The form attached to the file itself says it contains fifty-three items. It's initialed by Brigitte and a co-worker—the second counter. That number is correct—I counted the pages myself. But the computer says the file should have fifty-seven items."

"So someone entered the wrong number into the computer."

"Maybe. But that's what's strange about it. You see, I checked the photocopy in the file too, and it also says fifty-seven items."

"But—then how could it be a photocopy . . . ?"

"That's exactly the problem, you see. They're different. It looks as if Brigitte made a new inventory after the original was photocopied."

"So why didn't she correct the other records as well?"

"She can't. At least not directly. The photocopies in our own inventory files are closely restricted. No one is allowed access except for two clerks and their supervisor. We submit and request the inventory slips through a window. They do the copying, then return the originals to us. They also make the computer entries, and no one else can change those electronic records. We can call them up on our screen, but we can't alter them. And we can look at the photocopy, as I just did, but only in the presence of one of the clerks."

Karin and Pavlak looked at each other. The glass in the yellow phone booth was beginning to collect condensation and obscure the view of the street.

"But, how do you correct an error like this, then?" Karin asked.

"It's not easy. There rarely is an error—or if there is, we don't discover it. We don't have time, you see. One person makes the inventory, a second verifies the item count, we submit the inventory for recording, and move on to the next file. The next day, we pick up the inventories that have been photocopied, attach the original to the Stasi file, place it on the shelf, and that's that. We have so many, we almost never go back to one that's finished. If an error has to be corrected, there's a procedure for requesting the correction, but Brigitte never made such a request. I checked."

"You say a co-worker initialed the count. Are her initials on the copy attached to the file? The one that's correct?"

"*His* initials, in this case. It's a man. Yes, his initials are on both versions. I asked him about it, and he's as puzzled as I am. He says he doesn't remember Brigitte asking him to do a second count on a file that had already been closed. Yet the initials are his. At least—they *look* like his."

"So what happens now?"

"I'm not sure. I told my superior about it." Again Ursula hesitated. "You didn't . . . you didn't by any chance . . . I mean it's strictly forbidden, of course . . . and Brigitte of all people would never . . ."

"I didn't what?"

"Well . . . find four items—pieces of paper probably—that looked as if they might have come out of a file? I can't imagine that Brigitte would remove anything from a file. She was so proper about everything—and removing something from a file is a grave offense. I mean . . . you understand, of course."

"Of course. No, I've been through all of Brigitte's papers, and there was nothing like that in them, I assure you," Karin answered. "I'm sure Brigitte would never have done such a thing."

"No, of course not. There must be some other explanation, but—well, it is a bit odd, you see."

"Yes. That's probably what Brigitte's note was about. She probably meant to remind herself to make the corrections in the other records as well."

Ursula sounded relieved. "Yes, that's it, isn't it? You know, it's strange, though, that she would go back to a finished file at all. That's what puzzles me the most. We do thousands, you see."

"I guess that's something we'll never know."

"Yes, I guess so." Ursula sighed. "I'm so sorry about Brigitte. So young."

"Yes—I know. Thank you, Ursula. You've been very kind."

"Not at all."

Karin replaced the receiver. The glass in the booth was now completely fogged over, and she and Pavlak stood side by side in what might have been a time capsule. Rain pattered lightly on the fiberglass roof above them, and only the muffled hiss of tires on wet pavement reminded them there was a world outside.

Pavlak broke the silence. "She stole four sheets from Siegfried Schliemann's file and sent them to Judith by registered mail. Why would she take that risk? What was on those four pieces of paper?"

Karin was staring out at the dark shapes that moved like shadows beyond the fogged glass. "And where are they now?" she whispered.

16

Ten hours after the phone call to Ursula Lund at the *Gauk-Behörde*, Pavlak was roaring south in an ancient Peugeot that bucked and rattled fearfully on the crumbling pavement of the A-4, an old East German Autobahn. With the mystery of their adversaries deeper than ever, he had decided against taking a train out of Berlin. For all he knew, there were more than the two they had seen. Maybe many more. The risk was too great that someone would be watching the train stations. So his problem was how to get to Dresden. The passport he had gone to such trouble to retrieve was now a millstone around his neck. He would have to show it to rent a car, which would create another paper record. He considered simply buying a car with the cash in his pockets, but that too would involve registration and another computerized record.

It was Karin who suggested they contact a Turkish couple, cousins of Turgat. They were, she confided to Pavlak, illegal aliens. Brigitte had shared their secret with Karin one day while railing against Germany's immigration laws, which, though the most liberal in the world, were still immorally restrictive in her opinion.

Fortunately, Brigitte's address book was one of the items Karin had salvaged before leaving the apartment. She thumbed through it in vain for the address and had almost given up when she discovered a separate section in the back of the book apparently dedicated solely to Turkish acquaintances. There, scrawled hurriedly in red ink, were the names Mehmet and Cigdem Asul. The couple had entered Germany late, after the great influx of guest workers was finished. By the eighties the country's doors had squeezed tighter, and the only way most Turks could get into Germany was on a tourist visa. The Asuls secured visas for a three-day visit and took a train to Berlin. Then, with the help of Turgat and a circle of friends and relatives in Berlin's Turkish community, they simply melted into the city's millions and disappeared. If there was anyone in Berlin who might help them, these could be the people. The family connection would mean a lot to the clan-minded Turks, and they would certainly share Pavlak's aversion for contact with the police. Pavlak and Karin waited until early evening, hoping to find Mehmet home from work.

The apartment house in Berlin's *Neukölln* section was almost identical to Brigitte and Turgat's. It was gray stucco, stained nearly black by a combination of Berlin's damp drizzle and the tons of carbon particles that the city's traffic spewed into the atmosphere each day. A German maid wearing a blue apron was mopping the ground-floor entryway and threw them a dark look when they crossed the wet floor on their way to the stairs. The bare bulb that was intended to light the fourth-floor hallway was evidently burned out, so they fumbled in the semi-darkness to locate apartment number 404.

A thin, wiry man of about sixty cautiously opened to Pavlak's knock. His hair was almost completely white above a brown, leathery face. He smelled of factory grease and dried sweat, and his dark eyes were sharp with suspicion. Behind him, peeping shyly over his shoulder, stood a plump woman perhaps ten years younger. She wore the ubiquitous kerchief that identified Islamic women in Germany as unmistakably as the yellow Star of David once identified Germany's Jews. The kerchief, at least, was worn voluntarily.

Karin introduced herself as Turgat's sister-in-law, and relief immediately flooded both dark faces. The door swung open and the husband waved them inside with a Turkish newspaper that trembled when he gestured, whether from a physical condition or from nervousness, Pavlak did not know.

Their reaction to the tall American and the sister of their cousin's wife was one of typical Mediterranean warmth. They already knew about Turgat's murder. Apparently the news had spread quickly through the Turkish ghetto. Karin described the events of the previous thirty-six hours, leaving out only the BND identification and the 9mm pistol that was tucked into the back of Pavlak's belt. In fact, Karin did not know about the weapon. Pavlak had considered it wiser not to tell her.

The Turkish couple listened intently, occasionally interrupting to ask for clarification of an unfamiliar word, or to give Mehmet time to translate something for his wife, whose German was obviously weaker than his. The man's solicitousness toward Karin surprised Pavlak, who knew how atypical it was for a Turkish man to show deference toward a female.

When Karin finished, Pavlak took over. He needed new papers, he told Mehmet. A passport, preferably American, and a German driver's license to match. Or he would settle for a German passport, but in that case he would also need matching personal identity papers. He handed the husband a sheet of four uncut passport photos taken by an automatic photo machine an hour earlier. They had made photos of Karin as well, but both agreed that a replacement for Pavlak's American passport was the first priority.

"I'm trying to find out who murdered my wife and my little girl—and Brigitte and Turgat. Can you help me?" Pavlak asked simply.

Mehmet took the photographs into hard fingers but only glanced at them. He stared for a long moment at the stained floor, then raised his head.

"It is possible. I know some people. But very expensive."

"How much?" Pavlak asked.

An exaggerated southern shrug was the answer. "Do not know exactly," came the response in pidgin German. "But too many money. American Passport—good job—maybe ten thousand. Maybe more." His expression presumed that this line of action was out of the question.

"Fine," Pavlak answered immediately. "We'll pay."

The brown eyes widened for a second, but quickly resumed their enigmatic Turkish calm. "You have money," the old man smiled. "Good. Everything possible with money."

Indeed, Pavlak thought. That, at least, was one thing you could count on the world over.

"How long will it take?" Karin asked.

"Don't know. Many time maybe. Three weeks maybe. Month—maybe two."

"I need it in two days, maximum," Pavlak said flatly. "I'll pay what it takes to get it."

The old Turk studied him silently, then nodded. "I try."

Pavlak gave a slight bow. "Do you have a car?" he asked.

"Yes. Old car."

"Can I rent it?"

The old Turk dug into his pocket and wordlessly handed Pavlak a key with a safety pin attached. "Green Peugeot. There." He gestured toward the street. In return, Pavlak thrust a wad of bills toward him, but the Turk waved his hand angrily.

"No money!"

"Forgive me," Pavlak apologized. "Turks are kinder than Americans—or Germans."

At that, the angry frown transformed into a smile. Pavlak extended his hand, and the old man took it in a strong grip.

Pavlak and Karin accepted an invitation to dinner and devoured an eggplant dish heavily seasoned with garlic, accompanied by stuffed olives and yogurt. After the meal, Mehmet offered Karin their bed and Pavlak a spot on the worn couch for the night. He did not say where he and his wife would sleep, and Cigdem had not yet spoken a single word. They could stay as long as they needed, Mehmet insisted. It was for Turgat's sake. His poor cousin.

Pavlak thanked them for the offer and suggested to Karin that she accept.

"What about you?" she asked.

"I'm leaving Berlin—now."

Her eyes widened. "What? It's almost ten o'clock. Are you crazy?"

"I have to. Time is critical. They have endless resources. Sooner or later they'll find us."

"It can wait until morning. Get some sleep first."

"I can't." He looked directly into her eyes. "I'll be back as soon as I can find out who Siegfried Schliemann is—or was. It might take a day. It might take a week. I won't know until I get to Dresden."

"Then I'll go with you."

"No," Pavlak answered sharply. "It's less dangerous alone.

I'll be harder to spot. You stay here and don't leave this apartment unless absolutely necessary."

The old man had moved to Pavlak's side and looked at Karin sternly, wordlessly lending his support in a show of male solidarity.

"My friend here will take care of you," Pavlak said, laying his arm across the shorter man's shoulders.

Karin fixed Pavlak with a cool stare, but kept her lips tightly closed.

"You can contact your ex-husband if you insist," Pavlak continued in a conciliatory tone. The coldness in her eyes discomfited him. "But call from a phone booth and don't tell him where you are." Karin finally opened her mouth to object, but Pavlak raised his hand. "I know you trust him. But remember, *his* phone might be tapped too."

Now, on the Autobahn headed south, the Peugeot's headlights fought weakly against the blackness of an overcast northern night. Pavlak began to regret his haste. Dresden was a two-hour drive under the best of circumstances, and the old Peugeot was not the best of circumstances. He would arrive after midnight and then face the problem of finding a place to sleep without showing a passport. He had scarcely closed his eyes in the past two days, and he soon realized that keeping them open and on the road was a battle he could not win.

Seventy kilometers south of Berlin, Pavlak veered onto an exit and drove through a village, then down a narrow country road until he found himself in open farmland. After about five miles, he located a grove of fir trees around a curve from the nearest farm house. He backed the Peugeot deep among the trees until it was out of sight from the road, then, leaving the key in the ignition, he locked the doors, and made himself as comfortable as possible in the tiny car.

An hour or two of sleep, he reasoned, would at least refresh him enough to finish the drive.

He awoke with a start. The sun was fully exposed over the eastern horizon. Both his feet were numb from cold, and his side ached where the hand brake pressed into it. His right hand was swollen from its collision with the BND agent's head, and so sore he could barely grip the steering wheel. For the first time, it occurred to him that he might have broken a bone. Another moment of panic arrived when the Peugeot whined and coughed but refused to start. He smelled gasoline. The carburetor was flooded. He waited five minutes, then tried again. Finally the engine sputtered to life, belching smoke from the exhaust. In another ten minutes he was back on the Autobahn, feeling as if he had spent the night in a washing machine. At least his eyes stayed open now, if only from the cold. The Peugeot's heater did not work.

As soon as he crossed the Elbe into Dresden's downtown, he stopped at a phone booth and checked the directory for Siegfried Schliemann. There were several dozen Schliemanns listed, but no Siegfried. Pavlak was not surprised. Before reunification, not one in ten East Germans had a telephone. German Telekom was burying cable at a heroic rate, but it would be years before the system could be brought to a par with the western side of the country.

At 9 A.M. Pavlak parked the Peugeot in front of the *Schauspielhaus*, then walked around the old theater to the city's administrative building. He located the *Einwohneramt* and gave his name as Jürgen Schliemann from Frankfurt.

"I'm using my vacation to look up relatives in the east," he told the clerk with a foolish smile. "My father, God rest his soul, spoke often of Uncle Siegfried in Dresden, but I've never met the man, and unfortunately I lost my address book to a pickpocket in Berlin. Could you possibly . . . ?"

The clerk, a sullen young man with drooping eyelids, turned without a word and walked away. It would take a long time, Pavlak thought, to purge forty years of bureaucratic arrogance from the East German soul. Twenty minutes later, Pavlak walked out again, clutching a scrap of paper with the words, "Schliemann, Siegfried Mathus, 141 Bernerstrasse, 01069 Dresden," scrawled on it in pencil.

At the turn of the century, the city of Dresden was so beautiful it was known as the "Florence of Germany." But on the night of February 13, 1945, a firestorm ignited by allied bombs leveled the city, and today, much of Dresden is a nightmare of socialist architecture, drab concrete apartment buildings lined up in endless, dreary rows.

Pavlak found Bernerstrasse in the quarter known as Gorbitz, a housing project built in the seventies and eighties. The street was an asphalt path cutting through a maze of concrete boxes in which, for years, thousands of human inhabitants had striven to maintain the belief that there was purpose in such a life. On the second pass, he located number 141 and eased the Peugeot into a row of even shabbier Trabants. The German skies had resumed their relentless drizzle, and Pavlak hunched his shoulders against the damp and the cold as he dodged the puddles on the sidewalk.

For miles, every building in sight was exactly six stories high. Six stories was the maximum allowed by East German law before an elevator had to be installed. Pavlak climbed a stairwell that smelled of stale urine and finally knocked politely on a scarred metal door at the top. After a long wait, a man who looked about seventy but might have been younger opened it a crack. He was unshaven and wore blue workman's trousers held up by frayed suspenders. His feet were bare. The pale blue eyes that looked into Pavlak's face had long ago abandoned all hope for this life. It was a look Pavlak had seen many times before, in Hungary, in Czechoslovakia, in Poland—everywhere that a worker's paradise had left its stamp on human souls. The watchtowers and machine guns were gone, but men of Siegfried Schliemann's stamp would be prisoners forever. Pavlak guessed in an instant that this disheveled old man, if he *was* Siegfried Schliemann, was not a threat to anyone. Maybe Brigitte's note meant nothing after all.

"Herr Schliemann?"

"Wer fragt?"

Pavlak hesitated, then opted, on the spur of the moment, to give his real name. "My name is Pavlak—John Pavlak." The old man's eyes gave no flicker of recognition.

"And who is that?"

"I'm—an American—a historian. I'm writing a book about the German Democratic Republic. Or rather about the position of the church in the GDR. I understand you worked with the church years ago, and I was hoping you would speak to me for a few minutes."

Schliemann was still blocking his way, one hand resting on the back of the door, prepared to slam it shut in an instant. The frown deepened.

"Where did you get my name?"

"From the church."

"Who in the church?"

"A Mr . . ." Pavlak pretended to search his memory for a name. "A Mr. Grünewald—in Berlin. He gave me a list of people who had trouble with the government because of religious activities. Your name is on it."

"Never heard of such a list."

"Few people have. It was given to me in strictest confidence. Please don't mention to anyone that I told you of it. May I speak to you for a few moments?"

"Why do you do this?" the old man asked skeptically. "The past is past. Why do you bother me now?"

He was still blocking the door. Pavlak considered clamping a hand over his mouth and forcing him inside. Maybe he could frighten him into talking. But the thought had no sooner entered his mind than he dismissed it.

"Many people do not believe the things that happened here, Mr. Schliemann." Pavlak said in a softer voice. "Many people in the West—in America—still believe that Ulbricht and Honecker at least meant well. The real story must be told. Please. Only a few minutes."

The old man shifted his weight to the other bare foot and stared over Pavlak's shoulder at nothing.

"All right," he said with a heavy sigh. "Ten minutes. No more. Agreed?"

"Agreed."

The door opened wide enough for Pavlak to squeeze through. He was shocked at the sight that struck his eyes. Magazines and dirty dishes littered the linoleum floor. There was a stench of cooked cabbage, spoiled fruit, and what might only be described as the miasma of old age. An odor of living rot. A huge gray cat lounged on the windowsill and stared at Pavlak with watchful suspicion. Apparently Schliemann lived alone. He raked a stack of magazines off a chair and motioned for Pavlak to sit.

"Have you lived here long?" Pavlak asked with what he hoped was an ingratiating smile.

"Five years. I was supposed to get an apartment in 1982, but . . ." His voice trailed off.

"But you were arrested that year," Pavlak finished.

"You're well informed."

"Not really. That's about all I know. Can you tell me why they arrested you . . . and what happened?"

The old man laughed mirthlessly. "Why did they arrest me? You want to know why? Who ever knew why? I did not like them. I said so. They heard about it. That was enough."

"What about your church work?"

"What about it?"

"Did you . . ." Pavlak drew a deep breath. He didn't even know what he was looking for. How could he know what questions to ask? "Did they . . . was your church work a factor in the arrest?"

"Of course. I worked with young people. We took walks. We went camping. We read the Bible. Very subversive. I took their time away from the FDJ, perhaps."

"What did they tell you when you were arrested?"

"That I was an enemy of socialism. That I was spreading bourgeois superstitions. That I was seducing good socialist children to believe in such superstitions."

Schliemann took a long, bored look at his watch.

Pavlak had hoped that, once he started, the old man would ramble and reminisce, but apparently that was not going to happen. He tried another tack.

"Have you applied to see your Stasi file?"

"No."

"Why not?"

"Why should I?"

"Aren't you curious about what's in there?"

"*Quatsch*—garbage is in there. I know that. Why should I care?"

"But . . . aren't you interested in how they found out about you? Who informed?"

"I know who informed. I knew before they arrested me."

"Who?"

"Peter."

"Peter?"

"Mein geliebter kleiner Bruder."

Pavlak felt as if he had walked into a brick wall in the dark. "Your *brother* informed on you?"

"Of course. Peter was one of them. That was the only way to live well in the GDR, and he always wanted to live well."

"I see." Pavlak swallowed, recovering. "And . . . uh . . . you're certain that your brother informed on you?"

"Absolutely certain."

"What . . . what did your brother do? For a living, I mean?"

Schliemann shrugged. "He was Stasi, of course. He never said so, but I knew it. We all knew it. You weren't allowed to live in the West otherwise."

Pavlak's heart leapt into a higher gear. "He lived in the West?" he asked, as casually as he could.

"In Frankfurt. He was head of a trade mission there. At least that's what he said."

Suddenly the old man threw back his head and laughed. "I'll tell you something funny. He was with me when they arrested me. The fools arrested him too." The old man laughed again, a hard, humorless laugh. "They put handcuffs on him. Peter made a terrible scene."

Then, as quickly as it had come, the laughter was gone, replaced by a bitterness with no bottom. "Caught in his own net. Served him right. It was a mistake, of course. I'm sure he was free within hours. I know for a fact that he was back in Frankfurt two days later. I was still enjoying the hospitality of the state, of course."

Pavlak chose his words carefully. "When you and your brother were arrested, did Peter have any papers with him?"

"That's what he was so mad about. They took his brief-case." Schliemann shrugged. "I'm sure he got it back when they freed him."

"Is your brother still alive, Mr. Schliemann?"

"Oh yes. Alive and well and living on Crete. You see, our socialist masters rewarded him generously for whatever it was he did." Schliemann uncrossed and recrossed his legs. "And now they are cast down. Our former masters. Now we have justice." Pavlak could feel the hostility in Schliemann's gaze. "Only—they are not cast down, Mr. Pavlak. You say you defeated them—you Americans—but you defeated noth-ing." He gestured toward a window. "They still sit in the same offices. They still live in luxury. And we . . ." He waved his hand, then looked at his watch and stood. "Your ten minutes are up, Mr. Pavlak. Mr. American. Mr. Freedom. Bringer of justice. Good day."

"Mr. Schliemann—do you have your brother's address?"

Schliemann's eyes narrowed. "Why?"

"I want to talk to him. I want to find out what happened. As I said—I want people to know."

"I have it," Schliemann said after a long silence. "We have a sister in Rostock. She sent me the address. I save her let-ters. They are all I have left." Suddenly tears welled in the old man's eyes. He wiped them quickly away with a sleeve. "I haven't seen or spoken to my brother since my arrest, Mr. Pavlak. I don't want to see him, ever again. But, if you can make trouble for him—even a little trouble—yes, I will give you the address."

Pavlak waited while Schliemann drew a bundle of letters from a drawer and searched through them. A quarter hour later Schliemann still had not found the address, and Pav-lak's heart fell. Then, on the third run through the letters, the old man uttered a cry of discovery. He borrowed Pavlak's pen and copied something onto the back of an envelope.

"Here, Mr. Pavlak," he said, extending the envelope. But when Pavlak grasped it, Schliemann held tight. For a few seconds both men held the paper clamped in their fingers, a fragile bridge between them.

"What's the matter?" Pavlak asked.

"I don't know . . . I . . . Mr. Pavlak," he said with an edge of desperation in his voice. "I must confess something to you."

"Yes?"

"My brother must never know that I gave you this."

"Mr. Schliemann," Pavlak urged gently, "the Cold War is over. The Soviet Empire . . ."

"I am afraid of my brother, Mr. Pavlak," Schliemann blurted in a thin voice. "Even now, I am afraid of him." And suddenly the old man was crying in earnest, sobbing into his sleeve.

Pavlak closed the door quietly on his way out.

17

Before Germany's communications network was spun off into a semi-private corporation, the telephone system was a state monopoly under the administration of the Postal Service. Most German post offices still have phone booths dedicated for long-distance service. On his way back to Berlin, Pavlak stopped at one in the town of Luckau and asked to make a transatlantic call. The clerk threw a switch and pointed toward booth number two. It was just after 2 P.M. in Germany—8 A.M. on the East Coast of the U.S. Arthur Trask would be at work. Pavlak punched in the number and waited.

"Trask," said a rough, impatient voice.

"Pavlak," he replied, mimicking the big man's tone.

"John! Thank God. We've been worried to death. Where are you?"

"I'm fine. I'm in Germany. Anything happening over there?"

"Are you kidding? The FBI is all over the place. They want to talk to you. They know everything, John. They know you came to the plant. They know we went to Varryville for dinner. They know you're in Germany. One of them grilled me for an hour last night. Natty-looking guy."

"Streat?"

"Yeah, that's his name. Streat. He asked me if you knew anybody in Berlin."

So Streat had gotten as far as his registration at the Hotel Eger. "What did you tell him?"

"Nothing. Told him we just had dinner in Varryville, talked about old times, talked about Judith and Tasha. I said you told me you were going to disappear for a while, but that you wouldn't tell me where you were going. He asked me if you mentioned that German girl."

"Brigitte?"

"Yeah."

"What did you tell him?"

"I said I'd never heard of her. I think he believed me, but I don't know, John. This is over my head. What kind of trouble are you getting an old man into?"

"Probably not half as much as I'm getting myself into. Did they talk to my father?"

"And your brother, and everybody else you even breathed on when you were here. I'm telling you, John, this Streat guy wants you bad. For all I know he might even have the German police looking for you too."

"Yeah, he might."

"What are you going to do?"

"Just what I set out to do."

"John, listen to me. I think you should come back home. Disappearing like this looks damned suspicious. I think Streat thinks you had something to do with the bomb. You better get back here and straighten things out."

"Not yet. Something very weird is going on over here."

"What?"

"I don't know yet, but I'm going to find out. Just keep your ear to the ground for me, okay? I'll be in touch."

"What if the German police find you?"

"They won't. I'm staying with some Turks—friends of Brigitte's in Berlin."

"Have they got a phone?"

Pavlak thought back to the dingy apartment and tried to recall a telephone. "To tell you the truth, Arthur, I don't know."

"Well, what are their names?"

"You don't want to know, Arthur. It's just one more thing you might have to lie about. I'm sorry I put you in that position anyway."

"Let me worry about that. How can I contact you if something happens?"

"What could happen?"

"For Christ's sake, John, what if there's an emergency? I mean what if your father dies or something?"

"Bury him."

There was a long silence on the line.

"Don't talk like that, John," Trask scolded sadly. "Your father's a hard man, but he loves you. He doesn't deserve that kind of talk."

"All right, Arthur, I won't argue with you. Look, when I've finished what I came here for, I'll be back. And don't worry about Streat. I'll give him a call and soothe his feathers. Anyway, without me around to harass, maybe he'll find the real killer. I gotta go."

He hung up over Arthur's protest and dialed another number. This time a female voice answered.

"FBI. Can I help you?"

"This is John Pavlak, calling for Darryl Streat."

"Oh! He's been expecting your call. I'm sorry, he's not

in just now, but I'll have him return your call. What number are you calling from?"

Pavlak hesitated. "Nine-one-one," he said tersely, and dropped the receiver onto its cradle.

He was in Berlin before three. Mehmet was at work. Karin and Cigdem, kerchief still on her head, were stringing green beans and communicating volubly via gestures and a jabber of mutually unintelligible languages. When Pavlak walked in, Karin laid aside the aluminum pan in her lap and stood facing him.

"You look exhausted," she said simply.

"I am. But we may be onto something. I'll tell you later. Now I have to sleep."

With that he lowered himself to the floor and, to the horror of his hostess who motioned frantically toward the bedroom, fell instantly asleep.

He awoke a few minutes before midnight when the soft babble of the women's voices was interrupted by the rasp of a key in a lock. Mehmet walked through the door with a smile on his face. It was all arranged, he announced proudly. The American passport was not possible, but a German one would be manufactured, along with a matching *Personalausweis*. The initial demand was for DM 8,000, but he had negotiated the price down to DM 6,800. He had given the man a DM 500 down payment. Pavlak reached for his wallet, but Mehmet refused to take any money. They would wait until the goods were delivered, he insisted.

"And when will that be?" Pavlak asked.

"Three days. The best I could do."

Pavlak nodded. "Can you trust this man?"

"Of course," Mehmet smiled. "Turk!"

A comment about the trustworthiness of forgers, no matter what their national origin, rose to Pavlak's lips, but he stifled it.

"I must go now," Mehmet continued. "You stay here." He pointed at the sofa, wished Pavlak good night, and walked out the door again.

When Mehmet was gone, his wife gathered some items from a small table and stepped into the bedroom, closing the door behind her. Pavlak and Karin were alone.

Karin turned to him. "Well?"

Pavlak sat on the couch beside her and told her about his visit with Siegfried Schliemann. "The brother's the key," he concluded. "I'm going to pay Mr. Peter Schliemann a visit."

The strain of the past sixty hours was beginning to show in Karin's face. Her skin was drawn, and her eyes tired. "Poor Gitti," she whispered. "Why did she have to find that file?" She looked quizzically at Pavlak. "What caught her attention? And why did she send it to Judith?"

"Peter Schliemann was a Stasi agent. My guess would be that Brigitte found something in his brother's file that would compromise somebody—maybe somebody in the BND. At least that's one explanation for why the BND is following us. Maybe she sent it to Judith because Judith was an investigative reporter. Maybe she wanted Judith to help her look into it. Or maybe she wanted Judith to print something about it. I don't know."

"Print it where? In an American newspaper? If that's what she wanted, why wouldn't she send it to a German paper?"

"Maybe she wanted to deal with someone she knew and trusted. If it was going to cause a major scandal, then an American paper would serve as well as a German one. The German press would quickly take it from there. In fact. . . ," Pavlak raised a finger, "maybe that's why she did it—to protect herself. Maybe she thought if the scandal broke in the U.S., no one would think of looking for a clerk in Berlin."

"If that's true," Karin said grimly, "she was wrong, wasn't she?"

"Somebody got wind of it. But who? And how? Brigitte must have told someone. Someone close to her. Someone who betrayed her to the BND—or whoever murdered her. Any ideas?"

Karin shook her head. "None. I can't imagine that Brigitte knew anyone involved with the BND in any way." Karin stood and paced. "All of this is speculation anyway. We don't even know for sure that the file had anything at all to do with Brigitte and Judith."

"That's why I'm going to have a talk with Mr. Schliemann—Peter, that is."

"What are you going to say? You can't just walk up and ask him if he was involved in four murders."

"I'll think of something. I'll have to. He's our only lead."

"When are we going?"

"*We're* not. I am."

Karin's eyes flashed. "What do you expect me to do? Sit here and string beans until you get back?"

"Karin, listen. I'm sure the FBI has the German police looking for me. They know I was in Berlin. They know about Brigitte. We have to assume that by now the police are looking for you too. You still want to talk to the police? Easily done. Just get caught at a passport check on the border, and I'm sure you'll get your chance."

"All right, I get the picture," Karin replied sullenly. "When do you leave?"

"When I get a new passport."

"Will you fly out of Berlin?"

"I'm not flying. I'll lease a car using the forged papers and drive. With the fighting in the Balkans, it's too risky to go overland to Greece, so I'll head for Italy and take a ferry to Heraklion."

"Are you crazy? That'll take three days. You can fly there in a few hours."

"I know." Pavlak replied carefully. "But if I fly, I can't take this." He reached behind him and pulled out the pistol he had taken from Lederer.

Karin closed her eyes. Her lips formed a thin line. "Where did you get that?"

"I borrowed it from our BND friend, along with his wallet."

"Why didn't you tell me?"

"I had a suspicion you wouldn't approve."

"Your suspicion was correct."

Pavlak tried a grin. "Gee—so little time, and look how well I know you."

Levity, he realized too late, was inappropriate. Karin disappeared into the bedroom, slamming the door behind her.

As Pavlak was tucking the 9mm back into his belt in Berlin, Christopher Hopkins was opening a now-familiar door on the seventh floor at CIA Headquarters in Langley.

"We found him," he announced with an explosion of breath that betrayed his elation. He had been very worried about finding John Pavlak. The Central Intelligence Agency was not a law-enforcement unit. It sometimes did similar things—looking for agents who had disappeared, tracking down threats to a network, and so on—but in friendly countries, such matters were usually conducted with the cooperation and assistance of local law enforcement. Finding Pavlak without even letting the Germans know they were looking was a daunting assignment.

The FBI, of all people, had come to the rescue. Special Agent Darryl Streat was remarkably cooperative. Hopkins was not sure exactly what Streat's motives were. Perhaps he still hoped for CIA help in finding Pavlak, even though Hopkins had lied, on the DCI's orders, and told him that the Agency could not help. Or perhaps Streat just wanted to stay close to the CIA on a hunch. He had stated openly that he suspected Pavlak's activities had something to do with the CIA. Whatever the reason, Streat passed information liberally to the liaison office, and that information included a list of phone numbers belonging to, among others, a man named Arthur Trask.

At Christopher Hopkins' request—but over the signature of the director of Central Intelligence—the National Security Agency fed that list of phone numbers into a computer located north of Washington, D.C. When Pavlak called Arthur Trask from Luckau, his call was routed to a communications tower in the Hartz Mountains, beamed to a satellite over the Atlantic, then bounced back down to the East Coast of the United States where it was snatched out of the ether, not only by AT&T, but also by an antenna at a secret installation in New Hampshire. The computer north of Washington needed less than a second to match the number Pavlak had dialed to one in its memory bank. It responded to the match by sending a signal that brought an automatic tape recorder to life. That was the break Hopkins needed.

He had immediately called Frank Borning, CIA Station Chief in Bonn. Yes, Borning told him, the company had some resources among the Turks in Berlin.

"We're looking for an American named John Pavlak," Hopkins told Borning. "He's hiding out with Turkish relatives of a man named Turgat Onat."

"John Pavlak? Any relation to Gustaf?"

"His son."

"I see," Borning answered slowly. "We'll work on it."

As it turned out, the Agency's resources had little difficulty tracking down three of Turgat's relatives in the close-knit, expatriate community. Discreet inquiries were made immediately. The German cleaning lady at Mehmet's building recognized Pavlak's photograph. She had seen the tall man enter the building two days before. He came in with a young woman—short dark hair. She did not know which apartment they were visiting. That, she said haughtily, slipping a hundred mark bill into her apron, was none of her business.

Frank Borning, who had flown to Berlin to direct the search for Pavlak, used a secure line at the branch embassy on Neustädische Kirchstrasse to call Hopkins with the news. Scarcely five hours had elapsed since Pavlak dialed Arthur Trask's number.

"He's holed up with a couple of illegals," Borning reported. "We've put a watch on the apartment."

"Positive ID?" Hopkins asked.

"We haven't seen him, but we believe he's still there."

There was momentary silence on the scrambled line. "On the intercept he said he wouldn't be staying long," Hopkins said, worried. "How do you know he didn't slip away before you found him?"

"Because," Borning replied with a satisfied smirk that Hopkins, five thousand miles away, could not see, "we found another tidbit for you. The Turk is trying to buy false papers for him. We don't know what kind, or in what name, but we're working on it. Pavlak won't go anywhere till he's got them."

After Borning's call, Hopkins depressed the phone switch for three seconds, then dialed the extension for the DCI's office. Denham was in a meeting—as always. But he had left instructions that he was to be called out if Hopkins came up with anything.

"Tell him I'm on my way," Hopkins instructed the assistant who took his call. "It's important."

Now, to Hopkins' disappointment, the director acknowledged the news with a barely perceptible nod and no change in his expression. Instead, he drummed the ubiquitous pencil point on his desk top and stared at something on the wall over Hopkins' shoulder.

"So now what?" Hopkins asked after a full minute had passed. He tried to hide the peevishness he felt.

Denham pushed himself away from his desk, stood, and looked out a window across the rooftops of suburban Washington, D.C. He heaved a sigh. "Borning is a good man."

Borning? Was that it? Didn't *he* get any credit, for God's sake? "Yes—a very good man," Hopkins replied as pleasantly as he could.

"Have him pay Pavlak a visit. Find out what Pavlak knows. Maybe Pavlak hasn't learned anything about Fool's Gold yet. If he hasn't . . ." Denham stopped.

"Yes?"

"Tell him."

Hopkins' mouth fell open. "Sir?"

Denham turned to face him. "Tell Pavlak the whole story. That's our best chance of keeping him quiet."

"But . . . are you sure, sir?"

"You got a better idea?"

"Well . . . there *is* another possibility, of course."

Denham closed his eyes wearily. "Chris, he's an American citizen—an *innocent* American citizen. We can't just eliminate Pavlak like a rogue agent. There are too many people, too close to him, who know too much. That would be risking a scandal almost as bad as Fool's Gold." Denham lowered himself back into the leather chair. "This car bombing had nothing to do with us. He's on the wrong trail. Explain that—and the rest of it—to him, and he'll back off. He'll have to, under the circumstances. Wouldn't you?"

"Maybe," Hopkins said uncertainly. "But suppose he doesn't. His relationship with his father. . . ."

"Is strained at best," Denham finished for him. "I know that. I read the report. But Pavlak hasn't broken with his family completely. And as far as we know, he's a loyal American. He's a decorated veteran, remember? We have no reason to believe that he *wants* to cause us problems. When he knows the truth about Fool's Gold, especially how exposing it will hurt his family and gain him nothing, he'll drop this quest he's on." The director pointed at a document with a light blue cover that lay on the corner of his desk. "I'll have to admit that this decision is not unpremeditated, Chris," he said with a smile. "I took the precaution of ordering a psychological profile on Pavlak. Based on all the information we have about him, the shrinks are confident that Pavlak will toe a line if he knows where that line is. Basically, they say he's intelligent and extremely rational. He'll respond to reason. And reason will tell him we had nothing to do with his wife's murder."

Hopkins frowned. "I still think it's risky, sir."

"Of course it is. But so is letting him stumble around blindly and bump into Schliemann. I think it's less risky to give him the whole picture and get him off this wild goose chase he's on. Right now he's a loose cannon. Anything could happen."

Hopkins fidgeted in his chair. "Sin . . . Fool's Gold carries a very high classification. Borning will want . . ."

"I've thought of that. I'll order it declassified for twelve hours. We'll lock it up again before the list comes out. I know I'm bypassing the committee, but I have that authority in an emergency."

Hopkins frowned. "Still, classification changes are public record. If a snoopy reporter asks questions . . ."

"We'll explain that it was a mistake—quickly corrected. Look, I don't like it either, but at least it's legal, and ordering Borning to reveal classified information to a civilian with no clearance is definitely illegal. This is the best arrangement we can make."

Hopkins hesitated. "Well, I see your point, but it's a gamble. The whole thing is a gamble."

Denham smiled. "We'll cheat on the odds. Have Borning stay on top of Pavlak—even after he briefs him. Clandestine surveillance. Don't let him out of our sight. Not yet."

18

It was one o'clock in the morning, Central European Time, when Borning received his instructions in Berlin. He decided to wait until daylight. The apartment where Pavlak and the woman were staying was being watched by four-man teams, operating in two-hour shifts. This guy was not going to slip away from them. Hopkins had made it clear that the DCI himself was watching this closely, and Borning had used that information to bully the manpower he needed from the agency's staff in Berlin.

He grabbed a few hours sleep on a cot next to the company's communication center, then rose at six and gathered his team. At nine he arrived at the apartment house with replacements for the four bleary night watchers. To their displeasure, he ordered them to extend their shift another hour until his meeting with Pavlak was finished. If Pavlak panicked and ran, he would have eight agents surrounding the building. He was taking no chances.

As Borning entered the front door, two of the eight agents were hidden in a dented Mercedes van parked across the street. In several spots, rivets had worked out of the body, leaving small, corroded holes. Inserted into one of them was a tiny lens, invisible from the outside, that gave the agents in the van a panoramic view of the apartment house. Two more men sat in a car on a side street where they could watch the only rear exit in the building. They were munching sausages and black bread. A fifth man sat in a *Konditerei* on the opposite corner, drinking a leisurely cup of morning coffee. A sixth stood at a bus stop on the other side of the building, reading a newspaper. The remaining two strolled slowly around the block on opposite sides, keeping out of sight of each other. If it had been a normal clandestine surveillance, they would have made only one pass, then taken stations out of sight. But this was candy work. Just some harmless civilian, unarmed and not hostile, Borning had told them. Not a professional with trade craft.

And there was a ninth man. He stood in an apartment across the street, watching them all from behind a closed curtain. He was tall and thin, with long, delicate fingers. As he watched Frank Borning walk in the front door of the building across the street, he picked up a telephone and dialed the area code for the small town of Pullach, near Munich, in southern Germany.

Borning entered the building alone, climbed the stairs to the fifth floor—what the Germans called the fourth floor—and knocked loudly on number 404. After a minute of silence, he knocked again. Still no response. He fought off the sinking feeling in the pit of his stomach and rapped on the door a third time. Had they been watching an empty apartment? Then he tried the door lever. It didn't budge, but he heard a faint stir inside, then the scrape of a chain, and finally the door opened two inches. An older Turkish woman, wearing a black scarf on her head, peered up at him through eyes that were round with terror.

"Good morning," Borning said in German, smiling. "I'm

from the American Embassy. I've come to speak with Dr. John Pavlak."

The woman shook her head, said something in Turkish, then started to push the door shut again. "Wait!" Borning called. Instinctively his left hand shot out to catch the door.

Afterward Borning would admit that extending his hand was a careless mistake—one of several in this operation, caused, he would argue, by faulty information and thus faulty assumptions going in.

His palm had barely made contact with the heavy German door when a powerful hand snatched his wrist and jerked him violently into the room, wrenching his arm behind his back as it did so. Pain seared his shoulder, and Borning cried out, bending and twisting involuntarily to ease the pressure on the straining bone. Then a foot slammed into his ankles and swept his feet from under him. His face plunged to the floor. A split second later someone's knee landed hard on the middle of his back and crushed the last cubic centimeter of air from his lungs. The room went black.

He was unconscious, he estimated in his report, for perhaps thirty seconds, before the paralysis in his diaphragm eased and he was able to draw a shallow, painful breath. As he lay gasping for air like a landed fish, the room gradually took shape. Six inches from his nose stood the leg of a sofa. His arm was still pinned painfully behind him, and a heavy weight lay on his back, making his feeble efforts to breathe even more painful.

And there was something else. Something he had felt once before in Bulgaria, during a rendezvous with a threatened and panicking agent. It was the barrel of a pistol pressing into his neck.

"Who are you?" an American voice hissed in his ear. "What do you want?"

Training took hold. He made a conscious effort to relax his body and gather his wits. "Frank Borning, Third Secretary of the United States Embassy in Bonn." He waited a few seconds but got no response. "I've been asked to speak with Dr. John Pavlak. I have a message for him from Washington, D.C." The pressure on the bones in his shoulder eased slightly. "I'm just here to talk," he continued more hopefully. Nascent rage toward Christopher Hopkins was already building in Borning's mind. He had walked in for a quiet chat with a middle-aged civilian. Somebody should have warned him that this could get rough.

"Okay, talk," ordered a cold voice. The hard steel bored deeper into his neck. "Start by answering one of *my* questions. How did you find me?"

"They traced you from Washington," Borning gasped. "I don't know how. Ow!" He cried out as his arm was wrenched higher and fresh pain exploded in his shoulder. "I think it was through a phone call," he stuttered hurriedly, rushing the words. "You told someone where you were. They intercepted it." He prayed that the pressure on his arm would relent.

"Who are 'they'?"

"The Central Intelligence Agency."

"Is that who you really work for?"

Despite the chill in the apartment, a rivulet of sweat trickled down the side of Borning's nose. He decided not to answer Pavlak's question, even though he had not been expressly forbidden from revealing his affiliation. It was pretty obvious, anyway. Apparently the man on his back agreed, because he quickly moved on to another question.

"How many men with you?"

Borning hesitated. He had dealt with desperate men before and knew only too well how irrational their actions could be. The cold steel pressing into his neck was a dramatic reminder that he was a finger twitch away from death. And yet, the voice in his ear did not sound panicked. Angry and intense—but under control. "Eight," he answered. "The building is surrounded. They're only there to make sure you don't try to run before I talk to you. I have to explain something, then we'll all go away and leave you alone. I swear it." He tried not to reveal the pain he was in, but in spite of his best efforts, each gasp ended with a small grunt. "It involves your family," he croaked.

At last the pressure relented a little.

"Are you armed?" asked the voice.

"No."

"Kneel—slowly."

The adverb was unnecessary. The weight lifted from his back, but the powerful grip kept his wrist pinned against his spine. With difficulty Borning floundered to his knees and waited. At last his arm was released. Borning longed to massage the pained wrist, but he let it rest where it fell. The gun was still pressing into his neck. A hand came around his side and patted him down.

"Stand."

As the word was spoken, the gun pulled away from his neck. Borning stood slowly and deliberately, then turned. His adversary had backed six feet away, but the pistol in his right hand was pointed steadily at Borning's chest. He was a tall man, middle-aged, broad-shouldered, and muscular. The face was the one from the faxed photograph. But the set of the jaw, the dark fury in the stare—this was not the grieving college administrator Hopkins had described.

Out of the corner of his eye, Borning could see the Turkish woman crouched in a corner. The tall man motioned her toward a door in the rear of the apartment. *"Alles OK,"* he said, smiling. Borning took the cue and smiled at her as well. Just a little meeting between two Americans in Berlin. Nothing to worry about.

The woman scurried through the door, leaving them alone.

"Are you John Pavlak?" Borning asked.

"First of all, let's get something straight," the tall man answered. "If anyone else comes through that door, you will die immediately. Understand?"

Borning swallowed hard and nodded.

"As for who I am—assume I'm Pavlak and give me whatever messages you have."

Borning shook his head firmly. "I can't do that. What I have to say is for Pavlak's ears only. I'm not allowed to disclose it to anyone else. You have to prove you're him or the conversation is over. Can you show me a passport?"

The tall man stood motionless, pondering, for what seemed like ten seconds, then reached inside his jacket pocket, withdrew an American passport, opened it to the picture, and held it up.

Borning squinted. His eyes were not all they used to be, but he still resisted glasses. No matter. He could see all he needed.

"May I sit down?"

"No," Pavlak barked. "Talk."

"Before I do, I have to have your word that you will not reveal what I'm going to say to anyone. I must have a guarantee of absolute secrecy."

There was no response. Just the level stare and the dark hole in the end of the pistol.

"Dr. Pavlak. I believe, when you've heard me out, you'll understand that it is in your best interest, as well as your country's, not to repeat what I say. Do we have an agreement?" This was silly. If it wasn't on paper, what was the point of asking for a pledge? The man could still blab his guts out if he wanted to, and they would have no legal leverage to stop him. But Hopkins had insisted that an oral agreement was better than nothing. Moral pressure and all that. Bullshit, as far as Borning was concerned.

"All right," Pavlak nodded. "It's a deal."

"Good." Borning drew a breath. "I'm here on instructions from Washington. The Central Intelligence Agency has been in touch with an FBI agent who's investigating the murder of your wife and daughter. A man named Darryl Streat. I believe you know him."

Pavlak waited in stony silence.

"Yes, well—Mr. Streat has told us some things which indicate you may know something about an old intelligence operation—one that was folded some time ago."

"What things?"

"Excuse me?"

"What things did Streat tell you?"

"Streat has some telephone records. Shortly before your wife died, she made several calls to CIA Headquarters—calls that indicated she had some knowledge of this operation. It was code-named 'Fool's Gold.' " Borning raised his eyebrows. "Ever heard of it?"

"You're doing the talking, remember?"

Borning nodded. "All right. Fool's Gold started in 1976 and was wrapped up in 1989. It was actually run by the West Germans."

"You mean the BND? Your German counterparts?"

Borning nodded. "It involved an East German, an agent of the Ministry for State Security—the Stasi. His job was to procure western military technology and smuggle it into the Soviet Bloc. Actually, he was a double agent, working for the

West Germans. Over the thirteen years of the operation, he fed us information which led to the indictment of a number of western businessmen for exporting illegal goods to the Soviet Bloc, exports that were banned by COCOM. You know about COCOM?"

"The Coordinating Committee for Multilateral Export Control," Pavlak recited tersely. "Go on."

"Right. Anyway," Borning continued, "some of those companies were European, some American. We worked closely with the FBI and the Commerce Department to intercept the American shipments and gain the indictments. Other countries handled their own prosecutions, of course. The operation was quite successful. Also very long-lived."

"What was the East German's name?"

Borning hesitated. "I'm not at liberty to divulge that. Anyway, it's irrelevant."

"How did he operate?"

"His cover was a trade mission to West Germany."

"Where?"

Borning considered. His instructions were to tell all. It had been his own, spur-of-the-moment decision not to give Schliemann's name. Years of fanatical secrecy made this type of disclosure difficult for a career man. Why reveal any more than necessary? But then again, orders were orders.

"Frankfurt."

"Go on."

"Well, as you might imagine, there are difficulties in keeping this sort of operation going over a long period of time. If you burn everybody your man tells you about, his bosses will quickly catch on. And of course he has to show them some successes of his own or, at the very least, they'll transfer him to something else. Do you follow?"

A nod.

"Well, that made it necessary for us—the West Germans as well as the Americans—to, uh . . . to help this agent appear to be doing his job."

"You mean you helped him smuggle forbidden military technology into East Germany."

"Well, yes, sort of. We had to. Nothing of any real value," Borning added quickly. "Just goods we knew they would get anyway, or goods that were on the verge of becoming obsolete. But good enough to keep his people from getting suspicious. It was a tightrope. Some tough calls there, believe me. But we felt—and so did the Germans—that the things we were stopping were well worth the things we let get through."

"You mean *helped* get through."

"In some cases—yes." Borning studied the floor and shifted his weight. The next part was important. "Now, of course, Dr. Pavlak—you can see that this kind of operation would be very difficult for ordinary Americans to understand. I mean people who aren't involved with the complex world of espionage and interdiction." He cleared his throat. "If the press were to get wind of it, there would be a scandal of sorts, and it could greatly damage our ability to conduct such operations in the future. That's why it's so important . . . for the sake of national security . . . to keep this quiet, as you have assured me you will."

"You said it would be in *my* best interest," Pavlak interrupted. "What does it have to do with me?"

Borning drew another deep breath. Time to play the trump. "In order to provide these goods for our agent we had to get them into the Eastern Bloc. We did that with the cooperation of an American exporter who smuggled the items concealed in his own shipments of legitimate warehousing equipment." Borning waited, but there was no reaction. "It was your father," he added quietly. "Gustaf Pavlak."

Borning was prepared for either astonishment or a bored nod, depending on whether or not Pavlak already knew about his father's involvement with the CIA. If Pavlak knew, or at least suspected it—Borning would not be surprised. Even the most dangerous secrets tended to rattle around loosely within families. But Borning was not prepared for what Pavlak did, which was throw his head back and laugh.

"I don't think you understand," Borning continued peevishly. "If this had ever come out, your father would have been on his own, and he knew it. We would have kept quiet to protect our agent. He could have gone to prison. At the very least, he would have been ruined financially. Your father understood that risk and took it anyway. He's a brave man and . . ."

"Mr. Borning," Pavlak interrupted. "How much did you pay him?"

"He . . . received some compensation, of course. I don't know how much. As I said, he was taking a big risk."

"Right. And he would only have done that for a big gain. I know my father."

"I'm sure the gain was insignificant compared to the risk of losing everything he had worked his whole life for—and very possibly landing in prison to boot. You underestimate your father, Dr. Pavlak." Borning picked his words. "I was told that you and he don't get along very well. I can't believe, though, that you'd betray both your family and your country just for spite. From what I've heard, you're too big a man for that. Am I right?"

"Oh, can the bullshit, will you?" Pavlak snapped. "Don't worry—your dirty little secret is safe with me. I'm looking for a murderer, and your little spy games don't concern me."

"Precisely," Borning said. "That's the whole point of this meeting. To show you that our operation had nothing to do with the murder of your family. If you're looking in that direction, you're looking the wrong way."

"Uh-huh. Now I have some questions for you."

"Shoot—not literally, of course." Borning tried to laugh, but it fell flat. "Look, could you put that thing away? It makes me nervous."

"Good. It's meant to. First question. What role exactly did you play in the murder of my wife and my little girl?"

Pavlak raised the pistol and sighted along the barrel, straight at Borning's nose. The look in his eyes caused Borning's heart to seize, and he felt the blood leave his face. "I have no idea who killed your family. I just told you. . . ."

"You just told me a load of horse crap that would fertilize all the tulips in Holland. Second question. Who killed Brigitte Onat?"

"That was an auto accident. The German police told us . . ."

"Third question. Who killed her husband, Turgat Onat?"

Borning drew a deep breath. "Now that's a bizarre coincidence, I'll admit. The Germans suspect he was smuggling heroin from Turkey—probably a quarrel between dealers. Whatever it was, that case has nothing . . ."

"Fourth question. Why is the BND following me?"

"That's . . . that's ridiculous," Borning spluttered. "You're imagining things, Dr. Pavlak. You're upset—with good reason, I might add. But try to be rational. Don't you see that this thing . . ."

A leather wallet struck Borning in the chest and fell to the floor.

"Am I imagining that?"

Borning looked at Pavlak, then slowly bent his knees and

retrieved the wallet. He turned it over. An official identification beamed out in white from a dark leather frame.

"Where the hell did you get this?"

"Fifth question. How are you going to get out of here
alive?"

Borning looked into Pavlak's eyes. Something deep inside
them froze the blood in his veins.

"I was planning," Borning replied in a voice smaller than
he would have wished, "to walk out the front door."

"Just like that?"

"Just like that."

Pavlak's head pivoted slowly, almost imperceptibly, to the
left, then back to the right, then center again.

"Why not?" Borning asked. It came out as a whisper. This
was taking a very nasty turn. A line from the fact sheet leapt
vividly into his memory. The one about Vietnam and the
Distinguished Service Cross. The one Hopkins had brushed
off as ancient history. If Borning lived to get Hopkins on
the phone . . .

"Because I don't trust you," Pavlak said coldly. "Because
you're lying to me. Because people are winding up dead all
around me, and that makes me nervous."

"If there's more to this than I've told you, I don't know
what it is. I'm leveling with you, Pavlak. If you know something I don't—tell me. I swear I'll help you if I can."

"Turn around."

"What are you going to do?"

"Turn . . . around."

Borning turned slowly. The saliva in his mouth had
turned to glue. "What are you going to do?"

"That depends on you."

Thank God, Borning thought. At least the bullet wasn't
coming in the next second. "What do you want?"

"I want your men out of the way. I want out of here free and clean. Both of us."

"Both?"

"Are you going to tell me you don't know about Karin?"

"I was told you came here with a woman—short black hair. I don't know who she is."

"How do you communicate with the surveillance team?"

"Signals. I walk out the door with both hands in my coat pockets. That means the operation was successful, in other words that I've spoken to you as intended—and that's *all* we intended—and they'll melt away one at a time over the next twenty minutes." All but two, Borning did not say. The two in the van, who would continue surveillance indefinitely on instructions from Langley. Should he tell Pavlak? If he didn't, and Pavlak somehow found out . . . He preferred not to think about the consequences. On the other hand, it was his only ace in the hole.

"Go on," Pavlak said.

"Right hand in, left hand out means you weren't in the building, and they should maintain surveillance in case you show up later. Left hand in, right hand out means I think you're in the building, but I was unable to talk to you—maintain surveillance and detain you when you come out."

"And both hands out?"

"Both hands out is the red flag. It means I'm in trouble and need a rescue."

"And what will they do?"

"Depends on the situation. If somebody's tailing me, for example, they'll try to make a shielded pickup."

"What's that?"

"That means you maneuver a vehicle into a position where it's shielding your man from the tail, then you grab him and go."

"What if I'm walking beside you?"

"They shadow us—wait for an opportunity."

"To do what?"

"Whatever's necessary."

"Including shoot me?"

Borning hesitated. "Hopefully that wouldn't be necessary."

"What's the other signal?"

"That's it. We didn't do a whole lot of planning, you know. This wasn't supposed to be a hostile confrontation, just a simple meeting. I walk in and chat with you a while, then walk back out, and we all go home. I told you—the others were just here to make sure the meeting took place."

"I'll repeat the question," Pavlak said in a tone that sent a fresh shiver down Borning's spine. "What's the other signal?"

A bead of sweat rolled from Borning's forehead and stung his right eye. He tried to blink it away. "I don't know what you're talking about."

"The one that says leave me alone. Don't follow. Don't interfere."

Borning wished he could turn around and look into Pavlak's face. It was easier to tell when a man was bluffing if you could see his eyes.

"I walk out with the coat open," he said quietly. "Both hands in my pants pockets."

He could hear Pavlak move behind him, then the scratch of a pencil on paper. The scratching went on quite a while, long enough for Borning to feel the first hints of weariness in his knees—a consequence not of standing so long, but of the tension that had held him in an iron grip since he first landed on the floor beneath Pavlak's knee.

Finally there was more movement and then a knock on

the bedroom door. The door opened, and Pavlak's voice said in German: "Put on your coat. We're getting out of here."

Borning waited what seemed another eternity before Pavlak ordered him to turn around. A young woman stood beside Pavlak—short black hair, as the cleaning lady had said. Rather attractive. She looked nervous and scared. She wore a long coat and carried a handbag. Pavlak was now wearing a long, rather ragged overcoat. The sleeves were three inches too short for him. Borning caught a glimpse of the Turkish woman peeking from the bedroom.

"If you're not lying to me," Pavlak said, pointing the pistol at Borning's nose again, "then we're all going to take a pleasant little drive, after which I'll bid you a cheery good morning and let you go. If you *are* lying, then some people will probably get hurt. And you'll be the first one. Understand?"

Borning nodded.

"One more thing," Pavlak added. "I'm holding you personally responsible for the safety of my Turkish friends here. They're not involved in this in any way. If anything happens to them, I swear I'll kill you if it takes me thirty years to find you again."

Borning let out a slow breath. "*We* certainly won't harm them. I'm telling you, Dr. Pavlak, we're the good guys."

"Maybe."

The pistol sights never wavered from Borning's chest as Pavlak phoned for a taxi. A few minutes later, the three of them were waiting just inside the front door of the building. The gun was now in the pocket of Pavlak's overcoat but still pointed at Borning's back. When a horn sounded outside, Borning opened the door and walked out with Pavlak at his shoulder. The woman trailed close behind. Borning's overcoat flapped open, and he shoved his hands into his trouser pockets.

In the van across the street, a man muttered, "What the hell's going on?"

Fifty meters away in the corner *Konditerei*, another man held his third cup of coffee halfway to his lips and stared.

"Beats me," answered the second man in the van. "That's the back-off signal."

"Yeah, for the others, but that's the target with him—the guy we're supposed to tail. Now what do we do? Call in the team or not?"

"We back off. Back off means back off."

"But Frank told us to stick to this character after he left. Frank's leaving now."

"Right—and the character is leaving with him, and he's telling us to back off."

The first man frowned and squinted harder into the lens that made a rusty hole a quarter-inch wide look like a picture window. "Okay," he said frowning. "But I don't like this. I don't like this at all."

In the taxi, Frank Borning was thinking along the same lines. This scenario had not been foreseen. What was going to happen now? He was convinced Pavlak was a dangerous man, but he was not a psychopath. And the woman was with him. She was scared, and she looked at Borning with something like sympathy in her eyes. His instincts said Pavlak would let him go—if nothing happened to rouse his suspicions. Would the men in the van call in the chase team? Two cars were standing by for them on a round-the-clock watch. Borning's men were good, but Pavlak was no fool. If there was a tail, he would probably spot it. Borning prayed that his men would honor the back-off signal.

The taxi pulled away from the curb, made a left at the next block, and sped away. As it did so, a blue Mercedes pulled from an alley across the street from the apartment house, then made the same left turn.

Meanwhile, Borning was sandwiched in the middle of the back seat, with the woman on his right and Pavlak on his left. The barrel of the pistol gouged his ribs through Pavlak's coat. They had driven two blocks when Pavlak spoke.

"Get out your makeup kit."

The woman fished in her purse and extracted a small bag made of clear plastic. She held it and waited.

"The mirror. Give me the mirror."

With the mirror cradled in his left hand, Pavlak discreetly monitored the traffic behind them. He ordered another left turn, then a right. Then right again. Two more streets, then another right.

"You're making a circle," the driver protested. "Why don't you just tell me where you want to go and let me get you there?" He was a slender young man with a three-day beard and bloodshot eyes.

"We're sight-seeing," Pavlak snapped in a tone which did not invite further comment. The driver clamped his jaw shut and drove on.

After several more erratic turns, Pavlak ordered the taxi into Bismarkstrasse, and they headed toward the outskirts of the city.

A quarter of an hour had passed. Borning was getting nervous. Pavlak looked sullen and angry. Had Borning's men set the tail after all?

As they approached Theodor Heuss Platz, Pavlak drew a five-thousand-mark note from his pocket and held it high enough for the driver to see in his mirror.

"This is yours, cabby, if you do exactly what I tell you and do it fast."

The driver's mouth fell open. "You got it."

"There's a blue Mercedes two cars back. He's following us. There may be another car as well, waiting to take over—maybe more. Can you lose them all?"

The driver studied his mirror, then grinned. "No problem, *Chef.*"

They were almost beneath the next traffic light when it turned yellow. The cabby slammed on his brakes and skidded to a halt, forcing the cars behind him to do the same. Then, the instant the light turned red, he wrenched the wheel to the left, gunned the engine, and squealed into a U-turn just as the crossing traffic started to move. Borning looked to his left and caught a glimpse of a thin man sitting at the wheel of a blue Mercedes, staring in astonishment as the taxi flashed past him, now moving in the opposite direction.

Borning swallowed hard. It was not one of his, so who the hell could it be? Or was Pavlak imagining things? And even if the blue Mercedes was tailing them, would Pavlak believe him when he insisted it was not a company tail?

The cab driver roared the wrong way down one-way streets and sped through traffic lights, leaving angry shouts and shaking fists at every screaming turn. After ten minutes of terrifying recklessness, the taxi slowed.

"That should do it," the driver grinned.

Pavlak nodded. "Take us to the nearest hardware store."

A few minutes later, the car pulled up to a curb, and the passengers climbed out. Pavlak handed the driver the five-thousand-mark note through the window and threw in another hundred. For the fare and tip, Borning supposed. The delighted driver flipped on his "Occupied" light and roared away. Borning turned to Pavlak.

"It wasn't one of mine. I swear I never saw the guy in that Mercedes before."

"Shut up," Pavlak snapped. He handed the woman a DM 100 note and nodded toward the hardware store.

"Buy a piece of nylon cord," Pavlak instructed. "The shortest one they have." She hesitated, or so it seemed to Borning, then entered the store. He and Pavlak strolled down the street to the corner, then back again. The hard steel of the pistol raked Borning's ribs from time to time as a reminder. The woman appeared just as they approached the hardware store again.

"What are you going to do?" she whispered anxiously, handing Pavlak a small plastic sack.

"Give him some time to repent his sins. Let's go." He prodded Borning's ribs with the gun barrel again.

Half a block down the street hung a wooden sign that read, in chipped and peeling letters, *Zur goldenen Krone.* Pavlak nudged Borning in the direction of the sign, then through the door of the pub. Only a handful of patrons sat hunched over foaming glasses of beer. From their skin color and hair, Borning guessed them to be Arabs—Moroccans, most likely. The patrons eyed the threesome coolly as they entered the room, especially the woman, whose color was rich enough to be Mediterranean as well.

Pavlak shoved Borning into a booth and sat down beside him. The woman slid into the opposite seat. Pavlak ordered three beers, then stood up again when the waitress left.

"I have to go to the can," he said, looking into Borning's face. "Wouldn't you like to join me?"

"Not really," Borning said, trying to smile.

Pavlak leaned over him, and Borning could see the outline of the gun barrel pointed straight at his face.

"Reconsider," Pavlak said icily.

The toilet was tiny and stank. There was no urinal, just a filthy commode, splattered and stained with urine. Pavlak locked the door behind them.

"Turn around."

With the nylon cord, he tied Borning's wrists together behind his back, jerking the knot until Borning winced. Next, he shoved him onto the toilet seat, looped the remaining cord around both of Borning's feet, and secured it to the base of the bowl. He fed it through the rope on Borning's hands, then looped it around the metal pipe leading to the toilet. When he jerked the end tight, Borning could barely move.

"How are your sinuses?" Pavlak asked.

"Fine. Why?"

"Good. Then you won't suffocate."

Pavlak pulled the CIA man's handkerchief from his pocket, and wadded it into his mouth. With a pocket knife, he cut off a length of the leftover cord, and forced it into Borning's mouth as well, then pulled it tight at the back of his head. Borning's tongue was immobilized in the back of his throat.

"I'm very disappointed in you, Mr. Borning," Pavlak said, straightening. "I wanted to believe you about that Mercedes—I really did. The problem, you see, is that you bastards are the only ones who knew where I was. That's how I know he was your man. Now listen carefully. I'm going outside to have a leisurely beer and decide what to do next. If I hear one peep out of you in the meantime, I will come back and put a bullet into your head." He bent down until his nose was two inches from Borning's. "Somehow or other, you're mixed up in the murder of my little girl. I would be more than happy to blow your brains out. Think about that."

Pavlak unlocked the door, opened it a crack, and peered out. Then he pressed the button back into the locked position, eased himself out, and let the door fall shut behind him.

19

By five o'clock that same afternoon, Frank Borning slumped, exhausted, on a commercial flight from Berlin to Munich. He had spent an hour, bound and gagged in the stinking toilet, before an irate customer prevailed upon the bar's owner to unlock the door. Borning tried to pass the whole thing off as a practical joke, and the proprietor, who had his own reasons for not wanting to call his establishment to the attention of the police, finally waved him angrily out the door.

When Borning reported to Langley, Christopher Hopkins was astonished at the BND identification Pavlak had produced, and horrified that Pavlak had slipped away again. He instructed Borning to stand by and hung up. Forty minutes later, a coded telex arrived in Berlin, ordering Frank Borning to make contact with Krueger immediately. The message carried an authorization code belonging to the director of Central Intelligence.

An American liaison officer met Borning at the Munich airport and drove him to BND headquarters in Pullach, a few kilometers outside the city. Darkness had long since fallen when Borning entered the spartan office of the deputy director in charge of East German Affairs, Gerhart Krueger.

When East Germany ceased to exist in October of 1990, the entire Division of East German Affairs became obsolete, along with Krueger's job. He didn't mind. In fact the timing was perfect. He had planned to retire anyway, and the momentous events in Germany gave him the perfect excuse. Now he was busy mopping up the loose ends of an effort that had ended successfully after forty years of often deadly espionage, most of it within his own country. His *other* own country. His division had been a quiet but efficient part of a quiet and efficient Service. Let the Americans and the British get all the attention in the espionage game, Krueger maintained. Publicity does not mean a better operation. Often, in fact, it indicates the opposite.

Gerhart Krueger had matured quickly as a teenage soldier in the dying days of the Third Reich, then made his mark as an ambitious intelligence agent in the BND. He was quickly promoted to head of the *Abteilung für Industrieinformation.* When he took it over, the department was responsible for keeping track of the development of East German industry, particularly its military capabilities. Krueger expanded the department's responsibility to include information on western technology being smuggled into East Germany, and it was in that capacity that he personally recruited and ran the East German double agent who sat at the center of the operation the Americans had code-named "Fool's Gold."

It was through Fool's Gold that Krueger had first come into contact with the CIA's Bonn Head of Station, Frank Borning. They had known each other for many years now, and though neither particularly liked the other—Borning found the German arrogant, and Krueger considered Borning unpolished—they respected each other's professionalism and managed to get along.

"Klaus Joachim Lederer," were the first words from Borning's mouth as he grasped Krueger's hand for the obligatory German handshake. Borning held the grip overlong as he uttered the name.

"Klaus Joachim Lederer," Krueger mused cautiously, dislodging his fingers. "What about him?"

"Is he one of yours?"

"Hmm. Possibly. The name sounds familiar. Has he done something to irritate our gallant American friends?"

A leather wallet landed with a plop on the desk. "Explain that to me, please."

Krueger turned the wallet in his hand. "Ah, yes. Now I remember. A request for re-issue of his identification came across my desk a day or so ago. That's where I saw the name. He got mugged somewhere—Berlin, I think it was—and his wallet was stolen. But *mein Gott* Frank, where on earth did you get this?"

"From an American citizen who claims this man was following him. I'd like to know why."

Krueger met his gaze. "Wait a minute. Let me get this straight. An American ambushes one of our agents, beats him, steals his wallet, then tells the CIA that our man was *following* him? Did I hear that correctly?"

"I'm just repeating what he told me. What's going on, Gerhart?"

Krueger frowned. "This is confusing, to put it mildly. Let me ask a few questions, Frank, if you don't mind. Who is this gentleman? And why did he come to *you*?"

"He's a man whose wife and daughter were murdered last week in the United States. And he didn't come to me. I went to him."

"And why, pray tell, did you do that?"

"His name is Pavlak. Ring a bell?"

"Not Gustaf!"

"His son John."

Krueger's frown deepened and he leaned forward in his chair. "I believe, Frank, that you should tell me the whole story behind this."

Borning obliged, giving Krueger all the background information he had—about the murders, the FBI investigation, Judith Pavlak's phone calls to CIA headquarters, Pavlak's flight to Germany, and his own conversation with him in Berlin. As instructed by Langley, he omitted some embarrassing details of that meeting, as well as the detective work that was necessary to find Pavlak in the first place.

When he had finished, Krueger leaned his elbows on his desk top, placed the tips of his fingers together, and rolled his eyes to the ceiling. "Something I don't quite understand. How is it that our police are asked by your FBI to locate Mr. Pavlak, while it appears that the CIA was in touch with him all along? Or did I misunderstand something?"

"We were just lucky," Borning said lightly. "The FBI gave us some possible contacts in Berlin—friends of his and his wife's. He turned up at one of them."

"Ah, I see. Fortunate indeed. But . . . ," he frowned again, "why didn't the FBI give the German police that same information? Or perhaps they did, and our men in green were too slow to react. You 'beat them to the punch,' as you Americans say?"

Borning shrugged again. "I'm not privy to what the FBI told your police. You'll have to ask them. Presumably somebody screwed up somewhere along the line—probably the Fibbies. You know how it is. The information they gave us got lost in the bureaucratic pipeline somewhere—never got to your men, most likely."

Krueger smiled unpleasantly. "Yes, most likely that was it. And so, where is Dr. Pavlak now?"

"We're not sure. He's taken off again. We made no effort to detain him, of course. It wasn't our business."

"Of course. So tell me, Frank, if your FBI was looking for him—had the German police helping them, in fact—and you found him for them, why didn't you just call our police and let them hold him—or at least tell the FBI where he was?"

Krueger was enjoying the game, and Borning was beginning to realize it.

"Because, Gerhart," Borning replied irritably, "we told the FBI we would stay out of it. Our concern here is not the murders but the security of a joint operation—*your* operation, you'll recall. We cooperate with the FBI whenever possible, but to be honest with you, we have no interest in spreading the details of Fool's Gold around any more than we have to. And you would have done the same thing. Don't try to tell me you wouldn't."

Krueger's palms flipped outward in a gesture of wounded innocence. "Certainly. I understand. For heaven's sake, Frank, we've been around a long time, you and I. We know the ropes now, don't we? Well . . . I know nothing about this identification card other than what I've told you. And it appears that Mr. Pavlak didn't shed much light on it either. I'll have a talk with our Herr . . ." He flipped the wallet over again to expose the identification ". . . Herr Lederer. It's a bizarre coincidence, I must say. Maybe with Lederer's help we can get to the bottom of this. Where can I contact you?"

"I'll be at Stuart's," Borning replied, naming the liaison

officer who had driven him from the airport. He stood and extended his hand. Krueger rose to his feet, leaned across the desk, and met Borning's hand with a firm grip. The two men looked straight at one another, their hands locked in what might have been either friendship or combat.

"And one last thing, Krueger," Borning said, purposely using only his colleague's last name. "I know damned well something's going on here, and that you know more about it than you're telling me. When you're ready to come clean, give me a call."

Borning released the hand brusquely and spun on his heel. He had almost reached the door when Krueger spoke.

"Borning."

Borning took his time turning. The smug smile was gone from Krueger's face.

"Neither of us wants Fool's Gold compromised, right?" Krueger offered. "Think it over and perhaps it will occur to you that we should work together to stop Pavlak before this goes any further. As long as he's on the loose, we're at risk— your service and mine. It wouldn't be any easier to explain to the German public than to the American. And as for 'coming clean' as you Americans so picturesquely put it, I'll be happy to do so whenever *you* do. We Germans are not idiots, after all. I thought you had learned that by now."

Several retorts sprang to Borning's mind, but he rejected all of them. "I'll be waiting for your call, Gerhart," he said flatly, and walked out.

As the door fell shut, Krueger snatched up his phone.

"He's gone. Get in here *now!*"

A few seconds later a stocky blond man entered the office through a side door. The entire right side of his face was a mottled bluish-green color. The right eye was swollen shut.

"Blöder Hund!" Krueger exploded. "Here's your goddam-ned wallet." He tossed it onto the desktop. "Pavlak gave it to the Americans."

"So it *was* Pavlak," Lederer answered sullenly, doing his best to ignore Krueger's insult.

"Of course it was Pavlak, you idiot! I told you it had to be." Krueger shook his head in disgust. "The woman was supposed to lead you to him, and she did. So how is it a civilian—an American *Germanist*—saw two trained agents be-fore they saw him? And this," he snapped, gesturing at the wallet on his desk. "What stupidity is this? You're not sup-posed to carry that ID without specific authorization. Why on earth did you have it on you?"

Lederer's jaw was working sullenly. "I told you. The police were looking for him. There was always the chance that they would stumble onto us—start asking questions. The ID would have shut them up before they went too far. And what danger was there. . . ."

"What danger? Evidently there was the danger that you would be outsmarted, knocked senseless, and discovered. Now even the CIA knows we were looking for Pavlak. Born-ing is very curious. What the hell am I supposed to tell him?"

Lederer stared at the linoleum and made no response. Krueger paced and tore at a fingernail with his teeth.

"All right, listen," he said at last. "The only good news is that they've lost him too. It's time to forget about the doc-ument. Pavlak doesn't have it, or he wouldn't be here. But we have to find him just the same, before the Americans do. He's too dangerous to leave alive any longer."

"And the woman?"

"By now she knows everything he knows." Krueger picked up the wallet and slammed it into Lederer's chest. "Kill her too."

20

As Gerhart Krueger fumed in Bavaria, Pavlak and Karin were playing cards in a run-down hotel in the Scheunenviertel, a district in what had been, until recently, East Berlin. Until Mehmet secured Pavlak's new passport, Pavlak was effectively immobilized. After abandoning Borning in the toilet, he and Karin took the subway to Berlin's seedier side, home to many of the city's legion of prostitutes and pimps. They bought a bag full of food and a deck of cards, then went looking for a hotel. The second desk clerk they tried, a bald man in a sweater with a hole in the sleeve, was undisturbed by their lack of luggage, and instantly accepted a fifty-mark note in lieu of an ID. They registered as Herr und Frau Helmut Müller and settled in to wait.

The next two days passed in excruciating boredom. Pavlak did pushups and situps and ran in place. Karin read a novel by Heinrich Böll and, when Pavlak was in the shower, prayed, and meditated. At first she had been quiet and, Pavlak thought, distant. He had watched her nervously from the corner of his eye for the first few hours in their new location. Finally he could stand it no longer.

"Karin," he ventured, "I'm sorry about the rough stuff with that CIA man. And I'm sorry I was so . . ."

"It's not that," she interrupted. "It's not you. It's me. You did what you had to do. And you were right. You were right all along. We don't know who the enemy is, so we have to assume everyone is the enemy. And that's the problem for me now. That's what I can't accept. I don't *like* being suspicious of everybody. I don't like this feeling of . . . of . . ."

"Fear?" Pavlak offered.

She seemed to deflate in front of him. "That's a big part of it. But there's more. Anger, confusion . . . grief. I don't know. All of it together." She looked into his eyes. "I had just found something. Something so wonderful, so peaceful, so beautiful. Then this happened. And now. . . ." Her face crumpled, and she buried it in her hands.

She was sitting with her back against the wooden headboard, her legs extended and crossed on the bed in front of her. Pavlak sat down on the edge of the bed and put his arms around her quaking shoulders. Her head fell against his chest. "Look . . ." he began, then stopped, at a loss. "Oh hell," he sighed, stroking her hair. "I'm the last person to help you with a spiritual problem."

She laughed between her tears. "I know. But thanks for trying."

Pavlak kissed her hair, then instantly reproached himself and tucked her head under his chin instead. They rocked together gently until Karin's crying was finished. When she pulled back and smiled up at him, the old serenity had returned to her eyes, even though they were red and swollen. "That helped."

Pavlak released her and stood.

"John . . ."

He waited.

"How do you do it?"

"Do what?"

"Handle this. All alone. Whenever I think about them—about Gitti and Turgat and Judith and your daughter—the pain paralyzes me. I can turn to God for help. But you . . . ?"

Pavlak sat slowly on the bed again and stared at the floor. "Tasha," he said at last, "was my whole world. When I look back, I realize my life didn't start until she came into it. It's as if everything before her was just a dull dream. She gave me something—someone—to live for." He drew a breath and swallowed. "When she died, my life ended. And the nightmare started up again. The only thing that kept me going before, was Tasha. And it still is. I owe her one last service. And as long as I'm breathing, *that's* why." He raised his head and looked at her. "Do you understand?"

Karin nodded slowly, never taking her eyes from his face.

"Well," Pavlak said as lightly as he could. He slapped his thigh and cleared his throat. "It's late. We'd better get some sleep. You take the bed."

"Where are you going to sleep?"

"The floor. Don't worry. I'll be fine. I can sleep anywhere."

"But it's a double bed," Karin protested. "There's plenty of room for both of us."

Pavlak shifted from one foot to the other and shook his head. "Thanks," he smiled, "but I wouldn't trust myself."

Karin held his gaze as her expression turned slowly grave.

"I'm sorry," Pavlak said quickly. "I didn't mean. . . ."

"I'm not upset," Karin interrupted without changing her expression. "I'm flattered. And that's another problem." She stood, retrieved her handbag from the dresser and walked into the bathroom, closing the door quietly behind her.

The only other break in the monotonous routine occurred during the second night. Karin was wakened by a guttural groan, repeated several times. As the sleep cleared from her brain, she leaned over the side of the bed and touched Pavlak's shoulder. It was damp. Pavlak started violently, sat up, then lay back onto the floor without a word. A minute later Karin heard the sound of quiet weeping. She lowered herself from the bed to the floor beside him, eased her head onto his shoulder, and rested her arm across his chest. Suddenly, unbidden, a scene from her childhood sprang up before her. She was walking along a bicycle path beside the *Mittellandkanal*, holding her sister's hand. Brigitte's hand. A hand she would never touch again. In an instant, tears came to her eyes, and the two of them wept together. At last Pavlak gently nudged her away, and Karin climbed back into the bed. Neither of them had uttered a word.

The following evening Pavlak pulled on Mehmet's old overcoat and left the hotel at eight o'clock. He was back just after midnight, shivering and soaked, without the coat, but waving a brand new German passport wrapped in a plastic bag. A personal identity document in the name of Udo Jürgen Brandauer accompanied it.

When Pavlak picked up the documents, Mehmet assured him that he had followed Pavlak's hastily scribbled instructions to the letter. Mehmet and his wife were indeed followed as they left the apartment to get Pavlak's documents. When Mehmet eased out of his parking place in front of the apartment house, a Turkish friend pulled in directly behind him from a side street. Ten minutes later, the friend followed as Mehmet turned right into a narrow, one-way street, barely more than an alley. But then Mehmet's friend's car stalled in the middle of the block, and it took him ten minutes to get it started while a tall, slender man in a black

Volvo cursed and waved frantically behind him.

Mehmet's friend did not notice a second car, this one a Ford Escort, that approached the entrance to the alley and, seeing it blocked, rolled quietly away. The driver swore roundly in American slang and reached for a microphone suspended beneath the dash.

The forged documents had been ready as promised. The deal was completed, and Mehmet and his wife arrived at the appointed meeting place with Pavlak only twenty minutes late. Pavlak returned the overcoat over Mehmet's objections, paid for the documents, thanked them, and walked back into the rain.

Then, continuing Pavlak's instructions, Mehmet and his wife drove on to Frankfurt, where they abandoned the Peugeot and boarded a flight for Ankara. Their illegal sojourn in Germany was over. It was not until the plane was in the air that Mehmet discovered the ten thousand American dollars Pavlak had pinned inside the pocket of the overcoat.

As the Asuls stepped onto the tarmac in Ankara, Pavlak and Karin were just approaching Leipzig on the A-3 in a secondhand BMW that Pavlak had purchased with cash and registered in the name of the fictitious Udo Brandauer. Mehmet's story about the black Volvo that had tried to follow him to their rendezvous bothered Pavlak. Was it the same black Volvo that Lederer had sat in while watching Pavlak's hotel entrance five days earlier? If so, how did the BND find Mehmet—unless Borning told them, in which case he was lying when he said he knew nothing about the BND's involvement. But on that one point, at least, Pavlak had believed him. The astonishment in Borning's eyes when he saw Lederer's ID would have been hard to fake. Of course Borning was a career spook. Deception was his stock-in-trade.

On the other hand, the story about Fool's Gold was

plausible enough, and Pavlak had no difficulty believing that his father had participated. Gustaf Pavlak had never hesitated to take a risk if the potential gain was great enough. The trouble with Borning's story was that it did not explain the bomb that had torn his wife and daughter away, or the search of his house, or Brigitte's and Turgat's murders, or the BND man whom Pavlak had knocked senseless on a street in Berlin—or the black Volvo that followed Mehmet. It did, at least potentially, explain what had caught Brigitte's attention in Siegfried Schliemann's file. Presumably the missing document had something to do with his father and Fool's Gold. Pavlak remembered Brigitte's notation "Pavlak!" on her note to herself about the Schliemann file. Had her eye caught a reference to Gustaf Pavlak, or perhaps to Pavlak Equipment, Inc.? If so, then the missing pages may have indicated that Gustaf Pavlak had smuggled military technology into East Germany—technology of low value if Borning were to be believed. Brigitte, of course, would have had no way to know that the "smuggle" was a legitimate CIA operation, which would explain why she might take the risk of stealing the document and sending it to Judith. Pavlak knew Brigitte well enough to know that she hated spies of all sorts and would want to see Gustaf Pavlak exposed, especially since her friend Judith hated him so intensely and had spent so many hours convincing her what a villain her father-in-law was.

But the big question remained as obscure as ever. Pavlak could understand why the CIA and the BND were anxious to keep details of Fool's Gold out of the hands of news media in which no shred of civic responsibility remained. But would they kill four people—one man, two women, and a child—to avoid it? Surely the risk involved in those murders was greater than the danger of exposure. And if the CIA had killed the others, then they would have killed Pavlak at Mehmet's apartment, rather than send an unarmed man to negotiate. And yet, someone had the motivation to kill. Who was it? And what was that motivation? Perhaps the answer was tucked away somewhere in the mind of a traitorous ex-Stasi agent named Peter Schliemann.

With a phone call to a travel agent, Pavlak learned that the only ferry from Italy to Heraklion left from Bari on the Adriatic Coast. The ship sailed three times a month. Pavlak calculated that there was enough time to make the next sailing, even if he took care of some business along the way. The shortest route to Bari lay almost due south, through Austria and the Brenner Pass, but Pavlak headed southwest instead, toward Switzerland. The fifty thousand dollars he had brought with him was nearly exhausted. He had to replenish his coffers.

It was nearly midnight before he and Karin found another discreet hotel desk clerk, this one in the red-light district of Stuttgart. Two bored prostitutes held stations beside the door and eyed Karin coolly as she and Pavlak entered the hotel. With Pavlak's forged identity papers, they could have stayed in a comfortable hotel, but Pavlak explained that it was safest to leave no record of their route in case the German police—or someone else—managed to ferret out the name on his forged papers. Besides, this room was to be Karin's hideaway until Pavlak returned from Crete. Better to have no record of any kind in any computer, anywhere.

"*Personalausweis,*" the young woman behind the counter demanded.

Pavlak held out a folded hundred mark note. "I don't have it with me. Can you take this instead?" The clerk hesitated less than a second before pulling the note from Pavlak's fingers and tucking it into her brassiere. She handed them a key and turned back to her tabloid newspaper.

The room was dilapidated, and the view consisted of a brick wall across an alley six feet wide. When Pavlak opened the window, a faint odor of urine rose from the alley below.

Pavlak watched Karin carefully as she unpacked the few items he had bought for her before they left Berlin. She had been quiet and withdrawn all day. At last they took seats on opposite sides of the sagging mattress. Pavlak spoke cautiously. He promised to return from Crete in no more than a week. If he was not back by then, she was to move to a new hiding place.

Karin's face was drawn. She nodded silently.

Pavlak pressed on, reviewing plans for locating her again in case they got separated. They rehearsed every foreseeable scenario for another two hours until both were sure they understood every contingency. Karin kept a small leather-bound address book in her purse. She brought it out, and the two of them searched it for alternative hideouts in case anything went wrong. As far as possible, he was leaving nothing to chance, especially where Karin's safety was concerned. She seemed to be crumbling under the strain. The expression on her face was drained and preoccupied, and she avoided his eyes.

That night Pavlak again lay on the floor to sleep. He was still awake half an hour later when Karin quietly dropped onto the floor beside him. He pushed her gently back toward the bed, but this time, she clung firmly to his arm with both hands.

"Don't kill him," she whispered urgently. "Promise me you won't kill him."

The wooden floor pressed into Pavlak's back. He could feel desperation in Karin's fingers where they gripped his bicep. Her knee lay against his thigh. She supported her upper body on one elbow, and the dark shadow that was her face hovered over him. He wished that he could see her expression, but the tattered curtain across the window held at bay even the meager glow from the alley.

"I don't know that he's even involved," he answered. "I'm just looking for information."

"You know he's involved in some way. He has to be."

Pavlak moved his head in a nod, a nod he immediately realized she could not see. "It seems likely, yes. But even if he's part of the circumstances, that doesn't mean he had anything to do with the killings."

The grip on his arm tightened, and Karin's face dropped closer to his. He felt her breath wash softly over his cheek. Strange position for a would-be nun, he thought, but her voice scattered the thought as quickly as it materialized.

"But if he is involved in the murders," she whispered, "what are you going to do?"

"I don't know," Pavlak answered honestly.

She was silent for a moment. The fingertips gripping his arm relaxed. When she spoke again, it was in a different tone, less urgent, but more intimate. "What do you want, John Pavlak? What are you trying to accomplish?" Then she added in a whisper he barely heard. "Have you come here to die?"

Somewhere in the distance a drunken, dissonant chorus of *Mein Hut, der hat drei Ecken* wafted within earshot, then faded again as the revelers passed the entrance to the alley. Pavlak was startled by her question even though he realized that the same question had been tugging at some corner of his own mind, unacknowledged, for days.

"Why do you ask?" he countered, buying time.

"I'm not sure. Something I witnessed about you when that CIA agent came. Something desperate. Something . . . *careless.*"

"I thought I was extremely careful, under the circumstances."

"That's not what I mean." She was silent a moment, then explained. "It was in your eyes. You had no fear. Rage, yes. But no fear. That's what I mean by careless. Or maybe contemptuous is a better word. Contempt for life. Yours. His. Maybe even mine."

Pavlak said nothing.

"What do you want, John? Please tell me. What do you *really* want?"

"My little girl back," Pavlak said quickly, surprising himself. He moved his leg away from her knee, then pulled his arm free and sat up, facing the feeble yellow glow from the window. Karin still lay on the floor behind him. Somewhere in the distance a car horn blared angrily.

"But you know you can't have that," she responded. "It's something else you're after now. If you tell me what it is— if you even *know* what it is—I'll help you if I can."

A harsh light suddenly leapt through the crack beneath their door, making the shabby furniture visible again. The wooden boards in the hallway creaked as footsteps approached. There were two voices, speaking low, a man's and a woman's. The woman gave a short laugh as the steps passed their door, then they heard the sound of a key sliding into the lock next door. The door closed, then quiet settled again, except for a low mumble of voices through the thin wall. After a minute, the timer on the corridor light expired, and darkness dropped over them again.

"You know," Pavlak answered slowly, ignoring her question, "I envy you."

"Envy me?"

"Yes. I envy . . ." He took a deep breath. "Your faith."

There was a soft series of thumps next door, then silence.

"There's no need to envy faith. Anyone who wants it can have it."

"I wish that were true," Pavlak answered, "but it's not. I know. I've tried." He twisted around toward her. "Let's get some sleep."

Karin's hands found his face, and her soft palms warmed his cheeks. "Maybe I can help you. I don't know how, but maybe I can if you'll let me."

Pavlak gently took hold of her wrists. He was going to push her away, but something stopped him. The touch of her hands was like a balm, cooling and soothing his burning spirit. He tightened his grip. His mind told him to pull her hands from his face. But something else inside him wanted desperately to pull Karin toward him instead, wrap his arms around her, fall into her.

"No!" His own cry startled him. "I'm sorry, Karin. I can't." He tugged her hands from his face and laid them in her lap.

Karin said nothing, but Pavlak could feel her hurt, almost palpable in the dark, stale air that smelled of mildew and old urine. After a moment she climbed back into the bed.

"Good night then," she whispered in a voice tight with tears.

Pavlak lay back on the floor and stared into the darkness. After ten minutes Karin's breathing grew slow and heavy, but Pavlak could not sleep. Next door the squeak of a bed spring penetrated the silence. It was followed by another, then another, slowly at first, then faster until the squeaks fell into a steady rhythm. A woman's moans began to filter through the thin wall. The moans swelled and grew and finally broke in a high, thin wail that might have been either bliss or agony. It was the loneliest sound he had ever heard.

The next morning's good-bye was strained. Pavlak gave her most of his remaining money, then stood in awkward silence, feeling vaguely miserable. It occurred to him that she might have been back in Holzhausen now, never knowing anything was wrong. The mystery document was in the United States if it was anywhere at all, which meant it was him they had wanted all along, not her. It was his arrival that had thrown her life into turmoil and peril. Now she looked terribly small standing beside the bed in the shabby little room that would be her prison until he returned. "You've got the addresses?" he asked needlessly. "You know where to go if I don't get back on time?" She nodded. On impulse he kissed the top of her head, then turned and left. As he closed the door behind him, he resolved to finish his business on Crete as quickly as possible.

From Stuttgart he took the A-8 to Karlsruhe, then headed back south on the A-5 to Basel. In two hours, he was at the border. He held his breath while a border official on the German side punched his passport number into a hand-held computer terminal that fed the data via radio waves to a larger terminal in an office nearby. It took only seconds for the terminal to beep once. Number valid and not flagged. Pavlak hid the rush of breath that escaped his lungs. Mehmet's Turkish counterfeiters knew their business. Twenty meters away, a Swiss official threw only a cursory glance at the passport and waved him through.

In Basel, Pavlak paid a brief visit to the *Förster Bank* and opened an account, then made a transatlantic phone call to the home of Hoke Morgan and barked out his social security number with the last four digits reversed—the code to execute his letter of instruction. It was 4 A.M. in Lake Elm, but

Hoke Morgan, in a voice thick with sleep, thanked him profusely for the call and was still wishing him well when Pavlak hung up.

Next, Pavlak went shopping. He bought a new overcoat, clothes to replace the ones he had abandoned in Berlin, another small suitcase, and a large attaché case. Then he returned to the *Förster Bank* where he was immediately ushered through a series of locked doors into a small private office. Pavlak made his request, and a bespectacled little man with a hairless head and an utterly expressionless face bowed slightly and vanished. He was gone for ten minutes. When he returned, two bank clerks accompanied him, each carrying a pair of canvas bags with the bank's logo printed on the fabric. In his presence they counted out just over seven hundred thousand Swiss francs—the result of exchanging half a million dollars that the bank had received via wire from Lake Elm National Bank. The two clerks then stacked the bills into Pavlak's new attaché case with facile skill. Their faces wore expressions of professional boredom. For all the interest they showed, they might have been delivering a pizza.

Pavlak walked out the door with a firm grip on the attaché case, drove across town to a branch of the Swiss Federal Commerce and Agricultural Bank, and deposited all but ten thousand francs into a new, numbered account. From it, he would be able to draw funds from virtually any country in the world, simply by signing—not his name, but a number. He changed five hundred francs into Italian lire, and a thousand into Greek drachma, then walked out the door with the cash in his pockets.

On the way back to his car, he passed a young man with long stringy hair and a filthy green jacket, sitting on the sidewalk holding a sign that read, *Ich habe Hunger*. Pavlak handed the astonished beggar the empty, hundred-dollar attaché case and walked on.

From Basel, Pavlak drove south toward Lucerne and the Gotthard Pass. He began the climb through some of the world's most spectacular natural beauty. Soaring granite cliffs rose into the clouds on his left, while picturesque villages dotted a broad green valley on the right. When he reached an altitude of five hundred meters the first flakes of snow began to drift from a gray sky. At one thousand meters he was in a full-scale spring blizzard. He stopped in a small town and had a set of snow chains installed while he consumed a plate of *sauerbraten* at an inn down the street from the service station.

Then the drive grew tedious. Visibility fell to thirty feet. The BMW crawled into the swirling white mass while Pavlak strained his eyes to avoid plunging over a cliff. It was nearly 4 P.M. when he reached the Gotthard tunnel, but luck was with him. A train was just preparing to leave as he drove up. Following the gestures of a man dressed like an arctic explorer, Pavlak pulled the BMW onto the bed of the last car.

Five minutes later steel jolted against steel, and the train began to move. The gray light of the blizzard was quickly chopped off as the train sucked him into the base of the St. Gotthard massif.

A few seconds later, he sat in utter darkness, a darkness so intense he felt he was breathing it, like water. The roar of the rails, reverberating in the narrow granite tube, emulated a profound silence. After a few minutes, he opened his mouth and called "hello," but could not even hear his own voice. Soon he felt suspended in the blackness. Time was suspended. Life itself was suspended. He was reduced to pure mind, drifting in a world without sight or sound. Death, Pavlak thought, must be something like this.

And then he saw Tasha. She stared at him with intense, burning eyes, an ethereal ghost of light in the roaring darkness. His heart slammed. He stared at the apparition floating in front of him, unable to move his eyes away from it and unwilling, afraid it would leave him again. He forced his tongue to move.

"Are you afraid, Tasha?" he whispered soundlessly.

Two cars ahead of him someone lit a cigarette, and the brief, startling flare chased the apparition away. When darkness returned, Pavlak searched it desperately for his child, but it was too late. She was gone. "Am I going crazy?" he wondered aloud. He felt disembodied, invisible, dead. "Yes, I *am* going crazy," he whispered. He felt beneath the seat, and his fingers closed on the cold grip of the pistol. He raised the weapon and rested the barrel against his cheek bone. The cool touch was soothing. It penetrated the numbness and provided a point of reality. Pavlak focused all his attention on the dent in the thin flesh stretched across his skull. The train roared on. The darkness became eternal. Pavlak's body went numb. He could not move. Time stopped.

A screech of brakes pierced the roar, and his body shifted forward. Instantly his limbs came back to life. There was light, gray and feeble, then more, then an intense dot of it growing in the distance. Pavlak hastily replaced the pistol beneath the seat as an excruciating glare burst over him, and he hurtled free from the bowels of the mountain.

21

Exactly forty-one hours after Pavlak's ferry left Bari, the ship's landing bumper made contact with the dock in Heraklion. Except for an improbable two-hour layover on the tiny island of Patmos, the big white ship had ploughed doggedly through the choppy swells of the Mediterranean for the better part of two days and nights.

An hour after the landing, Pavlak signed the name Udo Brandauer in the register at the Commodore Hotel in downtown Heraklion. He was anxious to find Schliemann, but when he did, he wanted all his wits about him. Bad weather had made the trip uncomfortable, despite the soothing appointments of his cabin, and he had enjoyed only brief interludes of fitful sleep. He knew he would not be capable of thinking clearly until he got some rest. He found his room, locked the door behind him, then fell into a clean bed and slept for ten hours.

The next morning, refreshed and alert, he climbed into the BMW and took the northern coastal road west out of Heraklion. Endless olive groves climbed the hills on his left, while the magnificent Mediterranean stretched to the horizon on his right. Pavlak remembered his disappointment as a child on his first trip to the seashore. The "deep blue sea" was not blue at all, at least not on the North Carolina coast. It was murky green. Yet here on Crete the old rhymes rang true, for the Mediterranean on this early April morning was painfully, achingly blue. He pulled onto a rocky overlook and gazed out to the sea, with the snowcapped peaks of the Leuka Ore at his back. Pavlak turned slowly, 360 degrees, and drank in the sights and sounds and smells of Crete. The light was different in this part of the world. Brighter. *Whiter.* The colors were few, but all were cool and soothing. Against the blue of the sea, the land itself was white or gray, and the olive trees rippled in waves of silver as the breeze swept across their branches. To his left, out of sight beneath the horizon, lay the Peloponnesus. A little further to the right, on the eastern shore of the Aegean, was the coast of Turkey and the ruins of Troy. Was the sea that surged and soughed at his feet really "wine dark?" He found the metaphor strained. Even Homer had his foibles.

It was nearly noon when Pavlak reached the coastal city of Rethymnon. Even though it lacks a natural harbor, Rethymnon has existed since classical times and possibly before. The Venetians dug a harbor there in the Middle Ages, but maintaining it through the centuries proved impossible. By the twentieth century the city had slipped into a tenacious poverty that spared it the ugly modernization that plagued other Greek cities.

From a distance, Pavlak had seen the city's two spindly minarets—remnants of the Turkish occupation—struggling pitifully into the air above the shabby shops. As he drove through the narrow streets, made even darker by the jutting wooden balconies—another reminder of the Turkish empire—an aura of Medievalism descended. Here indeed, was a land that time had forgotten.

He swallowed a lunch of pork gyros in a restaurant in the old town, then asked the waitress for directions to the address Siegfried Schliemann had given him. She shrugged her shoulders and motioned for him to wait. A few minutes later, an emaciated old man wearing a dirty white apron emerged from the kitchen, wiped his hands on the apron, and scrawled a crude map on Pavlak's paper napkin. The old man explained the map with a jabber of incomprehensible Greek, accompanied by energetic, though equally incomprehensible gestures. Pavlak listened politely, thanked him, and left.

Following the map as best he could, Pavlak drove out of the town and guided the BMW up a steep, narrow road through the olive groves in the hills above Rethymnon. Though paved, the road was poorly maintained. Once, he waited while a middle-aged Greek with brown, leathered skin, coaxed a flock of thirty sheep across the road. Despite the black rags he wore and the rustic burlap knapsack slung over his shoulder, the man radiated a certain vigor. His step was sure, and his movements had the natural grace of one accustomed to outdoor life.

Something in Pavlak longed for the pastoral simplicity of such a life. But in the same instant, he knew it would never be. He, Pavlak, was one of the lucky ones. Born in the United States of America, educated, privileged, son of an immigrant who had lived the American dream. The irony of it all, as he watched the vibrant shepherd tending to his only concern in life, brought a bitter laugh to Pavlak's throat.

The broken asphalt soon gave way to crushed stone. The BMW bounced a few hundred meters further, always climbing, then the road turned a corner and ended abruptly at a massive wrought-iron gate. If he had followed the map correctly, this had to be the entrance to Peter Schliemann's estate. Beyond the gate, still higher up the steep slope, stood a huge house of gleaming white. The architecture was pretentious and grandiose, and the mansion looked out haughtily over the town of Rethymnon and away toward the Cyclades Islands, still invisible below the horizon.

The iron gate in front of him was the only break Pavlak could see in a stone wall that surrounded the house and grounds. The wall was eight feet high, and he could see shards of glass embedded in the masonry along its top. Apparently Peter Schliemann did not welcome visitors. The entire estate was freshly built. In places, mounds of earth still waited to be filled around the foundation of the wall, and more mounds protruded from the mud beyond the iron gate. From all appearances, Schliemann had bought one of Crete's ubiquitous olive groves, cleared a spot in the middle of it and constructed his castle. Treason, Pavlak mused, paid very well indeed. He climbed out of the car and, with the BMW blocking the view from the house, tucked the pistol into his belt and covered it with the tail of his jacket.

An intercom was built into one of the massive stone columns on which the gate hung. Pavlak pushed a black button and waited. After a moment the speaker crackled, and a female voice barked something in Greek.

"My name is Staffelberg," Pavlak answered in German. "I have come to speak to Mr. Peter Schliemann."

The speaker went dead. After several minutes Pavlak was about to push the button again when the speaker crackled, and an abrupt male voice said, *"Ja, bitte?"*

"Herr Schliemann?"

"Was wollen Sie?"

"My name is Staffelberg. Dr. Horst Staffelberg."

"What do you want?" the voice repeated.

"I'm a professor at Göttingen—a professor of German history—writing a book on East-West trade during the seventies. I'm here on vacation and wanted to speak with you a few moments, if I may. Your . . . sister gave me your address. I believe you once headed a trade mission in Frankfurt?"

There was a slight pause. "I'm sorry, I do not give interviews," the voice answered. "I could not help you in any case. Enjoy your vacation." There was a burst of static, and the speaker went dead again.

Pavlak pressed the button and waited. After a minute he pressed it again. After another minute, he began pressing it at five-second intervals until the speaker crackled back to life.

"Perhaps you did not understand me," the same voice said, now crisp with irritation. "I will not speak with you. Go away or I shall call the police."

"What about Fool's Gold?" Pavlak asked quickly. "Could we talk about that?"

There was a long pause. When the voice returned, it was smooth and amicable. "That, of course, is a different matter, Herr Professor . . . Staffelberg did you say? An interesting episode in our history. Yes, of course. I will be happy to speak with you about it. Unfortunately, I am indisposed at the moment. I have guests. Could you come for dinner tomorrow, say at eight? I could then be at your service the entire evening."

"Eight would be fine."

"Until tomorrow, then." The speaker crackled one last time.

Pavlak gazed up the hill toward the house, a hundred meters away. There was only one car parked in front of it—a black Mercedes limousine. There was no garage in sight, although the cinder-block foundations of some sort of outbuilding under construction lay in the mud at right angles to the house.

The twitch of a curtain caught his attention, but he could make out nothing behind it. He spun on his heel, climbed into the BMW, and headed back down the slope. At the first crossing he turned right, into a shepherd's trail, barely wide enough for the BMW, and followed it until it rounded a curve, out of sight of the main road. There he pulled the car under the olive trees and out of sight behind a mound of cut branches. Evidently spring pruning was underway.

Pavlak started climbing the hill on foot, staying beneath the trees. It was further than he had estimated, but at last the high stone wall loomed before him, hiding the house from view. He turned left and trudged along the wall. After fifty meters it made a corner and started climbing. Ten minutes later, the wall cornered again and began traversing back across the slope. Pavlak was now above the house. He turned his back to the wall and climbed higher, hidden from the house by the thick olive branches. When he thought he was high enough, he pulled himself into the sturdiest olive tree he could find and climbed as high as he dared before carefully parting the branches in front of him.

The estate lay spread out below him. There were perhaps five acres within the confines of the wall, with the house near the center. An English garden was being laid out behind the house. Wooden stakes and white twine marked the locations where trimmed shrubs were to be set. Several hundred were already in place. A wheelbarrow and shovels were strewn about, but there were no workmen in sight. As Pavlak studied the grounds, two enormous mastiffs wandered around the corner of the house. One lapped lazily at a water dish near a back door, while the other idly sniffed the air. After a few minutes, they drifted out of sight again.

Pavlak clung to the branches of the olive tree for a quarter of an hour before heading back to Rethymnon. On the way, he had to wait again while the same ragged shepherd urged his reluctant sheep across the asphalt in the opposite direction. When the last sheep straggled across, Pavlak dropped the BMW into gear and rolled forward again. He did not see the shepherd step behind an olive tree, swing the burlap knapsack around to his chest, and withdraw the microphone of a military field radio.

"Coming your way, sport," the shepherd snapped in the mean accents of a Liverpool slum. "Lose him and I'll have your balls for breakfast."

In Rethymnon a sympathetic young woman in the tourist information office gave Pavlak the name of a local doctor who spoke English. She was very sorry he wasn't feeling well and hoped he would recover soon.

At the doctor's office, Pavlak waited impatiently in a room full of whining Greek children and elderly Greek women wrapped in black from throat to ankle.

Crete, Pavlak mused, was a study in contrasts, a tourist mecca for northern Europeans, particularly the British who had played a decisive role in Crete's modern history. English tourists came south to shed their Anglo-Saxon inhibitions and their clothes and stroll nude on the white beaches. The local populace, on the other hand, consisted mainly of poor shepherds and olive growers who lived and thought very much as their ancestors from five centuries past.

When Pavlak and Judith had vacationed on Crete—years before Tasha's birth—he had seen a weathered peasant woman, perhaps in her fifties, riding on a donkey. It was hard to tell her age because the searing sun wrinkles skin prematurely along the Mediterranean. She rode side-

saddled on the donkey's back, swathed in black from head
to toe, a bundle of kindling tied to the donkey's haunches.
Pavlak had followed her stern gaze to where a group of
young men and women, mostly blond and blue-eyed, played
volleyball on the beach below her. They were laughing and
squealing and totally naked—oblivious to the old woman's
silent contempt. Stoic endurance, face to face with the fri-
volity of the decadent North, Pavlak had thought. Crete, no
doubt, would survive at its own timeless pace long after the
arrogant monuments of northern civilizations had crumbled.

On one of the rough benches that were the only furniture
in the doctor's waiting room, two teenage girls with upper-
crust British accents giggled and gossiped beside him. Pavlak
fidgeted and checked his watch. Nearly an hour passed before he was finally led into the presence of a sad-looking
doctor with incredibly dark circles under his eyes. Pavlak,
affecting a British accent, told the man he was suffering
from insomnia and exhaustion. His dear old mum had
passed away two weeks before and not even this trip to the
Mediterranean could ease his grief. Pavlak's hands shook
and tears rose to his eyes. If he could just get some sleep,
he sobbed, he was sure he could make it through.

The Greek doctor treated him to a glance rich with dis-
dain, then wordlessly scrawled a prescription for Triazolam
and waved him away.

At the pharmacy Pavlak asked the sales clerk where he
might find an architect. Following the clerk's instructions,
he located a dingy office two streets from the harbor. The
smell of salt and dead fish was heavy in the air. He spoke
German and switched reluctantly to English when the young
man to whom he was speaking lifted his shoulders in a gesture of non-comprehension. Pavlak explained in labored,

heavily accented English that he was visiting the island from Hamburg. He had stumbled onto a magnificent new house in the hills, and one of the locals had told him it belonged to a countryman, Schildmann, or Schliemann—something like that. He loved Crete so much he was thinking of building a summer home here himself. Were they by any chance the architects of that magnificent structure?

The young man shook his head. No, that would be Giannapoulos, four doors down.

Pavlak counted the doors and knocked. This time an attractive young woman with long shiny black hair, like raven's feathers, politely listened to his spiel. Yes, she answered in passable German, her father had designed the house for Herr Schliemann. The estate was almost completed now. Her father was very proud of it.

"With good reason," Pavlak smiled, summoning every ounce of charm he could muster. "A magnificent house indeed. I expect to build a house of my own here within the year, probably something on a similar scale. Would you happen to have any of the drawings at hand?"

Pavlak spent half an hour effusively admiring Mr. Giannapoulos' work, then drove to the quay and parked the BMW in a public parking lot on the waterfront. He walked six blocks to a rental agency and rented a delivery van.

The rest of the afternoon was spent shopping. As darkness fell, he loaded the last of his purchases into the van, then ducked into a restaurant specializing in health food for a leisurely meal that tasted like grass and fresh dirt.

Back on the sidewalk, he looked at his watch and frowned. It was fully dark now, but still much too early. With time to kill, he wandered the back streets of Rethymnon and eventually found himself sitting on a tie-up post at the dock of the silted harbor.

The Mediterranean was black now, and the lights of a luxury hotel twinkled in the distance where the coastline curved to form a shallow bay. At this time of year, the hotel would be no more than half full with tourists from northern Europe, mostly English and German, but with an occasional Frenchman thrown in, and perhaps the rare American who had stumbled onto the island seeking some off-season solitude.

It was July when he and Judith had come to Crete, and they had baked themselves on the white beaches, toured the island for hours in a rented Triumph, and marvelled at the great labyrinthine ruins of Knossos, where the minotaur terrorized the imagination of ancient Hellenes to the north. Ancient. That was the word for this land. After a stay in the timeless waters of the Aegean, even Germany's medieval castles seemed recent and trivial. Here on the Mediterranean men measured history not in centuries but in millennia. Here, Pavlak mused, gazing out into the black sea, had lived the great heroes whose exploits molded the Mind of the West.

He listened to the water lapping gently at the dock and shivered. The wind was cold and the quay deserted. He glanced up at a sky filled with stars and a quarter moon, the same moon Theseus once gazed upon, and Tantalus, and Thyestes, and Medea. A mad impulse came over him. In his mind's eye he saw himself dive into the black water and swim, blindly, out to sea, until he could swim no more.

Then he remembered Schliemann, sipping champagne in his mansion on the hill above, and Karin, huddled in a mean hotel in Stuttgart. The shades of antiquity vanished, replaced by the hard outlines of the present. There was still a job to be done.

Somewhere behind him a clock tower began to chime,

and he counted the bells. Midnight. Time to move. He strode away toward the van and did not see the figure swathed in black that slipped from a dark alleyway and followed.

The moon offered just enough light for the van to crawl up the mountain road with headlights off. Again Pavlak turned into the shepherd's trail and hid the van behind the same brush pile that had concealed the BMW earlier in the day. He studied the gentle motions of the olive branches. The breeze was blowing off the sea and up the slope.

From the van he pulled an aluminum ladder, a loop of climber's rope, and a plastic shopping bag that tugged heavily at his arm. With the rope and the ladder on his left shoulder, and the shopping bag in his right hand, he started to climb. Lederer's pistol nudged the small of his back at every step.

When Pavlak reached the wall, he set the ladder quietly against it, pulled some items from the shopping bag and carefully mounted until he could peek over the top. Floodlights were mounted under the eaves on every corner of the house, and they all burned brightly, bathing the grounds near the house in yellow light. The two mastiffs had already detected something. They were standing at attention beside the corner nearest him, facing his direction. This would be tricky. A few idle barks would not hurt, but he did not want the animals setting up a general alarm.

Pavlak reached into the bag and tossed a hand towel soaked in fish oil over the wall. The scent of the fish oil, carried by the wind, reached them quickly. They started to move, trotting cautiously in his direction. Pavlak tossed four balls of ground lamb over the fence, each one laced with one thousand milligrams of Triazolam, pulverized with the butt of the pistol. He jumped to the ground, grabbed the ladder, and sprinted away to his left, moving quickly out of the line of the wind.

Pavlak circled the wall until he reached the upper side of the compound, set the ladder again, and ventured another look. He was downwind of the dogs now and less concerned about attracting their attention.

At first he saw nothing. Then a shadow in the distance moved. He drew a pair of shiny new binoculars from the shopping bag. With their aid, he could just make out the two dogs sniffing and searching the ground in the soft moonlight. Presumably they had already swallowed the lamb. His main concern was that one of the animals might have reached the bait early enough to swallow all four clumps before the other one arrived, and for that exigency, a fifth ball of Triazolam-laced lamb still lay in the bottom of the bag, wrapped in plastic. Pavlak climbed down, hid the ladder in the shadows, and settled against the trunk of an olive tree to wait.

Half an hour later he looked again. One dog was clearly visible beside the house, stretched out on the ground and motionless. The other was nowhere to be seen. Pavlak searched the grounds carefully with the binoculars but found nothing. Maybe the missing dog lay hidden on the far side of the house, but he had to be sure. He had no choice but to carry the ladder back to the lower side of the estate and look again from there.

Pavlak moved to the exact spot where he had thrown the lamb across, climbed the ladder, and put the binoculars to his eyes. He found nothing. It was as if the second dog had disappeared into thin air—or perhaps he had wandered back to the other side of the house as Pavlak crossed to this one. That was a game they could play all night. Pavlak was pondering what to do when a faint sound directly below him

startled him. It was like a sneeze that never quite materialized. The wall was nearly three feet thick, so he could not
see down to its base. From the bag he pulled a piece of raw
leather, folded to four thicknesses, and laid it across the broken shards on the top of the wall. He eased his knees onto
the top, inched forward, and peered over the edge. The
other mastiff lay curled against the wall beneath him,
breathing erratically and noisily, but completely unconscious.

Pavlak hurried back down the ladder, secured the climbing rope to the butt of the nearest olive tree, then tossed it
over the wall. With both dogs out, there was no point in
climbing to the downwind side again. A moment later he
inched across the folded leather, then dropped silently to
the ground inside the compound, not four feet from the
unconscious mastiff. The climbing rope now dangled on his
right, ready for the escape when Pavlak returned.

He hoped, at least, that he would return.

The easy part was over. Next came the insanity, crossing
the lighted area, then entering a locked, occupied house. If
he did manage to get inside undetected, he had no idea
who, other than Schliemann and presumably a maid or two
might be waiting there. He looked at his watch. Two-thirty.
Even any night owls in the household should be asleep by
now. He couldn't see light behind any of the curtained windows on the second floor where the bedrooms were. Hug-
ging the wall to avoid the floodlights, he stole around to the
point at the back of the house that was directly across from
the cellar door. Pavlak leaned his back against the wall and
closed his eyes while he drew a long, deep breath. Then he
shoved himself away from the wall and made a silent dash
through the lighted area to a door which the architect's

plans had shown led to a short staircase down into the basement.

His shoulder collided noiselessly with the white stucco beside the door, and he froze, listening. Other than his own pounding heartbeat and labored gasps, there was no sound. But there was also no shadow to stand in, and the harsh glare of the floods beat down on him mercilessly.

From inside his coat, Pavlak quickly pulled a small steel bar. This was what he dreaded most. He had budgeted an entire hour for breaking down the lock and door jamb, and only hoped that he could do so in such tiny increments that no large noises would wake the household. He was a rank amateur at breaking and entering, and not at all sure the method he had in mind—forcing the door far enough away from the jamb to disengage the lock—was even possible.

Pavlak aimed the chisel point of the bar at the crack between the door and the wall, then froze with the steel bar in midair. "Careless," Karin had said. Of course. And she was right. He hesitated. No, there was no going back now. He aimed the bar once more, but the image of Karin came back unbidden. Karin in a seedy hotel in Stuttgart, helpless, waiting. "Tasha!" Pavlak whispered intensely, and without waiting to consider any longer, laid his left hand flat against the door and moved the bar forward. He was astonished when the door gave to his touch. He stopped, then pushed gently with his index finger. The door swung open a few inches.

Was it luck? Had a servant been careless? Or did Schliemann trust the wall and the dogs so much that he did not bother to lock the house? Perhaps the burglary rate on Crete was low, but still . . .

He pushed again until the doorway was a gaping hole, waiting, beckoning him into the black abyss within. Pavlak felt a chill race down his spine. He had planned to force his way through this very door. Now it stood open, inviting him in. Why was his foot so reluctant to move? He drew a deep breath, then stepped over the concrete ledge and onto the top step, then down another step, then another, feeling his way cautiously. At the fourth step, he turned and pushed the door shut behind him. In the stillness, the click of the latch falling home sounded like a cannon shot. He stood frozen in the darkness for a full three minutes, listening. There was no sound but the pounding of his own pulse. Burglary, he had once read, was addictive. Now he understood why. The excitement of standing, uninvited and undetected, inside an occupied home was almost sensual. It was violation—rape. Pavlak carefully replaced the crowbar inside his jacket and pulled out a pen light. Its tiny beam swept across a concrete floor still littered with the detritus of construction, scraps of wood and metal, pieces of aluminum conduit, a scrap of fiberglass insulation. The air was damp and cool and smelled faintly of sawdust and something chemical—a construction glue perhaps. Across the far wall, the beam swept an enormous wooden wine rack, and Pavlak noted that almost every orifice was filled with a bottle. Schliemann, apparently, was a connoisseur.

Pavlak picked his way as quickly as he could across the littered floor, taking care not to disturb any debris that might clatter. The stairway to the hallway of the east wing, the bedroom wing, should be ahead and to his right. Sure enough, the thin beam found another staircase, this one wooden, exactly where it was supposed to be. He climbed again, glad to be leaving the littered cellar. At the top of the stairs another door blocked his way. He grasped the knob and turned. Nothing happened. It was locked. That, at least, explained why the outside door was left open. Then he caught his breath and stared. A key protruded from the lock. He switched off the pen light, deposited it into a pocket, and pulled the pistol from his belt. The cold steel against his palm was reassuring. He turned the key softly, and the door gave way without a sound.

The faint glow from a night light in an adjacent room illuminated the hallway in front of him. Except for a narrow side table with an ornate mirror mounted above it, the corridor was empty of furniture. Pavlak moved quickly to yet another stairway—this one soft and carpeted. It led to another corridor on the second floor, and the big door at the end of that corridor led, Pavlak knew, into his destination—the master bedroom.

He eased his way up the stairs, then down the second-floor hallway. The thick carpeting made it easy to move soundlessly. Finally he stopped before an ornate double door of polished oak. A faint light leaked beneath the doorway. Someone inside was awake—or sleeping with a lamp on. Pavlak's heart beat painfully in his chest. Was this utterly insane? He could still turn around, retrace his steps, come back tomorrow evening as Schliemann had invited him to. And walk straight into a trap, if his suspicions were correct. No, this was his only chance to get the upper hand on Peter Schliemann. He had to do it, even if the whole thing was—careless.

Lederer's pistol was in his right hand, the barrel raised beside his ear. He took a breath, then wrenched the handle and threw the door open, leveling the pistol as he did so.

Straight in front of him lay an enormous bed, and in the middle of it, his legs beneath the covers, sat a man wearing a silk pajama top with the initials PJS embroidered on a lavender pocket. In his hands lay a thick, leather-bound book. A reading lamp, built into the carved bed head, glowed behind him. His hair was silver and immaculately trimmed, his features chiseled and strong. Peter Schliemann—if this was he—was a strikingly handsome man. He was probably nearing seventy, but looked ten years younger. Pavlak started to speak, then froze. He had seen that face before.

"Ah, Dr. Pavlak," Schliemann said calmly, lowering the book. "Good of you to come—though the hour is a trifle inconvenient."

Something moved behind him. Pavlak started to turn, then felt his skull explode.

22

"He's on the move."

Christopher Hopkins' voice was hoarse from lack of sleep. And he was catching a cold.

"He transferred half a million dollars to a bank in Basel. The FBI subpoenaed records from the bank in North Carolina . . ."

"Subpoenaed records?" Denham interrupted. "Why the hell haven't they frozen his assets?"

"They tried but couldn't get a court order. The truth is they've got nothing on Pavlak. Streat said he had to move heaven and earth just to get the subpoena. The Swiss will be useless, of course—you know their banking practices—but Borning has a team in Basel. They've staked out the bank where the transfer was made. If Pavlak shows up to get the money, they'll grab him."

"He won't show," Denham answered flatly. "Pavlak knows the transfer could be traced from this end. I'd bet the farm that his half-mil didn't stay in that bank more than an hour."

Hopkins shrugged. "It's all we've got just now."

"Then you haven't got anything," the director snapped. "Pavlak made a damned fool of the FBI first, then Borning, and now the rest of us." He slammed a coffee mug onto his desk so hard that a dollop of brown liquid sloshed across the mahogany surface. Denham's eyes were puffy and blood-shot. He had spent the previous evening at a reception in the Israeli Embassy, and he was in an ill humor. "For Christ's sake, we had the man in our hands and let him walk away while eight agents sucked their thumbs and watched. What are we? The Keystone Cops?"

Hopkins was not in a stellar mood himself. Not ten minutes earlier he had spoken on the telephone to Martha in Ohio. She needed more time to think, she told him. His house was a shambles, he had not eaten breakfast, and he was wearing yesterday's shirt. To top all that off, his dream assignment—his chance to show his stuff to the top brass—was turning into a nightmare.

"Borning was following your directions," Hopkins reminded the director, a little more sharply than he intended. "You said Pavlak would back off if we gave him the whole story, remember?"

"That was before we knew about this crap with the BND," Denham answered sourly. "Any more on Lederer?"

"Nothing. Krueger's stonewalling—sticking to the mugging story. Borning thinks he's lying. Krueger pretended not to know Lederer, but our files show him as an agent in the AII—*Abteilung für Industrieinformation*—that's Krueger's department. Krueger *hired* him."

"Terrific," the director snorted. "We get better cooperation from the KGB. Any chance that the lost ID was a setup? Somebody trying to sow dissension between us and the BND, for instance? Maybe one of ours? Some crackpot with a beef against the BND?"

"Not likely. He would have to know about Fool's Gold, as well as about Pavlak and his wife, not to mention our plans to contact Pavlak. That's even more fantastic than the mugging story."

The director grabbed a pencil and started tapping out a rhythm. "All right, what about Fool's Gold? Where do we stand on that?"

"We've interviewed everybody on our end, past and present, who was ever involved in any way. I've been over the file a dozen times. So have Olafson and Parker. Analysis put it through their ringer twice. It always comes up the same: a clean operation—modestly successful. No trace of dirt, nothing even remotely suspicious.

"Did you talk to the old man—Gustaf?"

"Of course. I had Erik Armand phone him. Armand's his old handler from Fool's Gold. He's stationed in Istanbul now, but he told Pavlak he was calling from Chicago.

"What did Pavlak have to say?"

"He's worried about his son. Wants to know what's going on—why we're asking questions about Fool's Gold again—thought it was finished years ago and so on. Just what you'd expect. If he knows anything, he's clever at hiding it."

"Yeah? Well remember, his son didn't buy his brains at Wal-Mart. Did the old man admit telling him about the operation?"

Hopkins shook his head. "Denies it emphatically. Says he never even told his wife. Armand thinks he's telling the truth."

"All right, what about the passport? Anything new on that?"

"We're reasonably sure Pavlak's got bogus papers, probably German, but we haven't been able to get a name or number. The Turks in Berlin are a tight lot. Either no one knows, or no one's talking. And that couple he was staying with when Borning found him are still missing. Vanished.

But the Germans found their car abandoned in a parking lot at the Frankfurt airport."

"What about the woman?"

"As far as we know she's still with Pavlak. The FBI says the German police are looking for her too. They want to talk to her about her brother-in-law's murder—and they're taking another look at the hit-and-run on her sister."

Denham tossed the pencil onto his desk. "Something stinks, Chris. It doesn't add up. Somebody, somewhere is dirty. We've got to find Pavlak again, and this time I don't want any screw-ups. Find him, detain him, and find out what he's onto. I don't know what we're sitting on, but it's not going to blow this agency to hell—not on my watch, understand?"

"No, sir, I don't."

Denham looked up sharply, but Hopkins plowed ahead, too exhausted to care. "You wouldn't let us eliminate him the last time we found him. Are you saying you've changed your mind?"

The director's face darkened. "I said, Chris, to detain him and question him. We'll decide where to go from there. That is, if you and Borning can get your hands on him again. So far he's running rings around you."

"We found him for you once already," Hopkins retorted. "If you had let us, Frank would have gone into that apartment armed, and none of this would have happened."

"Bullshit!" Denham exploded, jumping to his feet. "If Frank had gone in armed, Pavlak would have a CIA weapon now too, instead of just the one he got compliments of the BND. And we might have a dead Head of Station on top of that."

Hopkins' eyes were fastened on the floor. "Pavlak's not

ten feet tall," he said without looking up. "He's clever, I'll give you that, but he's not a killer."

"Oh, no?" Denham asked with a barely perceptible sneer. "You need to read his war record again. Some things a man never forgets."

Somewhere in the distance, bells were ringing. Homecoming. Somewhere. Pavlak's mother smiled, bent, and kissed his cheek, then Tom threw a baseball, hard, and Pavlak jumped as high as he could, but the ball sailed over his head. There was a crash of shattering glass. Then he was lying in a bed, his father standing over him, furious. He tried to hide, but his knees and elbows wouldn't move. The blows started, open-handed at first, then fists that thumped huge bruises into his chest and arms and thighs. He would have to stay home from school again. But no, it wasn't his father after all. It was Judith in a rage, and her little fists didn't hurt at all. Then she opened her mouth to bite, and the mouth was filled with sharp, pointed teeth, like a dog's mouth. And then she *was* a dog, a mastiff. "Daddy!" Tasha cried, terrified, standing unprotected in the open behind Schliemann's house, the dog between them. The dog turned and charged at her. Pavlak tried to run for Tasha, but something held his legs. "No!" he screamed.

"Halt's Maul!" a rough voice commanded. Then the toe of a boot connected sharply with Pavlak's ribs. He cried out and opened his eyes. A blur of light and dark swam in front of him, like a kaleidoscope without color. He was lying on his back, his arms above him. He moved his head and cried out again as a wave of pain gushed through it. His right hand moved instinctively toward his neck but jerked up

short with a clank of metal. It was chained to something. Confusion. He closed his eyes and tried to remember. He had entered Schliemann's house, climbed the stairs, opened the door. Then what? There was a face he had recognized. And that was the last thing he could remember. All right. They had not killed him. The battle was not over. Not yet.

He opened his eyes again and fought to make the blur in front of them come into focus. Beneath him, pressing up on his back was a hard cold surface. The silvery kaleidoscope swam in front of his eyes, then gradually resolved itself into a heating duct. Rows of pipes and conduits lay alongside it, then steel trusses beyond that. He was in the cellar.

Without warning, the boot flew into exactly the same spot again. Pavlak cried out again, and a face appeared above him, the mouth twisted into a malicious grin.

"Hat's dir gut getan, Junge?"

Pavlak had never heard the voice, but he recognized the face instantly. The right cheek was still swollen and discolored. Lederer. Pavlak's mind flew into overdrive. Lederer. The BND. Schliemann. Borning. If Borning was telling the truth about Fool's Gold, that would explain the connection between Schliemann and Lederer, a BND man. But if Fool's Gold was just a cold war relic, why did they kill Judith? And Brigitte and Turgat? And what did they want from him?

"The document, Dr. Pavlak," said a smooth voice in English. Pavlak twisted his head toward the sound, wincing at the pain in his neck.

Schliemann sat in a chair, one leg crossed over the other, hands folded in his lap. That face. Where had he seen it? It was much younger then. The hair was dark.

Schliemann wore a light blue turtleneck sweater and dark trousers with an immaculate crease. A fur-lined slipper dangled from the elevated foot. Every silver hair lay in perfect place, as if he had just stepped out of a salon.

"Tell us about the document," Schliemann said calmly. He was gazing dreamily into the distance somewhere, not even deigning to look at Pavlak.

"What document?"

This time Pavlak saw the kick coming, and tried to flinch, but nothing happened. The steel-toed boot impacted his ribs, and he cried out as the pain knifed through his chest. He jerked his legs again, but his feet were chained to something that looked like a furnace. He realized now that he was spread-eagle on the floor, every limb immobilized, helpless.

Schliemann raised a delicate hand. "Tut, tut, Klaus," he clucked. "Do be more gentle." Schliemann inclined his head indulgently toward Pavlak. "You'll have to pardon Klaus' manners, Dr. Pavlak. He's rather a proletarian sort, I'm afraid. You and I, on the other hand, can deal with each other in a civilized manner, can we not?"

"I know you," Pavlak moaned. "I've seen you before."

Schliemann laughed. "I assure you we've never met, Dr. Pavlak. If we had, I would certainly remember. A man of your resourcefulness is not so easily forgotten." Schliemann paused, and for a split second, something cold flashed in the complacent eyes. "My dogs, Dr. Pavlak. The poor creatures are really quite ill. I must tell you I take some offense at that. I'm quite fond of Hänsel and Gretl. It was hardly necessary to poison them."

"Sleeping pills," Pavlak grunted. "They'll recover."

Relief spread over Schliemann's features. "Well now, that truly is delightful news. I was deeply concerned. But tell me, Dr. Pavlak—why all this trouble? You didn't have to sneak into my house in the middle of the night for . . . what was it . . . research on German history, I believe? I fully intended to receive you for dinner tomorrow evening."

"I'm sure you did, you bloated little bastard."

Lederer made a move, but Schliemann's manicured hand signaled him to stay.

"Now, now, Dr. Pavlak. There's no need to be nasty. All right. You preferred not to meet me on my own terms. But you see, we are meeting—well, rather on my terms after all, are we not? You Americans always forget how small Europe is—how little time it takes for someone like my friend Klaus here to travel. When you mentioned Fool's Gold I knew it was you, of course, so I made a phone call. Klaus and his friend haven't had much sleep—but then neither have I." Schliemann inspected his fingernails carefully. "But did you really expect to surprise me? Did you think you were dealing with bumbling CIA agents again?" The pale blue eyes went hard. "You're out of your league now, *Herr Doktor*," Schliemann snapped. "You should never have come here. Oh, not that we wouldn't have come to you. Poor Klaus here was actually looking for you when you gave him such an unceremonious greeting in Berlin."

A smile crossed Schliemann's lips and he threw a teasing glance at Lederer who did not look at all amused. Schliemann nodded, and the boot flew again, more deliberately and much harder. Pavlak felt a rib crack and screamed in spite of himself. Then Lederer took aim and kicked again, then a third time, bone giving way to steel each time. Pavlak's whole body erupted in agony. He gasped vainly for breath, then a rush of nausea hit him, and he barely managed to roll his head to one side before he vomited.

"Oh dear, Dr. Pavlak. You seem to be quite unwell. I certainly hope it doesn't get worse. But of course it could." He learned forward and raised both eyebrows. "Much worse."

Pavlak struggled to suppress the heaving in his innards.

With the shattered ribs even the slightest convulsion of his diaphragm was excruciating. For the first time it dawned on him that he was being tortured. He threw the thought out of his mind and concentrated on Schliemann's face.

"What . . . do you . . . want from me?" he gasped.

"Oh, I believe you know the answer to that, Dr. Pavlak. The document, of course. We really must have it. And of course we will have it, sooner or later. It would be very much in your interest to make it sooner."

"Listen to me," Pavlak whispered hoarsely. "Call off the . . . goon . . . for a minute . . . and . . . listen to me."

Schliemann waited a long second, then nodded toward Lederer who reluctantly stepped back.

"This document," Pavlak gasped. "Are you . . . talking about . . . your brother's file?"

Schliemann drew a weary sigh. "Dr. Pavlak, really. It's not wise to stall. It only irritates Klaus and makes him more unpleasant. Just tell me where the document is, and we can end this little interview—perhaps even keep our dinner engagement tomorrow evening. He glanced at his watch. "*This* evening actually. I have a wonderful *Beerenauslese,* a Riesling from a little-known vineyard in Erden on the Mosel. Exquisite, Dr. Pavlak. I've been saving it for a celebration."

"And what . . . happens to me . . . if I tell you?"

Schliemann showed his soft palms. "As I said—we enjoy a pleasant bottle of wine, then you go your merry way. Of course we would have to detain you until the document is actually in our possession, but I assure you, Dr. Pavlak, I can offer you much more comfortable accommodations than this. It's up to you."

Pavlak's mind blundered desperately through a fog of pain. They would kill him as soon as they no longer needed him. Just as they had killed the others. His only hope was to pretend he knew where the document was. They would keep him alive as long as they believed that.

"It's in . . . North Carolina . . . the original . . . that is."

Schliemann's face darkened. "The original?"

"I made . . . four copies . . . sealed them . . . gave them to people . . . to hold . . . until I . . . get back . . . safely."

Schliemann's oily tone turned sharp. "You're really beginning to annoy me, Dr. Pavlak. And what you did—if you're telling me the truth—was extremely foolish. Because now you'll have to identify those friends as well."

"No chance," Pavlak croaked.

Schliemann nodded at Lederer who stepped over Pavlak's prostrate form and methodically delivered three kicks into the ribs on his other side. Despite Pavlak's determination not to cry out, he screamed each time the boot fell. He breathed pain and swallowed pain. He had never imagined it possible to feel such agony and still live.

Lederer sat down.

"One last time, Dr. Pavlak," Schliemann said smoothly, "where is the document, and where are the copies? If there really are any. Do be cooperative this time. I don't want Klaus to strain himself."

Pavlak blinked the tears from his eyes. "Fuck you," he managed to gasp.

"*Laß mich das Schwein . . . ,*" Lederer cried, leaping to his feet. Schliemann was quicker and stepped in his path.

"*Nicht doch. Lassen wir ihn ein bisschen nachdenken.*" It was the first time Pavlak had heard Schliemann speak his native language. "I believe you need some time to think, Dr. Pavlak," Schliemann said in English again. It was British English, pretentious and precise. "Perhaps a few days here will render you more reasonable. We can be patient, you see."

Schliemann stooped and picked up a four-foot piece of

steel conduit from the construction debris on the floor, then stepped closer, looking down at Pavlak with mock pity.

"You . . . ," Pavlak croaked. "You're the bastard . . . who killed . . . my little girl."

Schliemann's eyebrows ticked upwards. "Actually not, Dr. Pavlak. I honestly don't know who did that. Krueger, perhaps," he added with a questioning glance at Lederer who shrugged in reply. "You see, Dr. Pavlak," Schliemann continued, "killing the child was stupid. If she were still alive, I suspect you would be a trifle more cooperative. Now that she's dead, we don't have that leverage." He stooped beside Pavlak's head, the conduit resting lightly on his shoulder like a baseball bat. "But no matter. We'll get what we want through other means."

Without warning, the conduit whipped down across Pavlak's nose, crushing the cartilage. Instantly his mouth filled with blood, and his body convulsed, triggering a fresh explosion of pain in his whole torso. He wretched and vomit filled his throat along with the blood. He coughed, then wretched again, as, incredibly, the pain escalated with each convulsion, and wave after wave of nausea washed over him. He was sure he was going to die when finally the convulsions stopped, and he managed to draw an agonized breath. Blood and vomit covered his shirt and the floor around him.

Lederer and Schliemann watched in silence until the convulsions were finished.

It was Schliemann who spoke again. "You realize, of course, Dr. Pavlak, that this is only a taste of what's in store for you if you refuse to cooperate. Do think about that, won't you?" The conduit slashed down again, this time into Pavlak's exposed groin, and once more Pavlak screamed.

"And do keep quiet, won't you, Dr. Pavlak?" Schliemann smiled. "We all need some rest. It's been a beastly night."

He tossed the conduit disdainfully at Pavlak's head, and Pavlak flinched enough for it to strike his left eye rather than the broken nose. A moment later, his tormenters mounted the stairs, switched off the light, and left him in total darkness.

The next hour passed in hell. Every breath was a wracking agony. He tried to test the chains that bound him, but it was no use. The slightest movement was excruciating. And in the pitch black of the cellar, he could not even begin looking for a way to escape. There was nothing to distract him from his suffering, or from the hopelessness of the predicament.

"So this is how it ends," he whispered. "I'm sorry, Tasha. I couldn't protect you, and I can't avenge you. Evil wins. I'm sorry." Hot tears washed some of the blood from his cheeks.

By and by he discovered that if he lay perfectly still and measured his breaths, the pain subsided a little. He willed his limbs to remain immobile. After what he guessed was almost two hours, he urinated, and the liquid warmed his thigh. He wanted to weep but fought back tears to avoid the pain a sob would bring. He remembered what he had read about torture—about humiliation. It was not the wounds to the body that broke a man, but the wounds to the soul.

Self-recrimination set in. He should have waited. He should have surprised Schliemann away from his mansion and kidnapped him at gunpoint. He had been in too big a hurry. He thought of Karin in the hotel in Stuttgart, waiting. What would happen to her? Eventually they would find her, torture her, kill her too.

He did not know how long such thoughts chased through his fevered brain before he heard a noise, a scraping sound, like metal on metal. Then there was a hiss, like someone shushing him to silence. He held his breath, and it came again. Finally a thin beam of light pierced the darkness and landed on his face. At the same instant a distinctly British voice, not more than four feet away, whispered, "Good God, a proper mess you are, old boy."

Pavlak stared at the tiny point of light in confusion.

"Just keep still, and we'll get you out of here quick enough," the voice continued. The beam played across his whole body, dwelling on the chains at his hands and feet. The man knelt beside him, clenched the pen light in his teeth, and focused it on a pouch at his side. Pavlak was astonished to recognize the shepherd from the road up the hillside. The hard, weathered face was younger than Pavlak had thought. The man was about Pavlak's age, perhaps a little younger. Now he was wearing boots and camouflage fatigues in place of the baggy black pants and shirt of a Cretan shepherd. An automatic weapon of a type Pavlak had never seen swung casually from a strap across his chest.

"Who are you?" Pavlak whispered painfully.

"Never mind that now, old sod. Plenty of time when we're out of here."

"They could . . . come back," Pavlak warned.

"Could—but I doubt it. An old method, tried and true. Hurt you a bit, then, if you don't break right away—most do, you know—they give you a day or two of isolation. Time to lose your marbles—get hungry, thirsty, too weak to resist. By the time they come back, you're actually glad to see them. Start babbling your guts out."

From the pouch the Englishman produced what looked like an oversized Swiss army knife, made a selection and folded out a hack-saw blade, four inches long. He carefully wrapped his hand and the blade in a black wool cloth to muffle sound, then went to work on the chains. In ten minutes both hands were loose. Ten more and Pavlak was completely free.

"Can you walk?" the Englishman whispered.

"I'm . . . not sure. They . . . broke some ribs."

"Did they now? Well, suck it up, old boy. We've got a little ground to cover—and a wall to cross."

"The dogs . . ."

"I shot them—twenty-two with a silencer. Less humane than your method, I'm afraid, but rather more reliable."

"The lights . . . what if they see us? I can't run . . ."

"No light either. There's been a power failure—common enough on Crete, though this one's limited to just this house. Mate of mine cut the line. Up you go now."

Every movement brought fresh pain. It took two full minutes to get Pavlak onto his feet. "I can't make it," he gasped when he was standing at last. "Give me a weapon and . . . leave me here. I'll be ready . . . when they come back."

"No way, old sod. You're coming with me if I have to carry you. Here you go now."

They inched their away across the littered floor to the door. Movement helped. The pain was just as bad or worse, but the end of total helplessness made it more bearable. Once outside the house, Pavlak's rescuer pulled him forward more quickly, straight down a muddy path in what was to become the English garden, and toward the wall at its nearest point. The stars had already faded, and dawn was near. Pavlak gritted his teeth against the pain and tried to push his stiff legs faster.

They had traveled no more than thirty feet when a dark shape rounded the corner of the house and crouched in pistol-firing position.

"*Keine Bewegung!*" It was Lederer's voice.

The Englishman's response came in less than a second. Three rounds from the machine pistol struck Lederer, the first in the stomach, the second in the middle of his chest, and the third in the throat, flinging him backward. Somewhere above and behind them, two windows were thrown open, but at that instant the wall in front of them erupted with automatic weapons fire, raking the house over their heads. Pavlak saw at least four muzzles spewing flame from the top of the wall in front of them.

The Englishman dragged Pavlak forward at a run. Pain was now a giant blot. When they reached the wall, he was half pushed, half dragged up a ladder, then dumped down the other side and thrown into the back of a waiting Land Rover. Suddenly the firing stopped, and men were flinging themselves on top of him.

"Bloody hell," someone muttered, then the Rover was bouncing crazily down the hill, through the olive grove. Every jolt was excruciating. Pavlak concentrated all his energy on sucking oxygen, but it was no use. The broken ribs, the sprint to the wall, the all-consuming pain—oblivion opened up and Pavlak gratefully fell in.

" 'Ere now. I think 'e's fainted," a Cockney voice panted.

"Not surprised. They made a proper mess of him, they did. Nice job, actually. Excellent technique."

The Rover bounced onto an asphalt road and roared away toward a thin line of pink on the far horizon.

23

When Pavlak opened his eyes he found a face six inches away. It belonged to an unkempt old man with thick gray hair straggling over the collar of a gray shirt that had once been white. His beard was bedraggled, and neither the horned eyebrows nor the coarse hairs sprouting from his bulbous nose showed any sign of ever having been trimmed.

"Ow!" Pavlak protested as strong fingers nudged his broken nose a quarter inch to the left. He was lying in a room no larger than a walk-in closet. He tried to raise his right arm and found it bound to the railing of an examination table. An intravenous needle was taped fast to the arm, and a clear liquid dripped into his vein from a bottle hung on a nail in the wall. His tongue was thick and swollen, and he could taste fresh blood in his mouth.

The old man wrenched his nose again, and this time Pavlak snatched a handful of the filthy shirt with his free hand and shoved him roughly away.

The old man broke into a gleeful cackle. "American no sleep more, yes?" He tapped his nose and pointed at Pavlak's face. "I fix. Good like new."

"You're a *doctor*?" Pavlak asked.

"Doctor, yes. Very good doctor," he grinned.

"He's a bloody butcher is what he is," another voice answered from the doorway. It was the Englishman who had pulled him from Schliemann's basement.

"Not butcher," the old doctor grinned. "Good doctor. English," he said pointing at the man in the door. "English good. Come after war. Germans go. I help English."

"Stephan says he helps us," the man in the door said to Pavlak. "I had to rely on him once in the past, and about the best I can say is that I survived in spite of him."

Pavlak tried to lift his head and was instantly reminded of his broken ribs. He felt for them with his free hand and discovered that his torso was wrapped and tightly taped.

"Ribs okay," the doctor assured him, nodding vigorously for emphasis. "Five *kaputt*." He held up five fingers. "But okay. Take time."

"I don't have time," Pavlak whispered weakly. "I've got to get out of here."

"Forget that, old chum. You're in no shape to travel."

"Where am I?"

"Thilion. It's a village in the mountains, near the east end of the island. Stephan here will look after you until we can travel."

Pavlak closed his eyes and tried to concentrate. The all-consuming agony of Schliemann's basement was gone, but his whole body ached, and his mind refused to focus. He suspected that Stephan had provided an injection of pain killer, probably morphine.

"I left my car in Rethymnon," he murmured. "My passport is in it—and my money."

The Englishman reached into a pocket, pulled out a green German passport and Personal Identification Card, and handed them to Pavlak. "The BMW's hidden in a garage out back. The rental agency will have to get their van back on their own. We left it in the olive grove."

"I had a gun. . . ."

"I know. A Walther P-one, military version of the old P-thirty-eight, standard side arm in the German *Bundeswehr*. Very effective at short range, but a vicious bloody recoil."

"How did you . . ."

"Saw you tuck it into your belt when you got out at the gate the first time—through binoculars, of course. The weapon is Herr Schliemann's property now, I'm afraid."

"You were watching me?"

"From the moment you first drove up the hill to the house."

"Why were you . . . ?" Pavlak suddenly ran out of energy and abandoned the question. The Englishman answered it anyway.

"We were instructed to keep a watch in case you turned up at Schliemann's—which you promptly did—but to keep our hands off unless you got into trouble—which you also promptly did. Then we were to see to it that you stayed alive." One corner of his mouth puckered in an expression of frustration—or it might have been disgust. "A nearly impossible mission. How the hell was I to know when you got into trouble inside that house? Fortunately we heard you screaming. And suppose Schliemann had simply blown your stupid head off the minute you stepped into his house?" He shook his head. "Clients always want the impossible. They have no bloody idea."

"You're mercenaries?"

"Professionals," the Englishman corrected him.

"Who hired you?"

"No idea, old boy. I work through an intermediary. People like to keep their distance in case something gets bolloxed up. Insulates us a bit too—from trouble on the other end."

"Who was the intermediary?"

The Englishman smiled and shook his head.

"And I don't suppose you'll tell me your name either?" Pavlak asked.

"Don't really need it, now do you?"

"What can I call you then?"

"Call me . . . Jack."

"Thanks for pulling my ass out of the fire, Jack."

The soldier was an intense man, a little smaller than Pavlak, but hard as nails, with blue eyes like ice crystals. The eyes went suddenly cold. "Don't thank me," he said. "I'd blow your bleeding brains out if that was what I was paid for. I'm a businessman, not a missionary."

Pavlak nodded—or tried to. "So what happens now?" he asked.

"We wait until you can travel, then escort you safely off the island. That's what we're paid for—getting you off Crete in one piece. After that, you're on your own."

An image stole unbidden into Pavlak's mind: Lederer at the corner of Schliemann's mansion, pitching backwards in the gray dawn. "You killed a man . . ."

Jack made a wry face. "Stupid bloody bastard. Must have thought he was Superman. If he'd stayed behind the corner, he might have seen the sunrise this morning."

"Might?"

Jack shrugged. "Chances are one of my mates would have nailed him anyway."

"How many of you are there?"

"More than enough. Always more than enough. That's how you stay alive in this business."

Pavlak closed his eyes and tried to arrange his thoughts. "What's your fee for this?" he asked quietly.

Jack waited five seconds before responding. "Well, you don't purchase this kind of service for pennies, old chum, now do you? Your benefactor, whoever he is, has plenty of cash available."

"Yes," Pavlak said slowly. "He's a rich man. Listen—I've got to get a message to Germany."

"Forget it. We left a corpse back at Schliemann's. Now maybe Schliemann packs him up quietly and nobody's the wiser—but maybe he goes screaming to the police, right? I don't know, because I don't know what this is about." Pavlak opened his mouth, but Jack raised a hand. "And I don't want to know. We were told Schliemann was dangerous and that he might have as many as three men around to help him. That's all we needed to know. Now as of this minute, we're all invisible. Got that? No phone calls, no mail, no nothing. We don't exist—at least not until we're ready to make a run off this island."

Jack's tone encouraged no rebuttal and Pavlak uttered none, though his brain churned. What would Karin do if he didn't show up? She was expecting him no later than three days from now. Surely there was a way to get her a message. Should he give Jack more details and ask for help? No, the man was, by his own admission, a hired gun. Best not to trust him too far. And Karin had the backup plans. She knew what to do if he didn't show up.

And what about his father? It had to be Gustaf Pavlak who hired Jack. That meant that his father knew Schliemann, knew where he lived, knew his son might show up there, and had reacted typically to protect his dynasty. Then a thought struck Pavlak like a brick from a rooftop. Had his father ordered the car bomb? No. Impossible. He was a ruthless businessman, and a brutal, abusive father, but not that depraved, surely. Besides, he had been too obviously devastated by the news when Pavlak phoned him in Arizona.

And yet, his father had to be involved—deeply involved. In what? Pavlak still had no idea, other than his father's participation in an espionage operation known as Fool's Gold. The debacle at Schliemann's house had produced nothing new—well, almost nothing. Now he knew it was a document they were after. And Schliemann had mentioned a name. Krueger.

A few hours later the grubby old doctor helped Pavlak onto a chair in front of a mirror and went to work on the nose. Pavlak gave directions. "Up a little—no too much. Okay. A little to the right. It's crooked. Better." When the floating nose looked about right, the old man cemented it in place and fitted Pavlak with a leather harness that made him look like a prize calf on a halter. Pavlak resigned himself to a hospital visit at some time in the future. No doubt the nose would have to be re-broken and fixed properly another day. If he lived long enough.

The next eight days passed in aching boredom. Pavlak never once saw the outside of the house where he was staying. At least one of the mercenaries was with him every second. Jack was taking no chances of his stealing away on his own. Once, Pavlak managed to sneak a fleeting glimpse through a crack in a drawn curtain, but saw only a concrete wall ten feet from the window. Occasionally a vehicle drove past, not far from the front door—perhaps half a dozen times a day. If the house was on the main street through the village—and he knew from his tours with Judith that Cretan villages often had only one street—then it was a remote village indeed.

There were four rooms in the house. He and Jack and two of Jack's men slept on the floor in one of them. The two were not always the same. From time to time they would disappear, only to be replaced in half an hour by another two. Pavlak guessed that they were keeping guard some-where, perhaps at the approaches to the village, but whether they were keeping Schliemann's men out, or him in, he was not sure. In all, he counted six men, including Jack, al-though Jack was the only one who spoke directly to him. Pavlak occasionally heard the soldiers exchange a few words with each other. At least two of them spoke French. Another, who otherwise never said a word in Pavlak's presence, dropped a plate one evening and muttered an oath that sounded to Pavlak like Dutch, or Flemish, or possibly Afri-kaans.

His injuries healed more rapidly than he had expected. By the third day he could move around without unbearable pain. After a week he could breathe through his nose again.

He passed the time sleeping or playing chess with Jack, who proved to be a challenging chessman and a passable conversationalist. All in all, he was a man of more intellect than Pavlak had at first judged. He betrayed little about him-self but once mentioned service in the Falklands and alluded to at least one stay in Africa. Pavlak asked him if he had been a member of Britain's Special Air Service, but Jack pretended not to hear the question. Pavlak was sure he had guessed correctly. Small wonder then that Jack had made the snatch from Schliemann's house so easily. The SAS was arguably the finest elite military force in the world. They had pulled off hostage rescues a hundred times more com-plex than that one.

As the days dragged on, an image of Karin crept into his mind again and again. Where was she now? Was she safe? Had she followed his instructions? And what would be Schliemann's next move? Pavlak remembered the hail of gunfire when he was dragged over the wall, and it occurred to him that Schliemann could be dead, victim of a stray bullet. He asked Jack if the fire fight had made the news, and Jack shook his head. "Not a word of any of it, old chum. Your pal Schliemann seems to operate in a very private world."

Pavlak talked with Jack about cars, about women, about politics. Their liveliest exchange was about education. Jack, if he was telling the truth, had a year of university behind him, though he declined to name the institution and had nothing good to say about the experience. "Bloody waste of time," he concluded one day over the chess board. "After you learn to read and write properly, it's time to make your own way in the world—find your own furrow to plow. If you want to learn more, fine—you've got the tools to do it. School is for children. Show me a grown man lounging around a university, and I'll show you a bloody parasite."

Pavlak smiled and took his time replying. "What about the sciences?" he asked. "How do you learn science on your own? You need equipment, laboratories—all that."

Jack nodded. "Right. The sciences are an exception—all the useful branches of learning are. If they're worth anything, then they require that a man get his hands on the real world, literally, I mean, and the real world costs money. So the university's all right for that. I'm talking about the other rubbish—art, literature, history, that sort of thing. Bunch of wussies sitting around wasting their own time and other people's money."

"Wussies?"

"Good American term, eh?" Jack grinned. "Cross between a wimp and a pussy, I was told." He stretched and yawned. "Oh, don't get me wrong now. It's okay for somebody to do that kind of thing if they want. Read literature and history and all that. It's the universities I've got the quarrel with.

Let them what wants it do that sort of study on their own time with their own money—and learn to do something useful first. That's the main thing."

"Useful?" Pavlak asked. "You mean like rescuing a college administrator from a Cretan mansion? You know, I even teach a course now and then. German. So that makes me a useless wussy. Isn't rescuing me useless as well?"

"Well now, don't take it personal, old chum." There was a hint of embarrassment in Jack's smile. "Little school like yours—you've got close contact with the students. You can pass on something of yourself, something of your experience and understanding, apart from the stuff the students could learn just as well without you. At Oxford, or Harvard, or wherever, the bloody dons just stand up there like the little gods they think they are and shovel out crap to three hundred students they don't know and don't give a happy damn about. Why should he read me his bloody lecture? Why not just hand me a copy and let me read it myself?"

"Ah, but would you?"

Jack shrugged. "I would if I wanted to."

"But when you're twenty years old, how do you know you want to, until somebody makes you do it the first time?"

Jack squirmed forward on his chair and raised two fingers. "Couple of points to make here. First of all, why should I deal with the history of the Roman Empire at the age of twenty? Can't understand a damned thing about it, no matter how much I read, because I haven't lived enough. How can I know what it meant to be a legionnaire, or to run an empire, until I've been a soldier myself? And the second thing—how many bloody historians do we really need, anyway? Or literary scholars, for God's sake? Does half the population really need to spend its time reading treatises on the *Canterbury Tales*?"

Jack leaned back and laced his hands together behind his head.

"Now the tales themselves, that's a different matter—but you scholar types—you don't know squat about the literature itself. You can't, because you don't know squat about life. You spend all your time reading each other's tripe and posturing at each other until you think you and your kind run the bloody world. In fact, you're nothing but a bunch of buffoons—and what's worse, the most ignorant lot in all of humanity—living in a bleeding little fantasy world." Jack had worked himself into a nervous twitch.

"I've heard this a thousand times before, in one form or another," Pavlak sighed patiently. "And you know what . . . ?"

Jack shrugged sullenly.

"You're absolutely right," Pavlak said flatly.

Jack treated him to a puzzled stare, then a slow smile spread across his features. "And *you* know what, mate?" he said. "You're a strange man. Smart fellow, obviously. Bit stupid about the fights you pick, maybe, but smart otherwise. Can't figure you out."

"The puzzlement is mutual," Pavlak answered. He picked up a knight and slapped it onto a square behind Jack's line of pawns. "Check."

Jack studied the board, and his face fell. "Oh, bloody hell."

Eight days after they arrived at Stephan's house, Pavlak was awakened by a tap on the shoulder. Jack stood over him, fully dressed, with a purple beret on his head at a rakish angle and a canvas pack on his back. Pavlak raised his watch and tried to focus his sleep-filled eyes. One-thirty in the morning.

"Get your coat on, Professor," Jack whispered. "Time to travel."

Five minutes later he was shivering in the Rover as it careened down the mountains in an obvious hurry, driven by one of the mercenaries. Jack and Pavlak sat in the back. There was a car in front of them—a yellow Volkswagen as best Pavlak could make out—and another following half a mile or so behind. Jack was silent and subdued.

"Where are we going?" Pavlak asked.

"Hopping to another island."

"By ferry?"

"Sort of."

The ferry turned out to be a rubber dinghy dragged up on a beach. Pavlak guessed that the beach was on the north coast of the island, somewhere east of Heraklion. As Jack and Pavlak approached the dinghy in the dark, their shoe soles leaving faint impressions in the damp sand, Jack whistled once. An answering whistle sounded from some rocks about twenty meters away, and a man stepped out and strode rapidly toward them. In the pale moonlight Pavlak could make out an automatic rifle cradled in his right hand with careless ease.

Without a word, Jack and the second man strapped a life jacket on Pavlak, ordered him to lie flat in the dinghy, then pushed it out past the breakers and clambered in themselves. Jack bent his back to a set of wooden oars and the dinghy surged forward into the black Aegean. Twice, the man in the prow flashed a small light out to sea, and both times an answering flash traversed the black water. After twenty minutes, the dinghy pulled alongside a twenty-foot launch. Pavlak was helped, none too gently, up a rope ladder and into the launch before his traveling companions followed, pulling the dinghy after them.

Instantly, the launch sped away into the night, pounding brutally into the choppy waves. Every thud sent shivers of pain through Pavlak's body. The trip was cold, agonizing, and interminable. Pavlak said a silent prayer of thanks when, just before dawn, the pilot of the launch throttled the engines back and brought the boat around. Pavlak was lowered into the dinghy again, and this time only Jack followed him. Jack's powerful strokes quickly propelled them toward the massive looming shape of a cliff, black and foreboding in the darkness.

When the dinghy crunched into the sand, Jack helped Pavlak out of the life jacket, tossed it back into the dinghy, and drew a packet from his vest pocket.

"The rest of your papers and your money," he said quietly, handing the packet to Pavlak. "You're on Santorini. There's a tourist hotel about a kilometer that way. Look sharp and you'll find the path up the cliffs. From there you can get a cab into Fira. No ferries are running yet—too early for tourists—but there's a small landing strip where you can hire a plane to Athens—you've got plenty of cash—then take the ferry or fly back to Italy from there. Your BMW is waiting in a parking garage in Bari, a block from where you caught the ferry. The claim ticket is in the packet. That's it. You're on your own." He turned to go.

"Wait," Pavlak called. Jack turned, and Pavlak put out his hand.

"I told you," Jack said coldly, ignoring the hand. "I'm a businessman, not a bleeding missionary." He turned his back and waded into the cold surf, leaving Pavlak staring after him in perplexity.

By noon, Pavlak was resting in a hotel in Athens. The Acropolis rose majestically in full view from his window, but Pavlak was in no mood to enjoy the sight.

He slept four hours, then rose, showered, and looked at himself in the mirror. The brace and plaster on his nose attracted too much attention. He carefully cut both of them off with a razor blade. The nose was red and visibly crooked, but if he was careful not to bump into anything for a few days, he reasoned that it would heal well enough. He looked at the roll of tape that Stephan had supplied for his ribs, then tossed that into the wastebasket too.

At seven that evening he caught a night flight to Rome, then a train back across the peninsula to Bari to pick up the BMW. For most of the train trip, Pavlak reclined in his seat, planning his next move, and whispering a name to himself over and over again. Krueger.

24

Elizabeth called her husband at the embassy as soon as the letter arrived. A broad smile spread across Frank Borning's face as he sat at his desk, the green plastic receiver pressed to his ear. Holden Borning, the youngest of their three children, was a senior at Yale. He was their problem child, a slender, sensitive, and introverted youth whose bouts with depression had perplexed his parents since the onset of adolescence.

In his freshman year at Yale, Holden had somehow become obsessed with the scholastic honor society Phi Beta Kappa and had pursued induction heroically, semester after semester. Now Holden was a senior, and despite Herculean efforts, his grade-point-average hovered just below the cutoff point. The coveted award had not materialized, and during his Christmas visit to Bonn, Holden had been discouraged and depressed.

But now the dream was coming true after all. Holden Borning would be inducted into Phi Beta Kappa in two weeks, at the society's final meeting before graduation.

With a broad grin on his face, Borning replaced the receiver and told his secretary that he had an errand to run.

It had been a rough couple of weeks since the Pavlak fiasco in Berlin, but this more than made up for it. No matter how bad things got with his job, his family always came through for him.

At the entrance to the garage beneath the embassy, the guard in the booth smiled and waved, then pushed the button that unlocked the heavy steel door. Borning pushed it open and strode to his car, humming an old Elvis Presley tune. His son's success made him feel young again, made him remember the time when small successes could still brighten the whole world.

He drummed his fingers impatiently on the steering wheel as he waded through the security checkpoints at the wall, then nodded in answer to the last marine's snappy salute and sped away toward the center of Bonn.

Just off Market Square in the Sternstrasse in Bonn was a quaint little leather shop featuring handmade goods. Frank and Holden Borning had browsed there during his son's Christmas visit, and Holden's attention had been captured by a ridiculously expensive wallet made from kangaroo leather. They had both laughed at the price—DM 599, but Borning had seen the spark in his son's eyes as he turned the wallet in his delicate hands, and the father had decided then and there to buy the wallet when the next special occasion arose. And now it had.

He parked the embassy car in the public garage beneath Market Square and joined the noon-hour crowds in the pedestrian zone. The weather was typical: gray and chilling, with an occasional patter of light rain.

A bell tinkled softly when he opened the door of the shop, but there was no one in sight. He made straight for the display case where the wallet had been, and his heart fell. It was gone. He was contemplating what to do when his eye fell on the wallet, now in a different case to his right. As he stepped toward it, the bell tinkled behind him, and he heard another customer step into the shop.

"Komme gleich!" a female voice yelled from the storage room behind the counter. Borning's eyes were fixed on the wallet. The exterior was etched and burned with a scene from the Australian outback. Really rather tacky, the thing was, but . . .

He froze. Something small and round and hard was pressing into the small of his back.

"Tell me about Krueger," said a low voice in his ear.

Borning's first reaction was disbelief. Agents were looking for Pavlak all over the continent. How could the man be standing behind him in a leather shop in the middle of Bonn? He remembered the snub-nosed Colt .38 nestled in a holster beneath his left arm.

"Don't even think about it," Pavlak whispered intensely, pressing his weapon deeper into Borning's back. "Just turn around and walk out the door. Head for the university."

The purple curtain covering the door to the storage room parted, and a short, plump, gray-haired woman waddled toward them.

"Can I help you?" she smiled.

"Thanks," Pavlak answered. "We'll be back soon." He grasped the shoulder of Borning's overcoat and pulled him toward the door, as the saleswoman stopped short and stared. On the sidewalk Pavlak walked just behind Borning, keeping Borning's right shoulder in contact with his own left.

Borning willed his heart to a calmer pace and sized up his situation. Pavlak had positioned himself so that if Borning went for his weapon he would have to wheel 180 degrees before he could use it. And the street was crowded with lunchtime shoppers. Even if he could get the Colt in his hand before Pavlak shot him, the odds of wounding an innocent bystander were too great. Borning gritted his teeth. The sonofabitch had him again. At least for now.

They skirted Market Square and walked down Fürstenstrasse toward the squat, rococo towers of the university building that had once served as the residence of the Elector of Cologne. Borning approached its familiar, dull-orange wall, then stopped.

"Inside," Pavlak ordered tersely.

They passed through two sets of doors and found themselves in a closed courtyard, dotted with exhibits from a display of modern sculpture. "Keep going," Pavlak snapped, as Borning's steps slowed. Two more doors, and they had passed through the old building and were walking toward the broad expanse of lawn known as the Hofgarten. It was as big as three soccer fields, with benches scattered randomly across it, and no walkways. The field was flanked on both sides by rows of tall trees. Only a handful of students had braved the foul weather to munch on bread and cheese in the open air. Pavlak grabbed a fistful of Borning's sleeve and pulled him toward the trees on the right. Borning's pulse rose a notch. Here was Pavlak's mistake.

Frank Borning was good with weapons—the best in his training class at the farm near Quantico. And since then he had never missed an opportunity to hone his skills at the range. He could draw the .38 and use it accurately in less than two seconds.

Ahead and slightly to the left was a huge oak, about four feet in diameter at the trunk. Borning steered them subtly toward it. When they passed the tree, he would make his move, break away, get the tree between them for an instant—that was all he needed—and then put a bullet through Pavlak's brain. It would be a nasty affair, but the Germans would help hush it up. And who could blame Borning for using deadly force? His life was clearly threatened. What's more, it would end this little problem for the Agency—and for the BND—once and for all.

The tree was ten feet away. Borning began adjusting the length of his steps so that his right foot would make the step past the tree, allowing him to push off it as he ducked behind the trunk. He rehearsed the move in his mind. He would twist away from Pavlak and dodge behind the trunk, at the same time retrieving his .38. By the time Pavlak could react, Borning would be on the other side of the tree. Pavlak's natural reaction would be to chase him, so Borning would continue on around and put the bullet into the back of Pavlak's head, as low on the skull as possible. He had to be sure not to miss. If a stray bullet struck a bystander, there would be hell to pay.

They were two steps from the tree when Pavlak's right hand reached over Borning's shoulder, slid deftly inside his jacket and emerged with the .38. Borning gritted his teeth.

"Relax," Pavlak said. "I just want some information. The truth this time."

"I gave you the truth last time."

"Possibly," Pavlak conceded. "But not all of it."

They had stopped at a deserted spot beneath the trees. The ground dipped to form a shallow depression, and the sod was wet and spongy beneath their feet. Pavlak backed away.

"Turn around," he ordered.

Borning slowly faced him. "What happened to your nose?" he asked.

"Your friend Peter Schliemann broke it for me, along with half my ribs. Can't say much for the company you keep, Mr. Borning."

Borning's jaw dropped. "Schliemann?"

Pavlak nodded. "Schliemann and your other pal, Mr. Lederer. Remember? The one from the BND." Pavlak's eyes burned at him in a quiet rage.

"I don't understand. Tell me . . ." Borning began.

"No you tell me—about Krueger," Pavlak demanded.

"Krueger?" Borning repeated, playing for time. "Which Krueger? It's a common name. . . ."

Pavlak's hand emerged from the pocket of his overcoat, clutching Borning's .38. He leveled it at Borning's face. His thumb pulled the hammer, and Borning heard the trigger latch click into place.

"Wait!" Borning blurted. "All right. Krueger ran Fool's Gold."

Pavlak lowered the weapon and slid it back into his pocket. "He's BND?"

Borning nodded, almost imperceptibly.

"It's time to come clean," Pavlak ordered tautly. "My wife and child are dead, and I want to know why—right now. Judith had a document of some kind. Your buddy Schliemann nearly killed me trying to get it. What's in that document, and what does it have to do with Krueger and Fool's Gold?"

"Where did you see Schliemann?"

"At his mansion on Crete."

"And Lederer was there?"

"Very much so. He's dead, by the way."

Borning's eyes widened. "Dead?"

Pavlak nodded. "And so will you be if I don't get some information. Good information. Right now."

Borning hesitated. Schliemann was supposed to have been pensioned off and forgotten. And what the hell was Lederer doing on Crete? That sonofabitch Krueger. The bastard *was* lying. "Listen, Pavlak—I don't know what the hell is going on, but I'm beginning to want to know. I took the wallet you gave me to Krueger, and he denied even knowing Lederer. But he was lying. Something doesn't add up. Something about Fool's Gold is dirty. But you've got to believe me—it's on the German side. At least..." Borning hesitated. "At least, as far as I know it is. I told you everything in Berlin. This time the information's got to come the other way around. *You* tell *me* what you know. What's this 'document' you're talking about—and what has Schliemann got to do with it?"

Pavlak did not speak or move a muscle. The silence grew ominous. The .38 was back in Pavlak's pocket, but Borning could see the end of the barrel outlined against the fabric.

"Listen to me!" Borning pleaded. "I'm telling you the truth, for God's sake. We thought your family's murder had nothing to do with us, but since then, the Agency has gotten suspicious—and I mean all the way up to a very high level. We want to know what's going on just as badly as you do. Work with us. It's your only chance to get to the bottom of this thing."

No response.

"Look, I was unarmed in Berlin, remember? If we had wanted to blow you away, we could have done it then. No problem."

Borning felt the first cold trickle of rainwater pass from his saturated hair and down the back of his collar.

"What do you want from me?" he demanded in exasperation.

"A meeting with Krueger," Pavlak said evenly.

Borning waited a full five seconds, his brain churning. "I can arrange that," he said slowly. "But on one condition. First you've got to tell me all you know."

"Agreed," Pavlak answered. "But on a condition of my own."

"Name it."

"None of this goes past you. We work alone. You and I. You said the Agency was suspicious at higher levels. Well, forget the higher levels—and the lower levels. You tell nobody you even saw me today—and I mean nobody. Agreed?"

Borning chewed on his lower lip. It wasn't such a bad idea. Until he knew where the dirt was coming from, it was better to keep it to as few people as possible. Hopkins would howl eventually, but let him howl. For all Borning knew, Hopkins himself could be the dirty one. And there were Agency rules that allowed—even mandated—extraordinary secrecy in response to a suspected security problem within the Agency itself. The rules were notoriously vague—a very thin blanket to cover him in a situation like this, but a cover nonetheless.

"You got it. What do you say we get out of the rain and find a soft booth and a cup of coffee?"

Pavlak shook his head. "We're not pals yet, Borning. Maybe you're on the level, and maybe you're not. Time will tell. Sit down."

"Where?"

"Here."

"In the mud?"

"It's soft, isn't it?"

Reluctantly, Borning lowered himself onto the ground and winced as the cold water instantly soaked through his trousers. From this position there could be no surprise moves against Pavlak. Smart bastard. Good instincts. He would have made a hell of an agent.

In the relentless drizzle that drifted down from a leaden German sky, Pavlak related the events of the past weeks. He told Borning about Brigitte and Turgat, about his drive to Dresden and the meeting with Schliemann's brother, then about the trip south and the events on Crete. He didn't mention the false passport or Karin.

On his way to Bonn Pavlak had stopped at the hotel in Stuttgart, hoping against hope that Karin might still be there. The desk clerk told him that she had checked out "a week or so" earlier—which was exactly what she should have done, exactly what they had planned. For now, Pavlak could only hope that she had followed the rest of his instructions. He would have to find her soon to warn her about Schliemann, but he had decided that finding Krueger was a higher priority. His best chance of protecting Karin—and himself— was to get to the bottom of this.

Borning listened intently to Pavlak's account of his experiences on Crete, then had him repeat much of it. Although Schliemann had been well paid for betraying his country, the life-style Pavlak described was puzzling. He frowned when Pavlak recounted Schliemann's reference to Krueger. If it was true, it was proof that the pompous bastard was lying. With Pavlak's help, maybe he could find a way to nail Krueger.

When Pavlak finally finished, Borning sat silently in the mud for half a minute. He no longer noticed the cold and the damp. "All right," he said at last, "here's how we'll do it. I supply you with a microphone and a transmitter. It's tiny. We can sew it into the lining of your jacket. Then, when everything's ready, I'll call Krueger and arrange to meet him in Munich. We do it all the time—at a pub called the *Blaue Engel*. Only this time, you'll show up instead. I'll be outside in a company van, taping the conversation. There's just one thing," Borning cautioned. "You've got to promise me there'll be no heroics. No violence. We're just gathering information for the *Bundesverfassungsschutz*. They're responsible for German counterintelligence. They'll take care of Krueger and any others. I have a good friend there—a man we can trust. Agreed?"

Pavlak shook his head grimly. "No."

"What do you mean, 'no'?"

"I mean that I'm looking for answers, and I believe I can get some from Krueger—but only if we play it my way. Why would he tell me anything in your scenario? You think he's going to spill his guts if I offer to buy him a cup of coffee? And besides, I don't trust you. I'm not walking into any CIA traps. You should know me better than that by now."

"It won't be a trap. I give you my word."

Pavlak's mouth twisted into a humorless smile. "Really. And what's that worth, Borning? What's anybody's *word* worth in the 1990's—quaint old idea you have there. And this from a man who's made a life out of lies and deception. Forget it. We do it my way or not at all."

Pavlak outlined his plan, and Borning squirmed, remembering suddenly that he was soaked and miserable.

"Surely you don't expect me to agree to that?" Borning protested.

"Depends on how badly you want to get to the bottom of this. *If* you want to get to the bottom of it."

"I do, but . . ."

"Then this is your only choice. Yes or no?"

Borning thought it over. It was a hell of a gamble. If it turned out well, he would look like a hero. If it turned out badly, the best he could hope for would be separation with no pension—if not a prison sentence. It all depended on Pavlak, a man he barely knew.

"Tell me," Borning said, fastening a level gaze on Pavlak, "what's *your* word worth?"

"My life," Pavlak replied instantly. "My word is my life—the only thing that makes me worth more than a cockroach. I'm funny that way. If I say it, I'll do it."

Borning studied the dark face in front of him. It was cruelly lined, etched by grief, and drawn with frustrated fury. It was the face, as he had realized in Berlin, of a determined and probably very dangerous man. Yet despite that—or perhaps because of it—he believed what Pavlak told him.

"All right. Then will you at least give me your word that you won't hurt anybody, until after the meeting with Krueger is over, and after you and I have talked again? I have to cover myself in this. You've got to understand that. I can't help you commit a murder."

"I give you my word," Pavlak replied carefully, "that I will not hurt Krueger during this meeting, and that you and I will talk again before I take any action. But," he added grimly, "if you deceive me in any way, the deal's off."

"Fair enough," Borning nodded. "It's a deal. I don't like it, but it's a deal. When do I hear from you?"

"Soon. There's a phone booth on the corner of Martinstrasse and Hohlweg in Bad Godesberg. Do you know it?"

Borning shook his head. "No, but I'll find it."

"Good. Be there at eight o'clock tomorrow night."

Borning hesitated, then began slowly. "Are you sure you want to do this? Your father . . . for all we know, he may be involved in some way."

"I'm sure," Pavlak snapped. He turned and started walking away.

"Wait!" Borning called, struggling to his feet. "My weapon. Can I have it back?"

Pavlak turned. "Sorry. I need it worse than you do. Tell you what, though—I'll trade it for mine. Here."

He tossed something at Borning who instinctively threw up his hands and caught it. Then Pavlak strode away in the rain, leaving the bedraggled CIA station chief grinding his teeth over an empty soda bottle.

25

At precisely 8:00 P.M., the telephone rang in the booth on a quiet residential street in Bad Godesberg. Borning snatched it up. "Yeah?"

"There's another phone at a Shell station on Bergergasse. Be there in ten minutes."

The line went dead. Grumbling under his breath, Borning climbed back into his car and fumbled in the dash for a city map. When he screeched to a halt at the second phone, it was already ringing.

"Yeah?" he panted into the receiver.

"There's a pedestrian path from the dead end of Achterstrasse that leads into the walkway beside the Rhine. Seventy-five meters downstream is a bench. Leave the goods on the bench, wrapped in a newspaper."

The line went dead again. It wasn't easy, but Borning followed Pavlak's instructions, then felt challenged to double back and watch Pavlak pick up the miniature microphone and transmitter. That wasn't easy either. Pavlak had chosen a spot that was almost impossible to observe without being seen. Borning finally wedged himself behind a bridge support four hundred meters away, and from there watched, not Pavlak, but a boy of perhaps twelve make the pickup. He didn't try to follow. Pavlak, he knew, would check for a tail before exchanging the microphone for whatever tip he had promised the boy.

On the third evening, Pavlak called Borning at home. "How's the weather?" he asked.

"Typical," Borning responded, giving Pavlak the all-clear he had asked for.

"Yesterday, one P.M.," Pavlak said, enunciating each word carefully. "H-one-point-two, B-point-four."

The phone went dead. The call had lasted less than eight seconds. Borning picked up the phone and dialed Krueger's home number in Munich.

"Hier bei Krueger," a familiar voice answered.

"Gerhart? Frank Borning. Listen, something's come up on this Pavlak affair. Can we meet at the usual place, to-morrow morning at eleven?" As agreed, Borning added two days and subtracted two hours from the time Pavlak had given him.

There was a pause before the reply. "I'm very busy, Frank. I have an important meeting tomorrow morning at ten. Is it urgent?"

"Very."

"Could we make it the afternoon? Say three?"

"Sorry. I have to be back in Bonn before then."

"Well—all right then. I'll see you at eleven."

"Thanks Gerhart. It really is important, believe me."

"Of course."

Borning hung up the phone, walked to his desk, and opened a map of Munich he had bought that morning. He found the quadrant at H/B and with a ruler, measured in from the left vertical mark 1.2 centimeters and marked the spot on the bottom horizontal line with a pencil, then did the same at the top line. Finally he connected the two dots with a straight line. Next he measured up .4 centimeters from the bottom line and made a mark on the left vertical, then did the same on the right vertical. When he connected those dots as well, the two pencil lines intersected at the corner of Bernhartstrasse and Kleekstrasse, three blocks from the *Blaue Engel* where he and Krueger would meet.

The next day Borning took a 9:00 A.M. commuter flight out of Cologne to Munich. At 10:40 he was standing in a phone booth on the corner of Bernhartstrasse and Kleekstrasse holding the receiver to his ear and pretending to speak, but with his finger pressing the hook switch. At exactly 10:45, the phone rang. He released the switch.

"Yes?"

"How's the weather?"

"Typical."

"Take him for a walk down Elwertstrasse toward the *Deutsches Museum.* If you get as far as Istenallee, wait at the phone booth there."

"Listen, Pavlak . . ."

There was a click, followed by a brief silence, and then the dial tone. Borning checked the urge to grind his teeth. Pavlak's paranoia was beginning to get on his nerves. How the hell was he going to persuade Krueger to take a walk? They had never done that before. If Krueger *was* dirty, he would be suspicious about this meeting already.

Krueger was sitting in their customary booth at the *Blaue Engel* when Borning walked in. He stood and shook Borning's hand with a grip that was just slightly too firm, as always, as if intended to intimidate, rather than ingratiate.

"Nice to see you, Frank," Krueger began in his schoolboy

English, studiedly correct, but lifeless and heavily accented. He pronounced "Frank" as if it were the name of Charlemagne's tribe.

"How are you, Gerhart?" Borning responded, standing at the end of the booth. "Look, would you mind a little walk? I'd rather not speak in here today."

For just a second, Krueger's eyes narrowed, then the businessman's smile reappeared. "But Frank, I have ordered a *Birnenschnaps* for you. You never decline that."

Borning shook his head. "Not today, Gerhart. We have a lot of ground to cover and very little time." He faked a look at his watch. "I'm on a tight schedule."

Krueger was still sitting. "Really? What time is your return flight?"

"One something—before two, in any case."

"Very little time indeed. Why waste it walking in the cold when we can enjoy a drink here in a warm seat?"

Borning placed his hands flat on the table and leaned over Krueger. "Because I'm not sure this location is safe anymore," he whispered softly.

"Really?" Krueger whispered back. "Safe for whom?"

Borning caught what he thought was a hint of a sneer on Krueger's lips. Then it was gone, and Krueger was laughing.

"I'm joking, of course, old friend," Krueger laughed. "If you prefer, then of course, we shall walk." He stood and gathered up his overcoat from the seat beside him just as a waitress appeared with two schnaps glasses on a tray.

"Ah, just in time," Krueger exclaimed. He lifted one glass and held it up expectantly. Borning hesitated, then swept the other glass from the tray.

"To old friends," Krueger said.

Borning nodded and downed the schnaps with one gulp, savoring the aroma of pear in his nose as he exhaled.

"Thank you, Gerhart. My favorite, as you know." Borning pulled his wallet from his hip pocket, but Krueger waved him away and dropped a twenty-mark note on the tray. Generous, Borning thought. Very generous.

Outside, the air was bright and sunny, but bitterly cold for early spring. Borning carefully buttoned his heavy overcoat to make sure the receiver and the miniature recorder in the inside pocket stayed hidden. Pavlak had insisted on a portable receiver. No listening van. A van was too difficult to move, and Pavlak wanted ease of movement. He also wanted no one but Borning involved, so Borning would have to monitor their conversation himself—hopefully keeping the two in sight.

Krueger lagged outside the door of the *Blaue Engel* and lit a cigar—a difficult matter in the stiff breeze, requiring several tries.

"I didn't know you smoked cigars," Borning said.

"Rarely," Krueger conceded. "But I've come to enjoy them lately. This particular brand is Cuban. Care for one?"

"No thanks. I don't smoke. Where did you get a Cuban cigar?"

"I have my sources," Krueger laughed. He slapped Borning on the shoulder, a very un-Germanic gesture that immediately put Borning on guard. Except for the obligatory handshake, he and Krueger had never touched. There was something different about Krueger today. Or maybe Borning's nerves were just on edge. It had been a long time since his field days. It occurred to him that maybe Krueger was behaving a little oddly because he was nervous too.

"Beautiful day," Borning commented, as he led Krueger down Fichtengasse, then onto Elwertstrasse.

"Yes, but cold. Winter's last gasp, I'd say."

They crossed the street so that the Isar flowed past on

their right, separated from them by a narrow greenway with a few trees and an occasional park bench. Borning watched the faces and studied every tree. Pavlak was out there somewhere, watching. Presumably he would approach them when he was sure there was no tail. Borning hoped it would be soon. He did not like this plan, but he had to acknowledge a certain creative logic in it. Pavlak was surely the last person Krueger expected to see. If Krueger really was dirty—and really had been helping Schliemann find Pavlak—then Pavlak's sudden appearance should unnerve him. And once Borning withdrew and left Krueger alone with a man Krueger knew to be violent and in deep grief over his family, Krueger would make a mistake. Say something too hastily. Give the *Bundesverfassungsschutz* an opening. They would take it from there. Pavlak had never been trained as an interrogator, of course, but he had extraordinary instincts. He would get something out of Krueger.

Of course Borning had not mentioned it to Pavlak, but Krueger's mistake, if he panicked, might be to try to eliminate Pavlak. Borning hoped not—he was beginning to like Pavlak in a grudging sort of way. But this was a hard business, and with Pavlak wired, and the tape recorder spinning next to Borning's chest, Krueger would have a hard time explaining why he blew away an American citizen on a street in Munich—even an armed citizen.

"So what's the latest news on our friend, the younger Pavlak?" Krueger asked as the small talk died. "I assume he's the reason you called."

"Yes, as a matter of fact he is. I've spoken to him."

Krueger's step faltered only slightly. "You've *spoken* to him?"

"Yes. He called me yesterday at the embassy. He . . ."

"From where?"

"He didn't say."

"Oh, come now, Frank," Krueger snapped. "We both know you Americans have more electronics in that embassy than Siemens sells in a year, not to mention some special arrangements with *Deutsche Telekom*. Are you going to tell me you didn't trace the call?"

"All right, Gerhart. It was made from a phone booth in Berlin. We notified the police, of course, but he was gone by the time they got there."

"I see," Krueger answered with unconcealed skepticism. "So what did he have to say?"

"Where is Lederer, Gerhart?"

"Lederer?"

"Yes, you know—Lederer—the one whose ID was stolen by a mugger in Berlin. The one you pretended not to know even though you hired him yourself."

Krueger stopped walking and turned slowly. He fastened Borning with an icy stare. "I do believe, Frank, that you are calling me a liar."

Krueger's eyes were darts aimed at Borning's pupils. But to Borning's surprise, he noticed a tremble in Krueger's upper lip. The man was under a tremendous strain. They were on the right track.

"And you believe correctly, Gerhart," he said flatly. Their faces were six inches apart. "You've been lying to me all along on this one, and I'm getting pretty damned tired of it. What happened with Fool's Gold? I want the whole truth, and I want it now." Where the hell was Pavlak? This was moving too fast. Borning broke eye contact, turned, and started walking again. He was ten feet away before Krueger followed.

"I should take offense at this, Frank," Krueger said as he caught up with him. "We've known each other a long time."

"Bullshit," Borning blurted angrily. "You may have known me, but I haven't known you at all. I'm asking you again— where's Lederer?"

"I don't know. He's missing."

"Missing?"

"He disappeared about two weeks ago. We assume he was kidnapped—possibly murdered. But of course the possibility exists that he defected."

"Defected? To whom, Gerhart? The Cold War is over, remember?"

"We don't know. He may have gone underground under the protection of some industrialist or the other. That is, if he was—what's the phrase you Americans use—'on the take?' I believe you are implying that. Or have I misunderstood you, Frank?"

"Only halfway. Was Lederer involved in Fool's Gold?"

"To some degree, yes."

Borning searched the faces coming to meet them on the sidewalk. A mother in a pink parka, pushing a baby carriage. An elderly man in a shabby brown overcoat. Three schoolgirls carrying bookbags, gossiping and giggling.

"To what degree, exactly?"

"Oh please, Frank, just what is it you want? You know, your attitude is really annoying."

Time to fire both barrels. "It should be," he said, "because I believe that you and Lederer and maybe some others are dirty. You hired Lederer—no problem, that's your job—but you denied knowing him. You lied to me, and I'm trying to figure out why you would do that unless you're dirty. So why don't you tell me now, before I just take my suspicions to the BVS?"

"Why haven't you done that already?"

"Call it friendship."

Krueger's sneer was unconcealed this time. "All right," he said. "Just a moment—my cigar's out." He stopped again, pulled the lighter from his pocket and relit the cigar, puffing rapidly until the ember glowed. The schoolgirls and the baby carriage were long past them. Now the old man passed by with a tortured limp. There was no one else within one hundred meters.

"Now, where were we?" Krueger asked. "Oh yes—friendship. Tell me, Frank, just what is it Pavlak has said to you to make you suspect—an old friend?"

"He told me he paid a visit to Peter Schliemann and that he's living in luxury on Crete. Did you know that?"

"I had heard he moved to Crete. The luxury idea is probably exaggerated, though. We—or rather you Americans—paid him well, but not that well."

"Exactly. And that's not all. Pavlak says Schliemann and your friend Lederer tried to take him apart. As it happened, Schliemann slipped and let a name fall. Guess whose name that was, Gerhart?"

They were strolling slowly down the river walkway again.

"I have no idea," Krueger said coolly.

"Yours, *old friend.* Pavlak thinks you killed his wife and his little girl. He's an old Special Forces soldier, by the way—decorated for valor. And he has a hot temper. He's looking for you."

"He's wrong," Krueger snapped firmly. "It wasn't me."

"Then who was it—and why?"

Krueger seemed to be pondering his answer when a blue Mercedes glided to the curb beside them.

"Ah, here's my car," Krueger said, instantly pulling the back door open. "Let's ride for a while, shall we?"

Time stopped. As Borning was coming to grips with the sudden appearance of the Mercedes, his gaze caught the driver, and a flash of recognition interrupted his thoughts. Where had he seen that cadaverous face before? The hollow cheeks, the close, dark eyes?

Just before Krueger stepped into his line of view, Borning noticed the long slender fingers curled around the steering wheel. Of course. Berlin! It was the man who was following them when Pavlak's cab driver made that suicidal U-turn. It was even the same car.

Suddenly Krueger's fingers closed powerfully on Borning's right arm and drew him toward the open door.

"Climb in, Frank," Krueger commanded.

Instinctively Borning resisted the pressure on his arm. What else had he just seen? The driver's left hand was on the steering wheel. And his right hand lay on the seat, holding a newspaper. Why would he be holding a newspaper if he was driving? No, he wasn't *holding* the newspaper—his hand was *under* the newspaper.

The pressure on his arm had grown commanding, causing Borning's torso to twist to the left as his feet held their ground, thus putting Krueger behind his right shoulder. Instinct kicked in. Borning was not sure what was happening, but he was sure of one thing. He was not getting into that car.

Krueger's pressure turned into a shove as Borning twisted to face him, and Borning's left shoulder collided with the top of the door frame. He brought his right elbow up sharply, slamming it into Krueger's chin and staggering him backwards, then Borning's right hand dove for the pistol in his shoulder holster. But instead of the weapon, his fingers met only cloth. Then he remembered that he had buttoned the overcoat to hide the receiver in his pocket. With his left hand he jerked the lapel and ripped three buttons off.

It was too late. He heard the crack of a shot—he would later learn that it came from inside the car—and in the same instant felt something like a slap from a hickory switch hit his right elbow. There was a moment's delay before the pain from the shattered joint reached his brain. In the interim he saw Krueger's right hand rising toward him with a 9 mm pistol in it.

Suddenly a series of sharp reports erupted from the sidewalk close behind him. For a fraction of a second, Krueger's eyes met Borning's. The expression on Krueger's face was a mixture of surprise and pity—pity for what or for whom, Borning would never know, because an instant later Krueger pitched forward, facedown on the concrete at Borning's feet. Borning felt a bullet whistle past his face and willed his legs to turn loose, dropping him onto the concrete. No sooner did his back come to rest against the rear hubcap of the Mercedes than the wheel spun violently, throwing him to the pavement as the car sped away.

Then, just as suddenly as it had begun, all was quiet again—eerily, deathly quiet. Borning clutched his elbow and struggled back to a sitting position. The old man in the brown coat was lying on the sidewalk perhaps five meters away. For a second Borning thought he had been hit by a stray bullet, but then he saw the snub-nosed .38 clutched in both hands. With a start Borning recognized Pavlak in a fake moustache and dyed hair. Pavlak climbed to his feet and ran toward him.

Borning cradled the shattered right elbow in his left hand. Blood dripped from his fingers and began to pool on the sidewalk.

"How bad is it?" Pavlak asked, kneeling.

It was several seconds before Borning could find his voice.

"My elbow's shot to hell, but I'll live. What about him?" He jerked his head toward Krueger's prostrate form. Pavlak felt for the carotid artery.

"Dead. Is he Krueger?"

Borning nodded.

"I've seen him before," Pavlak said with a frown. "Him and Schliemann both, but I can't remember where. Did he tell you anything?"

"He said he didn't kill your wife and child."

"You believe him?"

"I don't know. Why didn't you intercept us?"

"I saw the tail. It was the guy from Berlin. I thought he was one of yours. I thought you'd double-crossed me. The only reason I got close at all was because I wanted to see Krueger's face. I had a hunch . . ." His voice trailed off.

Borning swallowed hard. He was beginning to feel ill— sick to his stomach. "Why . . . why did you shoot?"

"I don't know," Pavlak answered. "It was just a reaction when I heard the first shot and saw Krueger pull the pistol. I guess I felt like you were on my side. Funny, isn't it. . . ."

"They're crazy," Borning whispered. Reality was fading, and he was entering a dream. "I don't know what they thought they were doing, but the chances of getting away with it were minuscule. They're desperate."

In the distance, the first siren sounded.

"I've got to get out of here," Pavlak said anxiously, glancing in the direction of the siren.

"Pavlak."

"Yes?"

The pool of blood beneath Borning's elbow was spreading rapidly. The sidewalk began to writhe, and the grass beyond it turned bright yellow. "Find the document."

The grass went from yellow to black, then vanished.

26

A bell over the door tinkled warmly when Pavlak entered. Like most of Europe's few remaining family businesses, the little grocery had seen better days. The selection was limited, the prices high, and the merchandise covered with dust. If it weren't for free-spending tourists, Pavlak thought, this place wouldn't last six months.

A shriveled little woman, who must have been over seventy was deftly slicing pork chops on a butcher block behind the rear counter.

"Excuse me," Pavlak said in English. "I'm looking for a friend. My name is Arthur Smith."

The old woman pulled her head back like a frightened chicken and scurried through a door without a word. Pavlak heard excited whispering, then saw Karin's dark eyes peep around the corner. Seconds later she flung her arms around him and clung tightly to his neck.

"*Gott sei Dank,*" she breathed. "Thank God you're all right. I was so worried about you. I stayed in Stuttgart three extra days, hoping you would show up. It was the worst three days of my life. I was sure you were dead, like Turgat . . ." She broke off suddenly. "What happened to your nose?"

Pavlak glanced at the old woman, who stood to one side, now smiling benevolently. "The . . . gentleman I went to visit . . . rearranged it for me," he said after a pause. His arms were wrapped tightly around Karin's slender form, pressing her to him. He couldn't take his eyes off her face. It was a beautiful face, he decided. One that brought him a sense of joy and relief, a sense of . . . homecoming.

Karin's smile vanished. "Oh my God," she whispered, stroking the nose gently with her fingers.

"We'll talk later," Pavlak said. "Get your things."

"Where are we going?"

"Back to Berlin," Pavlak lied.

"How will we get off the island? The ferry . . ."

"I've hired a plane. He's waiting at the airstrip to fly us to Bremen."

"Can I have half an hour?" Karin asked.

"Make it fifteen minutes."

"Twenty."

"Ten."

She frowned. "That's not the way you negotiate."

"Hurry, Karin—please."

For an instant Karin gave him a curious look, then turned and rushed away, leaving him standing alone with the old woman.

"My name is Hagedorn," she said after an awkward silence. "I'm pleased to meet you."

Pavlak gently took the outstretched hand and smiled.

"Karin is such a wonderful girl," Mrs. Hagedorn blurted suddenly, answering his smile.

"Yes. How do you know her?" Pavlak asked, as if he didn't already know.

"We rent rooms. She and her husband—her former husband—stayed three weeks here on their honeymoon. We liked them very much and stayed in touch. We were sad when we learned of the divorce. But Karin is such a delightful girl. I'm sure she won't be single long." The old woman smiled and lifted an eyebrow.

"We?" Pavlak asked.

"My husband and I. My second husband. My first husband was killed—in the war."

"I'm sorry."

"It was a long time ago."

"Have you always lived on Wangerooge?"

"Yes. I was born on the island. I love it here. It's so quiet. We don't allow automobiles, you know."

"Yes, I know. I've visited the North Sea islands before. This is my first time on Wangerooge, though."

Another silence fell over them.

"You need anything for your trip back to the mainland?" she asked at last. "Any food? Take whatever you like. No charge." She indicated the whole store with a sweep of her arm and a generous smile.

"Thanks, I'll look around," Pavlak replied. He browsed through the old store, reminiscent of one a family friend operated in Lake Elm in the early fifties. When Karin appeared carrying an overnight bag, he picked up two bars of chocolate, mainly to please Mrs. Hagedorn. The old woman nodded and smiled and shoved three tins of sardines into his hands as well. Pavlak detested sardines, but thanked her anyway.

"And thanks for taking care of Karin," he added.

"Any time. She's such a lovely girl. A wonderful girl."

When the door closed behind them, Pavlak took Karin's light bag and slung it over his shoulder. "You have a fan," he teased.

"I know. It's a little embarrassing. She's match-making for me."

"I noticed."

Karin laughed. "You too, huh? Don't take it personally. In the four days I've been here, she's introduced me to four men."

Pavlak frowned. "That's not exactly keeping a low profile."

"I know, but . . . I couldn't tell her the whole story. I just said I was on vacation, waiting for an American friend named Arthur Smith. I told her I really just wanted to relax and read in my room, but she wouldn't leave me alone. I'm sorry."

"It's okay. If Schliemann had found you, you would know it already. By the way," Pavlak said as they rounded a corner, "I lied. We're not going to Berlin. We're going to Hamburg to catch a flight to New York. The tickets are in my pocket."

The small grass airfield at the eastern end of the tiny island was visible just ahead. Karin was slow to reply. "You could have discussed it with me first," she said coolly.

"I'm sorry, Karin, but there's no time for discussion. And nothing to discuss. You'll understand when you hear why."

A few moments later, the Cessna's engine noise discouraged further conversation. Pavlak and Karin sat squeezed side by side in the back of the four-seater as a taciturn pilot lifted them over the shallow sound and back to Bremen where Pavlak had left the BMW. On the drive to Hamburg, he had time only to recount the events on Crete. Bonn and Munich could wait. And anyway, he wasn't sure how she would react when she learned about Munich.

"Oh, my God!" Karin blurted before he had quite finished telling her about Crete.

"What is it?"

"I can't go to New York! Have you forgotten? I don't have a false passport like you."

"You do now," Pavlak said calmly. He reached inside his pocket and withdrew a German passport, slightly the worse for wear. Karin opened it and found her own photo looking back at her—the one Pavlak had insisted she make in the automat in Berlin when he had made his own.

"How did you get it?" she asked, her mouth open in amazement.

"Turks aren't the only ones with connections to forgers. I stopped by an American army base in Würzburg and looked up an old friend of mine. He's a First Sergeant now. He knows everything and everybody."

"Can you trust him?" she asked doubtfully.

"Absolutely."

"How can you be so sure?"

"He owes me."

"Owes you what?"

Pavlak's eyes never left the road. "His life."

The tone made it clear that he didn't wish to continue the conversation, so Karin dropped the forged passport into her purse and kept silent.

The jumbo jet was packed to bursting with passengers. Their seats were in the middle section, excellent for viewing a mindless movie starring Goldie Hawn, but ill-suited for private conversation. Pavlak tried to sleep but his eyes would not stay closed. They chatted idly for a while, then Karin picked up the flight magazine and started through it, cover to cover. Already the rush of excitement on Wangerooge, the gush of greeting, the warm hug—all seemed distant and vaguely embarrassing. An awkwardness had settled between them. They were, Pavlak reminded himself, still worlds apart.

It was three o'clock in the afternoon, New York time, when the jet touched down at Kennedy Airport. Two German tourists, Udo Brandauer and Elisabeth Schmeeling, separately endured the rude arrogance of New York customs officials, then found each other again in the lobby of the International Arrivals building.

Pavlak rented a Toyota Camry for the drive to North Carolina. He had decided to avoid airports as much as possible, for fear the FBI might be watching passenger lists. With Karin sitting silently beside him, he guided the Toyota over the Verrazano Narrows Bridge, across Staten Island, and onto the New Jersey Turnpike. This was Karin's first visit to the United States, and she stayed glued to her window in fascination. Pavlak felt only the detached disorientation he always felt when returning from abroad. Everything was familiar, yet foreign. The feeling would pass, he knew, in a day or two.

Once they were on the Turnpike, Pavlak set the cruise control at sixty-five miles per hour, removed his foot from the accelerator, and cleared his throat. It was time.

"There's more to tell, Karin."

"I know."

"You do?"

"Yes. You've been keeping something from me. I wondered when you were going to tell me. All right, whatever it is, I'm ready."

Pavlak drew a breath and told her about Bonn and his reunion with Frank Borning. He told her how Borning had admitted that Krueger was the BND man who ran Fool's Gold, and about their agreement to surprise Krueger in Munich.

"And what happened in Munich?" she asked.

"I'm getting to that."

While he searched for the right words, her hand came to rest on his forearm. "Just tell me, John."

In front of them a tractor trailer swung into the left lane to pass a camper, and Pavlak hit the brakes. He waited until their path was clear again before replying.

"I had to kill him," he said simply.

From the corner of his eye, he saw Karin's head drop to her chest. A moment later the first sniffle told him she was crying.

"I didn't set out to do it," he said with a twitch of his shoulders. "I had to. He was forcing Borning into a car. The skinny man from Berlin was driving it, the one who followed you to the subway station. They shot Borning. He's okay, I think. But they would have killed him, and then we'd have been back at square one. I had to do it. And besides . . . I just . . . I didn't have time to think. It happened so quickly," he added, aware of a note of desperation in his voice.

She murmured something he could not hear.

"Excuse me?"

She gave him an anguished look. Her eyes were red and her cheeks streaked with tears. "I said, why did you bring me here?"

Pavlak tightened his grip on the wheel. He nudged the brake, deactivating the cruise control.

"It's the only way I can protect you. Schliemann knows you're in this as deep as I am. And he's desperate. They were willing to kill a CIA agent—an American diplomat— to protect themselves. Think of what they would do to you. You can't spend the rest of your life hiding on an island. Besides," he added hesitantly, "I need you."

There was a full minute of silence before Karin replied. "How do you feel?"

"I feel fine. Why?"

"I mean about . . . Munich."

"I don't want to talk about it."

"Would you do it again?"

"If I had to."

They were into open countryside. The sky was still bright and warm even though evening was near. It was mid-April and the flat plains of southern Jersey were vibrant with fresh spring growth.

"Was he the one? The one who killed Brigitte and the others?"

"I don't know. The only way to find out for sure is to keep digging."

He glanced at her. She was staring out at the green landscape, but her jaw was set.

"What if it turns out that he wasn't the one?" she asked. "That it was someone else?"

Pavlak felt a rush of heat to his face. "Dammit, Karin," he exploded. "I told you! I *had* to do it. There was no choice."

"That's not what I'm talking about," Karin shot back. "If you find out it really was Schliemann after all, let's say, what will you do? I mean to him—Schliemann?"

"What should I do, Karin?" Pavlak demanded, "Say 'aw shucks,' and let him live out his filthy life in luxury on a Greek island?"

"You don't have to snap, John. I understand."

"Like hell, you do."

"Damn you!" Karin shouted. Startled, Pavlak glanced at her. Her fists were clenched on her knees, and rage shone through the tears in her eyes. "How *dare* you say that!"

Pavlak winced. "I'm sorry. I'm so wrapped up in my own hurt that I forget yours sometimes. And we're just . . . very different."

Karin took a deep breath. "Not as different as you think.

Maybe we argue because we're so much alike. Anyway, I just want this to have a happy ending. And we have a disagreement about what constitutes a happy end. By the way, you're going to get a speeding ticket."

The cars in the right lane were dropping rapidly behind them, one after the other. Pavlak looked at the speedometer. He was doing ninety. He released the accelerator and eased into the right lane. They crossed the Delaware River into Wilmington before either of them spoke again.

27

It was nearly midnight—6:00 A.M. Central European Time—
when they reached Petersburg. Twice Pavlak had caught
himself drifting onto the shoulder. When a billboard announced the presence of a Holiday Inn ahead, he stopped
and rented a double room in the name of Mr. and Mrs. Udo
Brandauer. To his amazement, Karin had to be shaken
awake when he had parked the car outside their room. Pavlak had been a poor sleeper all his life, and sleeping—at
least sleeping soundly—in a moving automobile was incon-
ceivable to him.

The room was wonderfully American, large and clean,
with two queen-size beds. Karin dropped onto one of them
fully clothed and was instantly asleep again. Pavlak pulled
the blanket off the other bed and gently covered her. While
she slept, he took a shower, then watched CNN for half an
hour before finally turning out the lights.

A few minutes later, Tasha came running to him, laughing
and alive, her dark eyes glowing, and her hair streaming
behind her. Pavlak snatched her into his arms, and, as he
hugged her warm cheek to his, a flood of indescribable joy

engulfed him. She was alive! None of it was true after all. The nightmare was over.

He awoke with a jerk. The room was quiet, and the faint, familiar scent of stale tobacco smoke was in his nose. Karin snored lightly on the bed beside him. Somewhere in the distance a siren wailed. The dream lingered only a second, like a distant echo, and then reality crashed in on him again. He knew that this time he was going to break. He rose softly, closed the bathroom door behind him, and shoved a towel into his face. It was nearly an hour before he eased the door open and fell back onto the bed, exhausted and empty.

At six he was awakened by the hydraulic whine of a garbage truck lifting a dumpster somewhere nearby. He dressed quietly, left Karin a note that said he would be back before ten, and slipped out the door. In downtown Petersburg, he found a franchise breakfast shop and ate a plate of soggy pancakes, topped with a syrup that tasted vaguely chemical. This too, he remembered, was America.

He asked the waitress for a telephone directory and flipped through the yellow pages until he found a gun and pawn shop that opened at eight o'clock. Frank Borning's snub-nosed .38 was corroding at the bottom of the Weser in Bremen, and after Crete, Pavlak felt naked without a weapon.

He was waiting at the pawn shop when the proprietor arrived to unlock the door. The man was middle-aged, a head shorter than Pavlak, and weighed at least three hundred pounds. He seemed incapable of smiling, but he was willing to do business, and twenty minutes later, Pavlak walked out carrying a plastic bag that contained a Ruger P89 Mark II 9 mm pistol and a shoulder holster. Three loaded magazines lay in the left pocket of his jacket, each packed with fifteen rounds. In his right pocket was a miniature twenty-two with an ankle holster. The guns were pawned items, not new. Pavlak asked for untraceable weapons, and the broker chose models that he was "positive" were stolen. The price for avoiding the paperwork, the permits, and the legally mandated waiting period was high. The fat pawnbroker was almost an honest man. But the power of money never ceased to amaze Pavlak. He was beginning to understand why corruption accompanies large supplies of cash the way worms thrive in rich soil.

At the motel Pavlak pushed the key into the door as quietly as he could. It was not yet nine o'clock, and Karin might still be asleep.

She was in the shower, and the television was on, still tuned to CNN. He picked one of the upholstered chairs beside a small round table by the window and sat down to wait. A few minutes later the faucet in the tub squeaked, and Karin stepped into the room, naked except for a towel held loosely at her throat. Pavlak's breath caught. He wanted to say something to warn her of his presence, but no sound came out. Her skin was rosy and damp from the hot shower and her wet black hair lay close to her head. She bent over the open travel bag at the foot of her bed and let the towel fall. At the same instant she glanced up and their eyes met. Seconds passed.

Pavlak cleared his throat. "You're beautiful," he said softly.

Karin straightened slowly, her hands at her side, her eyes still on his.

Pavlak felt his legs gather under him, felt himself rise from the chair, felt the magnetic pull of her body as he approached. He stopped a foot away. She smelled faintly of shampoo. Her right hand rose and came to rest lightly on his shoulder as her eyes closed. He heard her breath quicken as his left hand touched her side, then slid softly around to the small of her back. She was warm and damp and soft. His arm longed to pull her into him, but with a huge effort he forced it to remain motionless.

"Your plans . . . the Order . . . ," he whispered.

She shook her head. "I can't."

Can't what, he was about to ask, when suddenly she was in his arms, and her mouth pressed against his. Small fingers clutched furiously at the buttons of his shirt, at his belt, his zipper. Pavlak sank helplessly into her, drinking her, eating her, consuming her, and for a time the ugly world of death vanished, and an ageless world of life opened up and swallowed them.

Arthur Trask switched off the row of fluorescent lights that bisected the ceiling in his office and stepped out the door. It was late. Business was booming at Pavlak Equipment. They were operating three shifts, and the job of managing the plant was grinding him down.

"Getting too old for this shit," he muttered to no one as he fumbled in his pocket for his keys. That morning he had awakened with a new ache in his left hip, and he knew that at his age, aches did not come and go. They accumulated. He limped slightly as he walked to his car.

At the gate he waved to the guard on duty, then pulled onto Industrial Avenue, heading for home, a warm supper, and Edith.

As the big Pontiac accelerated, he thought about retirement. It was time. But what would happen to the company if he left? Tom Pavlak wasn't such a bad guy, really, but the kid didn't have what it takes to run a company like this. If Gustaf weren't still behind him, making the important calls,

Pavlak Equipment would be sliding down the tubes. And now it looked like the end was near for the old man—certainly the end of his activity at the company. Maybe it was time for Arthur to get out too, before Tom Pavlak actually got the authority that went along with his titles as President and Chief Operating Officer. If only John had stayed with the business rather than Tom. John Pavlak would have made a good businessman—a good anything, really. He was brilliant, that boy.

Arthur said a silent prayer for the older Pavlak brother, wherever he might be, and turned left onto Bark Street, named, so legend had it, for a vociferous Collie that once lived there. The headlights of an approaching car drew his attention to his rearview mirror. The car was closing fast— much too fast for a residential street.

"Damned fool," he muttered, and eased closer to the curb as the car swung out to pass him. As soon as it passed, brake lights flared, and the car stopped dead in the middle of the street. Arthur screeched to a halt.

"What the hell . . . ?"

The driver's door of the stopped car flew open and a man stepped out.

Carjacking was the first thought that flashed through Arthur's mind. He frantically shoved the shift lever into reverse and was about to step on the accelerator when he saw John Pavlak's face grinning at him in the glare of his headlights.

"John!"

Arthur threw open the door of the Pontiac and rushed to Pavlak with open arms.

"No!" Pavlak commanded, giving Arthur a stiff arm in the chest. "I've got five broken ribs that just healed, and I'm not having you break them again. Be gentle, okay?"

Arthur blinked, then restrained himself and took the

younger man gently into his arms. "God, it's good to see you, John," he said, patting him tenderly on the back. "Where the hell have you been? We've been worried sick about you. How did you break the ribs? And what happened to your nose?"

"Slow down, Arthur. All in due time. Listen, we can't talk here. Is your house safe?"

"What do you mean safe? I suppose so. Why shouldn't it be?"

"Nobody knows I'm here—especially not the FBI. Are they watching your house?"

"I think they did for a week or so, but I haven't seen anybody lately."

Pavlak shook his head. "Then it's still too risky. Where can we talk?"

Arthur stroked the stubble on his chin. "I know. The lake house. It's empty. We haven't opened it for the season yet. No time. That brother of yours . . ." he began darkly.

"Right," Pavlak interrupted. "Tell me later. Go ahead. I'll follow."

Arthur grinned and gave Pavlak a tap on the cheek that made his ears ring, then climbed back into his car.

"He certainly seemed happy to see you," Karin said when Pavlak eased back into the driver's seat of the Toyota.

"Arthur was the closest thing to a father I ever had, Karin. He's everything my own father wasn't."

They followed Arthur out of Lake Elm on U.S. Highway 29 toward the Yadkin River. Arthur made a series of turns down narrow asphalt roads, then pulled off to the right down a dirt trail through the woods until their path was abruptly blocked by a padlocked cable across the road.

Arthur climbed out of his car, opened the padlock, and tossed the heavy cable into the woods. They bumped along another half mile until the trail ended abruptly at a cabin overlooking the river.

"Jeez, I haven't been here since August," Arthur called, throwing the door of his car shut as if it were a toy. He stopped in his tracks.

"This is Karin, Arthur," Pavlak explained. "She's a friend. I'll explain later."

Arthur made a small, clumsy bow that brought a fleeting smile to Karin's face, then shuffled off toward the cabin, sorting his keys as he went.

The stale scent of dust and mold rose to meet them as they entered the cabin. Arthur fumbled in the dark for the breaker box above the kitchen counter and flipped on the main. Instantly the room was bathed in light from a bare bulb in the ceiling.

The cabin had been built in 1956 from the pine lumber cleared to make room for it. Ceiling, walls, and floor were all varnished pine that glowed warm and yellow in the electric light. It was tiny—only two rooms, a combination kitchen/living room and one small bedroom with a bath attached. A sofa and an armchair were both covered with sheets, but a small table in the kitchen area held four wooden chairs turned upside down. Arthur quickly flipped the chairs onto the floor and opened one of the cabinets above the sink. He pulled out three coffee mugs and a jar of instant coffee that had hardened to the consistency of concrete. Karin searched for sugar, while Pavlak put a pot of water on the stove to boil.

"Have you been home?" Arthur asked, watching Pavlak closely as he chipped at the coffee with the rounded point of a case knife.

"That's the last place I would go right now."

"Then you don't know."

"Know what?"

"Your father—he's not well, John. He had a stroke."

The knife paused in midair, and Pavlak lowered the coffee jar to the counter. "How bad is it?"

"He's partially paralyzed on his left side. Can't walk or stand. He can talk, but he almost never does. Just lies there and stares into space. It's bad, John."

Pavlak said nothing.

"He's out of the hospital now. Roser's taking care of him at home. They've hired some nurses. The—the deaths—hit him hard. He's been going downhill fast ever since Judith and Tasha . . ." Arthur flipped one huge hand nervously but did not finish the sentence. "He looked like hell even before the stroke—lost weight, wouldn't talk to anybody. He wants to see you, John. He's worried sick about you."

Pavlak picked up the jar and hammered at the stale coffee again. "I'll see him sometime, Arthur," he said grimly. "As soon as I can. I've got some questions for him—and for you too, as far as that goes. Does the term 'Fool's Gold' mean anything to you?"

"It's some kind of mineral, isn't it—looks like gold?"

"Iron pyrite—actually iron disulfide," Pavlak answered. "Has the same color as gold. Early prospectors would come across some of it and think they had struck it rich. Then they were left with about as deep a disappointment as a man can feel, I imagine. But I'm not talking about minerals. I'm talking about a CIA operation that involved Pavlak Equipment."

Arthur's eyes widened, and the big man sat back in his chair. "What!"

"That's right. Dad was part of it for sure—possibly Tom. I thought you might have known about it too."

Arthur stared. "Oh brother, I can't wait to hear this one."

Karin took the coffee jar and the knife from Pavlak's hand. "Go ahead and talk," she said in German. "I'll do this." She understood English well, she had told Pavlak on the way from New York, but she spoke it poorly.

Pavlak recounted the events of the preceding month, and Arthur listened intently, occasionally letting his mouth fall open, especially when he learned that Pavlak's call from Luckau had been intercepted by the CIA.

"Is that *legal?*" Trask spluttered.

"I doubt if it's illegal, at least not technically. Your phone wasn't tapped, after all. The call was probably snatched from a satellite by a secret antenna somewhere. Or maybe it was intercepted by a spy satellite over the Atlantic. Who knows? And who has jurisdiction over the ether?"

Trask shook his head. "Amazing. Scary."

Pavlak continued his story but omitted Bonn and Munich as he had at first with Karin. He might yet wind up in a German courtroom on trial for murder, he reasoned. The fewer who knew he had fired those shots into Gerhart Krueger, the better off he would be.

When Pavlak finished, Arthur frowned and scratched his ear. "You say Schliemann looked familiar . . . ?"

"Remember Dad's office at the old house—the one he added onto the east side?"

"Sure."

"Remember all the photographs he had framed on the wall beside his desk? Old photos from Germany, mostly."

"Jeez, he had a couple dozen in there."

"Right. And one of them showed three young German soldiers in battle gear, smiling at the camera with their arms on each other's shoulders. Remember it?"

Arthur was slow to reply. "Yes—I remember it," he said

apprehensively, watching Pavlak's every move.

"One of them was Dad—and one of the others was Peter Schliemann—I'm sure of it."

And the third, though Pavlak did not say it aloud, was a young Gerhart Krueger—the late Gerhart Krueger.

Karin set three cups of coffee on the table, along with a Mason jar full of sugar—also stale and hardened—and three teaspoons. "I'm sorry," she said in English. "There is no milk."

The coffee was bitter and barely drinkable, but in the chill of the unheated cabin, all three sipped it gratefully.

"Your Dad . . ." Arthur began carefully, "did not have anything to do with this."

"Borning told me he did, Arthur."

"I'm not saying he wasn't involved with this CIA scam thing—Fool's Gold, or whatever. He probably was. He loves this country."

"He loves money and power, Arthur. And nothing else."

Arthur shook his head. "Dammit, John, you're not fair to your father. I know you hate him, and I know why. I was around when you were growing up, remember? I told him many times he was too hard on you boys, that he would regret it one day. He wouldn't listen to me. He never listened to anybody. You know that. But just because you hate him doesn't mean he hates you. I know you think he does, but he doesn't. Gustaf thinks the sun rises and sets on you, John. Trust me. I know him better than you do."

"No, Arthur, you think you do, but you don't. He's a totally different man in his business than he was behind closed doors with his family. He's a smart, tough businessman to you. He was a goddamned tyrant at home. You see this?" Pavlak stretched out his left arm. The elbow bent grotesquely past the straight point. "He broke this arm for me when I was eight years old. Slammed me against a brick wall."

"I know about that."

Pavlak stared. "You do?"

"He told me when it happened. He felt terrible about it."

Pavlak leaned in. "Then why didn't he ever apologize to me, Arthur? And why didn't he stop doing that kind of crap? I've got other scars—so has Tom. And the beatings weren't the worst of it, Arthur—it was the words, the rage, the ridicule." Pavlak broke off and clamped his jaw shut.

"All I'm saying," Arthur insisted, "is that he wouldn't kill Judith to cover up something he did—if that's what you're thinking. And I almost believe it is."

"That's exactly what I'm thinking."

Arthur closed his eyes, then opened them again and stared accusingly at Pavlak.

Slowly Karin rose and crossed to Pavlak's side of the table. Standing beside his chair, she pulled his head into her breast and kissed his hair. Arthur's mouth fell partly open as he watched. Pavlak pulled out the chair beside his, drew Karin gently into it, and turned back to Arthur.

"He has to be involved, Arthur. How else did he know I would eventually latch onto Schliemann, and that Schliemann would try to take me apart when I showed up on Crete? He sent a squad of mercenaries to protect me, remember?"

Arthur studied the top of the table. "I can't answer that one. Maybe . . . I don't know. Maybe it wasn't him."

"It was Dad, and you know it. Who else could it have been?"

Arthur glumly stirred his coffee and said nothing.

"Anyway, I have to find the document, Arthur. That's the

key to everything. By the way, how are things going with
Judith's will?"

Arthur shrugged. "I've hired a lawyer to do most of it. I
don't have the time . . ."

"Has anything unusual turned up?"

"Nothing."

"How about Judith's safe deposit box? Has it been opened
yet?"

Arthur nodded. "Couple of weeks ago. I was there. There
was another copy of the will, a life insurance policy, a passport, some jewelry, title to her car—that kind of thing. No
mysterious documents from East Germany, if that's what
you're asking."

"Arthur, do you have any idea—any idea at all—where
Judith may have hidden that document? Did she ever say
anything to you?"

Arthur shook his head. "This is all news to me, John. Did
she . . . maybe she burned it or something."

"She wouldn't do that, not if it was such an important
piece of paper. She'd hide it, maybe, if she thought it was
dangerous to have it around."

"Where?"

"That's what we've got to find out."

Arthur squirmed in his chair, and the old wood squeaked
in protest. "Jeez, John, I wouldn't know where to start. We've
gone through all the papers in the house—nothing there.
Where could she have hidden it?"

"I don't know. But we've got to find it. That's why I'm
here. If we can find the document, I believe it will explain
why all this has happened. Then we can get the FBI—maybe
even the CIA—involved. It was Frank Borning who told me
to find it, and he's CIA."

"Why don't you just drive up to Washington and lay all

this out to somebody up there?" Arthur asked.

"Because somebody in the CIA is part of it, but I don't know who. All I know is that it's not Borning."

Arthur looked puzzled. "What the hell are you talking about?"

"Remember what I told you about Berlin—how I had to take Borning for a ride in order for us to get away?"

"Yeah."

"The car that followed us—the blue Mercedes—it wasn't one of Borning's men."

"How do you know?"

Pavlak hesitated. "I know, Arthur. Don't ask me any more."

"You haven't told me everything?"

"No."

Arthur stared hard at Pavlak. "All right, I won't ask—now. But soon you gotta tell me the rest, you hear me? You're scaring me, John."

"I'm sorry. I just can't tell you everything right now. But believe me, the guy in the Mercedes was not one of Borning's men. I think he was German, probably BND. And the only way he could have found out where we were is if somebody in the CIA tipped him off."

"But Fool's Gold was a joint operation, wasn't it?" Karin asked in German. "Maybe the CIA told the BND they were going to contact you about the operation. Maybe the man in the Mercedes found out legitimately—either directly from the CIA, or indirectly from somebody inside the BND."

Pavlak stroked his chin. "It's possible," he admitted. "But we can't know that for sure. And we can't trust the CIA until we do."

"What the hell are you two jabbering about?" demanded

a frustrated Arthur Trask. "Speak English, for God's sake."

"Sorry," Karin smiled. "My English is not very good."

"Sounds pretty good to me," Trask answered. "And from the looks of things, I have a hunch it's going to get much better."

"Hunch? What is a hunch?" Karin looked inquiringly at Pavlak.

"Too complicated to explain now." Pavlak said, turning back to Arthur. "Listen, you're sure you haven't run across anything in Judith's things that could be that document? How about her files at work?"

"Positive. We've cleaned out everything she had at work already. But listen, maybe whoever searched the house found it."

"No, or they wouldn't have searched my apartment the next day. Besides, if they had it, Schliemann would have killed me on Crete. It's got to be here somewhere."

Arthur let out a blast of air. "Well, good luck. That's all I've got to say."

"Question. Was there a fireproof box in the house? I bought one for computer diskettes."

Arthur frowned. "I'm not sure, John."

"It's solid black, about so big by so big. The sides are two inches thick. It's heavily insulated, fireproof, waterproof. Judith joked about it when I brought it home. She said we should bury her jewelry in the box and save the rent on the safe deposit box."

"I don't remember seeing anything like that."

"Well that's a place to start. Look for it, will you, Arthur? I need your help on this. I can't move around freely because the FBI is looking for me. And as executor of her will, you've got a legitimate reason to be at Judith's house. If the box is

not in the house, look around the yard—especially the garden. She might have buried it or hidden it outside somewhere. Oh yes, check out the garage too."

"Okay."

"Well," Pavlak mused, "it's late. You'd better get home
before Edith calls the police."

"She's used to this. I've been working late for weeks.
Where are you two going to stay?"

Pavlak shrugged.

"How about here?" Arthur asked. "Edith would never
come out here without telling me. And nobody else would
even think of it."

Pavlak threw Karin a questioning look.

"It's your country." she answered. "You must tell me."

"See? She speaks great English," Arthur laughed. "So—
when are you going to see Gustaf? And what are you going
to say to him? Take it easy on him, John, for God's sake."

"The FBI—were they watching Dad's house?"

"Probably. But they wouldn't keep it under surveillance
forever. You've been gone for a month now, John."

"Hm," Pavlak nodded. "But I can't be too careful. Streat
would love to get his hands on me now, and I can't let that
happen. If I'm locked up they might as well paint a target
on my chest. Schliemann would have no trouble getting me
killed in prison. He obviously has plenty of money. And if
Streat charges me with Judith's murder, there wouldn't be
any bail." He waved a hand at Arthur. "Don't worry. I'll get
to Dad somehow. Soon. I promise."

"Be prepared, John. He's—he doesn't—he's not himself
anymore." Trask heaved his huge frame out of the chair. "So
when do we talk again?"

Pavlak stepped into the living room and lifted the receiver
on a telephone beside the couch. A reassuring buzz sounded

in his ear. "Good, it's connected. You can call me here—but only from a phone booth. Don't call me from your house or from work. If I contact you, I'll give my name as—Norman."

"Norman?"

"Got a better idea?"

"Guess not. Okay—keep in touch." Arthur started to leave, then turned back. "These guys you're onto—Schliemann and Krueger and whoever else is in it—they got to Judith here. Don't forget that, John. Streat isn't the only one you've got to worry about. In fact, Streat's probably the least of your problems."

Pavlak fingered his ribs gingerly. "Believe me," he said. "I won't forget."

28

Just before 2 P.M. the following afternoon, a white Ford van pulled into the driveway of the Pavlak estate, shifted down, and began the climb to the house. The words "Chimney Chaps, Inc., Professional Chimney Care Since 1952" were lettered on both sides, along with a Charlotte telephone number and a black top hat, cocked at a rakish angle. From more than a few feet away, it was impossible to see that the paint was still wet in places.

The van parked at the front door, and two black-clad figures emerged wearing the traditional top hats and black clothing of chimney sweeps. One was tall and broad-shouldered, the other short and slender. They carried clipboards and kept their backs to the street. The smaller of the two figures hit the doorbell twice. It was opened by a middle-aged black woman dressed in white pants and a sweater—Gustaf Pavlak's day nurse—who held a brief conversation, then disappeared into the house.

A few minutes later Roser approached the glass storm door that still barred the entrance.

"John!" she cried, raising her hands.

"Don't say anything," Pavlak commanded sharply. "Act

perfectly calm and open the door. Someone may be watching."

The smile vanished and Roser lowered her hands. She pushed the storm door far enough for Karin and Pavlak to slip through.

"Can you get the nurse out of the house for a while?" Pavlak whispered quietly.

"Yes. I'll ask her to go to the grocery store for some things. She's good about that—usually happy to have a chance to get out. Are you all right, John?"

Pavlak nodded. "We'll be in the living room playing Santa Claus with the chimney. Let us know when she's gone."

They walked into the living room, closing the double doors behind them. Pavlak proceeded to get his hands covered in soot, while Karin doodled busily on the clipboard until the doors opened and Roser stepped in. She ran to Pavlak and threw her arms around his neck.

"The nurse is gone. Oh John, he's been so worried about you. Are you all right?"

"I'm fine. This is Karin, a friend from Germany. We're on the lam, I guess you could say."

"On the lam?"

"It's an American expression—on the run—running away from the police."

Roser's expression darkened. "That man from the FBI— Streat—he calls us almost every day, wanting to know if you've contacted us."

"You know nothing. Understand, Roser? The next time he calls, nothing has changed. You haven't seen or heard from me."

"What . . ."

Pavlak stopped her, holding up his hand. "No time now. I'll explain it all later. Where's Dad?"

"He's in the den watching television."

Pavlak turned to Karin. "Stay here," he said in German. "This will only take a few minutes."

"No, I want to go with you."

"Let me do this alone."

"I want to meet him," Karin said firmly. Then she added, "My life's on the line here too, remember?"

Roser stared from one to the other.

Pavlak hesitated. "All right. But stay quiet. Let me do all the talking."

They walked the long hallway to the den in silence. At the door, Roser turned and put her hand on Pavlak's chest. "Wait—let me warn him."

She disappeared through the door while Pavlak and Karin waited in silence. They heard a low murmur, then Gustaf Pavlak's voice, suddenly audible, "Here?"

Pavlak twisted the knob and stepped inside. "Right here."

He stopped short in shock. His father sat in a wheelchair with a wool afghan over his knees. He was pale, and noticeably thinner. But it was his eyes that brought Pavlak up short. The ice in them had melted. They were the eyes of a broken man. It was a look Pavlak had never expected to see in his father.

"Where have you been?" Gustaf demanded peevishly.

Karin stepped around Pavlak and extended her hand. "My name is Karin Oertmayer," she said in German. "I am a friend of your son's."

Gustaf looked blankly from one to the other, holding Karin's hand limply in his own. Pavlak nudged her firmly aside.

"Dad, listen to me, and listen closely. We don't have much time. I know about Fool's Gold—the official CIA version, at least. I know about your old army buddies, Peter Schliemann and Gerhart Krueger. But there's obviously more to this than meets the eye. Whatever it is you've done, it's cost the lives of six people so far."

Karin's hand fell gently on his shoulder. "John . . ."

"Please, Karin," Pavlak interrupted, turning to face her. "You don't know him."

"If you're in any danger," Gustaf Pavlak said, "then you don't have to bark at me to get help. I've always protected you the best I could, and I always will. Now what do you want? Rose . . ." He indicated the door with a wave of his hand. Roser rose without a word and left the room. Gustaf's voice was gravelly and hoarse, and his consonants were slurred from paralysis, but the voice was stronger than his appearance had led Pavlak to expect.

"All right," Pavlak breathed when the latch fell shut. "What's the dirty little secret about Fool's Gold that people are getting killed over? What's in the missing Stasi document? Why did your old buddy Schliemann mash me up like a cooked potato?" Pavlak's voice rose and he took a step forward. "And tell me why my wife and daughter are dead. Tell me that, Pop."

The two men stared into each other's eyes. Karin reached for Pavlak's arm but her hand stopped midway and retreated.

At last Gustaf lowered his eyes to his lap. "Was it Peter who broke your nose?" he asked.

"You guessed it."

Gustaf nodded. "I'm not surprised. There is something wrong with Peter. I knew it even then." He put his hands to the wheels of his chair and turned himself slightly toward Karin. "We were in the Battle of the Bulge," he explained, looking at her instead of his son. "We overran a regiment of free French near Bastogne. In the retreat, they left many wounded men behind. Our orders were to take no prisoners. There was no one to guard them, you see. Every available man had been put on the line. We came across a French boy—maybe sixteen or seventeen—with shrapnel in his knee. We were trying to think of a way to hide him from the officers when Peter came up. Peter was a very good soldier," Gustaf added, his inner eye drifting away toward a gray German day in January 1945. We told Peter that we were thinking of hiding the boy under the hay in a barn. Over there . . ." Gustaf waved his hand vaguely toward his left, and Pavlak noticed that it had become an old man's hand, withered and pale. "Peter laughed. Then he shot the boy in the face. We had seen a lot of killing, but—he was just a boy. Younger even than we were. And the laugh." Gustaf shook his head. "Peter disappeared not long after that. We thought he had been taken prisoner, but I learned later that he deserted and made his way home to Dresden. He was not the only one to desert, of course. By that time we all knew . . ." Gustaf shrugged.

It was Pavlak who spoke next. "So he wound up in the Soviet occupation zone, and when the DDR was formed, he joined the Stasi."

"Yes, of course. Peter was very ambitious. Always on the lookout for his own advantage."

"No wonder you were such good friends."

Gustaf looked up sharply. "You won't believe me, of course, but Peter was never my friend. I didn't trust him. We were fellow soldiers, that's all. Boys, really. Teenagers. I liked Gerhart Krueger a lot more. He's dead, did you know? Gisela—his wife—called me yesterday. He was shot to death in Munich."

Pavlak glanced at Karin, who was staring hard at the floor, biting her lower lip.

"So whose idea was Fool's Gold?"

"Peter's. He and Gerhart ran into each other on the street in Bonn one day. Maybe Peter planned the meeting, I don't know. Anyway, they went for a drink and struck up a conversation. Peter was heading a trade mission in Frankfurt, but of course Gerhart knew he was probably Stasi, and apparently Peter knew that Gerhart was with the BND." Gustaf plucked at the afghan on his lap. "One day Peter approached Gerhart with the idea of spying for the West. Eventually they worked out a plan for Peter to turn over the names of Western companies who sold prohibited goods to the Soviet Bloc. I was still in touch with Gerhart—we exchanged Christmas cards. He knew about Pavlak Equipment and knew we did some export business, so it was natural for him to think of me when they were looking for a western company to help with the deception. They had to smuggle some things in to make Peter look good to the Stasi, you see. But you know all this, don't you?"

"Some of it. Go on."

"That's it. I agreed to do it. It was risky—the CIA told me I was on my own if we were caught. But things were tough just then. They paid me well, plus the company was paid for the machines we shipped, of course."

"Who supplied the goods you smuggled?"

"A CIA man."

"How did you get them?"

"He posed as a salesman. Drove to the plant in broad daylight and handed them to me, usually in a briefcase—sometimes a cardboard box. I didn't actually see them. They were usually wrapped in asbestos and surrounded with padding. Sometimes there were long tubes. I suppose those were rolled blueprints, or technical documents or something."

"What was his name?"

"He called himself Ralph Diepkin, representing . . . what was it? Oh yes—Atwell Distributing Company in Chicago. There really is such a company. And a Ralph Diepkin really worked for them as a sales representative. I called once out of curiosity. The receptionist told me Diepkin was out of town."

"How did you contact him?"

"I didn't. We would get an order from East Germany, then just before shipping, he would show up with the goods to be hidden in the machines."

"Pop, are you sure he was CIA? Are you sure the whole thing wasn't a setup?"

"Positive," Gustaf said tersely. "I'm not a fool, you know. I had Gerhart's word, of course—he's the one who first talked to me about it. He came to the US with his family on vacation. He left them in Washington and drove down to see me. That's when he asked me if I would work with him and Peter and the CIA."

"He could have been lying."

"I don't think so. Besides," Gustaf added with a sideways glance at Pavlak, "I checked it out. I asked Robert Neely to have someone from the CIA contact me. They did and confirmed that the operation was legitimate."

Pavlak laughed. "Great trust you had in Krueger, Pop— to go to a senator for confirmation."

"Why not? Neely owed me some favors. Besides, I was just being careful. It was serious business. And risky. And there was always the possibility that Gerhart was being taken for a ride himself, wasn't there? Especially with Peter involved. It was Peter I didn't trust."

"Yeah, I know. That's why you sent a gang of mercenaries to protect me, isn't it?"

"What are you talking about?"

Pavlak glared at his father. "You know exactly what I'm talking about."

"I didn't send anybody anywhere."

"Where is Peter Schliemann now?" Pavlak demanded.

"I heard he moved to Crete after reunification. I haven't spoken to him since 1987. He came here once, to make our business dealings look legitimate to his Stasi bosses. That was it."

"You're lying, Pop. You know it, and I know it."

Gustaf's pale face darkened. "That's a hell of a way to talk to your father."

"You were a hell of a father, weren't you?"

Gustaf shook his head. "You'll never let go of it, will you?" he said bitterly.

"All right, forget it," Pavlak snapped with a wave of his hand. "How was the contraband hidden?"

"Usually it was welded into the frame on a fork lift. That's what the asbestos wrapping was for—to protect the goods from the heat of the welding."

"How did you know where to hide them?"

"That was up to me. The bill of lading carried some dummy control numbers. They were codes created from the part numbers of the parts the goods were hidden in. That's how Peter found them when the machines arrived. Sometimes—not often—we got something too bulky to hide in a machine. We just packed it in a crate, labeled it as spare parts, and shipped it with the machine."

Pavlak shuffled his feet nervously. He had to be out of the house before the nurse returned. "Who else knew about it?"

For the first time, Gustaf hesitated before replying. "Your brother. We hid the shipments in the middle of the night.

A couple of times we were running three shifts, so the plant was never empty. When that happened we took a machine to the inspection building, locked the doors, and did it there. It never took more than an hour or two. Make the cut, pack the goods, weld, buff, and repaint. I'd say we did— oh, probably thirty shipments from 1980 to 1989. Then the wall came down, and—it was over."

Pavlak glanced at Karin, who gave him a "What else do you want?" shrug.

"I never saw Ralph Diepkin again," Gustaf continued suddenly. "He called me, though, a couple of weeks ago."

Pavlak stiffened. "What did he want?"

"The same as you. The same questions. I think he wanted to know if people could be getting killed over it. And I told him what I'm telling you—that there is no reason for murder, at least not now that the Cold War is over. The whole operation is irrelevant now. Diepkin—or whatever his real name is—emphasized that the operation should stay a secret forever, for the sake of the Agency, and so on." He shrugged. "That makes sense, I suppose. Oh, and he wanted to know where you were, just like everybody else."

"Who else?"

"Everybody. The FBI, Tom, Arthur Trask, a man from Avery named . . . Rankin, I think it was." Gustaf shifted uncomfortably in the chair. "What do you expect? You disappear without leaving any word and you attract attention to yourself."

Pavlak stared at the Persian carpet beneath his shoes, not seeing it. When he spoke again his voice was cold. "It doesn't add up, Pop. I went to see your old friend Peter."

"He isn't my friend."

"Sorry—your old 'acquaintance.' Judith got her hands on some kind of document from an old Stasi file in Berlin.

Karin's sister sent it to her. Both of them are dead now, Pop. And your old . . . colleague . . . Schliemann broke my nose and five ribs trying to find out where it is."

Suddenly Gustaf grew larger in his chair. His eyes burned with something of the old steel in them. "I'll kill that bastard. I'll . . ."

"You'll sit here in your wheelchair and behave yourself for once in your life," Pavlak said sharply. "You can't do anything now, remember?"

Gustaf Pavlak stared at his oldest son, opened his mouth, then closed it again without replying.

"Besides, your man got me out of it before Schliemann killed me. He was good, by the way. Very good. You should send him a bonus."

"I'm telling you, I don't know what the hell you're talking about."

"Right. Did Judith ever say anything to you about that document?"

"I hadn't seen her since she threw you out. You never should have let her get away with that. You could have had lawyers. You . . ."

"Just shut up, Pop, will you?" Pavlak could feel his face growing red. "Forget it. She's dead."

"You tell *me* to shut up?" Gustaf shouted back. "Your own father?" His wasted legs jiggled frantically. For a moment, Pavlak thought he might actually stand up. "My God—one day I hope you . . ."

He froze in mid-sentence, his fist suspended above his knee. Then suddenly he flinched, drew his elbows into his abdomen, and threw his hands over his face with a moan. Karin rushed forward as something like a sob burst from the old man, then, choking, Gustaf muttered something into his hands.

Pavlak bent over him. "What is it, Pop? Your heart?"

Gustaf stayed silent, his face still covered. Only an occasional shudder in the bent shoulders indicated that he was sobbing.

"Call a doctor," Karin pleaded in a thin voice.

Pavlak laid his hand on her arm. "He's all right. Get Roser."

A moment later, Roser rushed to Gustaf and tried to pull his hands from his face, but the old man resisted, keeping his frame bent resolutely over his knees. Pavlak motioned to Karin to follow him, and they retreated silently, leaving Roser on her knees with one arm around Gustaf Pavlak's bent shoulders.

29

The phone was ringing when Pavlak unlocked the door to the cabin. He fumbled for the light switch, then grabbed the phone on the fourth ring.

"Hello," he mumbled in an unnaturally deep voice.

"Norman?"

"Where are you calling from?"

"A phone booth beside the Seven-Eleven on Armonk and Main."

"Good boy."

"What do you think I am, John," Arthur protested, "an idiot? I may not be a college graduate, but I can follow simple directions."

"Sorry. Okay, what have you got?"

"Nothing."

"Nothing?"

"Not a damned thing—except that you're right about that computer box. It's gone. I spent two hours turning the place upside down. It ain't there."

"Did you look outside the house?"

"Of course I looked," Arthur shot back. "Jesus, John, give me a little credit here, will you?"

"What the hell are you so touchy about?"

"I'm tired, dammit," Arthur snapped. "It's almost eight o'clock and I've still got three or four hours to go at the plant. We're busy as hell, and your brother is—well, he's trying to run the place by himself now that Gustaf is sick. Makes things that much harder on me. I'm so far behind I can't even see the rest of the pack."

"If it's any help, I really do appreciate it."

"Yeah, I know. So anyway, as I was saying, I didn't find it, I looked all over the house, around the house, under the house. I practically took the garage apart. I dug around in the garden and the lawn—place looks like it was hit by a wild boar. I even rented a metal detector and searched it again. Nothing. It's not there."

Pavlak sighed. "Well, at least we know the document is probably in that box—and if she put it in a waterproof box, then she probably hid it outside."

"Great. That narrows it down to planet Earth. Tell you what—you take a shovel and fly to San Francisco. I'll start digging at Cape Hatteras, and we'll meet in Kansas."

"I've got a better idea," Pavlak smiled. "Knowing Judith, she probably told somebody something about this. And if she did, I've got a good idea who that somebody would be."

"Good luck. Streat talked to everybody in the county. If he didn't find anything, I don't see how you can. Besides— you shouldn't let yourself be seen around here."

"I'll think of something. Listen, thanks a million, Arthur. You're a great guy. Did I ever tell you that?"

"Not often enough. Wait a minute—don't hang up yet. Did you see your dad?"

"Yes—got in there this afternoon."

"And?"

Pavlak wrapped the phone cord around his index finger. "He's gone downhill pretty fast."

"Told you. What about Fool's Gold?"

"I don't know, Arthur. It definitely happened. He was very open about it. Told me details. But . . ."

"But what?"

"But he's leaving something out. He denied sending Jack and his gang of professional thugs to protect me, for example. He says Fool's Gold was all legitimate as far as he knows. Says he doesn't know why anyone would be killing people over it. He had some sort of attack while we were there—or seemed to. Couldn't or wouldn't talk after that."

There was a long silence. "What did you say to him, John?"

"I was a little rough on him, if that's what you're asking. So what? I didn't hurt him. Nothing I say or do has ever had any measurable effect on him."

"You're totally wrong, John. You're just too stubborn to see it. And listen to me, you little jerk. I don't care what you think of him—Gustaf Pavlak has been my friend for forty years. He's given me just about everything I've got. And if you don't lighten up on him, then I'll whip your skinny little ass for you, you hear me?"

"That's a strategy he'd certainly approve," Pavlak replied drily.

"I'm serious, dammit. Lighten up. He's sick, for God's sake."

"Go back to work, Arthur. And thanks again."

There was a silence, then the sound of the receiver slamming down. Pavlak thought of Arthur's Trask giant hand and wondered if the pay phone had survived.

"Great," he said to Karin. "Now he's pissed off at me too. That makes it unanimous."

"I'm not angry at you." She was slumped on the couch, exhausted, her eyelids drooping. "But I have been thinking about things. John, listen . . . what if it *is* your father?"

"Would I commit patricide? Is that your question?" Pavlak asked. He walked to the couch and sat down beside her. "When I was a boy, I spent hours fantasizing about killing him. Once I even planned it. I took a twenty-two-rifle from the closet in his bedroom and hid in a tree outside our house. I lined up a clear shot at the front door through the leaves. I was going to kill him when he came home. I remember wondering whether I should try for the head or just go for his back. Either way, I decided I'd empty the magazine just to be sure. But I was only playing a game, and I knew it. When it was close to time for him to come home, I ran into the house and put the gun back before he caught me with it." Pavlak rubbed his eyes. He too was tired. Very tired. "And now, after all that's happened . . ." he continued. "Would I kill him?" Pavlak stared blankly at the thin carpet beneath their feet. "I don't know."

At that moment, thirty-five miles away on Kenley Lane in Charlotte, Special Agent Darryl Streat paced his office like a caged tiger.

"Dammit," he swore. "Dammit, dammit, dammit! You should have run the tag immediately."

"Why?" Agent Fortson asked calmly. "There was no reason to suspect anything. It was no more suspicious than every other vehicle that's pulled in there in the last five weeks. We ran the numbers as soon as our shift ended. Standard procedure."

"Yeah," Streat shot back. "Except that this time it turns out to be a stolen tag—stolen right there in Lake Elm."

Fortson shrugged. "So what are you telling me, Darryl—that we should have broken procedure? On what grounds?"

Streat waved his hand. "No, you did everything right. I'm just frustrated, that's all. This case is busting my chops." He stopped pacing and half sat on the corner of the desk. "What's happening on the van?"

"Jeff and Lisa are looking, but it's a long shot. There are thousands of them. They're starting in Charlotte—it was a Charlotte phone number on the side."

"But no such company as 'Chimney Chaps?' "

Fortson shook his head. "Not now, not ever. At least, not legally incorporated and registered."

"What about the telephone number?"

"Belongs to a gay bar on Wilkinson Boulevard. Kinky place. Whips and chains on the walls, that kind of thing. I spent an hour there questioning the staff. Nothing. God-damned bartender blew me a kiss when I left," he added crossly.

"And you never got a look at their faces?"

"The glass in the van was darkened—one-way stuff. They kept their heads down coming out of the house, like they were studying the clipboards. The brims of the hats hid their faces. I got a photo, but it doesn't help."

"Let me see it."

Fortson reached into his inside coat pocket and handed Streat a Polaroid snapshot.

"It's him," Streat said grimly. "The tall one is him. And the little one is the missing German woman."

"How can you tell?" Fortson asked, rising to look over his shoulder. Streat handed him the photograph.

"I just know, that's all. It's his way of doing things. Jerking us around. Sending us on wild goose chases. God, I can't wait to nail this sonofabitch." Streat walked around the desk and sat down. "Tell Jeff and Lisa to forget the van. It's point-less. And it wouldn't be in Charlotte anyway, knowing Pavlak. Put them on the motels instead. Check out all relatives and friends. Don't forget the ones in Avery. And put a tail on the big man in Lake Elm. What's his name?"

"Trask?"

"Yeah, him. He's Pavlak's confidant. Sooner or later Pav-lak will contact him. Also put a watch on Pavlak's old apart-ment—request some local help for that. From now on, any vehicle that we can't identify at the old man's place—get on the phone and run the tag immediately. If there's any doubt, follow it."

Fortson was scribbling notes on a pocket pad. "Okay—got it. What about the spooks? You going to tell them their boy's back in town?"

"I haven't decided yet. We don't know for sure, after all. And so far, they haven't given me squat. I still think the CIA knows something they're not telling. Typical. Those guys get secrecy on the brain. They don't even tell their wives when they're horny. Anything new from the Germans?"

Fortson shook his head. "They're worse than the CIA. I talked to a guy in Bonn this morning. I asked him straight out—I said why should I give you anything, if you won't give me anything on Munich? They just want to talk to Pavlak about it, he says. I say, 'why?' He blows some more smoke, then drops me off the phone."

Streat pressed his lips together and slapped the surface of the desk. "This thing's got spook written all over it, I tell you. Frankly, I don't give a crap what the spies are doing—ours or theirs—but I've got a dead woman and a dead little girl, and one way or the other, I'm going to crack this thing."

"I don't know, Darryl. When you get right down to it, we've got nothing on Pavlak either."

Streat raised his index finger. "Not yet. But when we get our hands on him we'll get something. I don't know what he's been doing, but he's in this thing up to his eyeballs. Pavlak's the key, and he's back on our turf. Find him."

Foster Denham stood with his back against the wall and his arms folded. "When will he be well enough to travel?"

"He says he's ready to come now, but the doctors say he has to wait another week. Something about making sure he doesn't get an infection."

Denham had made one of his rare trips down the elevator at CIA headquarters and surprised Christopher Hopkins in his office. When he entered, Hopkins started to rise, then changed his mind and remained seated. Now he regretted the decision. It was awkward sitting while the director of Central Intelligence stood in front of him.

"Have you decided how to handle this?"

Hopkins shrugged. "They reconstructed the elbow the best they could, but the chief surgeon says twenty percent function is the best he could hope for—and it's his right arm. I'm leaning toward a disability discharge."

"And a reprimand?"

Hopkins pursed his lips and studied the coffee mug on his desk. The inscription on the side facing him said "Because you are so very loving." On the other side, he knew, were the words, "You are loved so very much." Martha had given it to him for Valentine's Day one year. He couldn't remember which one. "Frank's been a good man for over thirty years now," Hopkins said. "And he had some grounds for taking the initiative in this case."

"But he screwed up big time," Denham retorted. "And I don't care what the grounds were, he should have reported the contact with Pavlak. His actions were irresponsible. He deserves at least a reprimand—in addition to the discharge."

"Is that an order?"

Denham shoved his hands into his pockets with a shrug. "I told you it was your call. I just don't understand why you're so hesitant on this."

Hopkins measured his words. "Frank did turn out to be right, remember? Krueger was dirty. We don't know how yet, but we'll find out eventually. And he's claiming section G-four gives him the authority to do what he did." He scratched at his cheek with an index finger. "It's an arguable point."

"What's the BVS have to say?"

"Very little. You know how it goes. We'd be pretty close-lipped too, if it was our scandal. Looks like the guy in the Mercedes was named Volker Scholz, another one of Krue-ger's men. He's disappeared. They're looking for him."

"Do they buy Borning's story about what happened in Munich?"

"No. They say there's no way Scholz shot Krueger by mis-take. Frank's wrong. His elbow caught a nine-millimeter. Krueger got it with a thirty-eight. Four times. Nobody acci-dentally shoots a guy four times."

Denham leaned his shoulder blades against the wall. "Then it has to be Pavlak."

Hopkins said nothing.

"And Borning's trying to protect him," Denham added.

"Maybe. Or maybe he really doesn't know what hap-pened. It was over in a few seconds. He was dodging bul-lets—and he did get shot, after all."

Denham bucked himself away from the wall and sat down in a hard chair, the only vacant one in Hopkins' office. He was wearing an eight-hundred-dollar tailored suit, and his shoes shone like a mirror. Who shines the shoes of the director of Central Intelligence, Hopkins wondered silently.

"And what have they got to say about us?" Denham asked.

"Who?"

"The BVS—German counterintelligence."

"Holzhauer told me he wished we had come to them sooner. I pointed out that Borning went to Krueger right away." Hopkins sighed. "They're keeping it very low-key so far, not trying to spread the blame around. But they will— if they find an excuse. God only knows where this is going to lead."

Denham jumped to his feet abruptly and paced. "All right," he announced after a half dozen turns in the small office. "We have to be sure we get to the bottom of it on our end before they do. I don't want them coming to us with information about one of our own people."

Hopkins' eyes widened. "What do you want me to do? We've already been over Fool's Gold a hundred times. It looks squeaky-clean. But apparently it wasn't. I don't see what else we can do except wait for something to break— probably from the German side."

"We can find Pavlak," Denham said with a hitch of one eyebrow and a glance at the open door. "And if we find Pavlak, we find the document. Borning sent him back here to look for it, remember?"

"*If* he listened to Frank. We don't know that he did. And anyway, if he's here, he's in Fibbie jurisdiction, not ours."

"Theoretically."

Hopkins waited before replying. "Are you saying that we should look for him here?"

"I'm saying," the director replied, "that the rules are fuzzy in cases like this—and that they've been bent many times before, as you know damned well. I'm just not too keen on doing nothing, while we wait for the roof to fall on our heads. We can't arrest him or detain him, but we can help our colleagues in the Hoover Building locate him—indirectly, of course. Using some of our—contacts here."

The contacts, as Hopkins knew well, had often proved helpful to the CIA, particularly when the Agency needed some dirty work done. But he doubted how useful the Mafia could be in Lake Elm, North Carolina.

"I'll check into it."

"Good." Denham started for the door, then turned. "What about Schliemann—any word?"

"None. He's disappeared. Greek Police have confirmed that an exchange of gunfire took place at his house. Witnesses heard the shots, bullet holes in the house, and so on. Oh—and blood in the basement. Looks like Pavlak was telling Frank the truth."

"Have they found Lederer's body?"

"Negative."

"Maybe he wasn't killed after all," the director wondered aloud.

"More likely Schliemann did a good job hiding him. A living, badly wounded man, is a lot harder to conceal than a corpse."

"Mmm," the director answered absently. "By the way, how are things with the wife?"

Hopkins was caught off guard. "She's . . . I . . . I don't know. I haven't seen her in a few weeks."

"Still in Ohio?"

Hopkins' mouth fell open, then he closed it and swallowed once. "You know about that, huh?"

The director shrugged. "Word gets around."

Hopkins said nothing.

"This is a tough business, Chris," Denham went on. "After

we find Pavlak, take some of the time you've got coming and get things straightened out at home. There's no reason for Fool's Gold to cost you your family."

Hopkins stared at his desk calendar without seeing it. "It cost Pavlak his, though, didn't it?"

The director grunted—a noncommittal grunt. "Little people get ground up in the machinery sometimes. Hell of a world we live in, huh?" He walked out the door without waiting for an answer.

30

The radio bounded to life at 6 A.M. sharp, blaring something obnoxious that featured an electric guitar. With his eyes still closed, Tom Pavlak slapped twice at the off button and missed both times before reaching under the bed and jerking the plug out of the wall.

"Shit," he breathed into his pillow. Dottie was still asleep beside him. She could sleep through a brass band. For him, on the other hand, it had been a rough night—the latest in a long series of rough nights. For some unknown reason he could not sleep soundly anymore. Typically he woke up three or four times and had fitful, disturbing dreams. Now he faced the worst part of the day—the first half-hour of getting himself up and going. He had learned that once the blood was flowing and the muscles working, the weight of the night began to lighten.

Tom dragged himself out of bed, focussed as best he could on the night light that glowed in the bathroom, and stumbled toward it. On her side of the bed, Dottie slept on. Her serene, rhythmic breathing irritated him. He made up his mind to throw a scene that evening—insist that she get her lazy ass out of bed and fix him some breakfast in the mornings. Didn't he have enough to do, running the company now? Time she pulled her own weight, at least. And if she refused, then he would by God hire a cook and that was that. He had built maid quarters into the house and now they stood empty because Dottie refused to have "a stranger" living in her house. Well, enough of that crap.

He closed the bathroom door gently and switched on a bank of six high-watt bulbs over the mirror. While he waited for his eyes to make the painful adjustment, he considered this sleeping problem. The Pavlaks were notoriously bad sleepers. His father rarely slept soundly, and sometimes John had problems too. He had thought himself immune from that malady, but now it was finally his turn.

Tom nicked himself twice while shaving, and stumbled down the stairs with bits of toilet paper plastered to his chin. At least the grogginess was beginning to drain from his head. That was good. He was going to fire that sonofabitch Kramer this morning, and he wanted all his wits about him. Trask would intervene, try to talk him out of it, but he wasn't budging this time. No smart-assed floor foreman was going to yell at him in a production meeting and get away with it, no matter how many years he had with the company. Best to let everybody know right from the start who was boss now.

He dumped two slices of white bread into the toaster and gulped down a glass of orange juice while he waited. Before the toast was buttered, he felt his stomach turn sour. That was new too—like the sleeping.

With the toast in one hand and his jacket in the other, he pulled open the door to the garage. Two steps into the darkness, an infrared motion detector latched onto his body heat and automatically switched on the garage lights. The toast flew six feet into the air, and Tom screamed.

"Pipe down, it's just me," John Pavlak said irritably. He

was leaning against the driver's door of a silver Eldorado where he had been standing motionless for half an hour, to avoid triggering the garage lights again.

"Jesus H. Christ!" Tom swore. "You scared the shit out of me. How the hell did you get in here?"

"I have a key, remember? You gave it to me."

"What the fuck are you doing here, anyway? I thought you were in Germany or somewhere."

"I was. I'm back."

"No shit."

Tom Pavlak had his brother's athletic build but was three inches shorter. He had been a good high school athlete in his day, though not a standout like John.

"Why don't you just knock on the damned door like everybody else?" Tom demanded irritably. "Look at that— that's my breakfast. Landed butter-down too. Wouldn't you know it."

"I'm wanted by the FBI. What do you want me to do, come at noon with a brass band and cymbals?"

"Why did you come at all? What do you want from me?"

"I want to know everything there is to know about Fool's Gold. I want to know what your old pals from that spy game are upset about, and exactly why they're leaving corpses all over two continents."

The motion detector, finding no more motion, automatically plunged them both into darkness. Pavlak could hear his brother's ragged breathing. Tom took a step backwards and the lights flared again.

"Who told you about Fool's Gold?"

"Lot's of people. It's about as secret as Niagara Falls. Dad, incidentally, was one of them."

Tom's eyes widened. "When did you see Dad?"

"Yesterday—come on, Tom. It's going to be light soon,

and I've got to get away from here. For all I know, the FBI is watching this house."

"All right, all right. What's to tell? Some CIA guy delivered little packages. Pop and I welded them into the frame of a forklift. We shipped it. They paid us in cash. Basta. End of story."

Pavlak swiped his hand across his eyes. "Look, Tom, this is not a joke, okay? My wife and baby are dead, and some of your old buddies are out there somewhere looking to put me in the same condition." He took a step forward. "Now tell me what the hell is going down, *now*."

Tom stood his ground. "Or what?" he asked between clenched teeth. "You going to beat my ass, like when we were kids? Back off, big brother. You might still be man enough to whip me, but I swear to God, I'll hurt you. Hey . . . what the fuck happened to your nose?"

"That's one reason I'm a little testy. One of your spy friends busted it for me, along with a bunch of ribs. Man named Schliemann. Now, why did he do that, Tom? And listen—I'm not leaving you alone until I know everything. You got it? It's time to let me in on this dirty little family secret."

"I don't know what the hell you're talking about. Who's Schliemann?"

"You really don't know?"

"Never heard of him."

Pavlak knew one thing for sure about his brother: He had always been a lousy liar. If he were lying now, it would be written all over his face, but it wasn't.

"What did Dad tell you about Fool's Gold?" Pavlak asked in a more conciliatory tone.

"Nothing. You know the old man—secretive as hell—always has been. It's part of his power game. He said it was a

CIA operation, and that we were helping smuggle something behind the Iron Curtain. I figured maybe it was little cameras or something for spies. Who the hell knows? Dad said 'cut here, weld here, paint there,' and I did it. Once, when he was out of town, I took a briefcase full of cash from some CIA guy who called himself Diepkin. That's all I know."

"What about Crete?"

"Who?"

"Crete. It's an island in the Mediterranean."

"What about it?"

Pavlak decided to try another tack. "Has Dad said anything to you about what's going on with me? Anything about my being in danger, for example?"

"Look," Tom answered, shifting his weight impatiently, "Since the stroke, I see the old man maybe once a week— maybe less. I'm running the company now, not him. He doesn't talk to me at all about you. All I know is that the FBI thinks you killed Judith and Tasha. At least it seemed that way. I talked to some agent for a couple of hours one night right after you disappeared. That's it."

The garage went dark. Tom flapped his arms like a wounded eagle to make them come on again.

"Then it *was* him," Pavlak whispered to no one in particular.

"What?"

"Nothing. Listen, mind if I lie down in the backseat of your car while you drive out of here? If nobody's following, you can drop me a couple of blocks away."

An unpleasant smile crept over Tom's face. "Well, well. The mighty First Born. Finally need your little brother's help for something, huh, *Doctor Pavlak*?"

"Oh come on, Tom, don't start, okay?"

"You know, the irony of it is—Pop always thought you walked on water. But look at us now, big brother. You're making what—forty K a year? Living in that pig hole of an apartment—when you're not on the run from the cops. Yeah, Dad could really pick 'em, couldn't he? And old never-amount-to-anything Tom—I'm running his company for him."

"He told me what a bum I was too, Tom," Pavlak said wearily. "At least once a day. And he beat me up *more* than he did you. If he had a favorite, it was you."

Tom laughed without humor. "That's bull crap, and you know it. You got the belt more because he paid more attention to you, that's all—the mighty first-born son. But I'm the one who turned out to be somebody," Tom said fiercely, jamming his thumb into his chest. "And you? Look at you." He threw out his hand in disgust.

The two brothers faced each other silently while the timer in the motion detector made its round and switched the lights out again. This time it was Pavlak who brought them back on as he stepped forward and grabbed a fistful of his brother's shirt.

"Forget the ride," Pavlak said in a hoarse whisper, his nose an inch from Tom's. "I'll walk. And as for your running the company—remind me to sell my stock."

He gave Tom a rough shove and walked to the side door.

"Hey big brother," Tom called, his eyes flaming. "We're not kids anymore. You ever put your hands on me again, and I'll fucking kill you."

Pavlak jerked the door open and slipped into the damp morning air.

Karin was waiting three blocks away in the Camry. "How'd it go?" she asked.

"Nothing like brotherly love," Pavlak said, climbing behind the wheel. He twisted the key and the engine roared. "He doesn't know anything. Let's go. Time to get a good day's sleep before we visit the thriving metropolis of Avery.

31

Pavlak had considered, then rejected the idea of calling Diane Sweeney in advance. He was not worried about phone taps—no one, including Diane, would be expecting him to contact her—but he was afraid to give her any warning. She disliked him intensely, and there was no way to predict what she might do. On the drive to Avery, he stayed off the main roads, traveling on narrow, twisting, secondary roads where it was easier to spot a tail.

When they reached the sleeping town, Pavlak was amazed at how little it had changed. But then he remembered it had only been five weeks. It seemed like an eternity. At the first opportunity, he slipped off Main Street and threaded his way down residential avenues, avoiding the brighter lights. They drove past Kenneth and Audrey Rankin's house, and Pavlak noticed a light in Kenneth's study. One day this would all be over, and if he were still alive, he could tell his story to Kenneth and Audrey. But as soon as that thought entered his mind, something else said no. That would never be possible. They would want to hear a story, but what he was living was not a story. It was another life. And he would never fit into this one again.

"You can't go home again."

"What?"

"Nothing. The title of a novel by Thomas Wolfe. He was a North Carolina author."

"Yes, I've read him," Karin answered. "A very passionate man. Are all the men in North Carolina so passionate?"

"Only the crazy ones," Pavlak replied. "And they die young. Wolfe was thirty-eight."

"Maybe he didn't have a sensible woman around to keep him alive."

Two blocks from his old house, Pavlak uttered an oath and made a sudden turn.

"What is it?"

"A surveillance team, I think—in a Ford Taurus. It looked like two men. Question is, who are they? If it's the FBI, then they probably know we're back in town. If it's not the FBI . . ." His voice trailed off.

"So what do we do now?"

"The street behind my house angles toward Davis Drive. Diane's is the last house in the point of the triangle. There's nothing behind it but underbrush and briars. I can approach through there unseen. But whether or not she'll answer the back door is another question."

"You mean *we* can approach through there."

"No, I mean *I*. It's risky enough with one—even harder with two."

"Remember Thomas Wolfe? I want to make sure you don't die young."

"Don't worry. It's too late for that already."

"I'm coming," Karin announced with finality. Pavlak drew a breath to reply, then let it go.

He parked the Camry on Cork Street, and he and Karin stepped out of the car. The night was cool enough for their overcoats not to attract attention, although the turned-up collars would appear a trifle odd. Pavlak was wearing a felt fedora with the brim pulled low, keeping his face in shadow. He was well-known in this town, so he affected a slight limp just to make sure some casual gaze out a window did not recognize his gait.

They reached the rear of Diane's lot without meeting anyone, and Pavlak began picking his way through the underbrush with Karin at his heels. Briars caught and tore at his trousers. He knew Karin's bare legs were taking a beating, but she did not utter a sound.

Abruptly the briars ended, and they found themselves on a clean lawn. Diane's old, two-story, wood-frame house loomed over them. It had been a wet spring in Carolina, and the turf was spongy beneath their shoes. A small porch, now ramshackle, had been added onto the back of the house, perhaps in the fifties, and screened in. Pavlak and Karin mounted the dilapidated wooden staircase that ended at a screen door to the porch. Pavlak pushed, but the door resisted.

"Rats," he whispered. "She's hooked it from the inside."

One corner of the screen curled toward him. He slipped his finger through the hole, tore the rusty screen far enough to admit his arm, then pushed the hook up through the metal eyelet, and opened the door. In the pale moon shadow on the porch, they could make out an old bicycle, an assortment of potted plants—all dead—and several lawn chairs, folded and dumped in a heap. The door to the interior of the house had panes of glass at the top, though the view was blocked by a dark curtain. Pavlak held his breath and rapped sharply on the corner pane. It was almost ten o'clock at night. A knock on her back door was sure to alarm Diane, but there was nothing he could do about that.

He waited a full minute, then rapped again and called softly through the door, "Diane, open up. It's John Pavlak."

There was another delay, then suddenly they were standing in the glare of a bare bulb in the ceiling of the porch. Instinctively Pavlak pinched his eyes closed until they adjusted to the light. When he opened them again, he was looking down the barrel of a Smith and Wesson .357 magnum revolver with Diane Sweeney's terrified eyes right behind it. In quick succession, he saw recognition, then relief, then anger, and finally something like hatred, flash through those eyes. The curtain fell. He heard a fumbling at the latch, then the door swung open.

"You goddamned sonofabitch!" Diane hissed. The revolver was still pointed at Pavlak's chest.

"It's nice to see you too, Diane," Pavlak smiled. "May we come in?"

"I almost shot you, you know that?"

"I'm sure you won't pass up another opportunity. May we come in? It's important. It's about Judith—and people are looking for me, so I'd rather not stand in this spotlight any longer than necessary."

Reluctantly Diane stepped aside and motioned with the barrel of the pistol. Pavlak entered, and Karin followed him. He felt her hand take hold of his elbow and grip it tightly.

As soon as he walked through the door, the stench of stale cigarette smoke assaulted him, and his hand involuntarily rose to his face.

"What happened to your nose?" Diane demanded sharply.

"I walked into a door in the dark. Could we sit down somewhere? I only need a few minutes."

Diane was dressed in fuzzy pink slippers and a baggy sweatsuit that did nothing to flatter her figure. Her red hair was tied in the back with what appeared to be an old sweatband, cut in two. Her eyes were moist and bloodshot, as always, and she still had a habitual smoker's cough. She let out a ragged sigh and turned toward the front of the house.

"Not the front," Pavlak said quickly. "There are two men in a car just down the street. They might be able to see into the front room. Can we go in here?" He pointed at a door on his left.

"Who are they?" Diane asked.

"I'm not sure. Maybe the FBI. Maybe the people who killed Judith."

She stared, then nodded at the door beside him. Pavlak opened it and stepped inside.

His eyes met a scene of total chaos. It was her bedroom, but by all appearances, the bed had not been made in weeks. Pavlak stepped on a high-heel shoe and almost tripped. There was an oval-shaped, hooked rug at the side of the bed, but it was buried beneath rumpled clothes. The one chair in the room, an overstuffed armchair, was also heaped with cast-off clothing, including a black lace bra on the top. Odd, Pavlak thought when his eyes lit on the bra. Erotic under-wear was not something he would have associated with Diane.

If she was embarrassed by the disorder, Diane did not show it. "What the hell are you doing here?" she demanded. "And who is this?"

"This is Karin Oertmayer—Brigitte's sister. You probably heard Judith speak about Brigitte."

Diane's hard face softened slightly. "Oh yes. I'm very sorry about your sister."

Pavlak's mouth fell open. "You know about that?"

"Yes. Judith told me. The day before she died. Brigitte's husband had just called her. She was very shook up."

Pavlak decided not to wait for an invitation. He stepped

over the clutter and sat down on the side of the bed. The mattress, he noted, was much too soft. Diane probably suffered backaches.

"Did she—say anything else about Brigitte?" he asked.

Diane had stepped to a vanity and was rummaging around in the junk on top of it. At last she came up with a pack of Marlboros and a lighter. "She was scared to death," Diane answered, turning. "That's all I know. I figured it had something to do with you."

"You figured wrong. This was all Judith's baby. And I still don't know what it's about. I need your help, Diane. The past is past, so let's forget it for a few minutes, can we? I'm trying to find out who killed Judith, and I need any information you can give me. Specifically, I need to know what has happened to a document of some kind that Brigitte sent to Judith by registered mail. That document is the key to all this. Did she mention it to you?"

Diane lit a Marlboro, inhaled deeply, and blew the smoke toward the ceiling. "The FBI thinks *you* killed her," she said, ignoring his question.

"They're wrong."

"I know. Otherwise I would have shot you back there."

"So who was it?"

Diane shrugged. "I have no idea. All I know is what I told the FBI—that Judith was scared. She didn't tell me why. She just said she didn't think Brigitte's death was really an accident. I begged her to tell me more, but she wouldn't. She said it was too dangerous, and that the less I knew, the better."

"I'm surprised she told you anything at all," Pavlak mused.

"She told me because she wanted to give me something."

Diane opened a drawer on the vanity, withdrew a plain white envelope with no markings on it, and handed it to him. "She said if anything happened to her, I was to give you this."

"Me?" Pavlak asked, incredulous.

"Don't ask me why," Diane shrugged. "Anyway, she said to give it to you and not to say anything to anybody else about it. She stressed that." Diane took another long pull on the cigarette. The tip glowed and her eyes narrowed. "You had some kind of sick hold on her, you know that, John? Yes, of course you know it." She gestured vaguely with the pistol that still hung suspended from her right hand.

"It's been opened."

"I opened it. You disappeared before I had a chance to give it to you."

Pavlak's eyes met hers. "You had plenty of chances, Diane. The funeral—plenty of chances."

"All right," Diane acknowledged with provocative insolence, "I hadn't made up my mind to do it yet. Judith was dead, so what did it matter? The note is just nonsense, anyway, at least to me. Maybe it means something to you."

Pavlak unfolded a page of lined notebook paper, torn from a spiral binder. On it in pencil, in Judith's hand, was written: "Itch Bitch, 2,2,196."

"Mean anything?" Diane asked, sucking at the Marlboro like a child with a licorice stick.

"Maybe." Pavlak's face had darkened. "Diane, you should have given me this like Judith told you." He fastened her with an angry glare. "I'm not sure about this, but if it's what I think it is, your hanging on to it might have cost some people their lives. It damned near cost me mine."

Diane's reply was crisp and hard. "Then obviously I didn't hold it long enough."

Pavlak took Karin's arm. "Come on. Let's get out of here."

Karin was following him into the hall when Diane suddenly grasped her arm. "Hey, listen, hon. I don't know why you're with this jerk. Maybe it's nothing. But if you've got any interest in him, just remember—his last wife is dead."

Karin seemed to be studying Diane's face. "I'm very sorry," she said in English, then gently pulled her arm away.

"For what?"

"For . . . everything."

Diane laughed, though there was no humor in her eyes. "Oh God, lady. You're a goner." She was still laughing as they passed through the back door and down the rickety steps.

32

"What's a 'goner?' " Karin asked when the Camry had left the lights of Avery behind and slipped into the moonlit countryside. She was gingerly extracting a nest of blackberry thorns from her right calf. With nothing but the glow of the instrument panel to light the operation, it was going slowly.

"A what?"

"A 'goner.' That's what she called me. 'You're a goner,' she said."

Pavlak laughed. *"Du bist fertig—erledigt."*

"Why did she say that?"

"I suppose because you didn't kick me in the crotch when she gave you her version of my marriage to Judith. By the way, got a copy of Shakespeare on you?"

"A what?"

"We need the complete works of Shakespeare, preferably New Cambridge edition."

Karin stared at his face in the bluish-green glow from the instrument panel. "You're talking about Judith's note, right?"

"Right. It's a line reference. Years ago, Judith and I went to see a production of *Antony and Cleopatra* in London—

Royal Shakespeare Company. We hated it. Judith said the actress—I forget her name—played Cleopatra like an American rich bitch. I said no, more like an Egyptian rich bitch. Judith suggested that we compromise and call her an Itch Bitch."

Karin gave him a blank look.

"Well," he shrugged, "I guess you had to be there. That was before Tasha was born—when we still had some fun . . . Anyway, after that, we always referred to Cleopatra as the Itch Bitch—it was an inside joke. Back when we still joked."

"Why a line reference?"

"I have no idea. Judith knew Brigitte had been killed. She knew she was in danger, and I guess she wanted to give me a message if anything happened to her—and she didn't want anybody else to know what that message is."

"But why . . . I'm confused," Karin said. "Why would Judith leave a message for you? Why not just give the message—whatever it is—to Diane?"

"I don't know," Pavlak answered. "It must be something she didn't trust Diane with. Judith was no idiot. She listened to Diane's ravings against me because it was what she wanted to hear at the time, but she also knew Diane's limitations. Or maybe she just wanted to protect her from getting involved in something so dangerous. Who knows? And anyway . . ." He hesitated. "If it's about Fool's Gold, then it involves my family. I'd almost bet that the name Pavlak appears on that mysterious document somewhere. That would explain why the document caught Brigitte's eye in the first place. And it could explain why Judith wanted to communicate something to me—if that's what her note is about. We'll have to wait and see."

"So what is Diane going to do now?" Karin asked. "Will she tell anybody she saw us?"

"Probably. Probably called the police or the FBI the minute we left. That's why I dragged you through those briars in such a rush."

"So what do we do now?"

"Not much we can do, except lay low." He looked at Karin. "Sooner or later they'll find us. We can't run forever. But we won't be safe from Schliemann and his henchman until we solve this. We've got to stay out of jail long enough to finish the job. After that? We'll see." Pavlak kept his eyes on the road. "I did kill a man."

"That was self-defense—sort of," Karin said quickly.

"Sort of," he repeated. "But nobody can say for sure what will happen. Are you sure you want to stick this out? You're on the run with a fugitive—maybe a murderer. You might be better off going to the police and asking for their protection."

Karin leaned across the hand brake and laid her head on his shoulder. "No," she said. "I'll ride this to the end."

"Could be a rough end. And we haven't talked about it, but . . ."

Karin's fingers touched his lips. "I know," she said softly. "Don't worry about it. I'm the one who has to decide about the Order. And remember, I haven't taken any vows yet, so I haven't broken any."

"Are you sorry about that morning in Petersburg—when you came out of the shower?"

She was silent for a moment. "No," she answered firmly. "Not yet."

It was after midnight when they reached the cabin. They had slept much of the day and neither wanted to sleep again so soon. While Karin read a year-old copy of *Newsweek*, Pavlak climbed into the tiny, aluminum shower stall in the bathroom. With every movement, his elbows punched the sides of the stall and sent thundering booms through the cabin. His shower was almost finished when a small hand slipped through the curtain and touched his hip. Karin's naked body quickly followed it into the steamy shower.

"Need some help?"

"To do what?"

At great risk to Arthur's plumbing fixtures, they made love in the tiny stall. Only when the hot water ran out did they emerge.

Pavlak had just finished toweling Karin off, and she was starting to return the favor when the phone rang. They looked at each other. It was after 1 A.M.

"It can't be Arthur—not now," Pavlak said.

"Maybe it's a wrong number."

The second ring sounded.

"You answer it," Pavlak said, nudging her through the bathroom door in front of him. "Just say 'hello.' If it's not Arthur, hang up."

Karin snatched up the receiver in the middle of the fourth ring.

"Hello."

A look of relief spread over her face, and she handed him the phone.

"What's wrong?" Pavlak demanded as soon as the receiver touched his ear.

"Can't you at least say hello before you start barking at me?" Arthur complained.

"Sorry—I didn't expect you to call at one o'clock in the morning."

"You weren't there earlier, and I've been working at the plant till now. God-awful amount of work to do there. And your brother . . ." Arthur broke off.

"Yeah, I know," Pavlak replied. "He's a real jerk. Where are you calling from this time?"

"Same place. Only this time I think I've got company."

Pavlak caught his breath. "Who?"

"I don't know—a guy in a blue Ford. I could be wrong. But a car like that pulled in behind me on the way to work this morning. Didn't think anything of it at the time—and I don't remember seeing him the rest of the day. I was in and out at the plant, went home for lunch, drove over to the bank—that kind of thing. But when I left work a little while ago, I noticed a car behind me. There's not a hell of a lot of traffic in Lake Elm at this time of night, if you know what I mean."

"Where is he now?"

"He's parked down the street. It's too dark to see anything."

"Don't let him know you're looking at him."

"Yeah, okay—I'll try."

"Listen Arthur—it's probably the FBI. By now they have to know I'm back in the U.S., or at least suspect it. But it could be somebody more dangerous—a lot more dangerous. Are you carrying a gun?"

"Are you kidding? I never carried a gun in my life."

"Have you got one?"

"Got a twelve gauge shotgun."

"First thing tomorrow, go buy a pistol you can carry in your pocket. There's a legal waiting period, but . . ."

"Forget it, John. I'm not carrying a gun. All I could do with it is shoot myself in the foot."

"Listen to me Arthur . . ."

"I said forget it!" The big voice bellowed into Pavlak's ear. "I don't know anything about pistols, and I'm too old to learn."

Pavlak sighed. He knew Arthur well enough not to waste time arguing. "Okay. Look Arthur, there's a copy of Shakespeare's complete works in Judith's house. I need to get my hands on it as soon as possible. Tomorrow."

"What the hell do you . . . ?"

"Don't ask. Just get it for me, will you?"

"Shit."

"I'm sorry, Arthur. I'll pay you back for all this some day."

"No you won't. You don't have enough money. All you Pavlaks together don't have enough money for this." A heavy breath blew into the phone. "Can't you at least tell me what you want it for?"

"Judith left me a message. I'll tell you later how I got it. It's a line reference in Shakespeare. I've got to find out what that line is."

"So what's wrong with the book there in the cabin?" Arthur demanded irritably.

Pavlak blinked. "What are you talking about?"

"Edith's books. She's a high-brow type like you, remember? There used to be a Shakespeare book there somewhere. She reads that stuff while I fish. I tried it once, but it's gibberish to me."

Pavlak was motioning frantically to Karin. He covered the mouthpiece with his hand. "Look for a volume of Shakespeare here somewhere. Try that cabinet over there, the one with the books on top of it." He removed his hand from the phone. "Okay, Arthur, we're looking for it. If we can't find it, I'll still need you . . ."

"Here it is!" Karin called, holding up a heavy blue volume.

"Oh great, we found it. Never mind. Listen, Arthur, get off the phone and don't try to contact me again. No more phone calls—nothing. I'll figure a way to get you a message if I need you. Now get in your car and drive straight home.

Lock all the windows in your house and put the shotgun under your side of the bed."

"That's where it stays."

"Good. If anybody comes into your house at night, Arthur, don't ask any questions, you hear me? Shoot the bastard and worry about the rest later, you got that?"

"I hear you, John, but—I don't know if I could do that. And look, it's probably the FBI like you said. They won't break into the house."

"It's probably the FBI, but don't take it for granted. Please, Arthur. Schliemann and his crowd are dangerous— very dangerous."

"Don't worry. I'm gone now. You guys watch yourselves."

The line went dead. Pavlak lowered the receiver and stood staring at the rich wood grain on the wall in front of him. So many carefree hours he and Judith had spent in this cabin. The golden wood glowed innocently in the electric lights, so reminiscent of a simpler life. What had gone awry?

Karin was still holding the book in both hands. "What's wrong?"

"It's Arthur," Pavlak responded, shaking his head slowly. "I never should have gotten him into this. I wasn't thinking. If Schliemann gets to him, he'll find out where we are, then kill him. Now I have to figure out a way to protect Arthur too."

Karin laid the book on a chair and put her arms around his waist. "It's not your fault. He loves you. He wants to help you."

Pavlak kissed her on the top of the head. "But don't I owe him the same favor?"

"Of course you do. But right now there's not much you can do for him. Accept it."

Pavlak sighed and pushed her gently out to arm's length.

"Anyway, we've got Shakespeare," he said, changing the subject. "Let's find out what Judith wanted to tell me."

He picked up the big blue volume, found the index and turned to *Antony and Cleopatra*. He found the second scene of Act II and ran his finger down the line numbers in the left margin.

"Here it is. 'The barge she sat in, like a burnish'd throne, burn'd on the water.'"

Karin watched him expectantly.

Pavlak frowned and read the line again. " 'The barge she sat in, like a burnish'd throne, burn'd on the water.' " He laid the book down and began pacing slowly from one wall to the other, his brow creased in thought. Karin picked up the book.

"What does 'burnish'd' mean?"

"Polished—shiny, like brass or copper."

Karin read the lines aloud, her accent lending the poetry an odd teutonic coloring. She looked up. "Do you have any idea what it means?"

Pavlak was still pacing. " 'The barge she sat in . . . like a burnish'd throne. . . . burn'd on the water." A full minute passed before Pavlak stopped pacing and frowned at her. "I don't get it," he said. "I don't remember even hearing that line before. Maybe . . . maybe Judith . . . 'the barge *she* sat in.' Who's 'she?' What the hell was Judith trying to tell me?"

They spent the next hour reading and re-reading the line. They read all the lines around it in case the edition Judith used had slightly different numbering. They tried the same reference in Act I, scene ii, and Act III, scene ii, then other combinations of acts and scenes, in case Judith had made an error in the scene reference. Nothing helped, and they returned to the original line. Pavlak scoured his memory until nearly 3 A.M., but could find nothing. Finally Karin closed the volume firmly and pulled him toward the bed-room.

"Get some sleep," she ordered. "Maybe tomorrow something will occur to you. It has to mean something."

Pavlak nodded. "But I have no idea what."

"Could Diane be playing some kind of joke?"

"I doubt that she has this much imagination—besides, she wouldn't know about the Itch Bitch—and the note's definitely in Judith's handwriting."

They climbed into bed and Karin fell asleep almost instantly. Pavlak kept the lamp on the bedside table glowing and stared at a wall decoration Edith had made by gluing small seashells onto a crude painting of the sea. The shells were supposed to look like the beach, but they looked like shells glued to a painting.

Finally, Pavlak switched off the lamp and slid down onto the pillow.

"Water," he whispered to himself. "Water—burn'd on the water. Burn'd. . . ." He stared into the darkness. "That's it!"

Karin started. "My God, you scared me," she protested, putting one hand to her chest as Pavlak switched the light on again.

He seized her shoulders. "Karin, I know where the diskette box is. It's here."

"Where?"

"Right here." He was pulling on his pants.

"Where are you going?"

"Get dressed and put on your coat. We're going for a walk."

A few minutes later they were stumbling through the dark woods, following a path that led down the slope to the river and the boathouse. The moon was still up, but the tall pines shaded the path, and the night air was damp and cool.

"Is it there?" Karin asked, pointing. "In the boathouse?"

"Not the boathouse. . . ."

Karin stumbled and would have fallen if she had not clung to Pavlak's arm. She recovered her balance and they half-ran the last few yards, then walked onto the pier, their footsteps suddenly resounding on the wooden planks.

The pier was an elaborate one, with a wider, roofed-over section at the end forming a sort of teahouse over water. Arthur had built it at Edith's insistence and grumbled over every nail. But in the end, it was Arthur who used it the most, sitting in the shade to fish on hot summer days.

"You see that?" Pavlak asked, pointing to a dark shadow about chest-high in the middle of the teahouse.

"What is it?"

"Come on."

Pavlak pulled her the length of the pier until they stood beneath the roof. The chill of the black water rose through the cracks under their feet. Karin shivered and leaned against him. She could make out a round dome of some sort covering something.

"It's a grill," Pavlak explained. "A covered charcoal grill. 'Burn'd on the water.' " He separated from her and felt in the darkness for the grip on the cover. "Edith made Arthur build it here for barbecue parties. There's an ash bin beneath it and everything. Arthur said he was going to be damned sure Edith didn't burn down his pier."

The cover was cast aluminum. Pavlak lifted it and plunged his hand into the dark void beneath. At first his fingers met nothing, then they touched a rough grate Arthur had welded together from steel reinforcing rods.

"The grill is gone. Edith probably takes it in for the winter. I'm touching the grate the charcoal rests on." He swept his hand around the circumference of the grate. Ash crumbled into his fingers, but there was nothing else there. His optimism began to fade. Maybe he was wrong.

"The ash bin," he said and dropped to his knees.

"You must be getting black from head to toe," Karin warned.

"Ah, here we go," Pavlak said as the door to the ash collector swung open. Pavlak rummaged his fingers through the greasy ash. "There's a summer's worth of ashes in here. Arthur forgot to empty it last fall." His fingers struck something hard. He felt along the line of it until he reached a bump that moved. It was a carrying handle. His index finger hooked beneath it and pulled.

"Got it!" he announced breathlessly, pulling the diskette box from the bin. Clumps of ash tumbled onto the boards and fell through the cracks to the water. Pavlak slammed the box twice against the boards to shake off as much of the sticky ash as he could, the hollow thumps cutting through the night silence.

"Come on."

He covered the path with long strides while Karin half-ran behind him. At the cabin door Pavlak reached for the doorknob.

"Don't touch it!" Karin cried. "Let me open it." She twisted the knob, and the light from inside spilled over them. "Oh Lord, look at you—you're filthy. You can't come into the house like that."

"We'll clean later." Pavlak brushed past her and set the blackened box on the kitchen table. A small padlock, its works gummed with grease and ash, hung from a metal loop at the front of the box. Pavlak found a hammer and a pair of pliers and went to work on the lock. It took ten minutes to break it loose. He pushed the snap latches on the front of the box and heard two reassuring clicks. His eyes met

Karin's. "Here goes nothing." With his thumbs, he tilted the lid backwards.

The box was empty except for some paper lying in the bottom, folded as if to fit into a business envelope. Pavlak immediately recognized the cheap gray stock that pervaded the lives of East Germans during the country's forty years of socialist rule. Paper was the one thing the system had produced in abundance.

"That's it," he breathed. "The document."

The bundle was thin and light. He thumbed the pages quickly. There were four sheets. Paperclipped to the front of them was a note in Judith's handwriting:

> *John,*
>
> *Brigitte Oertmayer found these papers in a Stasi file in Berlin. I believe it has to do with smuggling illegal technology into East Germany. I am in the middle of an investigation, but I have just learned that Brigitte died in Berlin today. Turgat told me she thought she was being followed for the last several days. He believes she may have been murdered and that I am in danger. I am going to hide these papers and leave a coded message for you in case anything happens to me. I wouldn't even give it to you except that it involves your father.*
>
> *Judith*

There was a P.S. at the bottom, but no text. An arrow pointed to the right edge of the paper. Pavlak slipped the note from the paper clip and turned it over:

> *By the way, I haven't told anyone at the newspaper about this yet. Since it concerns Pavlak Equipment, I want to be sure before I make anything known. Needless to say, I*

haven't said anything to your father. The only person I've told about the document is Arthur Trask, hoping perhaps he could help me, but Arthur knows nothing.

J.

Pavlak stared at the slip of paper in his hand.

At that moment, two hard raps sounded at the door, causing both of them to jump. "John! You in there?" It was Arthur Trask's booming voice.

33

"What is it? What's wrong?" Karin asked.

The knocking resumed at the door, more insistent this time.

"John? It's me. Open the door!"

The note hung suspended in Pavlak's hand.

"John? Open the damned door, will you?" Arthur shouted.

Pavlak shoved the note into the pocket of his jeans and whispered frantically to Karin. "In the bedroom, quick!"

"What is it?"

"Go!"

As Karin ran for the bedroom, Pavlak dumped the document back into the diskette box and clapped the lid shut. He considered hiding it in a cabinet, then realized it was futile. Both he and the table were black with ashes, and there was no time to clean things—or to make up a believable explanation. Anyway, Judith's note, at least, was in his pocket, even though the gray papers were still in the box.

"Just a second, Arthur," Pavlak called aloud. "I'll be right there."

He dashed for the bedroom and slammed his shoulder into the door just as Karin was closing it, throwing her onto the floor. He leaped over her prostrate form, jerked open the drawer of his side table, and slipped his hand beneath a folded towel. The butt of the Ruger met his fingers, and he pulled it from the drawer.

"John, no!" Karin pleaded. "What are you doing!?"

"It's *Arthur!* He *knew.* He's the one who tipped off Schliemann and Krueger." Pavlak shoved the pistol into the back of his belt.

Karin's hand darted to cover her mouth, the dark eyes sending Pavlak a speechless plea. At that instant, a key scraped into the lock on the front door. Pavlak rushed from the bedroom and closed the door behind him. He was still ten feet from the front door when it burst open, and Arthur Trask's massive shoulders blotted out the doorway. His eyes were heavy-lidded and bloodshot.

"Jesus H. Christ, John, what took you so long?"

The bulky wool hunting jacket made the man look even wider than he was. Pavlak suddenly recalled a scene from his childhood, when Gustaf Pavlak still raised pigs in his backyard and slaughtered them at the first hard freeze. The memory that came to Pavlak now was of one particular hog, a large red one, that sensed danger and dashed madly from one fence to the other, desperately seeking to escape its fate. His father's first shot struck the hog in the jaw. The wounded animal screamed and hurled itself around the lot in even greater frenzy. Three more shots missed. Finally, Arthur Trask, young but already a giant of a man, stepped over the low fence, seized the three hundred-pound animal by two legs, heaved it into the air, and slammed it to the ground. Stunned, the hog lay motionless while Gustaf plunged a butcher knife into its throat. The event occasioned great merriment among the assembled neighbors, but John Pavlak, six years old at the time, ran from the hog lot in horror and hid beneath the porch.

"You going to talk to me or just stand there staring?" Arthur demanded.

Pavlak cleared his throat. "I'm sorry. Karin wasn't dressed."

Arthur spoke in a confidential voice. "I want to talk to you about her sometime, John."

"What's to talk about? Close the door, will you? It's cold."

Arthur took another step into the room, turned, and shut the door behind him. "I'm not sure, John, I just . . . how well do you even know this girl? Maybe I'm wrong, but you two seem kind of—romantic. Am I right?"

"Kind of. So what?"

"Well, it's just that—it hasn't been long, you know. People will talk. Just . . . be careful, that's all."

Pavlak backed away two steps as Arthur moved forward. He did not want the big man to see the pistol in the back of his belt. Not yet. "Arthur—what the hell are you doing here?" Pavlak asked. "I thought you were tired. God knows you look tired. It's nearly 4:00 o'clock in the morning, for God's sake. By the way, were you followed?"

Arthur unzipped the hunting jacket, shrugged it off, and laid it across the back of the old couch that doubled as an extra cot.

"I couldn't sleep," he explained, lowering himself heavily. "I kept worrying about you out here and wondering if you'd learned anything from Judith's message. And no, nobody followed me. The guy in the Ford followed me home and parked outside a block away. After I turned all the lights out, he waited a little bit, then drove away. I'm sure he's FBI like you said." Arthur sat forward on the couch and tapped the tips of his fingers together. "You guys staying warm enough in here? Jesus, John, what's all this crap?"

He was looking at black marks on the carpet at his feet. Arthur's eyes followed the smudges to the kitchen and the blackened box on the table.

"What the hell is that?" he asked, pointing at the box. "This place is a mess. If I'd known you were going to treat my house like this, I'd have sent you to a hotel. What is all this black crap anyway?" He stood and moved toward the kitchen.

Pavlak followed a step behind and pulled out the first chair at the table. "It's ashes. Sit down, Arthur. This is what Judith's message led me to."

Pavlak stepped around the corner of the table and sat down at a right angle to Arthur. Arthur fidgeted nervously, and the wooden chair creaked and groaned. Pavlak reached for the box, extracted the gray sheets, and handed them to Arthur.

"What is this?" Arthur demanded. Pavlak noticed that the papers trembled in his huge hands. "It's in some foreign language. Is it German?"

Pavlak said nothing.

"Looks like some kind of list. Hey—it says Pavlak Equipment on here."

Pavlak rocked forward in his chair. "Have you ever seen this before, Arthur?"

Arthur shook his head. "Nah. At least not that I remember. Maybe. We do some foreign business, you know. These numbers here . . ." He stroked the page with a thick forefinger. "They're not our numbers."

Pavlak heard a small noise and glanced toward the living room. Was Karin doing something in the bedroom, or was it the wind, or was the situation making him paranoid? He listened for a moment, but heard nothing more. Finally he took the papers from Arthur's hand. "To tell you the truth, Arthur, I haven't really looked at these yet. We just found them. The box was hidden in the barbecue grill out on the pier."

Arthur's eyes grew wide. "*My* grill? That one down there?"

Pavlak nodded. He was studying the document. It was typed using a poor-quality machine that needed a new ribbon. The letters were uneven, and the print faded. Age had further lessened its legibility. The edges of the cheap paper had already begun to turn brown and brittle. Near the top of the first page, imprinted at a slight angle, was a hand-stamped box containing the words: "STRENG VERTRAU-LICH; UM RÜCKGABE WIRD GEBETEN," in red letters. "Top Secret; Please Return." Just above the stamp, at the top of the page, stood the title "MINISTERIUM FÜR STAATSSICHER-HEIT" in capital letters, framed above and below by a heavy black line. It was dated 7 July 1982, and below the date were the letters "HVA." Pavlak knew the acronym. It stood for *Hauptverwaltung Aufklärung*, the Stasi division responsible for espionage against the capitalist West. Then, just above the top of the list, was typed, *"Im Ausland erworbene Güter ab dem 1.1.82. Sämtliche Güter sind mit Genehmigung des Direktors der HVA an Oberst Protschek des Komitees für Staatsicherheit der SU per Hinweise weitergeliefert worden."* "Goods acquired in Foreign countries since January 1, 1982. All goods delivered to Colonel Protschek of the KGB of the Soviet Union as per instructions and with the approval of the Director of the HVA." It was initialed by hand with the letters PS. Peter Schliemann.

Pavlak lifted the first page and found that the second, third, and fourth pages were a continuation of a list that began midway down the first page. The lines were typed on blank sheets, except for the red-lettered "STRENG VERTRAU-LICH" stamp that someone had pounded across the top of each page.

He flipped back to the first page and began examining the list. Each line contained four columns. The first was a date in European order, day/month/year. The dates varied, but in every case the year was 1982. The second column listed a shipper—*Absender*. And it was in that column that the words "Pavlak Equipment, Inc." leapt out at him—several times on each page. There were perhaps half a dozen other companies as well, though none appeared as often as Pavlak Equipment. He recognized one West German chemical company. One company was clearly Italian. Two others were probably American or English, although he had never heard of them.

The third column was headed *"Anzahl"*—quantity—and the fourth listed an item. The items were identified in different ways, some by a manufacturer, a name, and a number—most likely a model number. Others had brief descriptions. Most of the manufacturers listed were American, and all the ones that Pavlak recognized were electronics or defense industry firms, IBM, Intel, Rockwell, Grumman. . . .

And then his eye lit on the third line on the second page. The date was 17/3/82, the *Absender* was Pavlak Equipment, and the *Anzahl* was one. But it was the item that caught his attention. "DSMAC, TMHK cruise msl."

Pavlak looked at Arthur, and for an instant their eyes met.

"Any ideas?" Arthur asked. He reached for the papers in Pavlak's hand, but Pavlak jerked them out of his reach.

"Why don't you tell me, Arthur," he said evenly. The Ruger gouged his back, and Pavlak shifted slightly in his chair.

Arthur's hand still floated in midair where the papers had been. "I don't know what you're talking about," he answered, lowering the hand. His face had grown pale. "But listen—let me have those papers, and I'll find out. If it has to do with Pavlak Equipment, then your Dad will know. I'll take them to him tomorrow. You'd better not leave the cabin for a while now. The FBI . . ."

Pavlak was shaking his head firmly from side to side, though his eyes never left Arthur's. "It's no good, Arthur." He held up the papers. "There was a note attached to this— from Judith. I know you've seen it already."

Trask deflated in front of him, like a giant balloon. The big man slumped down in his chair, and his gaze fell to the floor. Pavlak held the papers in his left hand. The knuckles of his right hand rested on the seat of his chair just behind his hip-bone, six inches from the Ruger.

"You knew about Fool's Gold, didn't you Arthur? Why did you lie to me?"

Trask stared at the floor and said nothing.

Pavlak shook the papers in his left hand. "I've got the document now. I'll find out everything eventually." He lowered his voice. "It was you, wasn't it, Arthur? You had Judith killed."

Trask jerked his head up. "I didn't kill them," he said immediately and emphatically. "John, I swear . . ."

But Pavlak was already rising to his feet. His eye had caught a movement behind Arthur and sought it out. It was the doorknob slowly turning. In an instant, the Ruger was in his hand and pointing at the door.

Suddenly Arthur Trask's powerful hand gripped his wrist.

"Are you crazy?" Arthur screamed forcing Pavlak's hand up. The pistol fired, and the bullet splintered into the pine ceiling two inches from the molding at the top of the wall. In the same instant, the door flew open, and Peter Schliemann stepped into the cabin. In his hands lay a sawed-off shotgun levelled at Pavlak's chest.

34

"It's okay," Trask shouted to Schliemann as he tore the pistol from Pavlak's hand. "He's not armed. Put down the gun."

A mirthless smile spread over Schliemann's elegant features. His head was bare, but the silver hair was scarcely ruffled, even by the damp night breeze. A diamond ring sparkled on the pale hand clutching the pump grip on the shotgun. It was not, Pavlak thought absurdly, a hand that one would expect to see holding a sawed-off shotgun. And yet, the weapon lay easily, comfortably, in Schliemann's soft hands.

"The woman, Dr. Pavlak," Schliemann said in the same oily imitation of an upper-crust British accent that Pavlak had been forced to listen to while bleeding onto the concrete floor on Crete. Except for the ugly weapon in his hands, Schliemann might have passed as an Oxford don on vacation. "Call her," Schliemann snapped. "Tell her to come out with her hands on her head."

Pavlak made no response.

Arthur Trask had stepped away from Pavlak. He was holding Pavlak's pistol awkwardly, in both hands, with the barrel pointed at the ceiling.

"Get her, Trask," Schliemann barked, jerking his head toward the bedroom door.

"Look, Peter, he's unarmed now, so put the gun down. You promised, remember?" Trask turned to Pavlak. "We're just going to talk this thing out, John, that's all."

Pavlak had not taken his eyes off Schliemann's face.

"Get the woman," Schliemann commanded again. Trask hesitated, then awkwardly slipped the pistol into his belt before moving to the bedroom door. He knocked politely.

"Just open it and bring her out here!" Schliemann ordered, stepping sideways toward the couch.

Trask hesitated. Even through the fear, Pavlak felt something like pity for Arthur. The big man was so obviously out of his depth. Pavlak saw the look of self-doubt that crossed Arthur's face when Schliemann spoke to him. So this was how it had happened. The smooth, urbane manipulator had taken control of the ignorant giant. Arthur, Pavlak realized with a start of despair, was afraid of Schliemann.

Arthur pushed open the door to the bedroom and disappeared. He was out of sight no more than five seconds.

"She's gone!" he cried. "The window's open."

"Get her, dammit," Schliemann shouted. "You waited too long. Get her now."

Arthur dashed to the door, stopped, and turned. "We have an agreement, remember? I meant what I said."

Arthur was trying to act intimidating, but it fell short. Pavlak could see the contempt for him in Schliemann's eyes, even as Schliemann responded with a glib, "Of course, Arthur. Just as we agreed."

Seconds later Pavlak heard Arthur crashing through the underbrush on the far side of the house. Karin had a chance in the dark, he reasoned, if she found a good hiding place and didn't move.

When Arthur was gone, Schliemann looked back at Pavlak and his frown turned to a smile that did not reach the eyes. "Well, Dr. Pavlak . . . we meet again. Do step over and join me." He motioned to an easy chair opposite the couch.

Slowly, Pavlak obeyed. Schliemann lowered himself onto the couch with a sigh, resting the shotgun on his knee. He was wearing an overcoat of what appeared to be beaver fur. "Quaint accommodations, I must say," he remarked with a glance around the cabin. "Rustic. Very American, I suppose. Do you plan to stay long?"

"Fuck you, Schliemann. And the horse you rode in on."

Schliemann clicked his tongue. "Now, now Dr. Pavlak. That's why we Europeans are so contemptuous of Americans. It's your incurable vulgarity—the product of all this democracy you're so proud of. Give power to the common masses, and you become a common nation."

Pavlak saw Schliemann's gaze land on the diskette box on the table in the kitchen and rest there for a second.

"Oh you have money and power just now," Schliemann continued, looking back at Pavlak, "but your culture is hopelessly inferior. That is why democracy is doomed to be a footnote in history, as your Mr. Reagan might have said."

"Unlike communism," Pavlak retorted, "which I suppose you still believe to be the wave of the future."

Schliemann laughed—genuinely this time. "Communism? Oh, that is a good joke, Dr. Pavlak. No, communism is certainly dead. Actually it never lived. How could it? Marx was undoubtedly one of the greatest fools who ever lived—surpassed only by those who embraced his silly, idealistic rantings and turned them into a cult."

"Are you speaking of your former bosses?"

"Of course—among others. You have plenty of them here as well. Odd, isn't it? You have all this wealth and freedom, and yet there are millions among you who thirst for tyranny. And they will have it eventually. Of course, that sort always assume that *they* will be the future aristocrats, exercising the *noblesse oblige* of an intellectual aristocracy. Because that's what it was, you see—our Marxism—a rebirth of aristocracy. We simply substituted Marx's moral right for the old idea of divine right." Schliemann tilted his head back slightly. "No, Dr. Pavlak, in the great scheme of things, it is the strong who achieve power and wealth. It has always been so, and always shall be."

Pavlak thought he heard something outside the cabin door. He waited a few seconds, but nothing happened. He had to keep Schliemann talking—and the man's pompous vanity seemed, at the moment, to be his most vulnerable spot.

"And you're one of the strong, right, Schliemann?"

Schliemann shrugged. "I am a very wealthy man, Dr. Pavlak. Wealthy by virtue of my own wit and will. If I did not live in this deranged century, I would be, I suppose, a minor prince of some sort. You see, I don't really crave power. I am satisfied with simple wealth—and enough power not to have to tolerate bothersome people. Such as yourself." The unpleasant smile crept across his face again. "Incidentally," Schliemann continued, "I heard that an old friend of mine, Gerhart Krueger, met an untimely end in Munich the other day. Would you happen to know anything about that?"

"Yes."

Schliemann waited but Pavlak was silent.

"Well—would you care to fill me in on the details?"

"I killed him," Pavlak said evenly, holding Schliemann's gaze.

Schliemann cocked an eyebrow. "Did you really? Well, that's something of a relief. I heard that Frank Borning was with him at the time, and I was afraid perhaps the CIA had brought about Gerhart's demise. That would really have been disturbing because it would have meant that they know more than they should."

"They know everything," Pavlak said on impulse. "I told Borning myself."

For an instant, the smug mask fell away, and Pavlak knew he had found a nerve.

"You're bluffing, Dr. Pavlak," Schliemann smiled, recovering quickly. "I heard you speaking to your large friend, Mr. Trask. You couldn't have told Borning anything of consequence because you don't know anything of consequence, do you? You bluffed me once—about distributing copies of the document. A clever lie at the time, but . . . you won't fool me twice."

Schliemann stood and felt his way to the kitchen table, walking sideways to keep the gun on Pavlak. At the table he hefted the weapon into one hand and with the other opened the box and withdrew the document, then made the same trip in reverse. He smiled and folded the document into the pocket of the beaver coat. "You see, Dr. Pavlak," he said. "The CIA knows nothing—and they never will."

"It was clever, I'll grant you," Pavlak began, "but . . ."

"Clever?" Schliemann exploded, feigning offense. "It was *brilliant.* Absolutely brilliant. It was the stunning achievement of my career. All the more so because I had detractors early on, those who thought it was crazy—who said we could never fool the CIA into smuggling America's technology to us."

He settled deeper into the sofa, and his hand relaxed a little on the polished wood of the pump grip.

"The KGB was particularly pleased, as you might imagine. And of course they took all the goods. Not a single shipment ever remained in Germany, not even for twenty-four hours.

The gentlemen from the committee were always on hand when a shipment arrived."

"So," Pavlak said slowly, "the CIA thought they were shipping minor goods to maintain the cover for a double-agent in place . . ."

"And they were," Schliemann interjected quickly. "In fact some of those goods were not so minor. That was a fringe benefit, you see. I actually persuaded the CIA to send us some pretty valuable technology on purpose—technology hidden in the shipments by your father. Dear old Gustaf . . ."

Schliemann's counterfeit smile had turned to genuine mirth. He was enjoying himself now.

"But Arthur hid the real goods in the same shipments for you, didn't he?" Pavlak said, as the pieces began to fall into place. "The CIA thought they were giving you copper for gold, when in fact, you were giving them the copper, and they were giving you Fort Knox."

Schliemann nodded contentedly. "And best of all, they arranged for it to reach us without the usual risk of detection by your Department of Commerce. As I said, Dr. Pavlak— brilliant. 'Fool's Gold' indeed. But which was the gold, and who were the fools? You can see why the Russians were so pleased. Oh, I am a living legend in Soviet intelligence circles, Dr. Pavlak. I am what your Mr. Le Carre would call a 'Master Spy.' Do you mind if I smoke?" He pulled a long cigar from inside the beaver coat.

"I mind if you breathe," Pavlak said tersely.

Schliemann ignored him and dug in his pocket for a lighter.

"How did Arthur procure the goods?" Pavlak went on. "Surely it's not that easy to buy large quantities of sensitive items."

"Not easy, Dr. Pavlak—but not all that difficult either. At

least, not when you're supposedly purchasing for domestic consumption. It's getting the goods out of the country that's difficult. You see, Mr. Trask had nothing to do with acquisition. *We* provided the items. He merely shipped them for us."

"You mean you just walked into a shop somewhere and bought a guidance system for a cruise missile?"

Schliemann's eyebrows rose. "I see you did get a look at the list. No, as a matter of fact, that guidance system was probably *the* intelligence coup of the last decade." Schliemann smiled with unmistakable pride. "We *stole* it, Dr. Pavlak!"

"Stole it? How do you steal a cruise missile?"

"Not the missile. Just the guidance system—a portion of the guidance system, actually. You see, there are three phases to it. I forget the acronyms for all but the last, most critical phase. That's the DSMAC. Stands for "Digital Scene-Matching Area Correlator." It actually matches a camera view of the final approach to the target with a picture stored in the computer's memory. Makes for incredible accuracy. Your navy can send one of those missiles through a particular window in a building seven hundred miles away. Our gallant Russian allies couldn't figure out how you did it." With his left hand, Schliemann delicately replaced a misplaced hair at his temple. "The DSMAC is manufactured at a plant in the midwest," he continued. "A truck hauling parts for a prototype of the Tomahawk was hijacked in Pennsylvania in 1982, the year before that particular missile was deployed. Two members of a military escort were wounded. The operation lasted less than three minutes."

"You're lying," Pavlak said evenly. "An incident like that would have been headline news, and I never heard of it."

Schliemann chuckled. "Odd, isn't it? I was rather surprised myself. But you see, the operation was only possible because of a series of security breaches on the American side. Sloppy. Very sloppy. The affair would have been most embarrassing for your military and intelligence circles. Evidently some very powerful people were scared enough of the consequences that they managed to hush it up. But they carried out an extraordinary search for the missing system. We had to get it out of the country quickly."

"And Arthur Trask shipped it for you—with the CIA itself guaranteeing safe passage."

Schliemann nodded. "Beautiful, isn't it?"

"But there are still two things I don't understand. How did you get Arthur Trask to do it, and where did you get so much money for yourself? I'm sure your Soviet bosses were pleased, but surely they didn't reward you that well—at least not with hard currency."

Schliemann found the lighter, flicked it, and puffed until the tip of the cigar glowed red. Clouds of aromatic smoke drifted above his head. "Related questions, really, Dr. Pavlak. Your Mr. Trask was persuaded by the prospect of great wealth—and he received it. You can imagine, of course, how valuable all this technology was to our Soviet comrades. Money, in such instances, is no object. Mr. Trask drove a very hard bargain."

"Arthur?" Pavlak asked doubtfully.

"Well, actually, *I* drove a hard bargain on Mr. Trask's behalf, though neither he nor the Russians knew I was doing so."

"And I bet it was you," Pavlak said slowly, "who handled the transfer of funds to Arthur."

Schliemann nodded. "Precisely. All in cash, of course, mostly American dollars—some West German marks. Brought into Bonn by diplomatic pouch, transferred to me in various clever ways, and eventually deposited in one of Mr. Trask's accounts in Switzerland."

"Except for a little commission that you retained for your services—and deposited in your own Swiss accounts."

Schliemann blew a cloud of smoke into the air. The cigar was at least eight inches long. "Of course. My little commission was fifty percent—which still left Mr. Trask a very wealthy man. He has over two million US dollars in Switzerland." Schliemann's face darkened suddenly. "He *had* them, that is. The damned fool just spent much of it very stupidly."

Pavlak's mind was churning. "So why did you need Krueger and Lederer and the other one—the cadaver man—the man driving the Mercedes when I shot Krueger?"

"Ah yes, the BND." Schliemann frowned. "That was perhaps a mistake. You see, there were two tiers to the operation. Pavlak Equipment was only one. Gerhart Krueger ran another in West Germany."

"And Krueger's motivation was the same as Arthur's? Money?"

"Not exactly. Gerhart had an unfortunate weakness, a fondness for young girls. And he liked to hurt them a little. As I said—an unfortunate weakness. One night such a girl died. Gerhart was horrified—absolutely devastated."

"Let me guess," Pavlak said coldly. "Did you by any chance have anything to do with his finding this particular girl?"

"As it happens," Schliemann said with a smile, "I had a hand in the matter."

"And she didn't really die."

"Oh yes, her death was real enough—although Gerhart didn't cause it. He just thought he did."

"You sonofabitch," Pavlak whispered.

Schliemann took a long pull on his cigar and let the smoke curl slowly from his mouth and nostrils. "Not really,

Dr. Pavlak. The girl was nobody. Her life was worthless. I'm a realist, Dr. Pavlak. And the reality is that the weak perish. I didn't make the world. And it's hardly my fault that I am one of the strong."

"You're confusing strength with ruthlessness. You're a sociopath, not a prince."

"In your view, I suppose so," Schliemann shrugged. "I've heard such words before from people trying to find excuses for losing to me. Fortunately, your view is of no real concern. Anyway, the incident with the girl made Gerhart most cooperative. He was desperate to keep it a secret, especially from the Service. As for Lederer—and Scholz, whom you refer to rather picturesquely as the cadaver man—they belong to me. They were both Stasi agents. I saw to it that Gerhart hired them. We placed them there partly to gather intelligence, and partly to keep an eye on Gerhart. You see, I didn't really trust him. I was always afraid that he would confess everything in some moment of moral hysteria. It was really rather a relief to me when you eliminated him."

Schliemann flicked the ash from the cigar and laughed. An impulse to lunge at his throat seized Pavlak, but he fought it down. Schliemann would kill him before he was out of the chair.

"To tell you the truth, Professor, if you hadn't killed Krueger, we probably would have. The only reason we let him live so long was to avoid arousing the suspicion of the CIA."

"We? Who's we? The Stasi is no more. You're unemployed, remember?"

"Retired, Dr. Pavlak. Semi-retired, that is. The only thing delaying my full retirement is this last little annoyance. As for the 'we,' I was referring to Lederer and Scholz. Lederer is wrapped in chains at the bottom of the Mediterranean now, but that's just as well. He was becoming a liability anyway. And since Munich, Scholz is on the run from the CIA and the BND. He's a matter of some concern, of course, since he knows enough to cause difficulty. You see, after reunification I put both him and Lederer on my private payroll. And naturally they don't want to expose themselves as former Stasi agents, so they were well-motivated to keep silent. Anyway, Scholz must be desperate now. He'll contact me for help eventually, and I'll deal with him then."

"Kill him, you mean."

"Possibly."

Pavlak laid his hands in his lap and stared at the carpet. He listened for a while, but heard only the wind. "Brilliant," Pavlak murmured, looking up. "Brilliant indeed. You double-crossed everybody—the CIA, the KGB, the Stasi . . . everybody. Do you really think you'll get away with it?"

"Oh, I already have. Except of course for this stupid bureaucratic mistake—and even that would have been no problem but for the unfortunate coincidence of the Oertmayer woman finding the file."

"What 'bureaucratic mistake' are you talking about?"

"The existence of this document, of course." Schliemann patted his pocket, then the complacent expression on his face suddenly turned hard. "That little idiot of a lieutenant," he said through clenched teeth, "the one who arrested me. . . . I saw to it that he was transferred to the Sixth Directorate and spent the rest of his career checking passports on the Polish border." The complacency quickly returned. "This document and two copies were in my briefcase when the fool arrested my brother and detained me. I was released quickly, of course, and you can be sure there were repercussions for all involved. Anyway, the copies and the original were to be removed from the files and destroyed. I was told they had been, but this one obviously was overlooked. This is the original. I suspect a clerk was told to destroy the copies and did so—assuming that *kopien* did not refer to the original."

"And so your little game was blown after all."

"No, not blown. Not yet. And it won't be. You see, I have the document now. And I will soon have the only people alive who have seen it."

"So you plan to kill us."

"Oh no, Dr. Pavlak. Your friend Mr. Trask would never stand for that. He's really extraordinarily fond of you—and quite angry with me for our little *tête a tête* on Crete. I had a devil of a time persuading him to come here tonight. I convinced him that, since you seemed to be on the verge of finding the document, we might be able to follow you and then retrieve the document before you had a chance to look at it. That, of course, was unlikely, especially since we had to shake an FBI tail first. But your friend wanted to believe it. And secondly, he saw that this was his best chance of saving you."

"Saving *me?*"

"Yes. I pointed out to him that your bringing this episode to light would greatly embarrass some very powerful men in your military establishment and Central Intelligence Agency, men who do not take kindly to public embarrassment. If they find out what a fiasco Fool's Gold really was—and especially if they know you can expose the cruise missile debacle—well . . . they will silence you for good."

"And you as well," Pavlak added. "If the remnants of the old KGB don't get you first for siphoning off half of their money."

Schliemann shrugged. "It's true that my motivation in this affair is very strong. But you see, this is how I convinced Mr. Trask that we could make a financial arrangement that would leave everyone contented." Schliemann's eyes narrowed. "The fool had the gall to threaten me. He says that if I harm you, he will go to the authorities himself."

"You mean Arthur believed that you could buy my silence after you murdered my wife and child?"

"I had nothing to do with that," Schliemann said simply. "And Mr. Trask knows me well enough to know I would not have killed her until I had the document in my hand."

Pavlak leaned forward in his chair, and Schliemann raised the barrel of the shotgun a centimeter. "Do you mean," Pavlak asked in a tight voice, "that *Arthur* arranged the murder?"

"I'm not sure," Schliemann frowned. "I can't imagine that. Can you? It was, of course, through Mr. Trask that I learned there was a problem. He called me immediately after your wife showed him the document. The poor man was in a panic, but it's difficult to believe he would kill her, isn't it? As I told you on Crete, it may have been Gerhart. I told Gerhart about her, and then later about you. I needed his cooperation to find you, you see. Gerhart was terrified, and scared men do stupid things. But . . . simply killing the woman without getting the list was pointless. Of course, I did send Lederer and Scholz to search her house and yours for the document, but they wouldn't have killed your wife without my authority. The truth, Dr. Pavlak, is that I honestly don't know who killed her. I would have done so eventually, but someone moved too soon. I suspect . . ."

"Go on."

"Well, she told Trask she had approached the CIA, so they knew something was going on . . ."

A woman's shriek, very close, startled them both.

35

The shriek was followed by the sound of a struggle. Schlie-mann whirled and started to rise. Pavlak was already gath-ering his legs beneath him, when Arthur Trask called through the closed door.

"Got her!"

Schliemann turned quickly and saw Pavlak with his hands braced on the arms of the chair. His face darkened. "Now don't be a fool," he warned, pointing the shotgun at Pavlak's face.

Pavlak sank back into the armchair just as the door burst open.

"It's okay," Arthur Trask was pleading. "I'm not going to hurt you. Calm down, will you?"

He was holding Karin in a bear hug. Her feet dangled a foot above the ground and her arms were pinned to her sides. She struggled until she caught sight of Pavlak, then let her body go limp. Trask set her gently onto the floor.

"I thought I had lost her," he said to Schliemann. "But when I got back to the cabin, she was standing right outside the door, listening."

"Ah yes," Schliemann said to Karin. "The sister of the

young woman who started all this trouble, I believe. Good that you found her, Trask," he added with what sounded to Pavlak like malice. "Sit here, Miss—Oertmayer is it?"

"Schmeeling," Karin corrected him, using the name on her forged passport. She crossed slowly toward Schliemann and the couch.

"As you wish," Schliemann smiled. He stood. "Here—please have my seat. As Mr. Trask indicated, we're here to hold a little conversation. Let's switch places, Dr. Pavlak, shall we?"

Pavlak stood slowly and moved to the couch as Schliemann circled him, keeping a careful distance. Schliemann crossed to the chair where Pavlak had been sitting, but stayed on his feet. Pavlak did not sit down. He tried to smile at Karin, but she only looked at him with numb, terrified eyes.

"It'll be okay," he said in English.

"Sure it will," Arthur Trask boomed, striding toward them from the door. "You're in no danger here. Peter—put down the gun now. Put it down, will you?" Trask stopped at the end of the couch.

"He's going to kill us, Arthur," Pavlak said quietly.

"No, no," Arthur protested with a painful grin, showing the palms of both hands. "He and I made a deal. We're going to work out something here."

"You're a fool, Arthur. He spent the last ten minutes bragging about his exploits. The only reason he would do that is because he knows I'll be dead before the night is over. He's going to kill all of us—you too."

The blood drained from Arthur's face.

"Sit down, Dr. Pavlak," Schliemann ordered. His tone was crisp and cold. "Now."

Pavlak turned slowly and lowered himself onto the couch beside Karin.

Arthur stared at Schliemann. "What the hell are you doing?" he demanded. "We had an agreement here."

"And we still do, of course," Schliemann assured him. He let the end of the shotgun drop so that the weapon was pointing at the floor, but he made no move to put it down. "We're going to talk a little, that's all. Have a seat." He motioned to the remaining space on the couch.

"As soon as you sit down, he'll start shooting," Pavlak warned. "He wants us lined up like sitting ducks."

"Don't listen to him, Mr. Trask," Schliemann laughed, waving a hand as if Pavlak were teasing. "We have an agreement, like you said."

Trask took a step toward Schliemann, and Schliemann took a corresponding step backward. "Then put the gun down, Peter," Trask said. His right hand rested on the grip of the Ruger tucked into his belt.

The two men looked at each other, Schliemann smooth and calculating, Trask coarse and angry.

"I can't do that, Arthur," Schliemann said calmly. "Dr. Pavlak is obviously frightened. He would attack me the minute I put the gun down. We have to talk first, make them understand our offer, then I'll put the gun away."

The skin behind Arthur's ears was turning crimson. The last time Pavlak had seen that happen was when he was sixteen years old and spending the summer sweeping the plant at Pavlak Equipment. Another employee, a young man of about twenty and a former all-state fullback, had made the mistake of cornering a female employee in the break room. When the woman screamed for help, Pavlak was the second person to reach the room, right behind Arthur Trask, and he had watched the fullback exit the plant unceremoniously through a closed window.

"He has a shotgun, Arthur . . ." Pavlak began.

"You won't hurt him," Arthur growled at Schliemann, taking another step forward. "I told you I wouldn't let you hurt him."

In a flash, Schliemann whipped the shotgun around and pointed it squarely at Arthur's chest. "You're really quite a specimen," he said in a cold voice, all pretense of affability gone. "The archetypal naive American. Did you really think I could let them live after they've seen the document?"

Arthur took another step. His entire face was crimson now, and the muscles of his jaw worked convulsively. "You aren't going to hurt him. I told you."

Schliemann gave a short, malicious laugh. "And how will you stop me? Your hired thugs aren't here now, are they?"

In spite of the shotgun, Pavlak climbed to his feet. "Arthur—it was you? *You* hired Jack?"

"Sit down!" Schliemann ordered.

Schliemann retreated one more step, and Pavlak saw the back of his thigh contact a rough wooden desk that stood against the wall. There was nowhere else for him to go. Pavlak reached Arthur in two strides and grabbed his arm. "Wait!" he pleaded.

With a wave of his arm Trask flung Pavlak onto the floor and lunged. The explosion came immediately, and Arthur thudded to the floor at Schliemann's feet. Pavlak struggled to stand as Schliemann worked the pump, ejecting the spent shell and slamming another one into the chamber. Just as Pavlak reached his feet, the barrel swung toward him. For a split second, he stared into the hollow steel tube from which his death was about to come. He wondered briefly how it would feel, then instinctively ducked his head and twisted to catch the blow on his shoulder, as if it were a club instead of fragments of metal traveling at ballistic speeds.

To his left, very close, he heard two quick snapping sounds, followed by another deafening explosion as the shotgun fired again. Pavlak's immediate reaction was disbelief. How could Schliemann have missed from this distance? Or was he dead? Was this what it felt like?

Two more snaps sounded. Pavlak looked for the source and saw the .22-caliber boot gun he had bought in Petersburg clutched clumsily in Karin's hands. Her eyes were pinched shut as she fired. Schliemann was spinning away from the desk, the shotgun still in his hands. He turned 360 degrees and stopped with the shotgun now pointed at Karin. Beside him, Pavlak heard three empty clicks, then silence. The drum in the tiny pistol only held four cartridges, and Karin had fired them all.

Schliemann worked the pump again. He was panting. His silver hair was ruffled now and a handful of strands straggled over his forehead. For five seconds they stared at each other, then the familiar, malicious smile crept over Schliemann's face.

"A feisty lady you have there, Dr. Pavlak. I underestimated her."

He winced, and Pavlak noticed for the first time that one of Karin's rounds had found its mark. A bloodstain spread slowly on the thigh of Schliemann's trousers where the great fur coat stood open.

"That hurts," Schliemann said. "You know—I've never been shot before."

"Maybe you'll die. That will save somebody the trouble of shooting you again later."

Schliemann snorted. "Hardly. A minor wound, that's all. An annoyance. I will outlive you all by a great many years.

But now, I believe I will behave more prudently and kill her first."

Pavlak stepped in front of Karin.

Schliemann drew a heavy breath. "Oh please, Dr. Pavlak. But all right, if you . . ."

His speech ended with a cry as Arthur Trask's right arm swept his feet from under him. The shotgun slammed against the floor and slid free. Pavlak dove for the gun as Schliemann rolled frantically to his knees and lunged. He was a heartbeat too slow. Pavlak snatched the weapon from under his fingers, rolled on his shoulder, and came up on one knee. He ended up four feet away, sighting down the sawed-off barrel at Schliemann's face.

Schliemann was on hands and knees, his right hand still planted on the pine board where the shotgun had lain. The fur coat dragged the floor on each side of him, making him look like some kind of ragged animal. The two men stared into each other's eyes, and Pavlak saw the blood drain from Schliemann's face. For a few seconds there was no sound except for both men's breathing.

Finally Pavlak raised one eyebrow and whispered. "Looks bad, doesn't it?"

Schliemann swallowed hard. When he spoke, his voice was hoarse and barely audible. "Are you going to kill me?"

"No!" Karin cried from the couch. The empty pistol fell from her hand and clattered onto the floor. She covered her face with both hands. "Please no," she whispered again, not to Pavlak but to someone unseen.

Pavlak heard a rasping breath, then a cough. He glanced at Arthur, lying motionless to Schliemann's left. A pool of blood was spreading from beneath his chest. Pavlak moved his gaze back to Schliemann's face.

"Yes," he said quietly.

He waited just long enough for the horror to sink into Schliemann's features, then pulled the trigger.

The recoil rocked Pavlak back on his heels but he kept his balance and immediately ejected the shell—an old hunter's habit. Then he dropped the shotgun onto the carpet and crawled to Arthur.

"Call nine-one-one!" he shouted to Karin. "Tell them to send an ambulance right away."

"I can't!" Karin shouted back. He looked up and saw her trembling and pale on the couch, then remembered that she could not possibly give a police dispatcher directions to the cabin.

"Help Arthur," he cried, scrambling frantically to his feet. "Try to stop the bleeding."

He snatched up the phone. It was dead. Pavlak shouted a curse and rushed outside. He had no idea where the telephone leads entered the cabin, so he started at the nearest corner and began feeling his way around the cabin in the dark. For the briefest instant, he let himself wonder about the consequences of killing Schliemann, but there was no time to dwell on the question. If Arthur still had a chance, it lay in getting help quickly.

Darkness impeded his search. The tangled shrubbery that surrounded the cabin added yet another obstacle. At last his fingers lit on a piece of conduit leading up from the ground beneath the kitchen window. He followed it upward, searching for the top of the conduit. From there the wires would be exposed briefly as they entered the connecting box before being fed into the crawlspace beneath the house. He was already thinking that he would have to find a flashlight and a knife for stripping the insulation from the wires when a sharp edge pricked his finger. Four tiny, severed wires protruded from the top of the conduit just above knee height.

He located the opposite ends extending from the box above and tried to pull them together. It was impossible. Schliemann had not only severed the lines, he had cut out a three-inch segment so they could not be spliced together without additional wire.

Pavlak rushed back into the house and found Karin kneeling beside Arthur, who lay on his side now. She was pressing towels into his back with her thighs while she held more towels against his chest with her arms. The shotgun blast had turned his right lung into a sieve. A lesser man would have died instantly, but Arthur Trask was not easy to kill. Not easy. But not impossible either.

"Get your bag," Pavlak said quietly.

"We can't leave him!"

He laid his hand on her shoulder. "He's dead, Karin."

For a long moment, Karin stared down at the motionless hulk beside her. Finally, she climbed to her feet and stood, her skin pale and her shoulders trembling.

"We've got to get out of here, Karin. Go. *Please.*"

Karin searched his eyes for a second, then walked to the bedroom. Pavlak pulled the Ruger from Arthur's belt and tucked it into his own, then retrieved the .22 pistol from where Karin had dropped it. As an afterthought, he picked up the shotgun and wiped it clean on the corner of the blanket that covered Arthur, then dropped it back onto the carpet. Karin emerged from the bedroom with a coat in one hand and her handbag in the other.

The Camry started with a roar, and Pavlak gunned it down the narrow lane through the trees, scattering gravel as they went.

36

The call came while Christopher Hopkins was in a meeting with Foster Denham. As he trudged back down the hallway toward his office, serious thoughts of resigning were kicking around in his head. He kept telling himself not to succumb to anything so plebeian and vulgar as a midlife crisis. And certainly not to respond to the collapse of his marriage by quitting his job, buying a sports car, and going in search of his lost youth. Besides, quitting as an assistant deputy division director in the Central Intelligence Agency was not exactly like resigning as vice president of an insurance company. This was one company you could never really leave—and the company never really left you.

The meeting with Denham had not gone well. The BND had positively identified the fingerprints. The body in that cabin in North Carolina was Peter Schliemann. And now the BND was speaking cagily of "irregular circumstances" in the hiring of Lederer and Scholz. That almost certainly meant they were Stasi plants. To make matters worse, the White House was warning Denham sternly that an espionage scandal was to be avoided at all costs. American policy was to support the democratic movement in Russia, and any rise in tensions would favor hard-line opposition in Moscow. So now what the hell were they—was he—supposed to do?

It all kept coming back to John Pavlak. He had to find him, and soon. The FBI had sniffed out a rental car that someone meeting Pavlak's description had turned in at the Raleigh-Durham airport, but the trail ended there. And the Mafia was doing no better than the FBI.

Hopkins turned into his office, started to sit, then noticed the pink message slip on the seat of his chair. Someone had called the Agency switchboard and asked for Frank Borning. The caller gave his name as John Pavlak. Hopkins snatched up the note and dashed next door into his secretary's office. "When did he call?" he screamed, waving the note.

The secretary, a career civil servant in her fifties, shot him a stern look. Her boss was getting out of control, and she meant to serve notice that she was only going to put up with so much of it.

"About ten minutes ago. Switchboard routed the call here as instructed for all of Mr. Borning's calls. I tried to page you, but I was told you were in a meeting and couldn't be disturbed."

"Shit!" Hopkins shouted, stomping the carpet. Beads of sweat had appeared on his forehead. In the hallway, two women who were passing by glanced in curiously.

"Mr. Hopkins," the secretary began, calmly removing her glasses. "I don't appreciate . . ."

"Shut up! Did he say he would call back?"

The secretary's face went white. When she finally replied, there was a coating of ice on every word. "He said he would call again in thirty minutes."

Hopkins looked at his watch. Twenty minutes to go. He spun on his heel. "Get me the director's office—*now*."

. . .

The trace began the instant Pavlak's call came in. It took less than ten seconds. State-of-the-art equipment pinpointed the phone booth at a bus station in Annandale before the operator even patched the call through to Hopkins' office. The only trouble was, Hopkins' hands were tied. He could hardly issue a request for the local police to pick Pavlak up. The best he could do would be to notify his contact with the Carlucci family as soon as the call was over. There *were* some disadvantages to doing things illegally.

"Hopkins," he barked into the receiver, affecting a nonchalance he did not feel. The door to his office was closed. Denham stood in front of him, holding a small speaker to his ear.

"Why can't I speak to Frank Borning?"

"Who is this, please?"

"You know damned well who this is. Get me Borning."

"I'm sorry, I don't believe I know anyone by that name."

Pavlak sighed heavily into the phone. "All right, we'll play little games. I have information and documentation concerning Fool's Gold. I will bring it to CIA Headquarters tomorrow and present it to the director of the CIA—only. Have someone prepared to receive a tourist named Micky Morton, preferably before the tour starts. Tours bore me to death."

There was a click and the line went dead.

Hopkins shot a questioning look at the director.

"Interesting," Denham said simply.

Pavlak paid off the cab driver and joined a throng of people already filing slowly into the reception building at CIA Headquarters in Langley, Virginia. Three rows away in the parking lot, two men in a black Buick sedan watched the tourists entering the building and occasionally compared one of them to a photograph on the dash. When Pavlak emerged from the taxi, the man on the right snatched up a car phone.

In the crush at the door, Pavlak found himself standing behind a short man wearing a cheap hairpiece. It was supposed to be light brown but had acquired a greenish tinge.

"I wonder if you can tour KGB Headquarters?" the man asked loudly to no one in particular. Several people chuckled. An elderly gentleman on Pavlak's left remarked that he thought that now you could. "Yeah, but could you get back out again?" Green Wig quipped. His accent was gutter Brooklyn, as thick as a salami sandwich. A few people laughed politely. Pavlak sighed. This was precisely why he hated tours. They attracted damned fools the way manure attracts flies.

The line moved with inexplicable sluggishness until it was finally Pavlak's turn to pass through the door, and he saw the metal detector. It caused no concern. He was not carrying a weapon.

The man in the cheap wig passed through in front of Pavlak, and the detector emitted an electronic scream. "Oops—forgot to leave my machine gun in the car," Green Wig joked. A young security man in a gray pinstripe suit smiled politely and held out a basket in which Green Wig laid keys, small change, and an old-fashioned Zippo cigarette lighter. When he passed through again, the detector uttered no protest.

Pavlak stepped through the detector and followed the crowd. To his dismay, the comic in the green wig was just raking the last of his change from the basket and fell in step with Pavlak as they started down a broad passageway.

"You a spy?" Green Wig asked.

"Yes."

"Really? For who?"

"For the Confederacy."

Green Wig cackled insincerely. "For the Confederacy, huh? The South's gonna rise again, huh? That's funny. So you're a spy for the Confederacy and the South's gonna rise again. That's a good one. You from the South, really? You don't talk like a Southerner."

"I don't talk like you."

"You don't? Coulda fooled me. I don't hear no accent at all."

Pavlak scanned the route ahead for a chance to escape. The crowd was splitting to enter two separate doors into a small auditorium. Maybe if he hung back, Green Wig would make his choice first, and Pavlak could head for the other door. He slowed his steps, but his nemesis did the same. Suddenly Pavlak stiffened as Green Wig seized his elbow in a firm grip.

"This way, Mr. Morton," Green Wig said softly, at the same time pulling Pavlak toward a narrow hallway on the right. Pavlak followed, and the man released his arm. At the end of the hall they were met by a guard in a glass booth who searched Pavlak again with a hand-held metal detector, followed by a pat-down. He nodded to Green Wig and pressed a button that unlocked the door to yet another hallway. After a series of turns and another security check, Pavlak found himself on a narrow escalator that seemed to descend forever. He had seen nothing like it except in the London Underground. At the bottom of the escalator, they entered a subterranean hallway with yellow fluorescent lights. The movie, *Dr. Strangelove*, came to Pavlak's mind, but he could

not remember exactly why. The corridor was deserted, and
their footsteps echoed in solitude until Green Wig led him
onto another escalator heading up. At the top, another corridor, another security checkpoint, and then an elevator that
rose several floors before more corridors and more turns.
Pavlak had not seen a window yet, but he guessed they were
a couple of stories aboveground by now. Finally, his guide
stopped abruptly, opened a door, and motioned him
through.

The room was small. From the sound-absorbing panels
on the walls and the close smell, Pavlak assumed it was a safe
room, regularly monitored for eavesdropping devices. It was
true then, what people said about paranoia in the spy business. Well, it was no doubt justified, even in one's own headquarters. Thousands of people worked there. Who could say
the KGB had never bribed a janitor, or an electrician, not
to mention officials in posh offices? No matter how thorough the background check, no one could guarantee how
a person would react when facing the prospect of sudden
wealth. Arthur Trask had demonstrated that.

"Wait here," his guide said tersely and closed the door
behind him.

The room had recessed fluorescent lights and a thin, hard
carpet of nondescript brown. A wooden conference table
and six wooden chairs were the only furniture. Pavlak sat
and waited. He pulled off his jacket in the stuffy room and
laid it across the table. An instant later, the door opened,
and a man in a blue suit closed it behind him. He was
younger than Pavlak, but he looked pale and wrung out, like
an old washcloth. His hair had once been sandy, but now
looked almost blond because of the white strands scattered
through it. As he offered his hand, Pavlak noticed tiny beads
of perspiration on his upper lip.

"Where's the director?" Pavlak demanded, taking the out-stretched hand without enthusiasm.

"He's tied up."

"Then untie him and get him in here. I'll wait."

Pavlak sat down again. Christopher Hopkins crossed to the chair across from him and sat down.

"The director has asked me to represent . . ."

"Forget it. I talk directly to Foster Denham or I don't talk at all. End of conversation."

"Mr. Pavlak . . ."

"Good. You admit you know who I am. That's a step in the right direction. Get Denham, please."

Hopkins folded his hands, but even folded they trembled, so he slipped them discreetly into his lap. "Mr. Pavlak, I promise you I will convey every word of what you have to say to the director—personally. He's a very busy man. Surely you can understand that."

"I understand," Pavlak said evenly, "that he doesn't want to get close to this if he doesn't have to. He has to. Please—we're wasting time." Pavlak pulled a paperback book from his pocket and opened it. It was a translation of a French novel entitled *The Turnaround.*

After a minute of tense silence, Hopkins sighed heavily and pushed his chair back. "Wait here," he said coldly. "It might be a long wait."

Pavlak looked up. "I have to leave by five o'clock. And I've arranged for some unpleasant things to happen if I'm not out of here on time. Look," he added with a sigh, slapping the book shut, "I'm here to cooperate. I want no quarrel with you. I believe we can arrange things so that you get what you want, and I get what I want."

"Which is what?"

"A long life," Pavlak said simply. "A life of staying out of your way while you stay out of mine. Get the director. Please."

Hopkins tried to read Pavlak's face but met only a level stare. "Wait here," he repeated.

Pavlak returned to his novel and had time to read a chapter of dialogue between a Soviet spy and an Orthodox priest in Paris. It was fascinating. The Russian, a man named Igor, started the book as a rational atheist, but had slowly become a believing Christian. Pavlak paused to take a look at the author's photograph on the jacket cover. His name was Vladimir Volkoff. The face was round, the hair thin above a very Russian-looking goatee. From an emigré Russian family, no doubt. Pavlak was trying to decide whether or not the spy's conversion was plausible when the door opened and Foster Denham walked in, followed by Hopkins.

The introductions were brief and civil, but no one smiled.

"So, what information do you have for us, Mr. Pavlak?" Denham asked, taking a seat.

Pavlak held up a sheaf of papers, folded once, lengthwise. "I believe this will explain everything." He selected the first page, laid it on the table, and slid it toward Denham. Denham took it without a word and started reading. He spent ten minutes studying Pavlak's narrative, as Pavlak fed him the pages, one at a time. As Denham finished each page, he handed it to Hopkins, who seemed to be growing more nervous by the minute. The document related every relevant detail of Pavlak's experiences since Judith's murder, including his first meeting with Frank Borning in Berlin, his capture and rescue on Crete, and finally the document in Arthur's barbecue grill. Some details were passed over, such as the names of the Turks in Berlin. It was also unclear exactly what part Karin had played in the events. But every detail about Fool's Gold and Schliemann's manipulation of the CIA and BND was there. Denham clearly blanched when he was reading about the theft of the Tomahawk guidance system, and Pavlak knew the passage had struck a sensitive spot.

The last page covered the events at Arthur's cabin, except that Pavlak concluded abruptly, offering no details on the bloodshed. He explained that Schliemann had attempted to kill them all, had in fact wounded Arthur Trask, and was himself killed in a struggle which ensued.

"Why," Denham began carefully when Hopkins looked up from the last sheet, "did you put all this in writing? Why didn't you just tell us yourself?"

"Because it has occurred to me," Pavlak said calmly, "that you would have a very powerful interest in seeing this entire episode suppressed—particularly the revelation about how the Soviet Union was able to develop super-accurate cruise missiles of their own. An interest perhaps powerful enough for you to silence me permanently."

"That's absurd," Denham retorted. "You've been reading too many spy novels. We don't operate that way."

But Pavlak had seen Christopher Hopkins' glance at Denham and knew by the look on his face that the option had at least been discussed.

"Maybe," Pavlak said coolly. "In any event, I felt it was in my best interest to provide myself some insurance. This is it. Along with this," Pavlak added, reaching into his jacket again. The director accepted another thin sheaf of papers, also folded lengthwise.

Denham examined the papers, then looked up calmly. "This is a photocopy. In the deposition, you said the document was an original typescript."

"It is," Pavlak said evenly. "That's part of my insurance."

"And what's the rest of your . . . insurance?"

"The rest of it, gentlemen, consists of copies of my deposition, along with additional copies of the document. One of each has been placed in a sealed envelope and mailed to a number of law firms throughout the United States and Europe. One of them has the original."

Hopkins glanced at Denham, but the director's face was inscrutable.

"I suppose," Hopkins began,, "that some instructions accompanied these sealed envelopes?"

Pavlak folded his hands, and turned his gaze toward the younger man. "The instructions are simply to hold the documents as one would a will. They are to be held for one year, and I specified my intention of renewing each agreement annually. Incidentally, I have paid them all handsomely for this service. If in any given year, I fail to renew the agreement, or in the event of my death, under whatever circumstances, the envelopes are to be delivered immediately to various organizations in the world press—although I also stipulated delivery to Senators Brentwood and Dellett of the Senate Intelligence Committee . . . two gentlemen who, as I'm sure you know, are not particularly friendly toward your agency."

"That wasn't very smart," Denham said coolly. "None of it."

"Maybe not," Pavlak conceded. "But it was the only way I could think of to keep you gentlemen on my side."

Hopkins was squirming at the director's side, his face passing from pasty white to crimson and back again. "Listen here, Pavlak," he snapped, "what the hell do you think you're doing? This . . ."

Denham laid a hand on Hopkins' forearm, and Hopkins fell silent. "How many of these . . . envelopes have you sent, Dr. Pavlak?" the director asked.

"I won't give you a number, but I will say that there are more than ten—also that I don't know all the names myself. As I'm sure you already know, I have a companion. She sent out half of the envelopes under the same terms. I don't know where she sent hers, and she doesn't know where I sent mine."

Denham shook his head ever so slightly and smiled. "Did you really think," he asked, "that we would beat the names out of you?"

"I didn't know," Pavlak said calmly. "But I preferred to be cautious."

"You certainly are that. What exactly do you want, Dr. Pavlak?"

"Two things. The first one is easy. I want to be left alone—and alive. I have no interest in exposing anyone's dirty laundry, or in causing an international incident. I don't really care about Fool's Gold—or you—one way or the other, and I will not make any of this public. Of course, you will have to pass the terms of this agreement to your colleagues in the BND."

"And the other thing?"

Pavlak slid his chair closer to the table. "I want the FBI off my back. I had nothing to do with my wife's murder, and I think you know that. And I want no consequences from what happened at Arthur Trask's cabin."

"And what exactly was that?"

"Schliemann killed Arthur Trask. He was going to kill me and Karin too."

"And it was you," Denham ventured, "who prevented him from succeeding?"

Pavlak ignored the question. "As I said—I want no consequences. I don't have time for jail or a legal battle."

Hopkins exploded. "Why are we listening to this? This guy is . . ."

"Calm down, Chris," Denham said smoothly. "We're just having a conversation here, that's all. So, Dr. Pavlak—what makes you think we can help you with this criminal investigation the FBI is conducting against you? We have no influence there," he added, turning his palms toward the ceiling. "We don't operate inside the United States."

"Have you ever been to a meeting in the Hoover Building, Mr. Denham?"

Denham looked Pavlak in the eye and smiled. "I see your point, but what you're asking is highly irregular, as I'm sure you know. Even if I were to make such a delicate request of the FBI director, chances are it would be turned down. There are a lot of people involved—local law enforcement, and so on."

"I have tremendous confidence in you, Director Denham." Pavlak said evenly. "I believe you can pull it off, and I believe you will. If I'm charged with killing Schliemann, my plea will have to be self-defense, which means I'll have to explain the circumstances surrounding the incident. *All* the circumstances."

"I see your point, Dr. Pavlak," Denham conceded. "All right. I'll do my best. Is there anything else?"

Pavlak eyed him intently before replying. "My wife and child are dead. Schliemann thought you killed them. Was he right?"

"We have no idea who killed your family, Dr. Pavlak, but it certainly was not this agency."

"Not directly, maybe. But you have a history of using outsiders for your dirty work. Remember the assassination attempts on Castro?"

The director's eyes rose to the ceiling. His right hand

made a strange gesture, sweeping the table in front of him as if searching in vain for a pen. At last he leaned forward and placed the tips of his fingers on the table.

"I will give you some information we learned through ATF. Actually . . . we helped them out a little on this. I'll tell you on the condition that you swear absolute secrecy. It's not classified, but no one is ever to know where you learned it."

Pavlak nodded.

"The explosives that killed your wife and daughter were of Czech manufacture—Semtex to be exact, a plastic explosive favored by terrorist groups—the PLO, the IRA, and so on. The detonator was activated by a radio signal. They found fragments of the receiver. The receiver is a Polish device."

Pavlak's breath caught in his throat. "Are you telling me," he asked slowly, "the KGB, or what's left of it?"

Denham let his manicured fingers fall flat on the table top. "I've told you all we know. We were curious ourselves, since it seemed to be your wife's murder that was driving you into areas that we were concerned about. But this agency was not—I repeat—*not* involved in that bombing in any way. In fact, up until a few minutes ago, we had no proof of anything at all wrong with our intelligence operation. We certainly had no reason to silence your wife." He waited a few seconds. "Do you believe me?"

"Your business is treachery," Pavlak replied, looking squarely at Denham. "You're professionals at it. Let's just say I have taken note of your denial."

"Does that mean you intend to keep looking for the people who killed your family?"

Pavlak did not reply.

"Dr. Pavlak," the director said at last, glancing down at his hands, then back into Pavlak's eyes, "I won't insult you by claiming to understand your anger. I won't even ask you to drop this quixotic quest. You're obviously not a man to be put off easily. But I'm asking one thing in return for our cooperation with you." Denham leaned closer to the table. "If you run across any more connections to Fool's Gold, or any other intelligence operation linked to this agency, present or past, you're to inform us immediately."

"How would I do that?"

Denham pulled an index card from his pocket and scrawled a telephone number on it. "Call this number at any time, twenty-four hours a day."

Pavlak stretched his legs out under the table. He touched something and saw Hopkins' torso bob as he withdrew his foot.

"What kind of information, exactly, are you looking for?" Pavlak asked.

"I think you know the answer to that one," Denham said after a long silence.

Pavlak's eyebrows ticked slightly higher. "Yes, I think I do. But the only one I know of who's still alive is Scholz—and I suspect the BND will take care of him for you." Pavlak looked at the ceiling. "Nevertheless, if I run across anyone else who knows anything about Fool's Gold, I will let you know. And in return, you will get the FBI off my back and otherwise leave me alone. Agreed?"

Denham nodded slowly. "Agreed. That is . . . as far as this agency is concerned. I don't know about the FBI. I can only promise to do my best. You have my word on that."

"And how good do you expect your best to be?"

"I would anticipate," Denham answered carefully, "that I will succeed."

"And you understand that if you don't, my assurances are no longer binding."

"I understand."

"I believe that covers everything, gentlemen," Pavlak said, standing.

The director looked at Hopkins and nodded. Hopkins rose and left the room.

"Just one more thing," Denham said when the door fell shut. "You mentioned that the sealed envelopes would be delivered if you or the German woman die. What happens if she's killed in an automobile accident—or if you have a heart attack?"

The door opened again. The man with the green toupee stood in the doorway, waiting.

Pavlak laid both hands on the table and looked squarely at Denham.

"Pray for us," he said calmly.

Denham met his gaze in silence. Pavlak nodded curtly and followed Green Wig out the door.

When he was gone, Hopkins entered the room and closed the door behind him. The director had not moved from his chair.

"Well?" Hopkins asked.

"I think Borning was right."

"About what?"

Denham stood and rubbed the back of his neck. "He would have made a hell of an agent."

Hopkins shifted his weight from one foot to the other. "You know," he said. "I felt a little sorry for him until he came here today. Now I don't care what happens to him. He's an arrogant jerk."

"True," Denham said absently, rising to his feet. "Now listen—get to a phone and call outside immediately. Tell our contacts not to follow him under any circumstances. Tell them we're finished with them and see to it that they're paid. Then call the German Embassy and arrange a meeting with BND liaison in one hour. I'll be there." He walked toward the door.

"Wait a minute!" Hopkins blurted. "You're not just going to let him walk out of here and disappear?"

The director turned. "Chris, do you have any idea what would happen if that cruise-missile story hit the press? That's a scandal that would make Watergate and Iran-Contra look like peccadillos."

"You mean . . . that story's *true?*"

"I didn't say that. I said it would cause a scandal if it hit the press." Denham had scooped up Hopkin's pen from the table and was examining it as he spoke.

"But . . . ," Hopkins spluttered, "what if he's bluffing?"

"What if he isn't?"

Sweat rolled into Hopkins' eyes and he wiped it away with the back of his hand. He realized suddenly that he was feverish. Maybe it was flu. "You mean—that's it?"

"Yes, that's it. We just have to hope he keeps his word— and lives a long time. But after all, Chris, he's not a disgruntled former operative like Philip Agee. He has no reason to hurt us. We've assumed that from the start, and we were right. And he's not asking much from us. He wants to be left alone, which we can certainly do, and he wants off the hook for killing Schliemann, which we can arrange as well—even if it means going through the president and pleading national security. Actually, he saved us a lot of trouble by eliminating Schliemann. Now Scholz is the only one left who might cause trouble, but I expect our German colleagues to handle him. Other than that . . ." Denham shrugged. "The Russians certainly aren't going to publish this, and neither will any former Stasi officials. On something of this sensitivity, there wouldn't be more than a handful of very highly placed people who know enough to damage us, and they're all trying to keep low profiles now— if they haven't already disappeared into South America somewhere. No . . . with any luck, we're home free." He frowned. "Provided, of course, that Pavlak doesn't still manage to get himself killed."

Hopkins swayed on his feet but said nothing.

"Chris . . ."

"Yes?"

"Start your vacation. Now."

37

From CIA headquarters Pavlak took a taxi back into Washington, then a subway, two buses, and finally a long walk through Georgetown until he was positive he was not being followed. One last taxi brought him to a motel in Alexandria where Karin waited nervously, fingering three thick manila envelopes lined up across the bedspread. They were addressed and prepared for overnight delivery via Federal Express to CBS News, the *New York Times*, and the Honorable Frederic Dellett, United States Senate.

When Pavlak arrived, he greeted her with a smile and held up his fist with his thumb on the inside, the German equivalent of crossing one's fingers for luck. They quickly checked out and climbed into the Oldsmobile Pavlak had bought after turning in the rented Camry. They drove three hours to a vacation cabin on the Savage River, near Avilton in Western Maryland.

On the way, Pavlak turned into a small state park and stopped the Oldsmobile beside a picnic table. Nearby, a metal trash can was chained to a steel post. He dumped the three envelopes from the motel into the trash can, doused them with rubbing alcohol, and threw in a match. The flames were three feet high when they pulled away again.

In Maryland they stocked the cabin with food, then hid the Oldsmobile in the garage. Pavlak had made over twenty calls before finding a cabin with an attached garage. If the FBI managed to get a lead on the car, he wanted no chance of it being spotted before he knew that Denham would keep his word.

It was not a long wait. Every day Pavlak drove to Westminster to pick up a copy of the *Charlotte Courier* at a specialty news shop. They were in the cabin only four days when the *Courier* reported that the mysterious shotgun deaths in a cabin on the Yadkin River near Lake Elm had been ruled a murder-suicide. The second body had been identified as that of a former East German trade official named Peter Schliemann who was visiting Arthur Trask on a fishing vacation. Apparently the two had argued. The article went on to say that the FBI had been called into the investigation because of a possible connection to the car-bomb murder of Judith Lyles and her three-year-old daughter, and the subsequent disappearance of her husband, John Pavlak. One of the shotgun victims, Arthur Trask, had been employed by a company owned by the Pavlak family. An FBI spokesman, whose name Pavlak did not recognize, reported that the incidents were unrelated. He added that the FBI was in contact with John Pavlak and that he was no longer wanted for questioning in the case. The investigation into the Lyles murder was continuing.

It was all at least halfway plausible, Pavlak decided, reading the article aloud to Karin for the second time. He found it noteworthy that a single article contained the information he needed about both Arthur's and Judith's murders, and he assumed that the FBI had used a reporter, either with or without the reporter's knowledge, to send him this message.

Of course it could all be a trap to lure them into the open. The only way to find out was to walk into it and see if it snapped shut on their necks. The next day, they packed the Oldsmobile and drove the nine hours to Avery.

Mrs. Ekelwood, it turned out, had evicted Pavlak *in absentia*, wanting nothing more to do with a fugitive from justice. She told him that Kenneth and Audrey Rankin had packed up his belongings and taken them away. She didn't know where, and she didn't care.

At the Rankin house, Audrey Rankin fell on Pavlak's neck with a small cry as soon as she opened the door. Kenneth appeared, pipe in hand, and eyed Pavlak from a polite distance. To Pavlak, their friendship already seemed a distant memory. He thanked them both for their kindness, made up vague lies to answer their questions, and tried to pretend that they did not seem like strangers to him.

It was already dark when they reached the house. The crime-scene seals were gone from the doors. Pavlak opened the back door with his key and walked in. The house was cold and the air was stale. It still bore the marks of the search and of dozens of feet trampling over it, gathering evidence. Pavlak and Karin spent the rest of the evening stuffing things back into drawers and making the house at least temporarily liveable.

The only room they did not touch was Tasha's. Pavlak stepped inside once, gazed silently at the chaos on the floor, then walked out again, closing the door behind him.

By midnight they were finished. So far there had been no phalanx of police cars screaming up to the house, and no sudden blast from a bullhorn to warn them that they were surrounded. They finally fell into the queen-sized bed in the master bedroom, exhausted.

At three o'clock, Pavlak still lay awake, listening to Karin's rhythmic breathing beside him. He rose quietly and walked down the hall to Tasha's door. For a moment he hesitated, then pushed it open and flicked on the light.

The room was small, only about half the size of the master bedroom. A twin bed stood askew in the middle of the room where someone had pulled it. The carpet on the floor was light blue. Pavlak had wanted pink, but Judith would allow no sexist stereotypes. A set of wooden bookshelves, painted white, stood against one wall. The shelves were empty now, the children's books torn and scattered across the floor. A matching chest of drawers stood beside the bookcase with small garments draped in confusion across the open drawers.

Pavlak recognized a blue-denim jumper he had bought her for her third birthday. The hurt swelled inside him like a balloon. He turned quickly and almost walked into Karin who stood behind him. For a second their eyes met, then Pavlak brushed past her without a word and disappeared down the hallway. Karin turned out the light in the little room and quietly closed the door.

Pavlak was lying on his back in the darkness when she climbed into bed.

"Do you want to talk?" she asked.

Pavlak said nothing.

"What *do* you want?"

"What I can't have," he whispered.

She laid her hand against his face. It was damp. "I'm sorry," she said.

"Me too," Pavlak whispered. "And somebody else is going to be sorry too," he added bitterly.

A few minutes later a series of small shocks traveled

through the bed frame. Pavlak turned and wrapped his arms around Karin's shuddering shoulders. She buried her face in his neck.

"What is it? What's wrong?"

"It's no good," she sobbed.

"What's no good?"

"Us."

The sobs subsided slowly, and when she spoke again her voice was unsteady, but the tone was determined. "I have to leave. Go back to Germany. It should be safe for me there now."

"Karin. . . ."

She laid her fingers gently on his lips. "John . . . I've been thinking about it since the cabin. I have to get away from you for a while—go back to the Order and sort things out." She sighed. "The five months I spent with the sisters were the happiest of my life. I had found a joy—a *serenity* as you call it—that was like nothing I've ever known before. Then all this happened, and now it's gone."

"Karin, listen to me . . ." Pavlak pleaded, hitching himself up on one elbow. "This will be finished soon. Then we can start over. Please don't leave me now. I need you." He hesitated, then added softly, "I love you."

Her fingers found his face. "I love you too," she whispered. "That's the problem. I love you too much. I feel like I'm choosing you over God."

"Does it have to be one or the other? Do you really believe God will abandon you if you stay with me?"

"No. I'm afraid *I* will abandon *Him.* This crusade you're on—this obsession—John, I'm terribly afraid it's going to destroy you. Even if you succeed . . . I'm afraid it will destroy you." She dropped her hands from his face. "And I'm afraid it will destroy me too. I thought I was stronger than you, at least in matters of the spirit." Her head rolled reluctantly from side to side on her pillow. "But I'm not." She raised herself on one elbow to face him. "Maybe I can come back," she said hopefully. "I don't know. Right now I'm too confused to do anything. I was happy when I felt that God was carrying my life, but now . . . now *you're* carrying it, and I'm scared, John. I'm terrified of you—not physically, but terrified just the same."

"Karin, listen to me. *Listen* to me!" It was Pavlak's turn to seize her head in both hands. "You *have* changed me. You've given me hope. I want to live now . . . and I want you with me."

"But not enough to stop killing?"

In the trees behind the house a whippoorwill struck up its mournful call. Slowly Pavlak released her head and eased onto his back. He could hear her breathing, sense her presence in the darkness, waiting.

"I'm sorry," he whispered.

The whippoorwill called again.

"So am I."

A car passed slowly on the street outside. Odd, Pavlak thought. At this hour. Minutes passed as he listened to the gentle sound of Karin's breath beside him. He silently begged her to speak again. Say she would stay. Say something to lift this awful weight from his heart. Then he realized that she was probably doing the same. And he *wanted* to speak, but there was nothing to say.

Karin's voice intruded on the silence. "Promise me one thing. It's all I ask of you. Something just for me."

Pavlak waited.

"Promise me you'll pray for him." Pavlak opened his

mouth to protest, but Karin rushed on. "I know it sounds crazy, but I only ask that you try. Just honestly *try*. It doesn't have to take more than a minute."

Pavlak tried to make out her features in the darkness. "All right, Karin. If I find him—and if there's time—I'll try."

Her fingers touched his chest, and they made love like two lost lovers, shipwrecked on an endless sea.

When Pavlak was a boy, Douglas Airport in Charlotte was a little more than a paved landing strip. The terminal was tiny and the concourse a concrete sidewalk covered with a corrugated metal roof. Now, forty years later, Charlotte-Douglas International processed over two hundred flights a day, and the new terminal offered the decadent appointments of modern airports everywhere. Passengers moved from the warmth and comfort of the terminal to the warmth and comfort of the aircraft without ever touching the ground. It was as if one traveled in moving buildings.

Karin was quiet and subdued. Pavlak fidgeted nervously with a newspaper.

They had spent a week in Avery. A dozen news organizations had called for interviews, and Pavlak had turned them all down, although he did talk to an FBI Agent named Forsyth who visited the morning after they arrived. Agent Forsyth was a squat, overweight man with thin gray hair, older than Streat who, the agent told him, had been reassigned. Forsyth was old enough, Pavlak surmised, to know the rules of the game and follow them. Pavlak looked into his tired eyes and knew that this was no hotshot who might balk at orders he found suspect. Forsyth never asked him where he had been for the past six weeks, and he left after an hour. The only hint he gave about the course of the investigation came when he mentioned that the Bureau was working with the DEA on a possible link between Judith's motorcycle gang and a certain drug lord in Colombia. A hired drug hit, he added offhandedly, seemed the likeliest scenario.

Now, as the last of the passengers filed through the gate and onto the waiting jumbo jet, Pavlak reflected on the previous month and a half. It had been a time like no other in his life—not even Vietnam—and he knew it had changed him forever. It wasn't just Schliemann and Arthur. *She* had changed him. The puzzling thing was, he wasn't sure how.

That morning they had spoken little and eaten little, opting instead for a long silent walk along the shores of Lake Norman, clinging to each other amid the scent of honeysuckle.

Now it was almost 6 P.M. and US Air flight 892 for Frankfurt was in final boarding. Pavlak began to feel disgruntled and irritable. He didn't know why or toward whom.

"You'll call when you get to Holzhausen?" he asked.

"It'll be six o'clock in the morning, your time. Want me to wake you?"

"Of course."

The gate attendant glanced at her watch and eyed them impatiently. All other passengers were on board.

"I have to go."

"Yes."

"John?"

"Yes."

"Stay alive for me . . . please."

He managed a smile. "I'll do my best."

She kissed him, then disappeared down the square tube into the waiting aircraft.

Pavlak paid his parking fee, then accelerated down Airport Boulevard. Instead of taking the left exit that would put him onto the Billy Graham Parkway toward I-85, he kept to his right and headed for I-77 South. For half an hour he threaded his way through traffic into Charlotte's coveted southeast side, where ostentatious estate homes mingled with slightly more modest symbols of American prosperity. The lots were typically an acre or more, the lawns manicured, the houses freshly painted and surrounded with azaleas blooming in profusion. This was the New South, the land of bank executives and yuppie lawyers.

The street lights had come on by the time Pavlak finally pulled up to a white, two-story house with green shutters. He counted four chimneys. The vinyl siding was immaculate, and a red Audi sat on the concrete driveway. Evidently the U.S. government paid better than he imagined. Or maybe family money played a role. One never knew.

He rang the doorbell twice, then waited. Someone approached the door, but did not open it immediately. Pavlak looked straight into the tiny glass lens of the peephole, giving whoever stood on the other side a full view of his face. A second later the door was snatched open and Special Agent Darryl Streat glared at him.

"What are you doing here?"

"I came to see you, obviously."

"I'm flattered. Now get the hell out of here."

Streat tried to slam the door, but Pavlak caught it with the heel of his hand. "Wait a minute, I just want to talk to you."

"Move your arm or I'll break it."

"Five minutes, that's all I ask."

Streat hesitated.

"It's about Judith's murder."

"Haven't you heard? I'm not on that case anymore."

"I know. But it hasn't been solved either. I need your help."

A sudden fury burned at him from the detective's eyes. Streat lunged, seized Pavlak by the throat, and shoved him backwards down the sidewalk.

"Listen, you sonofabitch," Streat was ranting, shaking Pavlak back and forth like a teddy bear. "I've been in the Bureau twenty-five years and I've never been yanked from a case. I don't know how you did it, but you've got a hell of a nerve coming here."

Streat's thumbs were becoming uncomfortable on Pavlak's windpipe. He grabbed the FBI agent's wrists and tugged, but Streat only squeezed harder. Pavlak brought his fist up sharply into Streat's solar plexus, and the agent doubled over.

"Are you crazy?" Pavlak coughed, massaging his Adam's apple. "I don't know what you're so mad about. I didn't kill my wife and daughter, and you know it."

Pavlak caught a movement out of the corner of his eye and looked to find a plump woman of about fifty staring at him from the doorway. Streat motioned to her, a wave that said everything was all right, though his bent posture and pale face belied the assertion. "It's okay," he choked. "Go back in the house."

Both men were silent for a few minutes as they nursed their hurts. Finally Streat spoke again, his tone bitter. "I don't know any such thing. Somebody had them killed, and as far as I'm concerned, you're still a suspect—not that my opinion counts for anything. And," he added, moving a step closer, "I know you killed two men—or at least one—at that cabin."

"That was a murder-suicide," Pavlak corrected. "Don't you read the papers?"

Streat laughed bitterly. "I've investigated more murders than you've seen on television, Pavlak. And I've learned a few things in the process. One of them is that a man who wants to kill himself with a shotgun, doesn't shoot himself in the chest with it. Too awkward."

"Oh?" Pavlak asked. "Were they both shot in the chest? Maybe it was the other guy. Where was he shot?"

"As if you didn't know."

"Humor me."

"All right—in the face."

"The face, huh? Well that makes sense. Sawed-off shotgun, wasn't it? He bent his face over it and pulled the trigger."

"Yeah," Streat said with an acid curl of his lip. "Then after he shot himself in the face, he picked up the shotgun and wiped his fingerprints off it. Suicides always do that. But what the hell . . ." Streat's face was glowing red now. "He held the end of the barrel about four feet away when he shot himself, so wiping off fingerprints after he was dead should have been an easy encore. *What do you think I am?*" Streat shouted. *"An idiot?"*

"So what makes you think I had anything to do with it?"

"Oh, can the bullshit, will you," Streat shot back, tossing his hand at Pavlak's face. "Your prints were all over the cabin. Your *clothes* were in the cabin, for God's sake. Your razor even. Piece of cake for a dog to match the scent with a pillow case from your apartment in Avery. Left in a hurry, didn't you? And you took a nine-millimeter pistol with you. Or did the guy who killed himself fire it into the ceiling, then go throw it into the river before he died? Oh, and I suppose he did the same thing with the twenty-two he used to shoot himself in the leg. Tell me, did he do that before or after he shot himself in the face with the shotgun?" Streat aimed a forefinger at Pavlak's nose. "Look, I know almost everything you've done since you got back to the U.S. I know exactly when you got here with the German girl—even what flight you came on. I know when you visited your father. I know everything but a few details."

"Like who killed Trask and Schliemann," Pavlak reminded him. "And who killed my wife and daughter."

Streat glared at him. "Like what was in the box."

"What box?"

"The box with the ashes all over it. The box you took out of the barbecue grill on the pier."

Pavlak decided not to take the bait. "Listen, Streat. I've just been trying to stay alive—and find the man who killed my family. I think you can help me."

"Why don't you talk to Forsyth? It's his investigation now."

"Because you were on the case a lot longer than he was. And you're a lot smarter than he is."

The FBI agent straightened gingerly and tried a deep breath. He winced. "My *dog* is smarter than Forsyth." He rubbed his midsection tenderly. "Why don't you ask your pals at the CIA?"

"I don't know what you're talking about," Pavlak said evenly.

"No, of course you don't. Look, I don't know what this is all about . . ."

Pavlak interrupted. "A minute ago you said you knew everything but a few details."

Streat plunged ahead. "But you're right. I'm smart enough to see that this is all tied up with the Germans and the CIA somehow, and obviously you convinced somebody—somebody very high up—that national security would be threatened if I continued to investigate the murders. So they

444   **Kurt Corriher**

called in that half-wit, Forsyth, and elbowed me into a ditch. End of story. You're home free. You got away with murder— literally."

"Nobody's going to get away with murder. Not if I can help it. That's why I'm here. You can believe me or not, but I have no idea who killed my little girl . . ."

"And your wife."

"Yes, and my wife. But I intend to find out, just like I told you in Avery."

Streat turned away in disgust and started back up the walkway.

"Why else would I have come here?" Pavlak called after him. "I'm home free, like you said."

Streat turned and looked hard at Pavlak. "What will you do if you find him?"

"Depends."

"On what?"

"Who it is. Where it is. What my options are."

"Suppose," Streat began, stepping toward him again. "Suppose it's somebody in a foreign country. Somebody beyond the reach of the law."

"Why? Is that what you suspect?"

"Just answer my question. Suppose you can't have him arrested. What will you do?"

"Kill him."

Streat's eyes met his and held them for a full ten seconds. "You know," he said slowly, "I believe you." The FBI agent tilted his head toward the sky and pursed his lips. Pavlak held his breath, waiting. "It was a plastic explosive," Streat said at last, his voice calmer. "Manufactured in Czechoslovakia. Terrorist goods. Tons of the stuff hidden in basements around the world. No way to know where this bomb came from."

Pavlak started to say he knew that already, but thought better of it.

"How was it detonated?"

"By a radio signal. Somebody was there to do it. Probably following her in a car—maybe a white Honda that was rented at Charlotte-Douglas by a mysterious Mr. Harold Greene who took a flight to Atlanta that evening. We can't find him. The rental car clerk has looked at pictures of so many Harold Greenes, she probably has nightmares about the name. Nothing. We're not even sure he was American. Could have been a false name, of course. Probably was, in fact. Anybody who had access to the devices he used is most likely a pro."

Streat drew a breath and threw a quick glance around them.

"The detonator itself was a common device," he said, looking back at Pavlak. "Swedish make, but available just about anywhere, including the United States. At least ATF thinks that's what it was. Not much to go on there." He raised his chin and scratched the stubble on his neck. "The interesting part is the unit that activated the detonator."

"The what?"

"The device that received the radio signal and set off the detonator, which in turn set off the bomb. We found a fragment of a transistor. It's Polish."

"Soviet Bloc stuff," Pavlak mused, pretending that he didn't already know what Streat was telling him.

Streat shrugged. "Except that there isn't any Soviet Bloc anymore, remember?"

"The Soviet Union is gone, but the people who ran it aren't."

"You think leftovers from the old KGB killed your wife?"

"I'm just thinking out loud, that's all."

"Well don't jump to any conclusions. Since the Iron Curtain fell, this kind of crap is flowing all over the place. There's a huge black market in military equipment from the former Eastern Bloc, and the Russian Mafia is shipping it all over the world." He shook his head. "Sorry, but what I've told you isn't much help. If it had been, I'd have nailed him a long time ago—the guy who killed your little girl."

"And my wife. You got anything else?"

"Nothing. Too many missing pieces. We needed more information. Something to narrow it down." He eyed Pavlak suspiciously. "I figured you could give us what we needed."

"You figured wrong."

Night had fallen around them and the first cicadas were warming up for the evening chorus.

"So what are you going to do now, Pavlak? What can you do that I couldn't?"

"I don't know," Pavlak replied truthfully.

"Take my advice, Pavlak. Go back to your little school and get on with your life. Even if you find the guy, your little girl will still be dead. I'm sorry, but that's . . ."

"What did you say?"

Streat took a quick step backwards. "Don't get excited. I'm just trying to help."

"No, no. You said, 'go back . . .' "

"Go back to your school and get on with your life."

"No, you said 'little school.' 'Go back to your little school.' "

"So?"

"Nothing. I just. . . . Nothing."

Pavlak turned and started toward his car at a trot, then caught himself and turned back. "Listen, Streat—thanks. I may have something."

He ran down the sidewalk toward the Oldsmobile, leaving the FBI agent staring after him with a puzzled frown.

38

Thirty minutes after leaving Streat's house, Pavlak walked in the front door of the Mecklenburg County Public Library on the corner of Tryon and Sixth. He was relieved to find that they carried a subscription to *Warrior Monthly* magazine. Pavlak asked for the March and April issues, then spent all his coins at the copy machine, plus two additional dollars in change from the check-out desk.

He drove to the house in Avery, plugged in Judith's ancient IBM Selectric and began typing letters. At midnight, he took a half-hour break for a salami sandwich and a beer, then returned to the typewriter. By two in the morning twenty-three envelopes were addressed, stamped, and stacked on the corner of the desk. He raked the bundle of letters into a plastic grocery bag and walked out into the night.

On the sidewalk he almost collided with Diane Sweeney who was walking her dog. In the pale light of the street lamp, she failed to recognize him.

"I'm sorry," she apologized, then took a second look. "Oh, it's you," she said coldly. "I heard you were back. What happened? I thought you would be rotting in prison by now."

"Sorry to disappoint you, Diane."

"Oh I'm not disappointed. You'll get there eventually."

Pavlak drew a breath to respond, then changed his mind and walked on, leaving her puffing furiously on a cigarette and glaring daggers at his back.

The round trip to the post office took fifteen minutes. When Pavlak unlocked the door again, his phone was ringing. He caught it before the third ring.

"I'm at police headquarters in Frankfurt," Karin said. "They were waiting for me at the airport."

Pavlak kept his voice calm. "What do they want?"

"I'm not being arrested. They want to question me about Brigitte and Turgat, that's all. At least, that's what they've told me. I'm exhausted, John. It's nine o'clock in the morning here. It's going to be a long day."

Pavlak found himself squeezing the phone. "Hang in there. You're tougher than you think. After all you've been through, a police interrogation ought to feel like a vacation."

"Easy for you to say. I've called Erich—my ex-husband. He's on his way here."

Somehow Pavlak did not find that news reassuring. "Fine," he said. "He'll help you. Don't worry about the police, Karin. Just tell them everything they want to know. Have they mentioned Arthur and Schliemann?"

"Not yet."

"They probably won't," Pavlak said, thinking the opposite. Streat would have briefed the Germans before he was pulled from the case. He and Karin had agreed on a story to tell if forced into it. It was very simple. They had left the cabin for a late night drive and when they returned they saw Arthur's Bronco parked in the woods. They decided on the spot not to return to the cabin but rather to drive on to

Washington. They had no idea what happened at the cabin. It was a story the FBI could easily shoot holes in, but the FBI was under orders to back off. Pavlak could only hope that the BND had managed to put similar pressure on the German police. In any event, Karin had committed no crime.

"Have they mentioned Munich?" Pavlak asked.

"No."

He breathed a sigh of relief. Krueger's killing was the only part of this whole thing that would concern the German police, other than Brigitte's and Turgat's murders, and neither he nor Karin were involved in those. "Okay. Anything else?"

"No, I just . . ."

"What?"

"Nothing. Good-bye."

It was 3:10 when Pavlak hung up the phone. He dropped into bed without undressing and slept until noon. At six that evening, Karin called again. She was at home in Holzhausen. The police had questioned her for four hours, all of it concerning Brigitte and Turgat and Berlin. They told her they would probably have more questions later.

"What did they ask you about the last six weeks?" Pavlak asked.

"Nothing."

"Nothing at all?"

"Not one word. It was almost embarrassing. It was obvious to everybody in the room that they were avoiding a huge chunk of time. I don't think they were very happy about it."

"You mean it was a hostile atmosphere?"

"At first, but it got better after a while."

Pavlak looked up at the mantel clock, it's pendulum swinging patiently. "You must be beat."

"Exhausted. I'm going to bed in a few minutes."

"Karin . . ."

"Yes?"

"I'm sorry . . ."

There was a silence on the line, then Karin's voice came back, choked with tears. "So am I. I have to go now."

Pavlak heard the receiver rattle onto its cradle.

For the next few days, he stayed close to his phone. There was little to do, and thoughts of Karin haunted his mind. He tried to distract himself with a computer chess game, but it didn't help.

On the fourth day, the call he was waiting for arrived.

"You still looking for Jack?" said a gruff voice on the other end.

"You know him?"

"Maybe."

"He would have been leading a team on Crete in early April."

"That was in your letter. I can read. How much is it worth to you to find him?"

Pavlak considered. "Five hundred."

"You're joking."

"That's a lot of money for an address."

The man on the other end gave a nasty laugh. "Who said anything about an address? You get a phone number, that's it."

"Not good enough," Pavlak shot back. "I want an address."

There was a silence before the man answered. "Then I take it you don't want Jack to know you're coming."

Pavlak considered his answer. He had a fish on the line. It could be a hoax, or it could be the real thing. If it was real, one false move and the line would go dead. He'd never know who called and never get him back.

"You take it wrong," Pavlak said firmly. "Jack's a friend of mine. I just need to talk to him."

Another laugh. "You're full of shit, pal."

"You're the one who's full of shit," Pavlak snapped. "You don't know squat." He hesitated half a second, then slammed the phone down.

Half an hour passed before it rang again. Pavlak picked up the receiver but said nothing. He could hear breathing on the other end.

"Okay, here's the deal," the voice said at last. "It's three thousand up front for the contact. You give me the message, and *I* talk to Jack, not you. For another three grand, I'll see if I can get Jack to call you, but I doubt he will."

Pavlak was pondering his response when the man went on.

"But if you want to surprise him, it gets expensive. There ain't no address. Jack don't give that to nobody. But I'll let you have the phone number for twenty grand—and you tell Jack you got it from a guy named Buster in Indianapolis. You tell him Buster answered your letter, and you went to Indianapolis to see him. He's short, stocky, dark brown hair, a scar over his left eye. That's the deal. Take it or leave it."

"I'll give you ten thousand for the phone number."

"The price is twenty," the voice said with cold finality. "We don't negotiate. I'm putting my ass on the line. Jack don't like surprises."

Pavlak let a few seconds pass. "How do we make the exchange?"

"You send cash to my box number. Registered mail. Nothing bigger than a hundred. After I count it, I call you with the number."

Pavlak was trying to identify the accent. Upper Midwest

maybe. "You must think I've got rocks in my head. I get the number, then you get the money."

The caller had obviously anticipated Pavlak's objections because his response was immediate. "Okay, here's the deal. You bring the money in a briefcase to a Mexican restaurant called Los Niños. It's on the corner of Eighty-sixth and T Street in Sacramento. Be there day after tomorrow, two o'clock in the afternoon. You're in Carolina, right? Wear a sweatshirt with University of North Carolina on it. Sit in a booth and put the briefcase on the opposite seat. Some-body'll give you the number and take the briefcase. The money better be there. *All* of it. Don't fuck with me or you'll regret it."

"Right. So I give you twenty thousand, and you give me a scrap of paper with Peter Pan's social security number. No deal. You get half the money up front. The other half after I make the phone call."

Pavlak waited. He could hear heavy breathing into the telephone receiver.

"How do I get the other half?"

"Next day. Same time, same place."

Another pause. "All right. Be there. And remember— Buster in Indianapolis. Short, stocky—scar over the left eye. And if you're jerking me around, pal, I'll fuck you from here to hell and back."

The line went dead.

Pavlak checked his list. He had sent two letters to San Francisco, half a dozen to Los Angeles, but none to Sacra-mento. He reached for the phone again and dialed Direc-tory Assistance in Sacramento. Yes, they had a listing for a Los Niños restaurant on 86th Street.

Pavlak hung up and considered his options. Maybe the caller was on the level, maybe not. A daytime meeting in a restaurant should be safe, which was exactly what the man wanted him to think—maybe as a sign of good faith, or maybe to put him off guard.

Pavlak stood and walked to his bedside table. He opened the drawer and checked the Ruger. He had still fired it only once, when Arthur grabbed his wrist in the cabin. Just to be safe, he should ditch the gun and buy another, he knew, but this one would be very difficult to trace if he had to use it again.

He snatched up the phone and called Instant Travel in Avery. The agent made a reservation that would bring him into Sacramento, via St. Louis, at 12:20 P.M. on Friday. That was cutting it very close, but the only other alternative would be to leave a day earlier, and he wanted to stay in Avery another full day in case a second call came in. Even if the man he talked to really could put him in touch with Jack, somebody else might be able and willing to do it on more attractive terms.

Pavlak reached for the phone one last time and called the FBI office in Charlotte. Darryl Streat was not in, so Pavlak left his number. It was urgent, he told the secretary.

The rest of the day came and went slowly. Streat did not return his call, and after five o'clock passed, Pavlak assumed the FBI agent was not going to help him. That would make things more difficult, but he would have to manage.

Bored, he climbed the steps to the second floor and walked toward Tasha's room. It was time to clean it up. Time to give away her clothes and toys. Time to face reality. He got as far as the door before the great hurt came. He let his hand slide off the knob and turned away. Before he took two steps, someone knocked loudly on the back door downstairs.

Special Agent Darryl Streat wore a dark suit and an even darker look on his face.

"Now what do you want?" Streat fumed, stepping through the door.

Pavlak was about to wish him a cheerful good evening, but checked himself. This was not the time for cheeky remarks.

"I need a trace on a phone number."

"So bribe somebody at the telephone company."

"Probably a foreign number. Probably British."

Streat eyed him in the dim light. "What do you mean, 'probably?' "

"I don't have the number yet."

"When will you get it?"

"Day after tomorrow, if all goes well."

Streat spun on his heel, took three paces away, then turned back. "Pavlak, goddammit! What are you up to now?"

"Can you get me the trace?

Streat drew a long breath and held it three seconds. "I could," he said in a rush of air. "But why should I?"

Pavlak scratched his ear. "Because you like me so much?"

The corner of Streat's mouth twitched up for a second, and Pavlak knew he had won a small victory.

"Tell me something, Pavlak. Will this be the last time I ever lay eyes on you? If it is, it might be worth it."

"Scout's honor," Pavlak promised, holding up three fingers.

"The scout salute is two fingers."

Pavlak did not move his hand. "I know."

Streat drifted toward the door, then back again. "Is this about the bombing?"

"Yes."

Streat's brow creased in thought. Finally he nodded once,

quickly, as if he did not want anyone to see. "But don't you ever ask me for anything else."

"Just one more thing."

"I said *nothing.* . . ."

"It's part of this request, not a new one. I'll need it in a hurry. I'll call you with the number around five in the afternoon, and I'll need a name and address by six. Can you do it?"

Streat passed his hand over his eyes. "Jesus H. Christ. *No,* I can't do it. What the hell do you think I am? A genie in a lamp?"

"How fast can you get it?"

Streat paced to the door, seized the knob, and swept it back and forth, fanning the living room and muttering to himself. "That'll be eleven in London. I'll need at least two hours," he said at last. "Maybe longer. Maybe a lot longer. And I'm putting myself into deep shit over this. Requests to foreign forces have to be approved in D.C. I'll have to invent some pretext for it."

"But you'll do it?"

"Yes, dammit, I'll do it. This better be good, Pavlak. You're still on my shit list."

He slammed the door behind him.

39

Los Niños was typical of Mexican restaurants on the West Coast that cater to secretaries on their lunch hour. The outside walls were white and topped with the obligatory red-tiled roof. Inside, Pavlak threaded his way through a maze of padded booths, upholstered in blue plastic, and finally settled on an empty one with a good view of the door. He dropped the briefcase onto the seat nearest the door and settled himself onto the opposite bench. Hoke Morgan had packed the case with twenty wrapped bundles of fifty-dollar bills, a thousand dollars in each bundle. Ten of them were now stashed beneath the mattress in Pavlak's room at the Holiday Inn on J Street.

Pavlak was wearing a sky-blue sweatshirt with the seal of the University of North Carolina on the front. It was faded from many washings, but the name of the university was still readable. He felt beneath it for the reassuring touch of the Ruger in his belt. On the wall beside him, a matador struck an absurd pose as an enraged bull thundered toward his cape. On the opposite wall hung a row of ornate sombreros. A decidedly un-Mexican waitress with blond hair and blue eyes took his order for a cheese enchilada and refried beans which Pavlak had no intention of touching.

It was late for the lunch trade, and only a few customers remained in the restaurant. Pavlak inspected them all. Three businessmen in gray suits lounged and joked four booths away. A young couple about college age sat side by side in a corner, gazing into each others' eyes. The girl's right shoe was off, and she stroked her companion's calf beneath the table. Pavlak did not know if they were in love, but they were obviously in heat. The scene stirred vague memories, but he decided against calling them up for closer inspection. The past was dead, and he had more serious matters on his mind.

It was ten minutes past two when the front door opened, and a boy, Mexican in appearance, with nut brown skin and high cheekbones entered the restaurant. He carried a stack of newspapers under his arm and began offering copies of the *Sacramento Bee*. The businessmen turned him away with a collective shake of their heads. The boy glanced at the lovers but made no move in their direction. He headed toward Pavlak, and Pavlak pushed his shoulders back and straightened his legs in order to dig some quarters from his pocket.

"How much?" Pavlak asked.

"Fifty cents."

The accent was purely American. Pavlak wondered if the boy had ever set foot in Mexico. He laid two quarters on the table and took a paper. As the boy raked the quarters from the table into his hand, Pavlak opened the paper and immediately saw the number scrawled in ink across the top of the front page. It started with 001, the international access number, then the country code, 44, for Great Britain. The city code was 1. Pavlak was surprised. Jack did not strike him as a Londoner.

The boy, meanwhile, laid his papers on the seat opposite Pavlak, beside the briefcase, and made a pretense of straightening his wares while he deftly slipped the briefcase under one arm and covered it with the newspapers. He was gone a moment later. Pavlak wondered vaguely why the kid was not in school, but let the thought go, snatched up his check, and walked to the cash register.

While the cashier rang up his bill, Pavlak stuck his head out the front door, gazed at the sky as if checking the weather, and then briefly stroked his right ear.

The nearest phone booth was four blocks away. When his bill was paid, Pavlak hurried to it and rang the FBI office in Charlotte. Streat himself answered the phone, took down the number from the newspaper and the number of Pavlak's room at the Holiday Inn, then hung up.

Pavlak let out a breath. So far, so good. If the number was what it was supposed to be, he would make the second payment the following day, then book the first flight out to London.

He took a taxi back to the Holiday Inn, washed his face with a steaming washcloth, and settled on the bed to watch CNN while he waited for Streat's phone call. It came much sooner than he expected.

"Is this some kind of joke?" Streat was screaming into the phone.

"It wasn't supposed to be," Pavlak frowned. "What did you find out?"

There was a long silence on the other end. Pavlak could almost see Streat counting to ten to calm himself.

"The Brits traced the number for me all right," Streat said in a lower voice that almost immediately began to crescendo again. "Do you know what that phone is? It's Buckingham fucking Palace! You gave me the queen's number!" Streat started shouting at full blast again. "The goddamned Brits are laughing their asses off at me over there. But you know what, Pavlak? I don't think it's so goddamned funny."

"Neither do I," said Pavlak grimly. "I was afraid of something like that." Then he added quickly. "I'm sorry, Streat. Somebody tried to pull a fast one on me. I'll get back to you." He hung up the phone, waited for the line to clear, then dialed a local number. According to the digital alarm on the side table, it was four o'clock on the nose.

"Asgood and Parker," said a pleasant female voice.

"This is Hawk," Pavlak responded, using the code the agency had given him. He was not sure why. Maybe they thought their phones were tapped.

"One moment, please."

While he waited on hold Pavlak felt his anger rising. He didn't really care about the ten thousand dollars, but he was mad at not getting Jack's number—and mad at being swindled. He scooped the Ruger off the bed with his left hand and jammed it into his belt just as the line came to life. This time it was a man's voice.

"Asgood. Is that Hawk?"

"Yes. Did you get it?"

"Was it the kid?"

"Of course it was the kid," Pavlak snapped impatiently. "Didn't you see my signal?"

"Yeah, sure, but—you know. We weren't expecting a kid."

"Neither was I. Are you telling me you didn't follow him?" Pavlak was poised to explode.

"No, no, we followed him all right. I was just checking to be sure. You're in luck because our man just called in. Not two minutes ago. The kid took a taxi to the south of town and passed the briefcase to a guy in a parking lot at a McDonalds. He was in a pickup truck. The guy didn't screw around. Looked into the briefcase, then lit out. Our man's still behind him."

"Where is he?"

"That's the bad news. He's on 1-80 West just past the Davis exit. Looks like your guy's headed for San Francisco. Want us to stay on him?"

"Like a leech."

"It'll get expensive."

"Your retainer should cover it."

"Sure, I just wanted . . ."

"I'm on my way to San Francisco," Pavlak interrupted. "I'll call a couple of times on the way. How good's your man?"

"Very. You said you wanted the best. You got it. He won't lose him. I'll alert some people in San Francisco that they're coming. Our man will have help when he gets to the Bay— assuming that's where the subject is going."

It was an hour before Pavlak finally snatched the keys to a Ford Taurus from the hand of an offended rental clerk. He drove two blocks to a phone booth and called Asgood again.

"Good news," Asgood told him immediately. "Or maybe it's bad. The subject left the highway before Berkeley and headed up into the hills. He took a dirt road that looks like a driveway of some kind. Our man didn't follow him any further. He's in the woods now, waiting for instructions."

"Tell him to wait for me. I'll be there in an hour and a half. Give me the directions."

"Uh—Hawk, listen. You understand we offer only detective services. Strictly above board. Strictly legal."

"Yes, I understand that," Pavlak said impatiently. "I only

want your man to tell me exactly where he went. I'll take it from there."

"Right. I just wanted to be sure . . ."

"The directions, dammit," Pavlak barked. "It'll be dark soon."

He made it to the rendezvous in a little over an hour, ignoring the speed limit on I-80 and praying he wouldn't run into a speed trap.

Asgood's man was everything Pavlak had not expected. He was not an inch over five feet five, had bowed legs, a sunken chest, and wore wire-rimmed glasses. He looked for all the world like Mr. McGoo. Pavlak followed him on a ten-minute hike to the top of a hill and quickly won some respect for the little man. Pavlak was panting like a sled dog when they arrived, but the private detective was barely breathing hard. He handed Pavlak a pair of binoculars and pointed.

"There. The dirt road that winds up through the woods. It might go through to another highway, but I doubt it. I'm sure he didn't spot the tail, so—unless there's something I don't know—he wouldn't be trying to throw anybody off. Nobody's come out since he drove in there, unless it was in the last fifteen minutes. I had to come down when I saw you coming."

Pavlak grunted approval and handed the binoculars back. It was almost dark. "What's your name?" he asked, as they started to descend the hill again.

"My friends call me McGoo."

Pavlak stifled a laugh. "Any chance he intercepted your calls?"

McGoo shook his head. "None. We scramble the signal." Pavlak's eyebrows rose in admiration, but McGoo shrugged.

"These days all the good agencies have that kind of equipment. Have to."

"What can you tell me about him?"

"I didn't get a real good look. He never came out of the truck. Your age. Maybe a little younger. Short brown hair, military-style cut. Military look about him. Wore a leather flight jacket. Tattoo on the back of his left hand. Couldn't see what it was. He smokes cigarettes."

"How big?"

"Hard to tell. Not as tall as you, I'd say. Bulky shoulders. Either a body-builder or naturally burly. Like I said, I only saw to about the middle of his chest."

"Anything else?"

"Tough guy. He had that look. Something in the eyes. Watch yourself," he added after a pause.

Pavlak nodded. "Thanks, McGoo."

He watched until the little man's taillights disappeared around a corner, then struck out on foot. The gravel drive shot up the mountain at a brutal angle. Pavlak understood why his man drove a four-wheel-drive pickup. If conditions were even slightly slippery, nothing less would make it. After a quarter of a mile, he came to an iron gate across the drive, secured with an enormous padlock. The gate barred vehicles, but not pedestrians. Pavlak decided it was time to leave the driveway and keep to the woods. It was too dark to see what was at his feet, so progress slowed to a crawl as he felt his way from tree to tree. Finally the terrain leveled off a bit, and at about the same time, he spotted a light in the distance.

Pavlak turned deeper into the woods and made a wide circle, keeping the light on his right. It appeared, from the hue, to be an outdoor halogen lamp on a pole, and it stayed in view as he made a 180-degree arc, proving that the light was higher than any buildings around it. Once on the back side, Pavlak turned and headed straight toward the light. A hundred yards later, the trees ended abruptly.

In the clearing in front of him stood a small wooden house with a tin roof. Three ramshackle outbuildings stood off to one side, and a halogen lamp—the one he had been following—bathed the entire scene in a pale violet glow. Beside the house stood a pickup truck. There was a light in one window of the house, but a curtain was drawn across it.

Pavlak surveyed the scene in front of him. There were two storage sheds, crudely built. He could see a wheelbarrow and what looked like a shovel, though it was too dark to tell for sure. The third building was a chicken house with a small yard in front of it, fenced in with chicken wire. One ladder led to a small square hole in the wall where the birds could enter. Pavlak noted that the ground inside the fence was scratched bare, even though most of the clearing was knee-deep in grass. That meant there were live chickens in the house, and live chickens had to be fed.

He circled around the clearing then slipped out of the woods and stepped up to the rough wooden wall of the chicken house. With his back against it, he inched around the corner to the back side, still out of sight of the house, although he could see the glow from the lit window illuminating the ground to his left. He had intended to sit with his back against the wall and rest, but the ground was soggy and moist. He had not felt cold in the woods. His light jacket, combined with the exertion of the climb, had kept him more than warm. But here in the clearing, a brisk breeze began to evaporate the sweat on his back, and he felt the first hint of a chill creeping into his bones. It would be a long night. Standing, he leaned his back against the rough board to wait.

At nine-thirty, the light went out in the window. Good, Pavlak thought. Early to bed, early to rise.

By midnight his legs ached so badly that he reluctantly slid down the wall and lowered his buttocks onto the moist earth. The cold and damp immediately seeped through the thin trousers. He tore off a few handfuls of grass and shoved them beneath him, forming at least a modest barrier between himself and the dampness. Pavlak pulled the jacket close around his neck and shivered.

He dozed fitfully until three o'clock, when the cold and damp had seeped so deeply into his bones that sleep was impossible. His hips and knees ached, and his neck was beginning to cramp from shivering. Every half hour he stood and did some calisthenics to loosen the cramped joints and generate a little heat. By five o'clock, when the first light began to soften the eastern sky, Pavlak was in a mood to meet the man who had put him through all this.

He had just dozed off again for the first time in over two hours when the slam of a screen door startled him awake. He scrambled to his feet, pulled the Ruger from his belt and swiveled his head around to the left, extending both arms with the Ruger in firing position. The footsteps drew closer, then stopped. There was the sound of metal clanging, then the squeak of a rusty hinge. The man had entered one of the other outbuildings. Pavlak's toes were numb. He tried to wiggle some circulation into them as a series of bangs and thumps emanated from the shed. They were still numb when the footsteps swished through the grass again, growing nearer. With his thumb Pavlak nudged the safety into the off position.

The figure that rounded the corner was carrying a plastic bucket full of ground grain and walking with his head down. He wore combat boots, army fatigue pants, and a soft, olive-green cap with the bill pulled over his eyes. Evidently the cold didn't faze him because his chest was covered only with a black body shirt. Pavlak's eyes strayed briefly to the masses of muscle in the shoulders and arms. Definitely a body-builder.

As the man raised his head to reach for the latch on the chicken-house door, he caught sight of Pavlak, six feet away with the pistol pointed between his eyes.

"Freeze where you are," Pavlak demanded in a low voice. He didn't want to be heard in the house if anyone were there.

He had anticipated several reactions, including an attempt to run. He did not anticipate what happened. The man simply lowered his huge shoulders and charged. There was time to fire, but Pavlak's finger refused to pull the trigger. He dropped his elbows to protect his abdomen, and the man's skull struck his right forearm. Suddenly the pistol was no longer in his hand. Pavlak felt his feet leave the ground and then he was hurtling backwards. As his back slammed into the grass, a shoulder buried itself in his belly, and pain exploded in his midsection. He tried to twist out from under the weight on top of him, but two powerful hands seized his throat and clamped tight. Pavlak worked his right arm free and smashed his fist into the face above him, but to no apparent effect, except that the man buried his face in Pavlak's chest, hiding the target. Pavlak continued to pummel the back of his skull, but the blows were harmless. He could feel his own eyes bulging from his face. Somehow he had to break the grip on his throat or he was going to lose consciousness.

Pavlak scooped his thumbs beneath the face on his chest and drove them into the man's eyes with all his strength. The head snapped back and around, then down again, and

Pavlak lost his grip. He clawed at the cheeks until one thumb found an eye again. This time the man hunched forward to protect his eyes, and Pavlak felt a nose against his cheek. He twisted his head, got the nose into his mouth, and bit down—hard. The cartilage crunched between his teeth and a bellow of pain shattered the quiet morning. The grip on Pavlak's throat loosened. He drew one leg beneath him, then swung it across the man's back as he heaved his shoulder with all his strength. His wounded adversary slipped off his chest, and Pavlak broke free. He rolled to his feet, just as the other man did the same.

They circled each other in the tall grass, crouched and panting like bulls in a ring. Blood streamed from the military man's nose and across his lips. Suddenly he lunged. Pavlak twisted to the side and avoided the charge with surprising ease. The man was strong as an ox, but just as slow. Then Pavlak's foot struck something hard, just as the second lunge came. Off balance, he was a split second too slow to escape the flailing hand that raked his belly, then caught the tail of his jacket and jerked him toward the ground. He whirled to his left, tearing his arms from the sleeves and leaving the man holding an empty jacket.

It was then that Pavlak caught sight of the hard object his foot had found. It was the Ruger, nestled in the grass at the mercenary's feet. In the same instant, the other man saw it too. He dropped Pavlak's jacket and dove. Pavlak had no chance to reach the pistol first, so he swung his right foot in a punting motion and caught the diving face flush on the top of his shoe. The head snapped back, and the big body jerked sideways. Pavlak reached for the gun, but the mercenary caught his wrist, hauled him to the ground, and tried to throw his weight onto Pavlak's chest. This time Pavlak jerked his knees up and caught the plunging weight on his legs. A split second later, he had the man's neck between his knees. Pavlak locked his ankles together and squeezed with all his strength. His adversary bucked and struggled, but Pavlak held on. He couldn't win this fight on the ground—not if the man broke free again. Sharp fingernails raked the skin from his calves and thighs. A thick hand plunged into his crotch, gripped, and twisted. Pavlak cried out in pain and struggled to dislodge the hand with both of his. He succeeded momentarily, but the hand kept punching back.

Then Pavlak's eye caught sight of the pistol, four feet away. He rolled and twisted until the weapon was within reach, seized it, and slammed the steel barrel into the close-cropped hair on top of his opponent's head. The scalp split, and blood poured from the wound, but the gouging and clawing continued. Pavlak fired a shot into the air, then planted the barrel hard against the top of the man's skull.

"Stop struggling or I'll blow your goddamned brains out," he gasped.

At last the heavy body went quiet. Pavlak released the neck, kicked the heavy shoulders away, and struggled to his knees, the pistol pointed squarely at the thick chest in front of him. For half a minute both men gasped for breath in silence.

"Who the fuck are you?" the man asked finally. "What do you want?"

"I'm Prince Philip, who else?" Pavlak retorted. "That's why I called the queen. Great joke. But not worth ten thousand. What's your name?"

The man was still blowing hard. Blood seeped down his forehead and into his eyes. He wiped it away with the back of a thick paw. "Smith," he said with a sneer. "How the hell did you find me?"

"Yeah, and I'm Jones," Pavlak shot back, ignoring the question. "Now listen to me, Smith. I'm real pissed off right now, so you'd be wise to cooperate. I want Jack's phone number—and an address—the real ones this time. And I want my ten grand back. And I want all of it right now." Pavlak raised the pistol until it was pointing directly in the man's face. "You've got to three. One . . ."

"Okay, okay. I don't have no address. And I meant to give you the phone number. Really. But then I got to thinking about it, and I decided not to fuck around with Jack. I told you—he don't like surprises."

"That's why I want the phone number," Pavlak retorted sarcastically, "so I can let him know I'm coming to tea. Give it to me *now*. Two . . ."

"Okay, okay!" He rattled off a number. "That includes the city code. It's in England. You have to dial . . ."

"I know. Listen, Smith. Think about that number for a minute, then say it again."

Smith recited the same number a second time, and Pavlak hammered it into his memory.

"If it doesn't get me Jack," Pavlak warned. "I'll have to come back again. So make sure your memory's not letting you down."

"It's the right number," Smith said sullenly, staring at the ground.

"It better be. Now where's my ten grand?"

"Fuck you. I gave you the number, now beat it. You were going to give me twenty for it. There, you've got it for half price."

Pavlak fired a shot a half inch past Smith's left ear.

"Jesus Christ! All right, all right. It's in the house. Are you nuts?"

"No, not nuts. I'm going to kill you calmly and rationally if I don't get my money back."

They walked toward the house, Smith in front, Pavlak three steps behind. If there had been anyone else in the house, Pavlak reasoned, they would have shown themselves when the shouting and shooting began.

"Wait here. I'll get it," Smith told him at the door.

Pavlak laughed, then his face went grim. "On your knees."

"What?"

"You heard me—on your knees, *now.*"

Smith looked once at Pavlak, once at the pistol in his hand, then dropped to the ground.

"Now crawl into the house, slowly, and take me to the money."

The house was tiny—only three rooms. It was remarkably clean, but cluttered with twice too much furniture. The walls hung full of antique weapons, sabers, and daggers, as well as Civil War rifles and a brace of muzzle-loading pistols. One wall contained nothing but antique handcuffs. There were also photographs of a younger Smith in uniform, one with a background of jungle vegetation. Pavlak would have liked to look more, but his attention was riveted on the crawling man in front of him. Smith, he knew only too well, was either very brave or very stupid, possibly both, and that made him exceedingly dangerous. Smith crawled to a chest of drawers and stopped. Pavlak's briefcase lay on the top of the chest.

"Under there," Smith mumbled.

"Then move it."

Smith placed one bulky shoulder against the chest and heaved it aside. With one finger, he lifted what appeared to be a loose board on the floor, then another, and another

until Pavlak could see stacks of clean, neatly folded under-
wear in what looked like a small box suspended beneath the
house.

"Move left," he ordered.

Keeping the pistol and one eye on Smith, Pavlak raked
away the clothes and exposed stacks of bills beneath them.
His ten thousand were there, and a lot more besides. Pavlak
searched through the cash twice with his free hand but
found no weapon. "All right," he ordered, "count out my
ten thousand."

Smith's eyes widened, and his mouth fell open.

"I'm not a thief like you, Smith. I came for *my* money, not
yours. *Move!*"

Pavlak's bundles of fifties were on top. Smith crawled to
the drawer and counted them out. When he finished, he
turned toward Pavlak. There was still a puzzled look on his
face. Pavlak jerked his head toward the briefcase. "In there."

When the cash was back in the briefcase, Pavlak pulled a
pair of antique handcuffs off the wall.

"Hold out your hand."

"I ain't got no key to that one," Smith protested.

"You'll think of something. Hold out your hand."

"Jesus, you guys from Carolina are weird."

Pavlak stopped, the cuffs in midair. "You dealt with another guy from North Carolina, not long ago, didn't you? A
man named Trask."

Smith stared at the wall and said nothing. Pavlak knelt
down and intercepted his vision. "You know, Smith, I *could*
change my mind about the rest of that money."

Smith quickly met his eyes, then dropped his gaze again.
"What do you want to know?" he asked sullenly.

"Nothing, really. I already know all you can tell me,

but . . . Jack did two jobs recently for somebody in North Carolina, a man named Trask, right?"

Smith shook his head.

"Come on, Smith," Pavlak warned. "You must have fifty grand in that box—maybe more. Be a shame to lose it, wouldn't it? And I bet you couldn't even call the cops about it, could you?"

Smith said nothing, but Pavlak saw from the look on his face that he was right about the money.

"Trask wanted one job, about six weeks ago," Smith replied. "Protection for some bozo in the Mediterranean. That's the only business we ever did with him."

"You're lying, Smith," Pavlak snapped. He felt an unreasonable fury rising in his spine and forced it down again. This was no time to lose control. "Trask wanted the woman killed too, didn't he? Don't bother to deny it. I know Jack was in on that job too."

Pavlak remembered Jack's words exactly. "Little school like yours—that's a different thing," he had said. Only Pavlak had never mentioned Avery or anything about the college. Jack could only have known so much if he had been there himself.

Pavlak raised the pistol and looked across the barrel at Smith's mangled nose. His finger was taut on the trigger, and he battled with himself. This man was close—very close to the man who killed Judith and Tasha. He was part of it. A small part, maybe, but a part. And Pavlak could kill him now. *Now.* With a twitch of his index finger. "Where did Jack get the Czech explosives, Smith? Where did he get the Polish detonator? *Answer me, damn you!*"

The pistol jerked, and a bullet pounded into the wall beside Smith's head.

"Don't shoot!" Smith cried, flinging his arms up. Sweat was mingling with the blood on his face and flowing into the black body shirt. "The IRA," Smith panted. "Jack has contacts . . . he got the stuff from the IRA. At least," Smith continued, twitching nervously, "I guess that's where he got it. Jack don't talk much."

But Pavlak was hardly listening. He was remembering Jack's strange behavior. His apparent fondness for Pavlak that would suddenly disappear in a cold insult. And the handshake he refused on the beach of Santorini.

Smith was terrified now, babbling and stuttering wildly. "But Trask had nothing to do with that. Not as far as I know. I never heard of Trask till later, till the protection job."

"What?" Pavlak murmured.

"I said it wasn't Trask had the woman hit. It was a guy named Caroon."

Pavlak felt his heart stop. "What did you say?" he asked in a hoarse whisper.

"The guy's name was Caroon. That's all I know. I swear it." Smith's eyes were filling with blood and sweat. He pawed at them absently, never taking his eyes off the Ruger in Pavlak's hand.

"What was his first name?" Pavlak asked. He felt as if the air in the room had turned to water—unbreathable.

Smith pinched his eyes shut. "It was . . . wait a minute. Just wait a minute, will you. I'm thinking. I swear. Shit, you're making me nervous, man. What's the matter with you? It was . . . it was . . . Cory! Cory Caroon. That's all I know, man, I swear."

The world contracted suddenly around Pavlak, crushing him.

"What's the matter with you, man?" Smith's voice rose to a desperate whine. "You look crazy, man. Don't kill me, please. Listen, it was just a job, you understand. I didn't know anything, man. It was just . . ."

"Shut up," Pavlak whispered.

Smith shut up.

Two minutes later, Smith was handcuffed to a water pipe in his bathroom. Pavlak figured it would take him an hour or two to work himself free. He ran out the door to the pickup and jerked the hood release. With the hood up, he snatched the cap off the distributor, and threw it into the deep grass.

Fifteen minutes later, he accelerated up the westbound ramp to Interstate 80. He had a better chance of catching a quick flight out of San Francisco than out of Sacramento, he reasoned. And besides, it was closer.

So he was flying east, just as he had planned. But not to England. This flight would take him back to Carolina.

40

The old woman sat with her hands folded together on the desktop. Soft hands. Unnaturally soft and pale. Old hands, Karin thought. Mother Angelika's face—it was the only other part of her body exposed—gazed on the young postulant benignly. Karin wondered why Mother Angelika still insisted on wearing the habit. It was almost unheard of anymore. But then, so were women like Mother Angelika. Perhaps that was why Karin was so afraid of her. She was foreign in a way. From another era, another world. Those old gray eyes, so serene now, had seen horrors Karin could not even imagine, did not *want* to imagine. This woman—a young woman then—had learned to know a concentration camp from inside the barbed wire. And she had survived. She was strong. Old and shrunken and feeble, but stronger, Karin thought, than anyone of her generation would ever be.

"We are glad to have you back, Sister Karin. We were quite worried."

"I'm very sorry, Mother. There was nothing I could do."

"Were you in danger?"

"Yes, Mother."

"And now?"

"I believe . . . *that* danger has passed." Karin's eyes dropped to her lap.

Mother Angelika took her time replying. "There is a new danger?"

"Yes, Mother. A . . . a spiritual danger."

"And this is why you asked to see me?"

"Yes, Mother." Karin drew a lungful of air and plunged. "I am afraid . . . I am . . . yes, afraid. Afraid that I will never be able to take my vows."

It was not as difficult as she had expected. And she did not feel as ashamed as she had expected to feel. Karin's brow furrowed deeper. What was happening to her?

"I see. And why are you afraid?"

"I . . . am involved. With a man. An American."

Karin's gaze tried to hold the calm gray eyes, but failed and sought refuge in the gently curving grain of the wooden boards beneath her feet. Old boards. Darkened with age. Older even, than Mother Angelika.

"I see." If the Mother Superior was shocked, she gave no sign. "Why has this happened, my child?"

"I have no excuses, Mother. I . . ."

"I did not ask for excuses," Mother Angelika interrupted calmly. "I asked for a reason. Do not feel compelled to punish yourself just yet. Search your heart for the truth. Were you overcome by physical desire?"

"I . . ." Karin found she could not speak. She shifted in the hard chair and tried again. "I don't think it was . . . that."

"Nor did I."

Karin looked up quickly, but Mother Angelika's face had lost none of its tranquility.

"You are too strong for that. There is more."

"I . . . I'm not sure . . ."

This time Mother Angelika drew a slow breath that could

have been impatience. Karin began to wonder if coming here was the right thing to do.

"Tell me about the American," the Mother Superior said simply.

"He is . . . not a bad man."

"That's an interesting way to phrase it. Am I to assume that he is also not a good man?"

"Oh no, I didn't mean that. He *is* a good man. In many ways, but . . ."

"Yes?"

"He is a very angry man."

Mother Angelika nodded but said nothing.

"And he is . . . a violent man."

"Has he hurt you?"

"Oh no, not me. Not . . . physically."

"Are you afraid of him?"

Karin hesitated. "No. Not in that way. He . . . has suffered much. His wife died. And his child. They were killed . . . murdered. He wants revenge. He calls it justice. I have tried to dissuade him, but I have failed." Again Karin's gaze sought refuge in the wooden boards at her feet.

"Has this man killed?"

Too late, Karin realized that she was going to cry. Tears spilled onto her cheeks. She fumbled in her handbag for a tissue, found one, and bought time drying her face.

"Yes, Mother," she answered at last, in a small voice. "Twice."

"And he is still angry?"

"Yes."

"Will he kill again?"

"Yes. Or be killed. I cannot stop him. And I . . . I don't really blame him for doing what he is doing. That's what frightens me." She hesitated. "Mother . . ."

"Yes, my child."

"You know my sister died."

"Yes. The accident."

Karin shook her head. "It was not an accident. She was murdered. He . . . the American . . . he found the man who was responsible for my sister's death. He killed him. It was not self-defense, Mother. He just . . . killed him."

Mother Angelika drew a long breath. "And did you witness this violence, my child?"

Karin nodded.

"I am very sorry."

"No, Mother. I'm not . . . I mean . . . it was horrible, but . . ." She stopped.

"But what?"

"I didn't want him to do it, because I didn't want to see it. But I was not sorry. I have tried to be," she added quickly, "but even now, I am not sorry. I'm ashamed of my feelings, but that's how it is. I'm unfit, Mother, do you see? How could I join the Order with such . . . such malice in my heart?"

Mother Angelika unfolded her hands and laid them flat on the desk. Her eyes rose to a spot on the wall behind Karin's head. There was nothing there, Karin knew. The walls were bare except for a single crucifix above the Mother Superior's head, on the wall behind her.

"When I was in Dachau," Mother Angelika began softly, "I saw men do horrible things. I learned hatred. A deep and profound hatred. As deep and profound, I thought, as God's love. I know now that I was wrong about God's love. And yet . . ."

Her voice trailed off, and her eyes looked into a distant world. Their usual serenity was replaced by something Karin had never seen there before, something intense and tragic and unspeakably sad. The transformation unnerved her. "And yet what, Mother?"

Mother Angelika's gaze returned to Karin's face, and their usual tranquility resumed. "Those men were brought down. Brought down by violence. And even today . . . when I have learned forgiveness and even love for them . . . I cannot say that I am sorry." She shook her head once, slightly, almost like an afterthought. "Are you in love with this man?" she asked abruptly.

"Yes, Mother," Karin whispered immediately, surprising herself. She had anticipated the question and had planned a long, complex answer.

"Are you certain?"

"Yes, Mother."

"Could it be pity you are feeling? Or pride?"

"Pride?"

"Pride that will not let you refuse the challenge. His challenge. To free him from the bonds of his hatred."

"But I have failed at that."

"And have you given up all hope?"

Karin hesitated. "I cannot."

"Why not?"

"Because . . . that would be giving up on him. Writing him off. Abandoning him."

Mother Angelika folded her hands again before replying. "Are you saying that you wish to return to him?"

Karin studied the boards for a long moment. "I came here," she began carefully, "to ask for your help in giving him up. I thought I was ready, but . . . how can I, Mother Angelika? How can I put him out of my life now? How can I return to the Order? How can I ever retrieve the peace and certainty that he took from me?"

"He has given you doubts?"

"About some things, yes," Karin answered in a tiny voice. She could not meet the old woman's eyes.

Mother Angelika waited, and the silence grew awkward.

"You did not answer my question, child," she continued at last. "Are you ready to give him up?"

"I want to be."

"But you are not."

Something inside her surrendered. "No, Mother. I am not."

"You have prayed?"

"Oh yes, Mother. Constantly."

"And have you found no answer?"

Karin shook her head.

"Then you must continue to pray. God will give you His answer in His time."

"Mother Angelika, could it be . . ." She stopped.

"Yes, my child?"

"Could God's answer possibly be that I should leave the Order and return to the American? Could that possibly be right? Could that possibly be God's will?"

The wrinkled old lips drew into a smile of infinite patience. "My child, it was God's will that his only son die in agony on a cross. Anything is possible. We must not question God. We must only obey."

"Mother . . ."

"Yes."

"Can you . . . can you tell me how to help him? Is there nothing I can do? I am afraid he will destroy himself. I am afraid there is no hope."

"There is always hope. Even in the concentration camps, there was hope."

"But I can see none for him, Mother. He has no faith. He wants faith, but cannot find it. And he suffers . . ."

Mother Angelika tilted gently forward. "And there, precisely, lies the hope you seek. For in suffering there is redemption—a remaking. If he survives, he will learn from his pain. And even if he cannot come to Christ, the Redeemer may come to him in his torment. You must have that faith yourself, child. That is your only responsibility. Now go. You have much to consider, and much to pray about. Do not despair. God will guide you."

One old hand rose from the desk and gestured, a gesture as light and soft as the stroke of a butterfly's wing. Karin bowed her shoulders once, then stood. "Thank you, Mother."

She closed the door quietly behind her.

41

The only Catholic church in Lake Elm was built in 1942 from quarried stone. The local Catholic population was, like elsewhere in the Anglo-Saxon and German South, an almost invisible minority. Thus St. Matthew's was narrow with a single nave and only two sections of short pews running down either side. But the ceiling vault rose to reverent heights, and stained glass windows set in soaring Gothic arches lent the sanctuary a modest grandeur. The colored glass depicted various saints, in two rows of bright colors, staring sternly at the worshipers. Each saint stood against an azure background that caught the early morning sunlight and cast a blue aura over the pews. Pavlak felt as if he had entered a tropical lagoon underwater. The church was cool, but the air smelled of incense and hot wax.

He walked softly down the aisle toward the crucifix that hung suspended over the altar, occasionally glancing left and right at the passing saints, but always returning his gaze to the Christ in agony. It grew larger and more distinct with each step.

He felt out of place, vaguely profane in this sacred setting. He would have preferred one of the more approachable

Protestant sanctuaries, but only the Catholic church was un-locked at this hour. He had not reached Avery until late the previous evening, and, exhausted, he had unplugged the phones and dropped onto the bed. But sleep had come only in a few brief and restless fits, until finally, before dawn, he had flung out of the house and driven to Lake Elm.

He reminded himself that the church was built by men, as surely as the hardware store across the street. Still, his cynicism could not completely dispel the aura of sacredness that surrounded him. He longed to stride back up the aisle and into the street, back into the secular world where he belonged. But a promise was a promise.

Pavlak drew a long breath. He was tired—beastly tired—from the long flight back to Charlotte, and the second night in a row with little sleep. His battered body ached in a hun-dred places. He was light-headed from dehydration, but Smith's fingers had bruised his throat so that swallowing was painful. Since flying out of San Francisco he had sipped half-heartedly at a cup of coffee but eaten nothing.

He slipped into a pew two rows from the pulpit and stead-ied himself with his hand on the back of the pew in front of him. The Christ on the crucifix seemed not to notice him, fixed instead on his own endless agony, his eyes rolled up-ward in an eternal unanswered plea for . . . what was it? Pav-lak studied the face, twisted in pain. Oh yes: "My God, my God, why hast Thou . . ."

A truck with a bad muffler roared past on the street out-side. Pavlak sighed. "Okay," he whispered. "Let's get it over with."

He tried to remember exactly what he had promised Karin during that moment in Avery, locked in her arms. He had promised to pray for the one who killed his daughter, pray for the man who swept away the only joy of his life.

Pray for the man's forgiveness, for his well-being. Pray for the blessing upon him. Pray for his happiness.

"Just promise me . . ." she had said. And he had promised.

"Father . . ." Pavlak began in a choked whisper, his voice a startling intrusion into the silence. "Father, forgive . . ." He cleared his throat, winced at the pain it caused, and tried again. "Father, forgive him . . . forgive him because . . ." He stopped. Seconds passed, then a minute. Pavlak could not go on. He let his forehead fall onto the back of his hand and rest there. "I tried," he whispered, closing his eyes. After a minute, he lifted his head again and sought out the crucifix, half-expecting the eyes to be turned toward him in bitter accusation. But they were still fixed upward in their grotesque and endless pain.

Pavlak pushed away from the pew and strode up the aisle.

Before buckling his seatbelt in the Oldsmobile, he reached beneath the front seat and retrieved the Ruger. It had not seemed right to carry the weapon into the church. Now, as he inspected the hard, cold steel in his palm, it felt foreign and detached, unreal somehow. He tucked it in the front of his belt inside his sport coat.

From the church, Pavlak drove to the white mansion on the hill and rang the doorbell four times at his father's house. A Mexican woman Pavlak had never seen before opened the door.

She was dressed in a cook's uniform, but looked half asleep and confused.

"I'm John Pavlak. I need to speak to my father for a few minutes," Pavlak explained, brushing past her. He was carrying a plastic grocery bag at his side.

"He's not here, Señor," the cook called after him.

Pavlak turned.

"He is very ill. In the hospital."

Lake Elm Memorial Hospital was only ten minutes from the Pavlak estate. Pavlak parked in the emergency room parking lot and took the elevator to the fourth floor and the suite of expensive, private rooms where Lake Elm's wealthier citizens chose to suffer their worldly fates. The only nurse at the nurse's station was a slender young woman with black hair and dark eyes who reminded him vaguely of Karin. She spoke immediately.

"Sir, visiting hours . . ."

"I'm here to see Gustaf Pavlak. He's my father. I'm about to leave on a long trip, and I have to see him before I go."

A light went on in her eyes. "Oh! Then you're John Pavlak."

Pavlak nodded, surprised.

"Someone just called for you."

"For me? Are you sure?"

"Yes. A lady with an accent. She said you were on your way here, and that she would call back in a few minutes. Go ahead. It's room four-thirty-two. I'll put the call through when it comes. And please don't stay too long. He . . . had a bad night."

"I understand. Thank you."

Pavlak turned and started down the hall. So the cook had wakened Roser. Why did she want to talk to him? Oh well, whatever it was, it didn't matter now. The door to room 432 was slightly ajar. Pavlak pushed it open and stepped inside.

Gustaf Pavlak was not asleep. The head of his bed was raised and he sat alone in the semi-darkness. Their eyes met.

"Hello, Pop," Pavlak said grimly, switching on the overhead light.

"Have you seen Roser?" Gustaf asked.

"No. The cook told me you were here." Something in his father's face stopped him.

"What's happened?"

Gustaf tossed one pale hand weakly. "It's over," he said. There was something like disgust in his voice.

"What do you mean 'over'?"

Gustaf tapped his abdomen. "Cancer. Here—here—everywhere. Stupid bastards should have found it months ago."

Pavlak took two slow steps and laid the plastic bag on the foot of the bed. The room swayed a little, and he fastened his gaze on a glucose bottle to steady himself. This was something he had not counted on.

"How long do they give you?"

"Couple of weeks. A month maybe." His speech was slow and slurred.

"You sound drugged."

Gustaf nodded. "For the pain." He pointed at the plastic bag Pavlak had laid beside his feet. "What's that?"

Pavlak picked it up and stared absently at his hands. Gustaf Pavlak, it had always seemed, would never die. An old reality was crumbling in front of him, and the effect was disorienting. Pavlak reached into the bag and his fingers encountered something soft. He squeezed, and the touch brought a scene from memory crashing into his brain, waking him from his trance. He peeled the bag away roughly.

"Remember this?"

It was a stuffed toy, a very worn and dirty facsimile of a raccoon. The tail was missing, and the head had been torn off and crudely reattached with green thread.

Gustaf Pavlak looked at the toy a long moment then rolled his head away from his son. When it rolled back a moment later, the eyes were moist.

"How did you find out?"

Pavlak said nothing, but stared into his father's eyes, letting his anger build.

Gustaf continued quietly. "I didn't know you still had that."

"I kept it as a reminder. A little memento of you, Pop."

Slowly, Gustaf extended a trembling hand and took the toy from Pavlak's fingers. "Caroon," he mused. "Even when you were old enough to say 'raccoon' properly, you still called him Caroon. I think it was your mother who added the first name—Cory. She was silly about things like that." Their eyes met. "Your protector," Gustaf breathed. "You slept with that thing until you were—what—twelve years old?"

"I was five, Pop."

Gustaf was slow to reply. "I did what I thought was best for you and Tom."

"Like hell, you did!" Pavlak lashed out. "You tore his head off in front of me, remember? It was time I learned to be a man, you said. Only girls slept with dolls. Remember?" Pavlak leaned over his father. His voice was hoarse with fury. "You did what you thought was best for Gustaf Pavlak—only—always."

Gustaf stared sullenly at the bedcover and shook his head. "That's not true."

"Oh yes it is. You wanted perfect children—so the world could see what a great father Gustaf Pavlak was. We were trophies to you, Pop. 'Children are a reflection on their parents,' remember? You said that a thousand times, whenever we misbehaved, or you thought we did. It was *you* you were worried about, Pop. You were afraid of being embarrassed, that's all. You never gave a damn about us."

"I knew the world was hard," Gustaf said, his weak voice rising. "I wanted you to be ready when you grew up. I had to fight a war . . ."

"For you the war never ended, Pop. You carried it on against your family."

"That's your mother talking!" Gustaf shot back. "She was soft. And she made you soft too, in spite of everything I . . . My God, what happened to your neck?"

Instead of answering, Pavlak turned to the door and closed it quietly, then switched the light off again. The morning was far enough along for them to see each other clearly, even with the blinds closed. But now the ugly black splotches left by Smith's fingers were less obvious. Pavlak gingerly touched his throat.

"Your soft, weak son nearly bit off a man's nose yesterday. This is my little souvenir from the fight."

Gustaf stared at him for a long moment, then his gaze drifted back to the stuffed toy in his hands. He turned it over and over without seeing it. "Is he the one who told you?"

"Yes."

Footsteps approached in the hall, passed, and continued down the corridor.

"How much did Schliemann pay you, Pop? Was it worth it?"

Gustaf shook his head slowly. "Peter gave me nothing— not directly. He never even knew that I was part of it. Arthur and I split the money, half and half."

Pavlak frowned. "But how did you . . . ? I mean . . ."

"Arthur told me about it when Peter made his offer. Arthur would never have done something like that on his own."

"Be a traitor, you mean? Yeah, I guess you're right. That's more your style, Pop. Anything for the money. As if you even needed it," Pavlak added bitterly.

"I needed it then. The company was in trouble. I wouldn't have done it otherwise."

"Oh, can it, Pop," Pavlak snorted. "Don't try to pretend

you have any scruples—a man who murdered his own grand-daughter to protect himself."

Gustaf looked up sharply, and his voice rose. "Is that what you think? You're crazy! I did it for *you*! I was trying to be your protector. Like Cory Caroon." He held up the ragged toy in a hand that trembled.

"My protector? You protected me by killing my wife and child?"

"I was trying to save Tasha for you," Gustaf insisted. "I knew how much she meant to you." His voice rose in pitch. "That goddamned bitch you married was going to take her away from you, and you were going to let her do it. I *had* to do something." The old man's blue eyes glittered. "Only . . . who was to know Tasha would be sick that day? Or that she would be in the car even so?" He shook his head. "Judith had her lying down in the back seat. He couldn't see her. He thought Judith was alone in the car. Bad luck—fate—I don't know what." He drew a weak breath and sank back into the pillow. "I'm not trying to dodge the blame," Gustaf went on. "I should have left it alone, but you . . ." he shook his head. "You left me no choice. I had to do something."

Pavlak was over him in a flash.

"You're not going to lay this on *me*," he croaked, his fists clenched in fury. "Every mistake you ever made was some-body else's fault. Remember the time you knocked a jar off the shelf in the basement and beat me with an axe handle because you said I put the jar too close to the edge of the shelf? Well, it won't work this time, Pop. *You* did this. You—and nobody else. You talk about being a man? Well, be man enough to take the responsibility for a mistake once in your life!"

Gustaf's failing eyes glared at him. "You wouldn't dare talk to me like that if I weren't laid up in this bed."

"You don't know how many times," Pavlak began after taking a moment to control himself, "that it's taken all my willpower to keep me from beating you to death—ever since I was big enough to do it. And even before. I should have killed you that day in the tree."

"What are you talking about?"

"When I was a boy. I climbed the pecan tree in the front yard and sighted at the door with the twenty-two. I was going to kill you when you came home. I wish I had."

Neither of them heard the footsteps. The latch clicked suddenly, and a nurse entered with a tray of medication in tiny paper cups. She started when she saw Pavlak.

"Sir, visiting hours aren't . . ."

"I'm paying for this goddamned room!" Gustaf Pavlak exploded. "I paid for half this hospital. He's my son, and he'll stay as long as *I* say. Now shut up and get out!"

Stunned, the nurse stared at him for a five-count, then walked forward and set a pill cup onto the bed table. "It's time for your medicine," she warned curtly, then marched out, her lips pressed together in fury.

Silence descended.

"Was Arthur in on the murders?" Pavlak asked at last.

Gustaf shook his head. "No. He came to me after Judith showed him the document. He was scared to death. I told him to warn Peter. Later, we knew Peter was sending two professional men to search Judith's house. And we knew when they were coming."

The old man had slipped lower in the bed. He struggled to pull himself up.

"I saw my chance to get rid of Judith and get Tasha for you," Gustaf wheezed, winded by the effort. "The police would think the bombing was connected to the break-in. They'd never know the truth." He looked up accusingly.

"And they wouldn't have, if you had let it alone. Everything worked perfectly. Except for the accident."

"A car bomb is not an accident, Pop. It's a murder."

"I don't deny that I meant to kill Judith. She deserved it."

"And you really expect me to believe you weren't doing it to protect yourself?"

"It doesn't matter what you believe," Gustaf shot back defiantly. "It's true. I did it for you, and I even took a *bigger* chance by killing her before we got the document. With her gone, finding the document was almost impossible."

More footsteps approached, then passed.

"Did you know that Arthur sent the same man to Crete?" Pavlak asked.

"Of course. Arthur came to me after your phone call from Germany. He was afraid Peter would kill you. I told him I'd take care of it, but he wouldn't let me. He said it was his fault. And he had the money to hire protection for you. Did I know anybody who could arrange it? I gave him the phone number."

"Where did *you* get it?"

His father frowned impatiently. "I have friends who have friends. It wasn't hard." He shook his head. "My sons, my sons." He glanced up at Pavlak and spoke louder. "Mc-Canless was here yesterday. He drew up a new will. I'm leaving you most of my stock. With what's in the trust account, you'll own fifty-one percent of Pavlak Equipment."

Pavlak shook his head in disbelief. "Are you crazy? I don't . . ."

"Wait. Just listen to me for once." Gustaf winced and pawed absently at his left side. "Tom can't do it. He can't run the company. I never really thought he could, but I had to give him a chance. Listen—I know you won't do it yourself, but find somebody . . ."

Pavlak exploded. "You think I came here to talk about the *company?*"

"All right," Gustaf said after a long silence. "Let's have it. What are you going to do?"

Pavlak felt his fingers tremble as they closed on the Ruger beneath his jacket. He raised the pistol and pointed the barrel into his father's face.

"Are you out of your mind?" Gustaf asked quietly.

Pavlak said nothing. The gun was not as steady as he would have wished. He nudged the safety off.

"Just tell me one thing," Gustaf said. "Are you going to kill yourself too?"

Pavlak shook his head. "I wouldn't give you that satisfaction."

"Then just how the hell do you expect to get away with this?" Gustaf demanded. "Everybody knows you're here. The shot will wake up the whole place anyway. Don't be a damned fool."

"I'll plead insanity, Pop. Shouldn't be too hard to pull that off . . . under the circumstances."

"Son . . ." Gustaf shook his head. If the old man was at all afraid, he gave no sign. "Son, don't do this. It's pointless. You'll spend the rest of your life in prison. At the very least, the state will rescind the will and leave you with nothing."

"I don't give a damn about the money, Pop. You'll never understand that, will you?"

"Everybody gives a damn about money, whether they admit it or not. You're no exception." Gustaf laughed bitterly. "Want to know something funny? I haven't slept all night because I was lying here trying to figure out how to kill myself. I've got nothing left but a few weeks of pain. I don't want to lie here and let them drug me into a vegetable. My life's over anyway. You kill me now, you'll be doing me a favor—but you'll be ruining your own life in the process. Don't be so stupid." He struggled to sit forward in the bed. "Look—just leave me the gun. I'll do it myself—when you're out of here. I promise."

The phone on the bedside table jangled. Pavlak hesitated. The phone rang again, and he picked it up with his left hand.

"Yes?"

"John?"

"Karin!"

"Oh, thank God. John—I'm sorry. I spoke to Roser on the phone a little while ago, and she gave me this number. She said you had just come by and were on your way to the hospital. I called once already, but you hadn't arrived yet. I've been trying to call you since yesterday. I was so afraid something had happened to you. Thank God . . ."

"I'm fine, Karin." But he did not feel fine. He felt weak and exhausted and lost. He had come here to kill his father, thinking it would be the easiest thing he had ever done. Had he not dreamed of it most of his life? And if ever a man deserved to die, it was Gustaf Pavlak. But it wasn't working. What justice was there in killing a man who *wanted* to die? The worst punishment he could give his father at this point would be to walk out of this ugly green room that smelled of alcohol, and leave him to die slowly.

"John?"

"Yes. I'm sorry. I'm here."

"John—what is it? What's happened?"

The situation was absurd. Out of his control. He stood holding the phone with his left hand, talking to a woman on another continent, while his right hand held a 9 mm pistol pointed at his father's head. And his father ignored him, picking instead at the matted polyester fur on a toy raccoon.

"I'm trying to finish my business here, Karin," Pavlak said without much conviction. "When I'm finished, I'll call you."

"Don't. I'm calling from the Frankfurt airport. My plane leaves in half an hour. I'll be in Charlotte at three-oh-five your time."

Pavlak's heart leapt. "You're coming back?"

"Yes, John. I know now that I belong with you. Whatever happens—I belong with you. You're my life."

"Karin! Thank God . . ." Then Pavlak remembered where he was, and why, and the surge of joy vanished. He fingered the phone and struggled to think. His right arm with the extended weapon was growing heavy. Gustaf had stopped picking at the toy and was watching him. There was a calmness in the drawn old face that disconcerted Pavlak still more.

"Can you meet me at the airport?" Karin asked.

"My father's dying of cancer," Pavlak heard himself say. "He's the one, Karin. He's the one who killed them."

"Her," Gustaf corrected. "I killed *her*—Judith."

"John . . ." From her voice Pavlak could tell that Karin was fighting panic. "Did you keep your promise?"

"I tried."

"Is he . . . is he there now?"

"Yes."

There was a long silence. The first rays of the new sun reached the blinds and stole through a crack to land on the back of Gustaf's hand as it lay like death on the sheet. Gustaf was staring into space, looking past the mouth of the barrel only a few feet from his face. Pavlak fingered the safety on the Ruger.

"John?"

"I'm here."

"In Stuttgart you told me you wanted to believe. Was that true?"

"I can't. I told you . . ."

"Listen, if you won't trust God, then please—please trust me. John?"

"I'm here."

"I love you. Please come for me."

His right shoulder was beginning to ache. He shifted his gaze back to his father's face and found the old man's features distorted in pain, his eyes rolling back in his head, both hands clawing at his belly.

Pavlak flipped the safety on, then jammed the pistol into his belt and snatched up the paper cup the nurse had left on the table. It contained three pills of various sizes and colors. He poured a glass of water from the pitcher on the night stand, then shoved the pills at his father. "Here. Swallow these."

Gustaf ignored him. His eyes were pinched shut. Pavlak laid the receiver on the table, lifted his father's head and pressed the cup to his mouth until the lips relented. When the pills disappeared into the black cavity, Pavlak poured a sip of water after them. Gustaf swallowed, then choked and coughed. Two of the pills spilled back onto the sheet. Pavlak picked them up and put them back into his mouth. This time he held the glass to Gustaf's lips and bent his head forward. He was relieved when the old man's Adam's apple bobbed up and down twice. From up close, Pavlak could see that the white stubble on Gustaf's neck and cheeks added to the pallor of his skin. The old man needed a shave. And his breath was foul.

Pavlak lowered his father's head slowly onto the pillow.

Gustaf's eyes were still shut, and his features still twisted, though the intensity of this surge seemed to have passed. Pavlak picked up the receiver and held it to his ear.

"Karin?"

"Yes. John, what's happening?"

"What time will you arrive?"

"Five past three."

"I'll be there." He stopped, then added. "I'm glad you're coming. Thank God you're coming. I missed you." He laid the receiver quietly onto its cradle, then turned and walked for the door. His hand was on the knob when his father's voice stopped him.

"John."

Pavlak waited.

"The pistol . . . Leave it here."

Pavlak did not move.

"Please, John."

Please. Pavlak could not remember his father ever saying that word to him before. He studied the dying old eyes, moist and glittering. They were filled with a silent plea.

Pavlak walked to the night table, laid the Ruger gently onto the blond wood, then started out again. At the door he turned. His father had picked up the pistol and was wiping the fingerprints off with a corner of the bedsheet. Gustaf looked up, and their eyes met. The old man nodded. Pavlak turned and walked out.

On the way to the car, Pavlak checked his watch. Ten hours until Karin arrived. God, how he had missed her. He unlocked the door of the Oldsmobile and started to climb in, then stopped short. Beside the car, a bed of azaleas was blooming in full spring glory, throbbing with pink and red. He stooped and pressed one flower to his nose. The scent was faint, but the blossom was exquisite nonetheless.

At last Pavlak climbed into his car and started the engine. Fifty-one percent of Pavlak Equipment. What the hell would he do with it? No matter what he did, Tom would make a royal scene. Maybe it would be possible to reconcile with his brother somehow. At the moment, anything seemed possible. Pavlak closed his eyes and gripped the steering wheel. "Take care of Pop, Lord," he whispered. He opened his eyes, pushed the lever into "Drive," and nudged the accelerator. His whole body ached, partly from the bruises and partly from weariness. He decided to take a shower when he reached Avery, then lie down for a few hours' rest. After that it would be time to meet Karin. . . ."